Other Titles by Cheryl Brooks

Cowboy Delight
Cowboy Heaven
Unbridled: Unlikely Lovers Book 1
Uninhibited: Unlikely Lovers Book 2
Undeniable: Unlikely Lovers Book 3
Unrivaled: Unlikely Lovers Book 4
The Cat Star Chronicles: Rebel
The Cat Star Chronicles: Wildcat
The Cat Star Chronicles: Stud
The Cat Star Chronicles: Virgin
The Cat Star Chronicles: Hero
The Cat Star Chronicles: Fugitive
The Cat Star Chronicles: Outcast
The Cat Star Chronicles: Rogue
The Cat Star Chronicles: Warrior
The Cat Star Chronicles: Slave
The Cat Star Chronicles Bundle: Slave, Warrior & Rogue
Sharing (Sextet Anthology)
Entanglements (Sextet Anthology)
Occupational Hazards (Sextet Anthology)
Mistletoe & Ménage (Sextet Anthology)
Dirty Dancing (Sextet Anthology)
Small, Medium, & Large (Sextet Presents)
The Lady Takes a Pair (Sextet Presents)
A Tale of Two Knights (Sextet Presents)
Midnight in Reno
If You Could Read My Mind (writing as Samantha R. Michaels

UNLIKELY LOVERS

Undeniable

CHERYL BROOKS

DERRYMANE PRESS

Derrymane
Press

Undeniable
Unlikely Lovers Book 3
by Cheryl Brooks
Published by Derrymane Press
Copyright 2014. Cheryl Brooks.
Cover design by Dragonfly Press Design
Cover image by Shutterstock
ISBN 13: 978-0-9838081-8-3

All rights reserved. No part of this book may be reproduced in any form or by any electronic or mechanical means including information storage and retrieval systems—except in the case of brief quotations embodied in critical articles or reviews—without permission in writing from its publisher, Derrymane Press.

The characters and events portrayed in this book are fictitious or are used fictitiously. Any similarity to real persons, living or dead, is purely coincidental and not intended by the author.

www.cherylbrooksonline.com

For anyone who has ever had the hots for a long-haired lead guitar player

ACKNOWLEDGEMENTS

My heartfelt thanks go out to:
My terrific critique partners, Nan Reinhardt and Sandy James.
My keen-eyed beta reader, Mellanie Szereto.
My pal and mentor in the self-publishing world, Marie Force.
My friends in IRWA for their support and encouragement.
My family for their love and understanding.
I couldn't have done this without you!

Chapter 1

Extraordinary talent, undeniable love…

৶ো

"Go ahead, babe. Order whatever you want. The sky's the limit." Bryce actually sounded nice, even generous. He was also smiling, which should have been Tracy Richard's first clue something wasn't quite right. That and the fact that their "dinner date" had turned out to be a quick trip through McDonald's drive-thru.

Leaning gingerly to her left, she glanced up at the menu. She already knew what she wanted, but she had to shout across Bryce to make herself heard.

"Your total is ten forty-three," a garbled voice said over the speaker. "Please pull up to the second window."

"Sure thing." Bryce eased the truck forward.

Somewhere between there and the pick-up window, he cracked Tracy in the nose with a quick, nonchalant backhand. The impact was so sudden, so unexpected, blood began flowing down her upper lip before her brain even registered she'd been hit.

I should've known. He'd been much too pleasant for far too long.

She didn't ask why he'd done it, but he told her anyway.

"I didn't like the way you ordered." The sharp edge in his voice sliced right through her, increasing her agony.

Tears mingled with blood dripped onto her white knit top. It was a safe bet she'd never wear that one in public again.

The fresh-faced boy at the pick-up window gasped in surprise. "Hey, is she okay?"

"Yeah, she's fine," Bryce replied. "She gets nosebleeds all the time."

"I–I'll give you some extra napkins."

"Sure, whatever." Bryce's tone accurately conveyed his complete lack of concern. "It's no big deal."

The boy stuffed the napkins into the bag and handed it to Bryce. "I put a wet-nap in there too. I hope you feel better, ma'am."

All Tracy could do was nod. Jumping out the truck was an option, but at the moment, she was too stunned to think straight, let alone move.

Bryce dropped the bag in her lap and drove on. "Don't bleed all over my food, bitch. And don't ever shout across me again. I hate that."

When she failed to comment, he added, "Don't you dare sit there and pout. I hate that even more."

At that particular moment, Tracy didn't give a damn about his likes and dislikes. All she wanted to do was to go home and try to forget why she'd ever in her wildest dreams considered him to be attractive.

"Are you just gonna sit there or are you gonna fix my dinner for me?"

Without even thinking, she reached into the bag and pulled out a napkin. After wiping her face and hands, she unwrapped his sandwich halfway and handed it to him, then she set his French fries in the cup holder on the console.

"Just the way I like it." He was smiling again—a creepy-crawly smile that seemed to come from a different personality altogether. "You'd make a good wife, wouldn't you?"

Not for you. Frankenstein's monster would have been a better match. Deeming it safer, she opted to reply with another nod.

"Quiet, too," he said. "I can't stand blabber-mouthed women."

At least I've made one correct decision today.

Tracy was beginning to wonder if Bryce truly liked *any* woman.

She'd certainly lost all desire for men. Practically every man she met turned out to be a controlling, foul-mouthed jerk. Sure, they all seemed nice at first, but after a few dates, their true colors began to emerge. One guy had even taken to driving by her apartment building late at night. She probably wouldn't have seen him if she hadn't been taking out her trash, but the thought of how often he might've been making that drive-by gave her the creeps. Bryce wasn't the first one to hit her, either.

Not that she'd been slugged enough to know the best way to deal with it. Perhaps a baseball bat would help. Or a can of pepper spray. Unfortunately, neither of those things would do her any good right now. The trick would be making it through this date without any more bruises. If Bryce thought buying her a burger and fries gave him the right to break her nose, she could hardly *wait* to see what he would do to her after a movie. Rattling a box of Raisinets during the show would probably get her killed.

Having gobbled down his chicken sandwich and fries at warp speed, Bryce waved a hand at the bag in her lap. "I'll eat that if you don't want it."

Tracy truly *didn't* want it, and with a rapidly swelling nose, she doubted she could taste it anyway. Already sick to her stomach, she decided it was best not to try. God only knew what he'd do to her for puking all over his pretty red Dodge.

She opened the bag, unwrapped her Big Mac, and handed it to him.

I'd rather cram it down his fuckin' throat.

She'd have felt less like a dupe if this wasn't their second date. Bryce hadn't exactly been Prince Charming during their first encounter, but he'd seemed decent enough that she'd given him the benefit of the doubt.

My mistake. She almost wished he'd hit her right off the bat. But then, the abusive ones seldom did. They liked to feel they had some control over a woman before they started pounding on her.

Not that Tracy enjoyed being controlled. The whole dominant male/submissive female scenario made her physically ill.

Unfortunately, she seemed to attract that type, and at the age of thirty-one, she wasn't desperate enough to put up with them and doubted she ever would be. No matter what, this was the absolute last Bryce would ever see of her, and it would be a cold day in hell before she went out with anyone else from that stupid dating service she'd joined. Thus far, they'd all been whiny-butt losers or obnoxious jerks. Bryce, however, fell into a category all his own.

Apparently, he wanted a woman who would cater to his whims and put up with his shit—a behavior so diametrically opposed to her own preferences, she could scarcely believe she was actually doing it, even in the interest of self preservation. To think, at one point she'd actually considered him handsome. Watching him eat the hamburger she should've been enjoying made her itch to slap the shit out of him.

Tall, blond, and reasonably well built, Bryce had recently been discharged from the Army, presumably having grown tired of being all that he could be. Tracy had no way of knowing for sure, but she suspected his discharge had been less than honorable.

A veteran of the war in Iraq, Bryce must've loved the way the Iraqis treated their women. If he'd stayed there, he might've found some other woman who was at least accustomed to the *idea* of getting the shit beat out of her on a regular basis. Then Tracy would never have met him and wouldn't be stuck in her current predicament.

I'm quitting after this one. Perhaps if she'd gone ahead and married her high school sweetheart the way her older sister Miranda had, she wouldn't be in such a mess. But no, she'd left him behind when she went off to college in search of greener pastures. She'd dated lots of guys—had even married one of them, albeit briefly—but now, with all the good ones taken, only the fuckwads were left.

Having watched Bryce consume the entirety of her dinner, Tracy took a cautious sip of her Coke, half expecting him to demand that she give him that as well. No wonder he'd told her to order anything she pleased. He'd probably known all along he'd be the one to eat it.

Unfortunately, swallowing anything after taking a fist in the nose was almost impossible. She considered throwing her drink in his face, but not for long.

"Thanks, babe," he said. "That was delicious. Great meal and a pretty lady. What more could a guy want?"

Tracy would've rolled her eyes if she hadn't been afraid he would respond by blacking one of them—that is, if he hadn't done it already. A peek at the mirror on the sun visor was enough to confirm her worst fears. The woman staring back at her looked like a cross between a raccoon and Rudolph the Red-nosed Reindeer. Her own mother wouldn't have recognized her.

So much for being pretty.

Stopping at a red light, Bryce smiled and took her hand, giving it a squeeze before pressing it to his lips. "You're so good to me. What did I ever do to deserve someone like you?"

Probably pulled the wings off of flies as a child or tortured bunny rabbits. Opting for silence, Tracy shrugged.

Mistake! His hand shot out as he seized her by the back of the neck and hauled her around to face him.

"Because I fought for this godforsaken country in a time of war!" he roared. "I deserve anything I want for having done that! You lazy-ass scum who stayed over here, enjoying all the comforts of home, wouldn't know anything about that, would you?"

Along with the majority of the general population, Tracy had never been in combat, but she was beginning to have some idea of what it was like.

With a snarl, Bryce flung her against the passenger-side door, slamming her head against the window. Her scalp split upon impact, and she felt more blood begin to flow, thankful that only her head was damaged. Fracturing her skull wouldn't have bothered him a bit, but a broken window would've sent him off the deep end.

As he drove away from the stoplight, Tracy dabbed the side of her head with a napkin.

"Don't you fuckin' bleed all over my truck," he snapped. "Fuckin' bitch. I've had just about enough of you. Forget the goddamned movie. I'm taking you home."

Home. She was about to thank God when a chill ripped through her.

He knows where I live.

After that other stalker, she should've known better. Cursing herself for being so stupid, she sat huddled in her seat, fully expecting to get punched simply for breathing. She was beginning to understand why so many abused women opted to sit tight and take it. With no idea what might incite further violence, they were afraid to do anything.

Fighting back was not an option. Tracy was no weakling, but as big as Bryce was, he would laugh at her for making the attempt—or her feeble efforts would anger him to the point of actually killing her.

She waited for the next blow, which never came. For one brief moment, she thought he might've decided she wasn't worth the energy. Nothing he'd done so far felt fatal, but it still hurt like the devil. As waves of heat and sickness washed over her, she focused on remaining alert, not even wanting to *think* about what he might do to her unconscious body.

Her apartment building lay just ahead, the most beautiful sight she'd ever seen in her life. As the truck screeched to a halt, she almost fell out the door in her frantic efforts to escape. Staggering to the steps, she clung to the rail, pulling herself up with arms and legs rendered nearly useless from pain and fear. She was almost to her door when his footsteps pounded on the stairs.

Gasping in horror, she struggled with her keys, desperate to get inside before he reached the landing. The dead bolt seemed determined to thwart her, and she screamed in frustration until it finally yielded. Slipping inside, she slammed the door one instant too late.

His foot was wedged in the doorway. "Let me in, bitch. I need to teach you some fuckin' manners. You can't just walk away from me like that."

"Get out of here!" she screamed. "Haven't you done enough?"

"Not anywhere near enough," he snarled. "You're gonna be sorry you treated me so bad."

"I treated *you* bad?" She would've laughed if she hadn't been so terrified. "Are you nuts?"

Making no reply, he muscled his way into her apartment. His first grab missed, and she stumbled across the living room to the kitchen, hoping to reach the stove so she could bash him over the head with a skillet.

She never made it that far.

Throwing her against the cabinets, Bryce seized her by the hair and began slapping her across the face until she collapsed and slid to the floor. For one brief moment, she thought he was finished with her. Then through the haze of pain, she saw him unbuckle his belt and unzip his fly.

No, he wasn't finished with her. He was only getting started.

ଚ୍ଚର

Joseph Manzetti had often been told to envision the success, to feel it, to live it, and it would eventually become a reality. This time, however, he couldn't pretend the screams he heard were the adulation of millions of rock fans crying out for more. He yanked off his headphones and listened. Those were *real* screams.

And they were coming from the apartment next door.

Tracy was a nice woman. Pretty. Friendly. She was a *nurse*, for Christ's sake. She certainly didn't deserve whatever was going down in her apartment.

No woman did.

Unplugging the cable, he headed for the door, his favorite guitar in hand. He had Gibsons and Fenders—including a Stratocaster with a tone unlike any other—but he'd never bonded with a guitar the way he had with that Ibanez. The last thing he wanted to do was break it over some asshole's head.

But a guy had to do what a guy had to do—whether he was wearing a pink thong under his jeans or not. He hesitated at Tracy's door, which, thankfully, was still ajar. Following the sounds of a struggle, he dashed into the kitchen in time to see a big blond dude drop his pants and grab Tracy by the hair.

"Open wide and suck it, you fuckin' cunt."

Okay. That does it.

Wielding the guitar like a battering ram, he darted in behind Tracy's attacker just as she drew back a fist and punched him in the nuts. With a roar, the man dropped to his knees as Joey slammed the body of his trusty Ibanez into the creep's right kidney. Flipping the strap over the guy's head, he spun the guitar until the strip of leather tightened around his neck like a garrote.

"On your feet, asshole," Joey hissed. Giving someone a foot taller and fifty or sixty pounds heavier the boot required some small degree of cooperation. He yanked on the Ibanez. "I said, on your feet!"

Instead of doing as he was told, her assailant attempted to pry the strap from around his neck—an action that cost him dearly because Tracy took advantage of the opportunity for further retaliation. Striking like a cobra, she bit his dick hard enough to draw blood.

With a scream worthy of a horror flick, he finally stood up.

"You should've done that sooner," Joey said. "Now, get your ass out of here."

With a knee in the ass to get him started, Joey propelled him through the living room and out the door. After releasing the guitar strap, he gave him a shove that sent him sprawling. "Might want to pull up your pants, dude. Your damn dick is bleeding all over the place."

"You little shit," he said between gulps of air. "I oughta kill you."

"I'd like to see you try." Doubling up the leather strap, Joey swung it with all his might, hitting the man across the face. He didn't stop swinging until he'd chased him down the stairs and out of the building.

After making sure the jerk got in his truck and drove away,

Joey ran up the stairs to Tracy's apartment, bolting the door behind him in case that asshole decided to come back.

If anything, Tracy's injuries were even worse than he'd expected. Her face was bruised and bloody and her eyes were almost swollen shut. Blood matted the hair near her temple, and her nose was twice its normal size.

Somehow, she managed a smile. "Way to go, Joey." A moment later, her head sagged as she slumped against the cabinet.

"Tracy!" He knelt beside her, frantically fumbling for a place to check her pulse—was it the neck or the wrist?—until he realized she was breathing. Passing out would probably save her some pain.

Jesus, what a mess.

He considered calling 911, but figured he ought to try to bring her around first. She might have a preference for which hospital she wanted to go to—or she might not want to go to a hospital at all. He could handle this.

Maybe.

He'd never been much use when it came to medical stuff, which wasn't surprising. He was a musician and a cook. Beyond sore fingers and the occasional cut or burn in the kitchen, he hadn't had much experience. Not like Tracy. She was really smart—had a college degree and everything.

Not smart enough to steer clear of abusive creeps.

Then again, considering the skeleton in *his* closet, he had no right to judge anyone. Opening a drawer, he pulled out a dishrag and a couple of towels, figuring the least he could do was to wipe off the blood before she woke up. She'd probably pass out again when she saw herself in the mirror.

Unfortunately, washing away the blood only made the cuts and bruises easier to see. The longer he worked, the angrier he got, and he wished he'd done more damage to that stupid jerk.

He should've brought his old acoustic instead of the Ibanez. The neck had begun to separate from the body, so breaking it over the guy's head wouldn't have been any great loss. After all, he wasn't one of those rich rock stars who could afford to smash guitars on stage. Still, the Ibanez had done a fine job, giving a whole new meaning to *Guitar Hero*.

Tears stung his eyes as he gazed at her once-lovely face. Since Geena had ditched him for her old boyfriend, he hadn't been interested in dating anyone but—

No. Tracy wouldn't go for his type. Not when she dated guys like the one he'd thrown out of her apartment—something Joey still couldn't believe he'd actually done. Evidently, the stories about an adrenaline rush causing superhuman strength were true. He only wished he'd gotten there a little sooner.

Story of my life.

Chapter 2

As the pain returned in full force, Tracy opened her eyes.

With his narrow face and hawk-like nose, she'd never considered Joey Manzetti to be particularly attractive. At the moment, however, he was a sight for sore eyes—and hers were most definitely sore.

"If it's any consolation, his dick was almost as bloody as your face."

She tried to smile, but her mouth hurt where Bryce had split her lip. "Thank God for small favors—and for you. I thought I was dead."

Joey's deep blue eyes conveyed understanding and concern. "For a second, I thought so too. Then I realized you were still breathing." A smile quirked the corner of his mouth. "Some nurse *I* am."

"You're doing fine—and as rescuers go, you were awesome."

"You were pretty awesome yourself." He sat back on his heels, his smile broadening into a grin. "I can't believe you bit him."

She shrugged. "Seemed like the thing to do at the time. Bet he won't ever try to shove his dick in anyone's mouth again. Talk about stupid…" Closing her eyes, she tried to wish the pain away without much success.

"Want me to call an ambulance?"

"No." Her head swam as she sat up. "I'm okay—or I will be in a few days."

He got up, rinsed out the dishcloth, and dropped it in the sink. "You're sure about that? You really scared me when you didn't wake up right away."

"Nothing wrong with me that won't heal up on its own."

"What about calling the cops?"

"Oh, God no. I can't deal with that."

"But what if he comes back?"

She shook her head. "He won't. Trust me, I know the type. No matter how tough he talks, he'll assume I've reported him and never show his face around here again."

Joey didn't seem convinced. "Yeah, well, the next time you're attacked, you need to scream louder. I had my headphones on and almost didn't hear you."

"There won't *be* a next time. In fact, I'm thinking of joining a convent. Men are too much trouble."

"Somehow I can't picture you as a nun," he drawled. "And men aren't *all* bad. Most of us are nice." He was obviously including himself in that category, but with black hair hanging to his waist in spiral curls, he certainly didn't look the part—more like the bad boy rock star type.

"Maybe, but all the good ones are taken. I haven't run across a single available man I'd give you a dime for in the past five years."

Opening the freezer, he took out several ice cubes and wrapped them in a dish towel. "Maybe you're not looking in the right places."

"Yeah, right. I'm sure I'd find better prospects if I hung out in strip joints and bars instead of logging onto that blasted Internet dating service."

"You haven't had much luck there, have you?"

"No, and bars are even worse. Any idea why I always attract obnoxious, abusive drunks?"

Kneeling beside her, he cupped her cheek and tilted her head back. "Maybe it's because you have such a sweet, understanding face." He handed her the makeshift icepack. "Here. Hold this on your nose."

Truth be told, her entire head needed an icepack. *Or a shrink.* "If that's the case, I'd better practice my Bitch From Hell look." She pressed the ice to the side of her nose and let out a yelp. What little strength she had left deserted her, and she slid sideways, sobbing. "I give up, Joey. I just flat fuckin' give up."

Joey put an arm around her shoulders, letting her lean against his chest. "I know the feeling, but there's no need to give up yet."

She peered up at him. "What do you mean, you know the feeling? Did something happen between you and Geena?"

"You could say that." He grimaced. "She moved out a few weeks ago."

"I wondered why I hadn't seen her around—or heard the baby crying. I'm surprised. You seemed so happy together."

"Yeah, well, *I* was happy—at least, I thought I was. Apparently, *she* wasn't. She packed up Darren and told me she never wanted to see me again—or rather, her mother told me that. She never wanted Geena to move in with me to begin with and seemed tickled shitless that whatshisname finally got jealous enough to want her back."

Tracy was appalled. "I can't believe Geena would do such a thing. She seemed like such a sweet girl."

"Girl being the operative word. I should've known better than to get involved with someone young enough to be my daughter."

"Maybe...but she *is* awfully pretty." A lovely blonde with natural curls and big, blue eyes, Geena had been a waitress at the restaurant where Joey worked as a cook. They'd seemed like a bit of a mismatch, but Tracy had always assumed it was the whole long-haired lead guitar player thing—an attraction Tracy could easily understand since she'd fallen for a few of them herself.

"Yeah. She's pretty, all right—pretty enough to make a fool out of me. I'm beginning to wonder if she ever loved me at all. She sure left me quick enough when her old flame showed up."

"What about Darren? Will you at least be able to visit him?"

"I asked about that. And do you know what she told me? She said Darren wasn't even my kid." He choked on the last word, his eyes filling with tears.

"Oh, Joey..." Tracy couldn't imagine loving a child and then having it taken from her—and worse, being told that it never really hers to begin with. Dealing with a miscarriage had been hard enough. "What did you say?"

"I told her she'd have to prove it. I'm still waiting for an answer on that one."

"What if it's true and he really *isn't* your child?"

"Then I guess I won't ever see him again." He squeezed his eyes shut as though fighting back more tears. "But enough about me and my troubles. Are you sure you're okay?"

"Yeah. I'll be all right eventually, but in the meantime, I'm swearing off men—probably for good."

Joey chuckled in spite of his tears. Obviously he thought she was kidding.

She wasn't.

"And I'm swearing off nineteen-year-olds—like I should've done a long time ago." His expression sobered. "Although that's probably not the only reason she left me."

She eyed him curiously. "Should I not ask about that?"

"I wish you wouldn't." He gave her a quick hug. "I don't want you to hate me too."

"Hey, as long as you don't go around beating up women and shoving your dick in their faces, I can't imagine too many other things that would make me hate you. I'm okay with most quirks, and considering some of the guys I've known, I'd have to be." She shook her head. "But I'm done with all that. If it happens, it happens. I'm not going to waste the time or the energy trying to find someone. Besides, right now, I'd probably even scare off the obnoxious drunks." She patted his hand. "Thanks for your help, Joey. I'm going to take a shower and go to bed. It's been a *very* long day."

"You're sure I can't do anything else?"

"Not unless you want to make sure Bryce is gone."

"No problem. If I catch him hanging around here again, want me to tie him up so you can kick the living shit out of him?"

While giving Bryce a taste of his own medicine was tempting, at the moment, she didn't have the energy or the inclination. "He's not worth the effort."

"Okay." Joey got to his feet. "If you need me, give a yell. I'm right next door."

He helped her to stand, then picked up his guitar and left,

closing the door firmly behind him.

Tracy locked her contrary deadbolt and put the chain across the door. Then she placed a chair in front of it—a precaution she'd never taken before—swearing never to give out her address to anyone ever again.

Stripping off her bloodstained clothing, she made the mistake of taking a quick look in the mirror before getting into the shower.

Nope, no guys will be chasing after me anytime soon. Even Santa would pass her by this year.

Shit.

It was bad enough having to see her patients and coworkers. Christmas was less than a week away. She'd have to face her family. Her parents were leaving soon to visit her brothers for the holidays, so she might be able to escape that confrontation, but her sister would give her hell.

And I deserve it. I knew better. I truly did.

Standing beneath the spray, she rinsed the blood from her hair, shuddering as the crimson water swirled down the drain, reminding her of the shower scene in *Psycho.* The metallic taste of Bryce's blood lingered on her tongue, and she opened her mouth, letting it fill with water and then spitting it out repeatedly, as though she could rinse away everything he'd said and done to her.

With a trace of irony, she recalled how painstakingly she'd applied her makeup in an effort to look nice for that asshole—that fuckin' asshole who'd reciprocated by beating her to a pulp and shoving his dick in her face. She'd rather be alone for the rest of her life than go through such pain and humiliation again.

Never again, she vowed. No matter who he was.

Never, *ever* again.

ꙮ

Joey went back to his apartment, his mind in turmoil. He'd never felt such rage before in his life. He'd actually wanted to kill Bryce after he saw what he'd done to Tracy—kill him so he'd never bother her or any other woman again.

However, rather than go tearing off on a vendetta, he turned to his music, knowing it would help him deal with the raging emotions. He'd lost count of the songs he'd written since Geena left him. This one was for Tracy.

A close examination of the Ibanez failed to uncover any damage—not a scratch or a dent to show what he'd done with it. Reconnecting the strap, he picked up the cable and plugged it in. Donning his headphones, he strummed a few chords and ran through some riffs.

Not even out of tune.

A melody flitted through his head, finding its way to his fingers. The raw emotion followed—the pain, the anger, the terror came pouring out of him. He scribbled down lyrics and notes until he'd purged himself of every thought and feeling he'd had since he heard that first scream.

By the time he'd finished, he had no idea how much time had passed.

His nerves had settled considerably, but Tracy was alone in her apartment, in pain, and probably still terrified. She'd said she was going to take a shower and go to bed. He imagined her washing the blood from her hair, crawling into bed, trying to sleep—possibly crying out when a nightmare awakened her. She had friends and family, of course, but now, when she needed them the most, she had no one to hold her and calm her fears. No one at all.

At least no one could hurt her while she was alone in her apartment. There was some consolation in that—unless that Bryce bastard started harassing her with phone calls. Joey wasn't convinced he wouldn't come back for another round. She should change her phone number, get better locks on her door, and start carrying something to protect herself, like brass knuckles or a can of mace—or even a handgun. He would keep an eye out, check up on her—stuff like that—and if he caught so much as a glimpse of that creep, he was calling the cops whether Tracy liked it or not.

He'd much rather she be mad at him than dead.

Chapter 3

Tracy didn't even bother to glance in the mirror after she dragged herself out of bed the next morning. She'd stared at her reflection enough times during the night to know she looked like death warmed over. The ever-present pain was reminder enough.

Shuffling into the kitchen, the first thing she noticed was the dried blood on the floor and the bloody dishrag in the sink.

I need coffee. Bad.

Ignoring the blood for the time being, she surveyed the coffee maker with a baleful eye. A few dregs were left from the day before, and she was almost desperate enough to pour it into a mug and zap it in the microwave rather than wait for another pot to brew. And yet, this was the first day of her new life, free of male influence, domination, or anything else.

You will not drink crappy coffee.

Pouring it into the sink, she purposely doused the bloody dishrag. "That's what I think of *you*, Bryce. You're nothing but nasty, day-old coffee." She almost laughed when the line from *Scrooge* ran on through her thoughts. *You're nothing but an undigested bit of beef, a blob of mustard, or an old potato. Yes, that's what* you *are…an old potato!*

Too bad Bryce wasn't a ghost like Jacob Marley. A ghost might've scared her to death, but at least they couldn't leave bruises. Her scalp tightened and her head began to pound.

I need caffeine.

She dumped the old grounds in the trash, rinsed out the brew basket, and had just put in a new filter when the doorbell rang.

Her heart took a plunge until she realized Bryce wouldn't have rung the bell. He'd have pounded on the door and yelled.

Coffee first. Visitor second.

She added the coffee, poured in the water, and headed for the door. Peering through the peephole at the tall, green-eyed redhead who stood in the hallway, she heaved a sigh of relief. *Melina.*

Tracy opened the door a crack. "Whatever you do, do *not* scream." She had no desire to wake Joey or anyone else in the building—or the dead, which one of Melina's screams was fully capable of doing.

"Okay…I won't scream," Melina said. "I promise."

Tracy opened the door the rest of the way. Melina didn't scream, but she gasped hard enough to trigger a major coughing fit.

"Gee, thanks, girlfriend," Tracy drawled. "That makes me feel *so* much better. Honestly, you've no idea."

"What happened?" Melina demanded as soon as she'd recovered. "Did you get hit by a truck?"

"In a manner of speaking, yes," Tracy replied. "As in thrown against the side of one."

"Ha, ha, very funny," Melina said with a smirk. "Details, girl. Give me details."

Tracy headed toward the kitchen. The coffee wasn't ready yet, but she wanted to be right there waiting when the moment arrived. "If it's all the same to you, I'd rather not relive the experience. It wasn't much fun."

Taking Tracy by the arm, Melina spun her around until the overhead light shone directly on her face. "Damn, Trace… Who did this to you?"

"Bryce Hancock. Remember him? The one I wasn't sure I liked but decided to go out with a second time because he was such a hottie?"

She seemed doubtful, holding her mouth in a puckered twist. "I think so—the tall blond dude?"

Tracy nodded. The coffee had almost finished brewing. *Thank God.* "Yeah. I don't know what his problem is exactly, but on the whole, I'd have to say he's a bit on the psychotic side—maybe delayed stress syndrome from serving in Iraq." *Close enough.* She filled up her mug. "Then again, I may be giving the war too much credit for messing him up. He may have already been nuts." A cautious sip burned her lip slightly. "Who knows? I only know I have no intention of ever seeing him again—unless it's in court."

Melina's gaze narrowed with suspicion. "You're pressing charges—aren't you?"

"I should, and if it weren't so much trouble, I'd consider it. As it is, he may be pressing charges against me because I don't think his dick is going to be functional for a while." Although she hadn't taken a chunk out of it, she certainly hadn't been gentle. "Would you like some coffee?"

Melina ignored the offer, her eyes perilously close to popping out of their sockets. "What did you do to him?"

"Let's just say he put his penis in a very dangerous place."

"You bit him?" She threw back her head, stomping her feet and crowing with laughter. "Oh, that is just too cool."

"It was the only thing I could think of to do—that and punching him in the nuts. Actually, my neighbor finished him off for me. You should have seen little Joey dragging him off with a guitar strap around his neck." Chuckling at the memory, she added, "I should probably bake him a cake for that."

"Or fuck him," Melina suggested. "Guys like that too, you know."

Tracy shook her head so hard she had to wait for her eyes to catch up with it. "Nope. Joey's a nice guy, but I've sworn off men. If I feel the need for intimate companionship, I'll find myself a nice lesbian—which I don't want right now, so don't try to fix me up with anyone. Okay?"

Dropping her chin, Melina gave Tracy her trademark round-eyed not-so-innocent stare. "Now, Tracy. Would *I* do that?"

Tracy didn't hesitate. "Yes. At least, you would if you knew someone."

"I don't know any lesbians personally," Melina admitted. "But I've been to a club in Louisville where you can find just about anything you could ever possibly want—gays, straights, cross-dressers, lesbians—you name it, and there's probably one hanging out there. The show's usually pretty good too. Female impersonators, mostly."

"Well, *if* I ever go—which I seriously doubt—it would only be for the show. No romantic encounters for me. Period."

Melina shrugged. "Can't say I blame you, but it would be fun to go there together sometime. It's only an hour's drive from Pemberton, and I think you'd enjoy it. Speaking of fun, you *are* still planning to go to the Barton Junction concert with me, aren't you?"

"If I'm not too scary-looking by then."

"Hmm..." With a finger beneath Tracy's chin, she tipped her face up toward the light again, subjecting her injuries to further scrutiny. "You should be able to cover up most of that with makeup. Any thoughts as to what you'll do with the extra ticket now that you haven't got a date?"

Considering the price Tracy had paid for that ticket, she was tickled shitless not to have to waste it on Bryce. "I should give it to Joey. He'd like that better than a cake anyway. He's a big rock star himself."

"Rock star?" Melina's eyes were once again agog with curiosity. "Really?"

"No, not really. He plays in a local band. I went to see them once. They're actually pretty good—although Joey sounds even better by himself. I hear him playing some of his own songs once in a while. Don't know if the band ever plays them or not."

"Go ahead and ask him," she said. "If not, I'm sure we could find someone else."

"No shit. I still can't believe we got such good seats."

"I know." Her eyes gleamed with excitement. "Center stage, seventh row! I can hardly believe it myself. I nearly had a fit when Janet told me."

"I've never had seats that good for anything in my life," Tracy said. "If I get a ticket at all, I wind up in the nosebleed section— which I should probably avoid for obvious reasons." She tapped her nose. "Still, it's nice to know that every once in a while, things can actually go my way."

"Oh, now, don't start feeling sorry for yourself," Melina chided. "We're going to see the best band in the whole world, and we're going to have a great time."

"You're right—and I'll be better by then, I promise."

"You go, girl." She gave Tracy a hug. "I guess Christmas shopping is out of the question?"

"I believe so." Tracy sighed. "I don't need to buy a whole lot more anyway. I've got the family covered and my Christmas cards sent out. I don't think I'll make it to the party tonight, though. Going back to work on Monday will be bad enough."

"I'll pass along your regrets, but that shithead ought to be in jail. You know that, don't you?"

"Yeah. I know. Right now, he's just another name on my Not Safe To Date list."

Melina snorted a laugh. "You should post that list on Facebook—or Tweet it."

"That's a thought—although they'd probably all gang up on me at once if I did. Don't think I'd survive that. My plan is to lay low and hope no man ever notices me again."

"In the meantime, you'd better get tested for HIV."

"Don't worry. I will."

Melina aimed her no-nonsense nurse look at her. "I mean *now*."

Tracy groaned. "If I go into a clinic or hospital now they're gonna want to know where all these bruises came from. I can't face that yet, Melina. I really can't. Trust me, I'll be just as HIV positive or negative a few days from now."

And every bit as determined never to let another man into her life.

No matter how hot he is.

೮೨೦೪

Joey almost had a heart attack when he heard Tracy's doorbell ring. Her friend probably didn't realize he'd been listening for screams—

or that he might be watching her from the peephole in his own door. After assuring himself that Bryce hadn't returned, he went back to practicing—without the amp or the headphones. He couldn't hear the notes as well, but the fingering practice was just as important.

He'd checked the parking lot at least every half hour since breakfast. A red Dodge Ram would be easy enough to spot, although he wasn't sure a guy who'd taken a fist to the nuts and a bite to his dick would feel much like stalking—not yet, anyway.

After her friend left, he wrote his cell phone number on a scrap of paper and took it with him when went to see Tracy. Neighbors had to stick together in times like these, and exchanging phone numbers was one way to help ensure everyone's safety—whether there were abusive boyfriends involved or not.

"Yep, I'm still alive," Tracy said when she answered his knock. Her lips were so swollen, she winced when she attempted a smile.

"Glad to hear it." He held out the slip of paper. "Here's my phone number if you ever need me. But I'm warning you, if I see anything suspicious, I'm calling the cops." Knowing he'd sounded a bit brusque, he softened his tone. "I hope you don't mind."

Fortunately, she didn't argue. "I'm willing to let it slide for now, but I won't be so forgiving if he comes back. Guess I'd better give you my number—although I'm really bad about letting my phone go dead. I think the battery's getting funky."

"Might want to get a new one."

She arched a brow—another action that appeared to be painful. "You and my friend Melina must be cut from the same cloth. Aren't you going to tell me to get an HIV test?"

"I *was* going to suggest it. I'm assuming some of that blood was his."

"Not much, actually. It's not like I held on to savor it." Her voice contained a teasing note—one he was far more familiar with than her sobs.

"When do you have to work again?"

"Monday. Hopefully I'll feel more human. Too bad I won't be healed up before Christmas. I can hardly wait to hear what my sister has to say."

"Can't blame you for that."

She glanced down, fidgeting with the paper he'd given her. "Thanks again, Joey. I–I think you might've saved my life. You could've ignored the screams."

"Not once I'd heard them. No way."

She gave him another painful-looking smile. "You're a great guy. Geena's probably kicking herself for letting you go."

His heart gave a lurch. "I doubt it." She might actually be thanking her lucky stars. If only he didn't play so much better when—

"Hold on a sec, and I'll write my number down for you real quick." Her stride never faltered as she hurried off toward the kitchen.

Joey had to admire her spirit. She wasn't exactly out painting the town, but at least she wasn't sitting around crying in her beer.

Definitely tough.

A few moments later, she returned with another slip of paper. "Here's my number, along with a little something for saving my life." She handed him a ticket. "I hope you aren't busy that night."

His mouth fell open when he read it. "Holy shit. Barton Junction? You're kidding me, right?"

"Nope. I'm going with a couple of friends. I got that extra ticket so I could take a date, but since I'm not dating anyone, I thought I'd give it to you."

"Thanks, Tracy. I don't care if I *am* working, I'll get off somehow. They're an awesome band."

Her smile seemed a little easier this time. "Nothing's too good for my hero." Leaning closer, she kissed his cheek.

Goosebumps raced over his skin and his groin tingled. In another second, his dick would be hard.

Whoa.

He cleared his throat. "Well, I, um, guess I'll see you later. Thanks again for the ticket."

"My pleasure." With a nod, she closed her door, leaving him

standing in the hallway, still slightly stunned.

Heroes didn't feel that way about the people they rescued, did they? The damsel in distress was the one who was supposed to gaze up at her hero with adoration—not the other way around. Never having rescued anyone before, he truly didn't know.

Perhaps that reaction was normal.

Or maybe it's because of what I'm wearing under my jeans.

If Tracy ever discovered *that* little secret, she'd change her tune in a hurry, just like every other woman had. Geena hadn't come right out and said it, but he was convinced it played a role in her abrupt departure. He couldn't help it if he played guitar better that way. *Among other things*. Still, he'd managed to keep it hidden from Geena for a long time.

But wouldn't it be nice not to have to hide?

He might know how that felt someday, but today wasn't that day. Not with Geena, and probably not with Tracy—no matter how forgiving she'd been of other men's quirks. He couldn't blame either of them. It wasn't their fault anyway.

It was all his.

Chapter 4

Monday morning could've been a lot worse. The outcries from her coworkers seemed tame in comparison to Melina's reaction. Beverly was properly shocked and, having recently rid herself of an errant husband, was in complete agreement with Tracy's intention to give up men forever.

"That's probably your best bet," the lanky blonde said with a firm nod. "The past two years with Jerry were enough to make me want to become a nun. Too bad I'm not Catholic."

"Me, either," Tracy said. "Although I'm not absolutely certain that's a requirement. I'll have to check into it."

"Let me know what you find out," Bev said. "I'm not sure I'd like wearing black all the time, but maybe the rules aren't as strict as they used to be."

"Will you two stop that?" Melina admonished. "There are lots of nice men."

Beverly pulled a bag of IV fluids from the Pyxis machine and spiked it with the tubing. "Name one."

"My husband," Melina replied.

Beverly barked a laugh. "You mean the man who cleaned under the hood of your car and threatened you with death if you drove it down a gravel road?"

"He worked hard on that," Melina protested. "I can see his point."

"Yeah, but why would anyone want to clean a car's engine anyway?" Tracy asked. "I'd have told him to get a life."

"Okay, so he *is* kind of anal," Melina admitted. "At least he doesn't deny it. Nobody's perfect. It's simply a matter of finding someone you love enough to ignore their quirks."

Tracy didn't think abusive husbands and boyfriends fell into that category. Some quirks were impossible to ignore. "Be that as it may, if Prince Charming comes knocking on my door, fine. But I'm not gonna go looking for him." She set her supplies on the cart. "If you all need anything, I'll be in room three putting in a PICC line."

Melina snickered. "And if Prince Charming calls?"

"Tell him I'm busy."

Tracy got the PICC line in place without a hitch and spent the rest of the day doing every procedure wearing a mask, whether it was required or not.

That's one way to hide a smashed face.

She told one patient she was wearing the mask because she had a cold, which was believable considering her inability to breathe through her nose. Makeup helped cover the bruises, but the swelling around her eyes was harder to explain.

"Allergies," she said to one elderly man, wishing it was the right time of year to blame bee stings or poison ivy. Then she hit on the idea of a peanut allergy, which was less seasonally specific.

Too bad I can't wear a mask on Christmas. Since their parents would be out of town visiting their brothers for the holidays, Miranda had invited Tracy to the party at the home of her new in-laws. Tracy had met Travis's family the day he'd married her sister so at least their first impression of her wouldn't be as the stupid chick who'd let some asshole beat the shit out of her. Telling Miranda the details of what she'd done to Bryce would have to wait until another time.

The trouble was, she *did* feel stupid. Looking back, she should never have gone on that second date with Bryce or should've at least jumped out of the truck right after he hit her. She could've called a cab or had Melina pick her up. *Why didn't I do that?* And if she couldn't understand it, why would anyone else?

You had to be there. She was willing to bet there were millions of abused women who would say the exact same thing. Anyone could talk tough and think straight when they weren't getting beaten to a pulp. Sure, she'd fought back, but only when convinced she was going to die no matter what she did.

Shaking off the frisson of fear, she finished her shift without incident, although lunch was difficult. Refusing to admit defeat by eating the hospital cafeteria's chicken noodle soup, she cut her hamburger into tiny pieces so she could get it in her mouth. She chewed it carefully, noting that her teeth weren't nearly as loose as they'd been the day before.

Lucky me.

Her luck was short-lived, however, because while crossing a crowded overpass on the way home the next day, her car's alternator light came on, and everything, including the CD player, slowed down and died.

Thankful that the grade of the road was slightly downhill, she put the car in neutral and pushed it over to the shoulder—alone. Not one of the irate motorists behind her offered to give her a hand. The tricky part was hopping in and setting the emergency brake before the car rolled any farther—which she managed to accomplish—although not without hitting her shin with the car door as she leaped inside.

Her cell phone was completely dead, and she was several miles from home. Still aching from her ordeal with Bryce, she climbed out of the car, locked the door, zipped up her coat, slung her purse over her shoulder, and started walking.

She hadn't gone far when a couple of guys in a van slowed down and shouted something at her, startling her into stepping off the edge of the pavement and turning her ankle. Evidently, they didn't find her red nose and swollen eyes appealing because they didn't stop.

Grumbling, she limped on down the road, ruminating on the mean, despicable natures of men. She didn't need them. A nice, butch girlfriend with a tow-truck would suit her needs quite nicely. Perhaps if she went to that club Melina mentioned she might find one who wouldn't mind her black eyes and swollen nose.

Not likely.

She had almost reached the off-ramp when a squad car pulled

up beside her. The cop riding shotgun rolled down his window. "Is that your car parked on the overpass?"

He had curly brown hair, blue eyes, and dimples. In another life, she'd have said he was cute. At the moment, however, he was simply another annoying male.

"Yeah."

"You'd better get it towed pretty quick or we'll have to impound it."

Her annoyance quadrupled. "I wasn't intending to leave it there."

"See that you don't," he said. "What happened to your face?"

"I ordered the wrong meal at Mickey D's."

"Very funny." He wasn't smiling. "Did your boyfriend do that to you?"

She thought for a moment. "He was more of a mistake than a boyfriend."

"Did you press charges?"

Oh, here we go... "No, and I'm not going to. I never want to see him again, not even in court."

"Wouldn't you like to at least see him thrown in jail?" With a shake of his head, he blew out a disgusted breath. "I'll never understand the way women think. How can we ever get the creeps off the street if victims don't press charges?"

"If everyone pressed charges, there wouldn't be any men left on the street at all—not that I have a problem with that." At the moment, putting the entire male population behind bars seemed like an excellent idea. Too bad there weren't enough jails.

"Aw, be nice, now." He was finally smiling. Sort of.

"I don't *feel* like being nice." Obviously they had no intention of offering her a ride. With a wave, she started off. "Have fun fighting crime."

Once upon a time, she would've teased and flirted and those two officers would've fallen all over themselves to give her a ride—or anything else she wanted. In her current frame of mind, however, walking on a sore ankle in the freezing cold seemed preferable.

She hobbled down the ramp and crossed the street. By the time she'd covered the two blocks to the nearest convenience store, she was so cold she couldn't feel her feet. Unfortunately, the numbness didn't extend to her ankle.

She reached the door just as the glass shattered and man in a ski mask ran out, brandishing a gun and knocking her to the ground. Pain shot through her leg as his footsteps pounded across the parking lot and faded away.

She lay there debating the wisdom of getting up. It seemed quite pointless, really. Sooner or later, someone was sure to knock her down again. A siren wailed in the distance. Perhaps if she stayed down long enough someone might put her in an ambulance and take her to the hospital.

Nah. Not hurt badly enough for that.

Rolling over, she sat up to assess the damage. A rip in her scrub pants exposed her knee, which was scraped, bleeding, and hurt like the devil. Her hip couldn't have felt much worse if she'd been kicked by an elephant.

Tracy struggled to her feet and went inside, grateful for the warmth. The best she could tell, the robber hadn't shot anyone—at least, no one else seemed to be bleeding—although several other people were in the process of getting up off the floor. "Is anyone hurt?"

"No." The clerk stood up, gaping at Tracy's face. "Except you. Did he do that?"

She shook her head. "He only knocked me down and tore up my leg. Someone else rearranged my face—although it wouldn't surprise me if they turned out to be cousins."

Lights flashing and siren wailing, a police car screeched to a halt near the door. The same two officers she'd met on the overpass leaped out and rushed into the store.

Oh, joy...

While they took statements from the other witnesses, Tracy bought a cup of coffee and box of sandwich bags. Filling one of the bags with ice, she held it on her knee while she called a tow truck from the payphone in the corner. She was about to call a cab when one of the officers—the cute one—approached, surveying her from head to toe. "You look worse."

"Thanks." She stared pointedly at the dark stain on the front of his pants. "So do you."

"Spilled my coffee," he mumbled.

"Really? I thought you might have an incontinence problem. If so, I could help you with that. I'm a whiz with catheters. One guy even kissed me after I got a coudé in him when no one else could."

He took a step backward as though she had a Foley in her hand. "I had one of those in me once. Never again."

"Yeah, well, someday when your prostate is the size of a grapefruit and you can't pee, you'll thank me."

His eyes widened in horror. "They can get that big?"

"Oh, yeah. Then you'd have to have it surgically removed or at least roto-rootered before you could ever pee again." Tracy derived a rather perverse satisfaction from his shudder.

Clearing his throat, he flipped over a page in his notebook. "Did you get a good look at the perpetrator?"

"Absolutely. Right after he knocked me down, I tripped him, yanked off his mask, and took his picture—or I would have if my phone wasn't dead." Noting his scowl, she added, "Sorry. If you guys had offered me a ride, I might be in a better mood."

"We aren't supposed to do that unless you commit a crime or the circumstances make it imperative. Some asshole sued the police department after he lost his job when his boss spotted him in the back of a squad car. The guy told his boss his car had broken down, but he didn't believe him and fired him anyway. And we don't open car doors when you lock your keys inside anymore because some other asshole sued us for screwing up his paint job."

"Assholes are everywhere," she agreed. "I've dealt with quite a few of them lately." Joey being the lone exception. "That last one had on a black jacket, jeans, and a ski mask. He had a gun, and he can run pretty fast. I can't remember anything else." She gave him her name and rattled off the number of her dead phone. "Can I go now?"

He nodded. "Got a ride?"

"Not yet. I was about to call a cab—and yes, I already called a tow truck."

His smile finally showed a trace of compassion. "If you'll stick around for a little while, we'll take you home. Just don't tell anybody we did it."

"I could pretend to be a hooker who got beat up by her pimp," she suggested.

His eyes swept over her again. "Hookers don't wear scrubs—especially not with Winnie the Pooh and Tigger on them. Not sexy at all."

"Good. I don't *want* to look sexy. I've had it with men. From now on, I'm sticking with women. They're a lot safer."

He snorted a laugh. "You've obviously never tangled with a pissed-off dyke. You'd be better off dating guys."

"I didn't say I wanted to date them. In fact, I don't want to date anyone—male *or* female—ever again."

As though scenting a challenge, he immediately turned on the charm. A slow grin spread across his face, dimpling his cheeks. "I'll bet the right man could change your mind."

Once upon a time, Tracy would've returned his smile and joined in the flirtation—or even been the initiator. Those days were gone. "I doubt it."

"Not even a man in uniform?"

Ignoring his cocky grin and twinkling eyes, she waved a dismissive hand. "Highly overrated."

"I dunno," he drawled. "You might feel differently after being interrogated in a police car." He rubbed his chin with his left hand, drawing her attention to his wedding ring.

It figures.

She peered at his name pin. "Oh, Officer Williams, you are *such* a bad boy. Somebody oughta spank your cute little butt."

His grin became a smirk. "Are you volunteering?"

"Nope. Just making an observation." Hitching her purse strap higher on her shoulder, she nodded toward the payphone. "Never mind about the ride. All of a sudden, I have this overwhelming urge to call a cab."

"Suit yourself."

"Don't worry. I will."

Chapter 5

With a trembling fingertip, Joey tapped the link to the lab result and sat staring at it as though reading his death sentence. Although he tried, he couldn't convince himself there was any possibility it might be a mistake. These tests were supposed to be one hundred percent accurate, and he knew they hadn't mislabeled anything. The samples had been double checked by everyone, including the required witnesses.

"You don't look very happy," Paulina said. "I'm guessing this has something to do with why we're now short a waitress?"

He glanced at his boss. Tall and heavyset with short, dark hair and a gruff voice, Paulina Stotts had a heart of gold, whether she liked for anyone to know it or not.

"Yeah," he said. "Sorry about that."

"Hey, it's not your fault she's a damn fool." She nodded at his phone. "What's the verdict?"

"Well…this doesn't say whether Geena's ex-boyfriend is Darren's father or not—"

"You mean that Trey Daniels she used to date? She dumped you for *him*?"

Paulina's expression of incredulity was some consolation, although it didn't improve his mood any. "Apparently. Anyway, it turns out I'm not Darren's father."

"You're a damn sight better dad than Trey will ever be. Best I could tell, he was a selfish, immature piece of shit."

Joey's attempt at a smile failed miserably. "You're only saying that to make me feel better."

She shrugged. "Maybe, but it's also the truth—at least, as I see it." Tying on her apron, she added, "So that's that, huh? She just takes the baby and leaves?"

"She already did." He switched off his phone and sat down with a thud in the nearest chair. "This only clinches the deal."

"Guess I'll have to hire someone else then." She pursed her lips. "What type of girl do you want this time?"

He finally managed a chuckle. "Sure you don't want to hire one that'll suit *you*?"

A pastry chef by training, Paulina had been the manager of Georgio's for several years before Joey finally figured out why she tended to hire such pretty waitresses. Unfortunately, she had yet to hire one who saw her as a potential love interest.

"Nah. No point in that. I'll just stick the 'waitress wanted' sign back in the window and run an ad in the paper. We'll see who takes the bait."

For his part, he hoped the next one really *did* prefer girls.

Geez. I'm starting to sound like Tracy.

For a microsecond, he thought about introducing his neighbor to Paulina. He wasn't sure Tracy would be interested in someone as butch as his boss, but if Bryce was any indication, Tracy liked her boyfriends big and tall—and Paulina certainly fit that description.

She clapped him on the shoulder. "Let's get started. If you'll take care of the *puttanesca*, I'll make the pizza crust—unless you'd rather work out your frustrations on the dough."

Joey wasn't sure which was more appropriate: kneading bread dough into submission or making the pasta sauce supposedly originated by Italian prostitutes.

"I'll make the dough."

෴

Arriving home exhausted and in pain, Tracy tossed her purse on the kitchen counter, plugged in her phone and her Christmas tree, and ordered a pizza.

She doctored her knee while she waited, and when the doorbell rang, her heart only stopped for a second or two. Maybe someday she'd stop assuming any visitor or phone call was Bryce coming back to hound and torment her. Peering through the peephole, she saw the delivery boy standing in the hall.

"Looks like you've had a rough day," he said when she opened the door.

"More like a rough week. Keep the change." She handed him the money, knowing full well that the "change" was all of thirty-five cents, took the pizza from him, and shut the door more gently than she would've liked.

This run of bad luck would end someday. Then she could smile and be charming to delivery boys and give them big tips instead of practically slamming doors in their faces.

Nobody's luck stayed bad forever, did it?

Then again, perhaps she'd used up her luck allotment getting such good seats for the concert. Melina's friend, Janet, had stood in line to get a number that determined her place in the queue to actually buy the tickets. Maybe it was *her* luck that was good, rather than Tracy or Melina's. Perhaps Tracy's streak of bad luck reached further back than she realized.

But what if there was no such thing as luck? What if this was punishment from God?

Didn't matter. The pizza was hot and delicious and much easier to chew than the chicken she'd had for lunch. She ate as much as she could hold, washing it down with a cold beer before falling asleep in front of the television.

When the doorbell awakened her, she glanced at the clock. *Eleven-thirty?* A frisson of fear shook her to the core. It had to be Bryce. No one else could possibly have a legitimate reason for wanting to see her so late.

Although she considered ignoring it, curiosity soon got the better of her. Tiptoeing to the door, she checked the peephole.

Joey stood in the hallway with his head hanging low and a defeated sag to his shoulders.

Now I'm really *curious.*

Shoving the chair out of the way, she undid the chain, turned the key in the deadbolt, unlocked the knob, and opened the door. She hadn't been mistaken. His expression was bleak, and an air of defeat hung about him like a dark cloud.

"Is something wrong?"

He nodded. "Sorry to bother you this late, but I had to talk to someone."

She opened the door further and gestured for him to enter. The remains of her pizza still sat on the coffee table. "If you're hungry, I could warm that up for you."

Having worked in the ER for a few years prior to switching to the clinic, Tracy understood the virtues of cold pizza and was of the opinion that nothing on a pepperoni pizza could possibly go bad, even if it sat out through two shifts.

"No, thanks. I'm not hungry." He sat down on the couch as heavily as a man his size could. "I got the results of the paternity test today. Turns out I'm really *not* Darren's father."

Tracy gaped at him for a moment before finding her tongue. "Do you believe the test? I mean, was it witnessed and legal?"

"Oh, yeah. I made sure of that. We did one test with me, Geena, and Darren, and then another one with Trey, her old boyfriend. Just wish we'd done it when Darren was born." Leaning back against the couch, he blew out a breath. "I'm so damned stupid. I wasn't even suspicious when he was born a few weeks early, and he doesn't look a thing like me."

Tracy nodded. "He always reminded me more of Geena. If I'd thought about it at all, which I didn't, I'd have realized that your darker coloring should've been the more dominant trait."

He stared up at the ceiling. "I can see it all now. She came onto me so fast I can't believe I didn't realize what she was doing. At least we didn't get married."

"That really would've been a mess."

"No shit. I don't have any legal claim to either of them. I should feel relieved, but I don't." He paused for a long moment before barking out a mirthless laugh. "Ever hear that Toby Keith song about some other man running his life when his ex remarries? That's how I feel—whether Geena and Darren were truly ever mine or not."

Tracy preferred rock to country, but she knew the song. "It seems odd that he would've waited this long. Darren is what, five months old? He's had more than a year to come back. What made him do it now?"

Joey seemed to sink further into the sofa. "That's my fault, actually. Geena…found something of mine. Something that freaked her out enough to go see him and tell him about Darren." The smile he gave her was as weak and humorless as his laugh had been. "And don't worry. It wasn't whips and chains or kiddie porn. Nothing that horrible, just something she didn't understand."

Tracy didn't understand, either. Not that it mattered. "Think she'll get over it and come back?"

"I doubt it—unless her Prince Charming turns into a frog."

She patted his knee. "Stranger things have happened."

Poor Joey. He looked so miserable. She had no idea what to do or say to help. Perhaps there *wasn't* anything for her to do. "But would you? Take her back, I mean?"

"I don't know. She said some pretty awful things to me. I know she was upset, but *still*…"

Tracy recalled what her ex-husband had said to her when he left. No. She wouldn't take him back. *No fuckin' way.* "Burned her bridges completely?"

"Maybe." He shrugged. "It's hard to say how I'll feel about her a year from now—or even next week." He blew out a breath. "I guess this is what I get for pretending to be normal."

Tracy had no idea what he'd meant by that and was too chicken to ask—aside from the fact that it was none of her business. "You know, a new baby can be very stressful. Maybe—"

"No. This isn't the first time I've been dumped—and for the very same reason—although there was never a baby involved before." Closing his eyes, he drew in a ragged breath. "Geena was pregnant and said she loved me. I thought it might actually work. Obviously, I was wrong."

Tracy hesitated, wondering if this was the time to commiserate.

Perhaps it was. "I was pregnant when I married Bob. Then I lost the baby, and he scrammed of my life like a scalded cat. Of course, I was devastated at the time, but it was probably for the best. He was way too stuffy."

"That must've been tough."

"I'm over it now—and like you said, at least you and Geena weren't married." She suspected that Joey's loss was too raw for him to see any silver linings as yet. That sort of thing only came with time.

"True." Seeming to have just noticed it, he nodded toward the rip in her scrubs. "What happened there?"

"It's a long story. Sure you wouldn't rather call it a night?"

"Try me." He rubbed his eyes with the heels of his hands. "I doubt if I can sleep anyway."

Tracy rattled off the events of her day, ending with her reaction to the doorbell.

"Sorry about that," he said. "I knew it was late, but—"

"No harm done. Really. I'm glad I was here for you. After what you did for me, I owe you one."

He traced the outline of her nose with a gentle fingertip. "Does it still hurt?"

"Not much," she replied. "Trust me, it looks a lot worse than it feels."

"Yeah. And then there are some things that feel a lot worse than they look."

By that she could only assume he was referring to a broken heart. "I know that feeling, too."

"Don't we all."

૱ᎯᏫ

Joey entered his own apartment, passing by the room he and Geena had shared without so much as a glance. Standing at the doorway of what was once Darren's room, he tried to recall the quiet, even breathing of his sleeping child—a child who wasn't really his.

Whether he was the boy's biological father or not didn't matter. Joey still missed him—missed everything about him, from changing his diapers to rocking him to sleep. He'd done his share of babysitting, especially after Geena went back to work. They'd worked opposite shifts to keep from having to hire a sitter or put him in daycare. Maybe that was part of the problem. He and Geena hadn't seen much of each other during those last few weeks.

Geena wouldn't come back. Her mother would see to that. Irene had disapproved of Joey from the very beginning, citing everything from the difference in their ages to his lifestyle as a musician—and she hadn't known the worst of it. She'd begged Geena not to move in with him and had repeatedly offered to help raise the baby. She'd won in the end.

If only she hadn't felt the need to gloat.

Whether he liked Irene or not, even he had to admit that she'd been right all along. If he'd listened to her, he wouldn't be facing such an unbearable loss now. He might believe he had a son—somewhere—but never having held Darren in his arms and grown to love him, he would've been spared the pain of separation.

Still, Geena had been like a breath of fresh air in his life, and for a time, he truly thought she would make a difference—perhaps even bringing about a permanent change. He turned out to be as wrong about that as he'd been about everything else. Of all the stupid mistakes he'd made in his life, that was the worst.

Darren wouldn't remember any of this, and there would be no need to ever tell him. Geena would probably destroy any pictures of the man she'd lived with for the first few months of her child's life. Darren would grow up only knowing Trey as his father. There would be no custody battles, no chance of a relationship of any kind with the boy. The war was over even before it began.

And Joey was the loser.

Chapter 6

After work on Wednesday, Melina drove Tracy to the shop to pick up her car. The new alternator was pretty pricey, but Tracy was pleased to have wheels again.

Melina's parting gift was a can of pepper spray. "Don't be afraid to use it if that idiot gets anywhere near you."

"Okay." Tracy wasn't convinced it would stop a guy like Bryce, but she took it anyway.

"I mean it, girlfriend. Spray his ugly mug with impunity and then give him a kick in the groin that'll make peanut butter out of his balls."

Biting back a smile, she climbed into her car. "I'll do my best."

After wishing Melina a merry Christmas, Tracy headed for home. Despite the fact that her breath still caught in her throat every time she passed a large red vehicle, she focused her conscious mind on Joey's situation rather than her own. Whether he was Darren's real father or not, Joey had loved the boy as his own and undoubtedly looked forward to celebrating the baby's first Christmas. Now he'd be spending it alone.

That so totally sucks.

Arriving at her apartment building, she scanned the vicinity before getting out of her car. Pepper spray in hand, she hurried to the door, catching a brief glimpse of the window overlooking the parking lot. If Joey was home, he was sitting in the dark. Even his tiny Christmas tree remained unlit.

No one answered her knock, either. Since Joey mostly worked evenings, this wasn't surprising, but it proved one thing. Geena hadn't returned.

Entering her apartment, she glanced at her own tree. There was something inherently sad about an unlit tree, and the first thing she did was plug it in. The soft glow instantly improved her mood, and she took a moment to count her blessings. She had good friends, a car that actually worked, and a neighbor willing to stick his neck out for her.

Life could be a helluva lot worse.

She considered calling her sister to apprise her of the recent encounter with Bryce's fists, but couldn't find the right words. In the end, she emailed her for directions to her in-laws' house. Miranda would have a fit when she saw her, but she'd pitch an even bigger fit if Tracy didn't show up.

Spending Christmas Eve alone was nothing new, and she saw no point in visiting Miranda simply to get the conniptions over with a day early. Not when she could snuggle up on the couch with a cup of hot chocolate and watch the marathon showing of *A Christmas Story*.

After seeing Ralphie get his Red Ryder BB gun for the third time, she decided to call it a night.

She awoke on Christmas morning, wondering if she should run over to Joey's apartment and wish him a merry Christmas. Something told her he was bound to be feeling pretty rotten—if he was even there.

She didn't have to be anywhere until eleven or so. The party would probably go on all day and into the night. She didn't have to stay that long, which was one nice thing about going to a party without a date—she could leave whenever she felt like it.

Tracy was in the process of pouring her first cup of coffee when the doorbell rang, triggering yet another frisson of fear.

I'd like to kill that man.

Twice.

Picking up the can of pepper spray, she headed for the door, fully intending to spray first and ask questions later.

Fortunately, she had the good sense to check the peephole. Joey stood in the hallway.

After undoing her numerous security measures, she opened the door.

"Merry Christmas." She did her best to sound more cheerful than he looked. "I knocked on your door when I got home yesterday. Guess you were working."

"Yeah. I was surprised at how busy we were. I was supposed to have the day off—what with the new baby and all—but I figured I might as well work rather than sitting home alone."

She laughed. "And to think, you could've come over here and sat through the *Christmas Story* marathon with me."

He managed a grin. "How many times did you watch it?"

"I drew the line at three. Want some coffee?"

He nodded. "Yeah. I'm going crazy over there all alone."

"Believe it or not, I'm actually feeling a little better. Still pissed as hell that I freak out whenever I see a big red truck or hear the doorbell, but otherwise, I'm not doing too badly. I've got a family thing to go to in a little bit. I don't know how long I'll stay, but—" She paused to consider the alternatives. No one would mind if she brought Joey along, and since he wasn't her boyfriend, she didn't see it as a date—more along the lines of aiding a fellow sufferer. "Would you like to come with me?"

He shook his head. "Not sure I'm up to that yet. I just came over to thank you again for listening the other night. I hated to bother you, but—"

"No worries, Joey. That's what friends are for. The holidays are tough enough as it is. I'm feeling better today, but I might be down in the dumps again on New Year's Eve."

"My band is playing at a party—otherwise, I'd probably be right there with you."

"Thank God for the gig, then." Reaching into the cabinet, she got out another mug. "Have a seat. Need cream or sugar?"

"No." He pulled out a chair and sat down at the table. "Black is fine."

She set his coffee in front of him and leaned back against the counter. "We're quite a pair, aren't we?"

"Yeah. Truly pathetic—at least, *I* am. Right now. I'd like to get drunk and—"

"And what?"

He gazed into the mug of coffee as though he might find the answer there. "I have absolutely no idea. Instead of getting a major kick out of my son's first Christmas, I'm trying to wrap my head around the fact that I don't even *have* a son." With a bitter smile, he added, "Almost makes me wish I'd slept around and had eight or nine kids with half a dozen other women. At least that way, I might have someone to visit on Christmas."

"No other family in Pemberton?"

"My parents are both gone and my sister lives in Connecticut. Guess I'll call her after while." He sniffed. "She'll be so pleased. She begged me not to get involved with Geena."

"The invitation's still open," Tracy said, although she knew he wouldn't accept. Had she been in his shoes, she didn't think she'd want to spend Christmas Day with a bunch of strangers, either—no matter how lonely she was.

"Thanks, but I'll pass."

"Can't say I blame you. Having to explain my beat-up face will be tough enough. I'd stay home if I could."

With a weary sigh, Joey leaned back in his chair. "So, what do we do now?"

Tracy had never seen a man look quite so defeated. Unfortunately, she was fresh out of helpful ideas. Melina's suggestion that Tracy fuck Joey as a way of thanking him for coming to her rescue flitted through her mind, but she immediately dismissed the notion. It wouldn't solve anything and could only end up complicating everything else. "I don't know. Eat chocolate and cry, I guess."

At least he smiled. "I've already done that."

"Me, too—although I'm not sure it helped much," she said. "Right now, I can't even *think* about getting involved with another man. It's as if Bryce killed that part of me."

"Yeah, that numbness of the heart is tough to overcome. Songwriters are about the only people who benefit from heartache.

I've written scads of songs in the past few weeks." A shy smile accompanied his glance. "I wrote one for you after I left here that night."

She didn't have to ask what night he was referring to. "Really? You'll have to sing it for me sometime." An awkward silence crept in on coattails of her casual remark. He'd actually written a song for her.

That's a first.

"Not sure it's ready to be performed yet. It's still pretty rough." He ran a shaky hand through his hair. "They're *all* pretty rough, actually. But that'll give me something to do."

"At least you're doing something productive. I'm not sure a smashed nose will help my career any—except as a way to help me relate to other abuse victims."

"See many of them?"

"Hardly ever—although I've seen a few post-op noses that look like mine. Maybe I should tell everyone I had to have emergency sinus surgery."

"That wouldn't explain the cut on your head."

"No, but—oh, hell. It won't matter what I do. Even if no one else says a word, I can almost guarantee my nephew will ask me what happened."

His eyes showed the barest glimmer of a twinkle. "Nosy?"

"Not exactly. Levi is mildly autistic and doesn't have the filter on his speech that most people have. He says what he thinks—and he's completely adorable."

Joey snorted a laugh. "Wonder what he'll have to say about Bryce."

"No clue, but I'm sure I'll want to print it out and frame it." With a brief chuckle, Tracy added, "Hey, would you look at us? We're actually laughing."

"Imagine that." He winked at her. "Must be the coffee."

"Nah. It's probably from talking about Levi. He always makes me smile."

"Hold that thought."

"Yeah, depression isn't a bit fun—especially on Christmas morning. We should be drinking eggnog and opening presents instead of crying in our coffee. Speaking of fun, are you still going to the concert with us?"

"Wouldn't miss it."

"At least I won't look like Rudolph by then—although I'll probably still need some cheering up."

"Me, too."

She gave him a smile, wishing it could've been more. She'd never known anyone who'd lost a family quite the way Joey had and suspected that time was the only cure. "I'm so glad you came over. I really do feel better now. Too bad I can't think of anything else to cheer you up."

With a shrug, he attempted another smile. "Maybe you could bring me some leftover turkey."

In an instant, his features contorted as deep, choking sobs racked his body. Tracy had seen a few men cry like that before—usually following the death of their wives, which was one reason why she'd traded hospital nursing for working in the outpatient clinic. She still saw sadness and death on occasion, but not the kind she'd seen working in the emergency room.

Setting down her coffee, she made a move toward him just as he came up off the chair and into her arms. She patted his back and stroked his hair the way she would've comforted a child.

As his sobs subsided, he stepped back, wiping away his tears. "Sorry. I shouldn't be such a crybaby when you've been hurt worse than I'll ever be."

She shook her head. "No need to compare us, Joey. It doesn't work that way. You were there for me when I needed help. Now it's my turn—and believe me, I understand what it means to lose a child. Having a miscarriage was devastating, but knowing that Darren will grow up with no memory of you at all…" She caught herself before saying more. "Sorry. Didn't mean to make you feel worse."

"No. That puts it in its proper perspective. I mean, at least he's still alive."

"True." With a start, she realized that the last time she'd gazed into Joey's deep blue eyes she'd been sitting on the floor, leaning against the cabinet in this very spot. Bleeding.

My, how times have changed.

"And don't feel bad about crying," she said. "It really does help."

"I'm sure you're right. I'm just sorry you had to be the one to deal with it."

"Don't worry about it. It's what I do."

෨෬

Joey had been so close to taking Tracy up on her offer. That way neither of them would have to face the day alone. Too bad he didn't know her very well. Somehow, the right to join in the family fun on Christmas didn't extend to casual acquaintances.

Then again, they'd been through hell together—or at least the aftermath. Plenty of people couldn't claim to be even that close. In a way, he wished he hadn't bothered her—even though they'd both felt better as a result. She had enough on her plate already.

Maybe that was all it was—the camaraderie of surviving some of life's more painful episodes together. Plenty of friendships had been based on less.

He tried to recall what he'd done on Christmas before he and Geena moved in together.

Not much. Georgio's was closed on Christmas Day, and if he'd ever played a Christmas gig, he couldn't remember it. He usually took advantage of the opportunity to get in some extra guitar practice. And, of course, there were always songs to write.

Figuring he might as well get something good out of all the emotional upheaval, he picked up the Ibanez and sat down. Time slid by as the words and notes began to trickle through. This was how he'd always dealt with time on his hands.

That and other things.

He played back the song, and though he wasn't completely

happy with one line of the chorus, he reminded himself that it was a work in progress. Flipping through the pages on the stand, he found the song he'd written for Tracy. He'd penned emotionally cathartic songs before, but they didn't always elicit the same feelings when he played them again.

Nothing was missing this time. The pain, the fear, and the anger remained—just as raw and bloody as they'd been the night those lyrics were ripped from his heart.

Great. Now all I have to do is sell it.

Which was easier said than done. Still, he should at least celebrate in some way. Finishing a song was, after all, an accomplishment of sorts. Perhaps not as momentous as saving the world or rescuing damsels in distress, but it was something not everyone was capable of and demonstrated at least some degree of talent.

Celebrations of that type had usually been private ones—special moments set aside to engage in the very thing that had sent Geena screaming out of his life. With a shrug of complete indifference, he realized that part of him was absent at the moment.

But not for long. It would come galloping back to the fore in a day or two.

It always did.

Chapter 7

Tracy did her best to cover her bruises with makeup, finally admitting defeat when it came to disguising the swelling in her nose. Whether she'd been stalling or not, she was the last to arrive at the home of Travis's parents, Grace and Adam York.

As she'd expected, before anyone else had the chance to comment, Levi took one look at her and blurted out, "Aunt Tracy! What happened to your face?"

Good ol' Levi.

Her smile became a wince as her lip split open. Again. "Nothing much. Just another bad date."

Levi scowled, reminding her, as always, of Daffy Duck on a rampage. His blond hair and green eyes didn't quite fit the character, but his exaggerated expression certainly did. "You shouldn't go out with those mean men. You should marry a *nice* guy."

"It's not like I haven't tried." She winced again as Miranda hugged her a little too hard. "I think it's time for me to give up."

"No," Levi insisted. "There are lots of nice men. Maybe they aren't very handsome, but at least they aren't mean."

Tracy shrugged. "I guess that's the answer. Only date the homely ones." Funny, she'd always considered Joey to be a bit homely—in a long-haired, exotic, guitar player sort of way. He was at least a nice guy. Tracy still didn't understand why Geena left him.

Miranda's eyes flashed with anger. "I hope the bastard rots in jail."

A simple nod would've sufficed—if Tracy hadn't known she'd get caught in the lie. Miranda would find out somehow. She always did. "He'll wind up there eventually."

Hang on…here it comes…

"You didn't press charges." Miranda's green-eyed glare was every bit as fierce as Levi's had been. "Did you?"

"No, I didn't." Why was it that no one else understood why she didn't want anything to do with Bryce for the rest of her life? "I gave almost as good as I got, and my neighbor clobbered him with a guitar and practically strangled him with the strap before booting his ass down the stairs—which was pretty impressive considering Bryce is easily twice his size."

She smiled as she recalled the vision of Joey marching Bryce out of her life with a bleeding penis and a purple face—the one shining moment in that entire fiasco. Biting Bryce's dick and punching his nuts had been instinctive and effective, but not nearly as enjoyable as watching him get the bum's rush.

She wished Joey had come with her if for no other reason than to bask in the glory of being her hero. Although, now that she considered the matter, he looked more like Alice Cooper minus the weird eye makeup than the typical hero.

Trust me to have a hero who breaks the mold.

"I'm glad to hear it—I think." Miranda shook back a lock of auburn hair. "You sure know how to pick 'em."

Understatement of the year. "No shit." She sniffed the air. "Do I smell turkey?"

"Of course you do," Levi said. "It's Christmas. What else would we eat?"

"I don't know, Levi," Miranda drawled. "What about roast beef and Yorkshire pudding?"

Miranda's husband Travis stood beside her, a smile dimpling his cheeks. "Damn, that sounds good."

Miranda hadn't had to settle for a homely guy in order to find a good one. Travis was adorable, and his brother Stuart gave new meaning to tall, dark, and handsome. Their cousin Alan was scruffy, but cute, and their respective girlfriends, Christina and Emily, were just plain beautiful. Tracy looked like a beat-up hooker out on bail.

And Joey could pass for my pimp. She pressed her lips together to keep from laughing—an action that nearly made her yelp in pain.

"No," Levi insisted. "Turkey is *much* better."

Travis's mother smiled at her newest grandson. "Good thing I baked one then, isn't it?" Her expression shifted to one of concern as her gaze landed on Tracy. "Oh, you poor girl."

"I'm okay, Grace," Tracy assured her. "Really." She glanced at the others, ending with a pointed look at her sister. "And please, don't any of you try to fix me up with someone. I'm not going on any blind dates or using a dating service ever again."

"But—"

She held up a hand, cutting off Miranda's protest. "I mean it, Sis. I really do. I'm done."

"Good," Levi said. "Can we eat now?"

"Absolutely," Tracy replied, grateful for the change of subject. "I'm starving."

Having cast aside any concerns about her attractiveness to men, for once in her life, Tracy didn't consider her figure while she enjoyed Christmas dinner.

Afterward, she laughed along with everyone else during the Dirty Santa gift exchange. Levi and Stuart fought like tigers over a pizza cutter shaped like the *Starship Enterprise*, with Levi emerging victorious. Tracy wound up with a handmade ceramic bowl that was the perfect size for fixing soup or casseroles for one.

Unlike Grace, who obviously enjoyed cooking for a crowd and being the matriarch of a large family, Tracy had no such aspirations. Miranda could have that job. *She* would stick to being the maiden aunt.

She'd have much more freedom and a lot less hassle. Besides, having a huge family was no guarantee that anyone would be around to care for her in her old age. She'd had plenty of patients whose children lived on opposite sides of the country. They managed…somehow.

When the gift exchange was over, Alan and Emily left to go to another party. Tracy gave it another half an hour, then hugged everyone goodbye and accepted two huge plates of leftovers from Grace, fully intending to give it all to Joey.

The funny thing was, she wasn't so much in a hurry to leave as she was anxious to see him. If he truly expected her to bring him some turkey, he was probably getting hungry—unless he dealt with depression by cooking. Some people did. Beverly had a tendency to bring batches of cookies to work whenever she felt rotten. Melina, on the other hand, took her frustrations out on her assortment of exercise machines. Since Joey cooked for a living, he would probably turn to his music for solace. Tracy wasn't sure what her own coping strategies were.

Chocolate, maybe.

Bundled up against the cold, she went out to her car and set the foil-wrapped plates on the back seat along with her nifty new bowl. Flurries swirled in the headlights as she drove home. A white Christmas, even this late in the day, always made her smile.

Turning on the radio, she discovered that hearing "Grandma Got Run Over by a Reindeer" could still elicit a giggle. Bing Crosby singing "I'll Be Home for Christmas" brought tears to her eyes, but that was normal, wasn't it?

Maybe I don't need a shrink after all.

The coping mechanism question still had her stumped. Beyond snow flurries and ridiculous Christmas songs, what else did she enjoy? Although she liked cats, her apartment building didn't allow pets. Perhaps she could buy her own house and become a crazy cat lady. And then there was her fondness for antiques. If she had a really big house, she could stuff it full of ancient furniture and display cabinets—or become a hoarder.

Probably not. She liked cats well enough and could appreciate the beauty of the occasional antique, but she preferred people. Funny, she'd never given it much thought before, but it was quite obvious that spending time with friends and family had improved her mood. Truth be told, despite all the flirting she'd done in her life trying to find the right man, she preferred the company of women—or at least men she didn't feel the need to impress.

So, I'll be a crazy lesbian cat lady antique hoarder.

Not that becoming a lesbian would truly end all of her

troubles—aside from the fact that homosexuality wasn't a conscious choice like deciding which shoes to wear. No. The sex of her significant other wasn't the issue. The question was whether or not she could find someone she could trust with her heart as well as her body. Thus far, she hadn't had much luck finding any trustworthy souls among the male population.

With Officer Williams's crack about pissed-off dykes still fresh in her mind, she knew that dating a woman didn't necessarily guarantee her safety or her happiness. She'd never been attracted to a woman in a romantic or sexual manner. Still, there was a first time for everything. Perhaps a more girly, non-violent type would be best.

Hmm…

ಶಂಧ

Joey hated to admit it, but he was waiting for Tracy to come home.

Loneliness will do that to a guy.

That wasn't the only explanation. He'd been lonely before. Now he had a neighbor he liked very much who'd had the shit beat out of her by another man. Concerned for her safety, he was still on the lookout for that truck—unsure of what he would do if he ever saw it. He only kept watching to protect her, not because he craved her company.

Well, maybe he did. There was no other excuse for dropping in on her that morning—which was stupid because Tracy's attitudes probably wouldn't differ from those of any other woman he knew. Then again, he had no way of knowing for sure unless he flat-out asked her. He'd never had the guts to do that.

It was too soon, anyway—for both of them. Geena and Darren had only been gone a few weeks, and Tracy was disgusted with men in general.

Yeah. Bad idea.

However, when a knock on his door had him peering through the peephole, he couldn't help smiling when he spied Tracy standing in the hall.

Opening the door, he leaned against the jamb. "Aww…you brought me some turkey, didn't you?"

"You bet. After I casually mentioned that my hero was a little on the skinny side, Travis's mom gave me at least half of everything she had left. And let me tell you, the woman can cook."

"Smells great." He stepped back from the door. "Want to come in for a while? There's something depressing about eating Christmas dinner alone."

"I know what you mean," she said as she breezed past him. "I've come to the conclusion that the reason I keep giving these jerks a second chance is that I don't care for solitude."

She carried the food into the kitchen and set it on the table.

Joey lifted the foil on one of the plates. The delectable aroma of turkey and dressing escaped, bringing back memories of holidays gone by. He didn't even want to think about those that lay ahead—although he didn't see how they could possibly be any worse than this one. "Want some?"

"I might have room for a bite or two now," she said. "I was too full to eat much dessert."

He unwrapped the other plate, revealing slices of pecan pie and pumpkin pie, assorted cookies, brownies, divinity, three kinds of fudge, and bourbon balls. "You're right. The woman can definitely cook."

"She did it all herself too. Miranda offered to help, but Grace wanted to do everything." She grinned. "Personally, I think she just doesn't like to share the limelight."

Being a cook himself, he could relate to that. "You might be right. So, did you have a good time?"

"Yes, I did—surprisingly enough. Once Levi and Miranda were done freaking out over my swollen nose, it turned out to be a fairly normal Christmas. I'm glad I went."

He waited a beat for her to say she wished he'd gone with her. She didn't. "I polished up some songs. All things considered, it was a pretty good day for me too."

Tracy sat down and perused the plateful of desserts. Until that moment, he hadn't realized how much he'd let slide since Geena left him. The table needed cleaning and so did everything else.

I really need to get my shit together.

She popped a bourbon ball in her mouth and chewed it slowly. "I figured that's what you'd do. On the way home, I was thinking about the things people do to cope with adversity, and about the best I could come up with was that I need other women—and chocolate." She snorted a laugh. "My other choice is to become a crazy lesbian cat lady who hoards antiques."

Joey's burst of laughter made him thankful he hadn't sampled the turkey yet. "I can understand why you might enjoy collecting antiques, but why would you want to be a crazy lesbian cat lady?"

"I like cats and I like women. I like being with them and talking with them—women that is, not cats. I think I'd have much better luck dating girls instead of guys."

"Maybe so, but would you really want to have sex with a woman?"

She selected a piece of fudge and took a bite of it before replying. "I'm not sure. I mean, just because I never *have* doesn't necessarily mean I never *will*."

Joey tried to keep a straight face and failed. He hadn't enjoyed a conversation this much in ages. "Haven't met the right girl?"

She arched a brow. "You're laughing at me. I'm actually quite serious."

"Sorry. The whole idea seems sort of…extreme."

"Extreme circumstances call for extreme measures. And besides, antiques are expensive, and cats aren't allowed in this building. As I see it, my choices are a girlfriend or death by chocolate."

Earlier that evening, Joey had toyed with the idea of getting soused. He suspected Tracy already had. "How many bourbon balls have you had today?"

"Just one. And no, I'm not drunk. I'm simply trying out a new perspective. I don't trust men anymore."

"You trust me, don't you? I mean, you're sitting here in my

apartment late at night."

She waved dismissively. "Yeah, well, you don't count."

His eyes widened. "Oh, really? How come?"

"You *rescued* me. Of course I trust you."

He scratched his head. Evidently, she wasn't attracted to him. At all.

Shit.

"My friend Melina told me about this club where there are all sorts of gays, lesbians, cross-dressers, and such. She said she didn't know any lesbians personally, and I made her swear she wouldn't introduce me to anyone, but I'm betting she knows somebody." After another bite of fudge, she continued. "Not that I'm looking, you understand. Now that I know what my best coping mechanism is, I can talk to my women friends to keep from getting too weird. In the meantime, I'm going to focus on living my life the way I want rather than the way anyone else thinks I should. Does that make sense?"

He wasn't sure how feasible her plan was, but it sounded good. "Maybe I should do the same thing."

"You should," she said with conviction. "I've only been thinking about it for a little while, and I already feel a hundred percent better—almost normal, in fact."

"Except for your attitude toward men. You weren't like that before, were you?"

"No. I was sort of obsessed with the idea of finding a husband. Now I don't care whether I find one or not."

Obviously she didn't consider the man sitting next to her to be husband material. Then again, if she thought she could develop an attraction to another woman, he might have a chance.

And his hair was longer than hers.

Nah. It would never work.

Chapter 8

Tracy spent the long Christmas weekend divesting herself of everything any man had left behind. She tossed out various toiletries and articles of clothing—thankfully, none of them belonging to Bryce—and was astonished at how much more room she had in her closets and cabinets.

That done, she tackled her own things. Since she no longer sought male companionship, her appearance need only be neat and clean rather than alluring. She kept only the bare minimum of makeup for special occasions. All non-essential toiletries went in the trash, leaving more room for moisturizers and lip balm that added no color or flair whatsoever.

She went through her clothes, keeping only those garments which were best suited to the weather and her own personal comfort. Anything tight or revealing went into a pile to be donated to charity. A few of her nicer outfits were spared for the occasional wedding or funeral, along with the matching shoes. Any footgear that pinched or altered her balance went in the charity box.

By the time she'd finished, she doubted she would ever face an overcrowded closet wrinkling issue again.

Following the purge of her bedroom and bath, she set to work on the rest of her apartment. She toyed with the idea of moving in case Bryce ever thought about looking her up again, but dismissed it. If he hadn't shown up by now, chances were he never would.

She pitched anything outdated from the refrigerator and pantry. Old books and magazines went in the recycling bin. The various knickknacks given to her by old boyfriends suffered a similar fate. As a result, her home was now neater and more spacious than ever before.

She ordered a new battery for her phone and made a vow to spend more time with her friends and less time in front of the mirror. She would eat whatever she liked and exercise purely for the endorphin rush. Instead of vainly attempting to please the entire male gender, she would please herself.

Logging onto the nefarious Internet dating service, she revised her profile to read that hell would freeze over before she dated another man, and that she was permanently retiring from the list of interested singles. She put all thoughts of love and sex out of her mind, and if she felt the need for the occasional orgasm, well, she'd always been better at achieving them for herself than any man had ever been.

In the past, she tended to classify men as fuckable or unfuckable and wondered what they were thinking about her. Did they find her attractive? Did they want to have sex with her, or did she fall into the not-if-you-were-the-last-woman-on-earth category?

Now that none of that mattered, she was left with far more brain time for other things. She might be a little lonely at times, but her life would be much simpler, not to mention less dangerous.

She went back to work with a spring in her step and a newfound sense of freedom. Her mother would undoubtedly chastise her for the lack of pride in her appearance, but in her opinion, she'd never looked better. She certainly *felt* better. She'd never realized how much time and energy she'd put into the endless—and ultimately fruitless—search for Mr. Right, and as that expenditure decreased, her stress level plummeted.

Any evenings spent with friends would no longer tick off her current boyfriend. Men could be so possessive and selfish. She liked to think she would understand if a man wanted to hang out with his buddies now and then. Why did they always have to take it so personally whenever she did it? She'd purchased two tickets to the Barton Junction concert with that issue in mind, thinking that whoever she might have been dating would have felt slighted if she'd gone without him.

That extra ticket was being put to a much better use now. Joey would enjoy the concert and wouldn't be there as her date. Sure, they might sit next to each other, but they didn't have to ride together. Joey was perfectly capable of getting to Evansville on his own.

Unless...

She and Melina had already agreed to split the cost of fuel for the drive. Sharing expenses with a third person would save them even more. The price of gas being what it was, Joey would undoubtedly appreciate the offer.

After checking with Melina, who seemed delighted with the idea, she wrote Joey a note and slid it under his door. It was a friendly gesture, nothing more, and one she would've made for anyone, whether he was her hero or not. Driving to Evansville together didn't make it a date, especially not with Melina along for the ride.

No. Not a date.

Definitely not a date.

ഌଔ

After all the heartbreaking news Joey had received lately, he retrieved the slip of paper from the living room floor with apprehension. Once he'd read it, however, his lips curled into a smile. Tracy wasn't precisely asking him for a date—he wouldn't even be alone in the car with her—but it was better than nothing.

He would accept, of course. Considering she'd given him the ticket free of charge, he couldn't very well turn down the opportunity to help her and her friend pay for the gas.

This Melina seemed like an interesting character, and he was anxious to meet her. Anyone who went to clubs catering to the GLBT crowd intrigued him, and might be a potential...

What? Co-conspirator?

Maybe.

He would take a wait and see approach on that issue. He still wasn't sure how high he stood in Tracy's esteem. True, he was supposedly her hero, but as far as she knew, he was nothing more than a cook who moonlighted as an underpaid musician.

He hoped to be more than that someday. Granted, he was a good cook. He'd been complimented often and rarely received any complaints. Georgio's was a nice restaurant too, not some truck stop dive. He was also a first-rate guitarist, an opinion shared by any number of people. Although at his age, a musician should've either achieved national success or given up the dream.

Joey hadn't given up yet. Unfortunately, he'd never had the luxury of devoting all his time and energy to his music, and his relationship with Geena had cost him dearly in that respect. Working alternate shifts to save the expense of daycare hadn't left him much time to practice—not that he'd regretted any of the time he'd spent with Darren.

That chapter was over now. Everyone from Paulina to his band mates assured him that a clean break was best.

Clean break. Actually, it had been more like a surgical excision. Hardly a trace of either of them remained. Geena's name wasn't on the lease—or even the mailbox—and never had been. That part of his life might never have happened.

And yet it had. He'd had a son—and now he didn't. The whole thing was so surreal—almost like a time traveler had popped in and edited Geena and Darren out of his life.

Tracy's place in that life was unclear. He was definitely attracted to her. Unfortunately, the attraction didn't seem to be mutual, making the idea he'd had on Christmas night seem more preposterous all the time.

But life did go on, and he'd spent the past few days giving his apartment a much-needed cleaning. The only remaining task was to get caught up on the laundry. With a sigh, he gathered up everything that needed washing and lugged it down to the basement.

He arrived in the laundry room just as Tracy bent over to reach into dryer. In that position, her sweat pants didn't leave much to his imagination regarding the shape of her ass.

Oh, yeah. Definitely hot.

His balls tingled. "Hey, Trace. Thanks for the note. Riding to the concert together is a great idea."

She stood up, brushing back a lock of hair that had escaped from her ponytail. "I thought so. It'll help save on gas, which is good because that new alternator wasn't cheap."

"I don't suppose it was." He set his laundry basket on the table between the two washers and began sorting through his clothes. "I haven't seen you since Christmas. Everything okay?"

"Oh, yeah. My HIV test was negative, I cleaned out my apartment, and I made a list of New Year's resolutions."

"Glad to hear about the test. I'm sure you're relieved."

"You got that right. One less worry."

Her smile did things to his dick he hoped she wouldn't notice. "I, um, cleaned up my place, too. No resolutions, though. I've never seen the need for them myself."

"First time for me," she said. "And don't worry. Finding a girlfriend wasn't on the list."

"Given up on that idea?"

"Not really. I've decided to go with the flow where love is concerned. You can't make resolutions about that sort of thing anyway."

She had a point.

"Any plans for New Year's Eve?"

Her sparkling eyes and the tilt of her chin suggested defiance, perhaps even pride. "For the first time in ages, I'm not going out. I'm staying home and watching the ball drop at Times Square all by myself."

"What? No New Year's kiss?"

Her laugh was a derisive huff. "Those kisses have never done me a bit of good. I'm having my own little party, complete with shrimp cocktail, a cheese ball, chocolate truffles, and pink champagne."

"Sounds good." Joey would've given a lot to be the one to hold her in his arms at the stroke of midnight, but unless he could smuggle her into the private party where he and the band were playing, the odds were against it. Especially since she obviously thought staying home on New Year's Eve was such a treat.

Her gaze drifted to his laundry basket. "I guess Geena forgot a few things, huh?"

Joey's heart nearly stopped. "Yeah, I, um, found a bunch of stuff in the bottom of the closet."

"I'm getting rid of all my lacy little bras and thongs. You can toss those into my Goodwill bag if you like—unless you think she'll come back for them."

Not a snowball's chance in hell. "I doubt it." He tossed the rest of the whites into the washer and closed the lid. "Thanks, but I've got a bag of my own started."

She frowned. "Aren't you going to put in the detergent?"

"What? Oh, yeah, right." Lifting the top, he threw in a soap packet. "Those little packets sure are handy," he said, desperate for a new topic of conversation. "This was supposed to be our last bucketful because Geena heard that toddlers have a tendency to eat them. Guess I don't have to worry about that anymore."

"True. I've never had to childproof my place, but I *have* sort of man-proofed it. No need to keep shaving cream or jock itch remedies on hand. I'm lovin' it."

He couldn't help but smile. "Do you *always* find a silver lining to every cloud?"

"Usually." She paused, frowning. "You know…maybe *that's* why guys feel like they can beat me up all the time. They figure I'll wind up thinking it's a good thing."

"Not all men are abusive, Tracy."

"No—just the guys I date."

Her cheeky grin made him want to kiss her until she couldn't see straight. Unfortunately, her lips were still sort of puffy. He might have to settle for kissing her somewhere else.

What a hardship.

He cleared his throat with an effort. "Have you considered trying a different type?"

"You mean only go out with homely guys? That was Levi's suggestion. He says they're nicer."

"I take it you don't believe that."

"I don't think it matters. Miranda's husband is gorgeous, and he's as nice as they come." With a slow wag of her head, she added, "I'm pretty sure I'm the problem. I only attract creeps."

"I doubt that." Unless, of course, she considered *him* to be a creep.

Maybe she does. But she did trust him. That had to count for something.

"Yeah, well, it's a moot point anyway." She flashed him a cheerful smile. "I'm done with guys."

If his reaction was any indication, men weren't done with *her* yet. The thought of stripping off her pretty pink sweats and kissing her all over made Joey's balls twitch and his dick drool. He wanted to suck her clit, sit her on his prick, and—

Folding the last of her scrubs, she laid them in her basket. "Goodnight, Joey, and if I don't see you before then, Happy New Year!"

"Same to you."

Joey watched her go, wishing he had the guts to call her back and do lots of crazy, wonderful things with her—starting with sex in the laundry room. Too bad she wasn't ready for that. Truth be told, neither was he. His dick might be willing and able, but he and Tracy both needed more time to recover.

Dumping the dark clothes into the other washer, he tossed in a detergent packet and closed the lid before heading back upstairs.

The New Year might not turn out to be a very happy one, but it would certainly be interesting.

Chapter 9

Joey slung his guitar strap over his head and plugged in the wireless transmitter before surveying the room—small stage, decent-sized crowd of typically noisy New Year's Eve revelers, and an open bar.

Oh, joy.

Lenny picked out a few notes on his bass for the sound check. "So, are you up for this?" With his tall, thin frame, Lenny always reminded Joey of a stick person playing guitar.

"Yeah. I guess."

"Look, dude, it'll get better. You knew you and Geena couldn't last."

Joey frowned. "Did I?" *Maybe I did. Nothing else has.*

"She didn't love you. She *used* you. Don't you get it?"

"No. Well…maybe I do, but it wasn't like that. At least, I didn't think it was."

"Here. Drink this. It'll help."

He stared at the glass of clear, colorless liquid that Lenny held out to him. "What is it, vodka?"

Lenny snickered. "No, dude, it's fuckin' water."

Joey took a sip. He wasn't kidding. It really *was* water.

"You know how dehydrated you get when you're on stage. Drink up."

"God, this is stupid. Here I am, playing a New Year's Eve gig, and I'm drinking water. What's wrong with this picture?"

"Dunno." Lenny shrugged. "It's what we do, you know?"

Yeah. He knew. Always playing for the party but never really a part of the festivities. Providing the entertainment instead of enjoying it.

No. That wasn't true. He loved playing in the band. And he

liked being a cook—although everyone told him he could do better. *Sure I can.* But with no more than a high school diploma in his resume, the doors weren't exactly open to higher-paying jobs. He still held out the hope that the band might make it big someday—and then what? Touring, recording, TV appearances?

Sex, drugs, and rock 'n' roll?

Of the three, he'd rather have sex with Tracy, let love be the drug, and have the rock 'n' roll be the stuff he and the guys had written rather than a cover of another band's success.

Success...

How would they know when they'd achieved it? A guest spot on SNL? Maybe. Earning enough money to quit the day job? That sounded good, but comparatively few musicians ever reached that point, and even fewer could rely on royalty checks enough to stop performing.

Not that many musicians truly wanted to do that. Making music was more than just a job. It was a need, a passion, and a way of life. The urge was always there. Paul McCartney was rich as a king, and he was still at it more than forty years after the Beatles broke up.

Holy shit. Has it really been that long? Then again, Joey was thirty-eight. The Beatles as a group had ceased to exist before he was born.

And yet, people still remembered them and still played their songs. When had *they* considered themselves to be successful? Deep down, he doubted they ever had. No one did—no matter how much talent they possessed or how many records they sold. Someone was always waiting in the wings, itching to jump up and knock you off that pedestal.

Comparing himself with other guitarists was no help at all because everyone had their own style. Still, considering the number of people in the world who picked up guitars and couldn't play worth shit, he was doing pretty well. He was no Eric Clapton, but the band actually had paying gigs. They weren't begging to play for tips in a dingy bar somewhere.

A recording contract was a reasonable measure of success. So was a number one hit. But even those didn't guarantee lasting success. The list of one-hit wonders grew exponentially every year. Maybe three albums would establish them as a bona fide talent—even though he could name several bands that hadn't stayed together beyond that third album.

And then, of course, there were the Rolling Stones.

I am so not going there.

He had two jobs that basically relied on the opinions of other people. Did they like the pasta or the riff? The lyrics or the sauce? If he'd had to guess he'd have said there were at least as many musical genres as there were varieties of cuisine. The fact that he excelled in two of the most popular gave him an advantage, but it also handicapped him. There were tons of Italian chefs and rock guitarists. What talents were necessary to distinguish him from either faction, and did he have them?

Music being his first love, he hoped his guitar playing outshone the cooking.

And now's the time to let it shine.

As he tore into the opening riff, his doubts disappeared. He belonged here—on stage with a pick in his right hand and the neck of a guitar in the other. The audience ceased to exist as he lost himself in the music.

The notes came instinctively. He knew the original version well enough to put his own spin on it—an extra note here, a hammer-on or a bend there. The Ibanez was really screaming tonight. Whether anyone else enjoyed his performance—or even noticed it—didn't matter.

And it doesn't get any better than that.

With the lacy thong holding his balls, his dick lay hot and hard against his stomach as the mental image of Tracy going down on him crowded out every other thought. With his mind's eye, he watched as Tracy peeled the thong from his body with her teeth.

Oh, fuckin' yeah.

The fantasy continued as she hooked her fingers through the rings that pierced his nipples. Her quick tug shot lightning bolts of pleasure all the way to his balls, stiffening his cock even further. Releasing him, she stripped off her bra, a sly smile touching her lips as she massaged her nipples into firm peaks. She crawled up over him, dragging her soft tits over his naked cock and on up his torso until they rested against his lips. Joey opened wide, sucking her warm flesh into his mouth, teasing her with his tongue until her moans of pleasure became the final notes of the song.

Breaks in the melody were her wet lips poised above his cock, her hot breath on his skin in the split second before sucking his cock deeply into her mouth. Her tongue bathed his scrotum, his sharp cry wailing from the amplifier as she sucked in first one testicle and then the other. The slide from one note to the next was his cock spewing a line of cum from her tits to her pussy lips.

He'd never had fantasies about any other woman that seemed so real or felt so hot. Not Geena or any of the others.

Tracy *inspired* him.

As the songs shifted to something softer, sweeter, her lips touched his, her tongue slipping into his mouth for a caress. The quieter runs were her whispered words telling him what she had planned. He would scream for mercy when she bit his ass, moan when she sucked his balls, and come all over the place when she tied him up and spanked him.

She'd lap up the semen running down his legs and then spit it on the strap-on she wore. The thought of her using his own cum to fuck him nearly had him jizzing in his jeans. Her hand slapped his ass in time with the beat, getting it red-hot and stinging before plunging into his manhole and fucking him until he came again.

His cock pulsed as pre-cum soaked the thong the way her pussy would drool all over his mouth. Now her pussy lips hung above his face, daring him to pull her down and suck her clit. Soft, wet…

Delicious.

When the last song in the set ended, the reverb echoed through his groin like the aftermath of Tracy's orgasm squeezing his dick.

Brad turned away from the microphone. "Holy shit, dude. What the fuck are you on?"

Joey stared back at him, dazed and undoubtedly glassy-eyed. "Nothing. What's wrong?"

"Nothing's wrong. I've never heard you play like that—you or anyone else."

Joey frowned at Lenny. "What was in that water you gave me?"

The bassist shook his head, scattering droplets of sweat from the tips of his hair. "Just plain water. Honest to God."

Then I'm high on sexual fantasies—and Tracy is the star.
Whoa.

"Whatever you're doing or thinking or feeling, don't stop," Brad urged. "You've got all the women out there creaming their panties."

Joey rolled his eyes. "Bullshit. You're the hot frontman. I'm—"

"Hey, baby," a sultry voice cooed as a pair of feminine hands snaked around his waist from behind. "You were awesome tonight. The way you shred that guitar drives me fuckin' wild."

Turning, Joey caught a glimpse of sparkling eye shadow and lashes so long he could hardly see the eyes beneath them. Dark, glossy hair fell in beckoning waves around bare shoulders—and they weren't the only parts of her that were bare. Her dress, if it could be called that, was a single tube of stretchy, sequined fabric that only covered her from her nipples to her pussy.

Red lipstick glittered on the mouth she pressed to his ear. "I want to suck your cock."

Joey blinked and took a step back. "Um…what?"

"You heard me." The lack of subtlety in her wink made him cringe. "But I bet you've already got ten girls waiting in line."

Joey had never been particularly interested in the groupie type and wished this girl had picked someone else to hit on. If the sound of her voice hadn't wilted what was left of his erection like a bucket of ice water, her overdone eye makeup would have done the trick.

Pasting on a smile, he shook his head. "Just one. And she's not here tonight. Sorry."

He held his breath waiting for Lenny or Brad to dispute what he'd said, then realized they would understand why he'd lied, and

Dave, the band's drummer, would be tickled shitless to step in. Getting laid afterward wasn't a reliable indicator of successful gig anyway—at least not tonight, and certainly not after the sizzling fantasies he'd had about Tracy. Right now, all he really wanted to do was to go home and see the New Year in with his dick in her pussy. This girl would be nothing but a poor substitute.

Too bad real people never lived up to the fantasy version of themselves. Experience had taught him that much. Nonetheless, he would've been happy to give it a go.

Dave took the girl's hand and kissed it. "I, on the other hand, am ready, willing, and extremely able." Only Superman could've actually heard her offer above the din, but Dave wasn't stupid, nor did he have a steady girlfriend—at the moment. He liked to play the field, and being attractive to women—rumor had it he was hung like a horse—he could take his pick.

"In that case, I'll leave you two alone." Joey flipped off the strap and set his guitar on the stand. After toweling off as much sweat as possible, he checked his pocket for his phone, grabbed his coat, and headed for the door.

The night was crisp and clear, and his breath hung in the air like smoke as he stepped outside. He would've preferred a warmer spot, but short of the restroom, there wasn't any place quiet enough for a phone call—nor did he wish to be overheard.

The frigid breeze cut through his sweat-soaked hair, and he pulled his coat tightly around him. Digging into his pocket for his phone, he tapped the screen, shivering—but was that a shiver of anticipation or simply his body's response to the freezing weather?

Probably a little of both.

Selecting her number, he put the phone to his ear.

సౌర

Tracy's phone played "I Will Survive," drawing her attention away from the television. Who the hell would be calling her at eleven-thirty on New Year's Eve? Miranda? Melina? She glanced at the ID.

It was Joey.

"That's weird." With a frown, she took the call, wondering whether he needed bail money or a ride home.

"Hey, Joey. What's up? Did the party get raided?"

"Nah, it's pretty tame, actually. I just wanted to call and wish you a happy New Year. Figured I'd better do it now before all hell breaks loose around here."

His thoughtfulness had tears filling her eyes. "Thanks, Joey. I really appreciate you going to so much trouble."

"No trouble at all." He hesitated. "You doing okay?"

"Sure am," she replied, doing her best to sound chipper. "I'm sitting here wrapped up in an afghan, eating shrimp cocktail, and watching *The Philadelphia Story*—you know, the old movie with Cary Grant, Katherine Hepburn, and Jimmy Stewart?"

"Must've missed that one."

"It's great. I'm trying to see if I can get more excited about Kate than Cary. Not sure I'm succeeding."

"Yeah, well, I've heard that both of them had sexual orientations that fell outside the mainstream."

"Really? How disappointing. At least, I *think* it is. Like I said, I'm still not sure where my own orientation belongs these days. Not that it matters." *Time to change the subject.* "How's the party?"

"Fine. We're playing pretty well. The crowd seems happy—although it could be the booze. It's really flowing tonight."

"I'll bet it is. Better watch out for the drunks when you leave."

"Don't worry, I will." He drew in a breath, hesitating as though unsure of what to say next. "I wish…well, I just wanted to make sure you were okay. I know you said you *wanted* to stay home alone tonight, but—"

"I'm fine. Really. You don't need to worry about me. I'm perfectly happy." Perhaps a smidgen on the lonely side, but that was to be expected. People weren't *supposed* to spend New Year's Eve all by themselves, were they?

"Okay, then. Guess I'd better let you go." He paused again. "Happy New Year, Tracy."

"Happy New Year to you too, Joey. You drive carefully, you hear?"

"I will. Bye now."

Switching off her phone, Tracy stared at the television. He'd sounded sort of sad—even more so than *she* should've been. After all, he was at a party.

With no one to come home to.

Of course. He missed Geena and the baby—and who could blame him? Aside from his sister in Connecticut, they'd been his only family. He was probably calling that sister right now.

Like I ought to call Miranda and the guys—and Mom and Dad. Her parents were visiting with her brother Craig and his family in Tucson, having spent Christmas with her other brother Darryl in Fort Worth. Tracy had gone with them the year before, but hadn't been able to get the week off this time. If she'd been in Texas, she might've avoided the Bryce incident altogether.

Lucky me.

When the movie was over, she switched to the network to watch the celebration in Times Square. As she popped the cork on her champagne, she couldn't help comparing this holiday with previous ones. The fact that Dick Clark wasn't on hand to ring in the New Year wasn't the only difference. She'd never been alone or sober—at least, not since she'd given up her ER position in favor of the clinic. Prior to that, she'd spent plenty of nights wishing she'd never taken that job.

Still, it beat seeing the New Year in alone.

Maybe.

No one made her stay home. This was her choice. She could've easily done something different.

Too late now.

She made the calls to her family. Travis reported that Miranda was working and Levi had already fallen asleep in front of the television. In the more western time zones where Craig and Darryl lived, the clock hadn't even struck midnight yet.

So much for that.

She drank a toast, only then recalling how much she disliked champagne. Didn't matter. She drank it anyway, then went to bed, thinking about the one person who'd been thoughtful enough to call *her*.

Maybe I ought to bake him that cake after all.

Or fuck him.

Nah. One look at her beat-up face and his dick would shrivel up to nothing. Better not take the chance.

Chapter 10

Tracy woke up the next morning with the headache from hell.

"Guess that's what I get for drinking champagne," she muttered as she staggered into the bathroom. "Should've stuck with tequila."

She stood for a moment, staring at her reflection in the mirror while debating the wisdom of letting her body deal with it versus the possible relief of popping some ibuprofen—or even going the "hair of the dog" route. Deciding that coffee might still be the best cure, she went out to the kitchen only to discover that the other time-honored remedy wasn't possible anyway.

The champagne bottle was empty.

She had no recollection of drinking all of it. Perhaps she'd poured it out after deciding it wasn't fit to drink.

The size of her head disagreed.

After putting the coffee on to brew, she returned to the bathroom and took the ibuprofen. A glance at the clock had her staring at it in frank disbelief.

Eleven-fifteen? Oh, surely not...

Since that clock agreed with the time on her watch, she was forced to admit she'd slept eleven hours.

Or had she? Drinking a whole bottle of champagne was bound to have taken longer than fifteen minutes. No telling when she'd actually gone to bed.

At least she'd been alone. No one would've seen her dancing on the coffee table or whatever weird shit she might've done. And she certainly hadn't awakened next to a strange man.

On her way back to the kitchen, she checked her room, making sure her bed was empty—which, of course, it was.

The one thing she remembered clearly was the phone call from

Joey. Sweet of him to do that. He really was a nice guy. *Maybe—*

Nah. Not going there. Men and Tracy Richards were incompatible.

A quick survey of the living room revealed that hers had been a rather tame celebration—the room was neat and tidy with no confetti or tilted lampshades. The coffee table was uncluttered, proving she'd at least had sense enough to clean up after her New Year's Eve party-for-one.

"Must've been on autopilot." She put two slices of bread in the toaster and poured a cup of coffee. A sip of the scalding brew sent shock waves through her swollen brain, and the toaster nearly triggered a seizure when it popped up. After buttering the bread, she took a seat at the table, landing in the chair like a sack of potatoes.

She'd eaten most of the toast and was working on her second cup of coffee when the doorbell rang.

Not Bryce. With those words repeating in her mind, she made her way to the door and squinted rather painfully at the peephole.

Joey stood in the hallway.

Knowing she probably looked as bad as she felt, she hesitated before turning the deadbolt. Then again, he'd seen her in worse shape.

She opened the door. "Happy New Year, Neighbor Joey." She let her fuzzy gaze roam over him. "Has anyone ever mentioned you look like Alice Cooper?"

"Yeah. I get that all the time. Only he's taller."

She made a painful attempt at a chuckle. "So, you're a mini Cooper, huh?"

"Now, that one, I *haven't* heard." His grin shifted to a more sober expression. "Hey, are you okay? I was kinda worried about you last night."

"I'm a little hung over, but otherwise intact." He'd obviously survived the night a hell of a lot better than she had. In fact, he was downright cute with his long curls and the sparkling studs in his ears.

Suddenly, the reason for Geena's desertion of him hit her like a brick between the eyes.

He's gay.

No wonder he seemed so safe. Geena had probably felt the same way when she was desperate for someone to pass off as her baby's father.

Well, no. Gay wouldn't work—not if he'd actually *believed* he was Darren's father. Bisexual maybe?

Evidently, she hadn't had enough coffee. "Coffee's hot. Want some?"

"Sure."

He headed into the kitchen while she bolted the door. After pouring him a cup, she sat down across from him. Funny how she'd never thought of him as cute before—gorgeous blue eyes and a friendly smile. Granted, the nose was a bit imposing, but *still…*

No. He had a dick and two balls and was therefore off limits.

If only she didn't like dicks so much. Liked sucking them and stroking them. Loved the way they felt inside her. Even liked watching them spurt.

Hmm…

"What time did you get home?" she asked.

"About three-thirty," he replied. "I only woke up a little while ago."

"Me, too—and I have no clue when I went to bed. The best I can tell, I drank a whole bottle of champagne—unless I poured it down the sink."

"Yeah, well, I wouldn't blame you for that. Never cared for it myself."

"Me, either, which makes drinking it seem so unlikely. Of course, the fact that I don't remember doing either one points to my having drunk it all. It's a wonder I'm still alive."

"Drink plenty of fluids and go back to bed," he advised. "You'll feel better tomorrow."

"Yeah. And after that, I'm swearing off the pink stuff. Tequila is my friend. It's never done this to me."

Arching a brow, he shot her a grin that might've been wicked, playful, or both. "Does it make your clothes fall off?"

She shook her head and immediately wished she hadn't. "Not so far," she said with a wince. "At least, not without help."

He drew a breath as if about to speak, but sank his teeth into his lower lip instead. Following an exhale that was almost a groan, he took a sip from his cup.

"Wait a minute," she said, frowning. "That line about tequila...isn't that in a country song?"

"Just because it's country doesn't mean a rock band's never played it."

"Ah."

Somewhere in the twisted haze her mind had become, this cozy morning-after scenario registered on a primal level. She was still in her pajamas, sitting across the kitchen table from the guy next door—a man she'd just decided was attractive—and he'd asked if tequila made her clothes fall off. Her traitorous body responded with tingling nipples and a telltale twinge in her core.

No fuckin' way.

She'd never considered what Joey might have hiding behind the fly of his jeans and couldn't quite picture him in an erotic context. This was certainly not the time to start—not when engaging in any activity more strenuous than sitting and breathing would probably make her skull explode.

"So, what *are* your New Year's resolutions?" he asked. "You never said."

"Not sure I should tell you. That way someone other than me will know when I've failed to keep them."

"Fair enough."

She was a tad surprised he didn't pursue the topic any further. "I guess I could tell you a few of them. First off, I'm not letting my apartment ever get so full of junk again."

"Sounds good."

"And second, I'm never buying another pair of tight jeans."

He cleared his throat. "I can understand that."

"Would you believe I used to try on jeans, and then buy a pair two sizes smaller? God, I was such an idiot. I had one pair that used to give me—" She stopped there. Yeast infections weren't a proper topic of conversation with one's male next-door neighbor, whether he was bisexual or not. "Never mind."

"Tight jeans are overrated," he said. "A relaxed fit with an elastic waistband makes them much easier to take off."

Tracy's heart took a break from its normal rhythm. Surely he didn't mean that the way it sounded—almost…suggestive. She stared at him, detecting no hint of a smirk or a wink as he sipped his coffee. He was perfectly serious. "Very true."

Then she realized he hadn't said anything about putting them *on*.

Joey's fantasies from the night before hadn't lied. Tracy was hot. *Incredibly* hot. Even in flannel Tweety Bird pajamas. The first three buttons of her top were undone, and if she was wearing a bra, it had nipples on it. Even if the pants had a drawstring waist, he could have them off her in no time.

He hitched in his chair, wishing he could unbutton his fly to relieve the pressure on his cock. Or better yet, have *her* do it. Then she could reach inside, pull out his dick, and suck it. He liked button-fly jeans—liked the idea of being able to walk around with his cock and balls hanging out for her to see.

And grab.

He glanced down at his empty cup. Did he dare ask for a refill and stay long enough to drink it?

She might be hung over, but she hadn't lost her powers of observation. "Want some more?"

What a loaded question. "Sure."

"How about some toast?"

He nodded. She was only being kind. She wasn't the type to have ulterior motives—didn't scheme to keep him there so she could sit on his prick and bounce that luscious ass on his nuts.

Luscious was the right word, all right. Even loose-fitting flannel couldn't hide the curves as she turned away from him. She wasn't even *trying* to be sexy, and he was about to come in his jeans.

A swift, downward glance revealed a bulge and a wet spot Tracy was bound to see as soon as he stood up. At least she had a hangover and he had on a black T-shirt. Maybe she wouldn't notice. Then again, she might assume he'd spilled his coffee. He had the choice of being a klutz or a horndog.

Decisions, decisions...

Tracy set a plate of buttered toast in front of him, then refilled his cup. "I'm glad the holidays are over. Guess I'll take down the tree tomorrow. Not sure I'm up to it today."

He was certainly *up*—for almost anything. Following a mental eye-roll, he wondered what the hell was wrong with him. He was hearing innuendo in everything she said.

Wishful thinking, no doubt.

"All I have to do with my dinky little tree is put a sheet over it and stick it back in the closet."

"Mine's a bit more involved than that, but not much." She stepped on the foot lever of the trashcan and dumped in the coffee grounds. "Whoa. Nothing like a few shrimp tails in the garbage to clear your head."

"I can take that out to the dumpster if you like."

Shuddering, she let the lid fall shut. "Thanks, I'd appreciate it."

"No problem." Now he could hide his bulging wet spot and seem heroic at the same time.

"I'm glad you came over—and not only to take out the trash. I've been meaning to talk to you about the concert next Saturday. Melina's picking me up at four-thirty. We're going to drive down and meet up with her friends at a restaurant somewhere and have dinner before we go to the stadium. Does that sound okay to you?"

"Sure. I'll be ready."

By that time, he might've figured out where to put his dick so she wouldn't notice it. Or maybe he would've fucked her by then, and she wouldn't care if he had a raging hard-on anytime he got near her. Even now, she might appreciate a hard dick as much as him taking out the trash.

No. For a woman nursing a hangover, the latter would probably score more brownie points.

"I'm still trying to decide what to wear," she said. "I need something that'll cover all my bruises and be comfortable. Right now, I'm leaning toward a long-sleeved sweater."

Hopefully, she'd wear a bra under it. The pajamas were driving him nuts. "You still have visible bruises—I mean, aside from the ones on your face?"

"A few," she replied. "I've got another week to heal up. Might not even need makeup by then."

He nodded. "Your nose is almost back to normal, and I can hardly tell you've got a black eye."

"That's good—not that it matters. It's not like I'll be meeting the band or anything." She studied him for a moment. "Do the guys on stage really notice anyone in the audience?"

"Depends on the lights," he replied. "Sometimes you can't even tell the people are out there."

"Then I definitely won't need makeup." She huffed out a breath. "Guess that idea was just my former vanity trying to reassert itself. I never used to leave the house without makeup on and my hair fixed. No point in bothering with it now."

She was right about that much. Tracy hadn't powdered her nose or combed her hair and Joey was already itching to nail her on the kitchen table.

As if she'd read his thoughts, she ran a hand through her disheveled locks. "Melina's so excited. She'll probably drive me up the wall next week trying to figure out what to wear. Of course, she'll look absolutely stunning no matter what she has on. She always does."

"You're pretty stunning yourself." The words were out before he could stop them.

"Um…thanks." Her puzzled frown suggested she'd simply been stating a fact, not fishing for a compliment. Clearing her throat, she changed the subject yet again. "You never said how your gig went. Did you guys play like rock gods and have the girls drooling all over you?"

Did he dare be honest about her role in his performance? Could he actually *tell* her he'd fantasized about her the whole time? After the way that last remark had fizzled, he opted to play it safe. "We played better than usual, actually. Must've been good vibes or something."

She nodded. "Or the stars were in the right alignment. Tough to explain, isn't it?"

"Usually."

Not this time. The reason was standing right there in front of him in her flannel pajamas, leaning against the kitchen counter, completely oblivious to her effect on him.

He was dying to give her a demonstration. His dick had escaped from the tiny thong long ago, and his fingers itched to play her body like a well-tuned guitar. Tracy had already found her way into his music. Apparently, finding his way inside her would take a while longer.

But it would be well worth the wait.

Chapter 11

Tracy's befuddled brain skipped back a few sentences. He thought she was stunning? Compared to what? A sledgehammer to the head?

Getting involved with Joey was a bad idea. They were both on the rebound—sort of—and every love affair/relationship she'd been a part of had gone south. To top it all off, he lived next door.

I'd like to at least remain friends. Somehow she couldn't see that happening with anyone like, well, like anyone she'd ever dated or been married to.

Still, he thought she was stunning, and she thought he was a cute mini Alice Cooper.

I really need to think about this when I'm not hung over. This wasn't a good time to do much of anything, except maybe watch the New Year's Day parades on TV. Unfortunately, she didn't feel like doing that, either.

In the end, Joey went home and she went back to bed.

Feeling much better later that evening, she considered knocking on Joey's door and asking him just exactly what he'd meant. Then she remembered he was supposed to be working the dinner shift at Georgio's. She couldn't even remember how she knew that.

Maybe she didn't.

One thing she *did* know was that she wasn't going to do any unsupervised champagne drinking ever again. Melina would've cut her off. Miranda wouldn't have offered it to her to begin with. If she'd been at a party and had to drive home afterward, she probably wouldn't have had anything alcoholic to drink at all.

Apparently, spending New Year's Eve home alone was not in her best interest.

Vowing to add that pertinent detail to her list of resolutions, she watched *It's a Wonderful Life* and then went back to bed wondering what the world would've been like if *she'd* never been born. Her family and her patients probably would've said she was a worthwhile addition to the human race. The jury was still out on how her men friends would vote. She, on the other hand, would've been much better off had none of them seen fit to make an appearance in that life.

෴

After his breakfast with Tracy, Joey went back to his apartment wishing he could've found an excuse to stick around longer. The more time he spent with that woman, the more he wanted her. Too bad she wasn't interested—yet. She hadn't recovered from the incident with Bryce physically or mentally.

He knew the feeling—the mental part of it anyway. After Geena dumped him, he'd lost interest in women. But that was changing, and he had faith that Tracy's attitude would also improve with time.

Going to that Barton Junction concert was perfect. It was a date without really being a date. He could get to know her better and meet some of her friends, increasing his connection to her. And if that didn't work, there was always Plan B—which was possibly the craziest idea he'd ever had.

True, it would kill two birds with one stone, but it could also backfire on him in *so* many ways. He would try the more conventional approach first and only use his alternate plan as a last resort. Even so, he had no intention of hiding anything from Tracy. In fact, he ought to tell her even before—

No. Not yet. He'd let her find it the first time she got into his pants. If it freaked her out, so be it. No more lies. No more secrets.

He put in his shift at Georgio's, and by the time he got home that night, his dick hurt from thinking about her asleep in the next apartment. Climbing into bed, he exposed his cock and gripped it in his hand. For a relatively small man, he had a decent-sized tool. Certainly no one had ever complained about the size or shape of it.

Not that many women were very vocal about such things—at least, not to a guy's face.

Did Tracy like the kinkier stuff? Would she like the way his cock and balls looked with a tight leather strap around them? Cock straps certainly made him hard—almost as much as wearing something a little more feminine. The first time he'd wrapped one of Geena's bras around his dick he thought he was going to fucking explode. Geena hadn't been home, of course. Too bad his pet fetish freaked her out.

Still, she'd lied to him, passed Darren off as his kid, and then left him when she found out about his stash of goodies. On the other hand, he may have simply provided her with a convenient excuse to leave when Darren's real father came sniffing around.

He might never know the whole story, but he was over it now. At least as much as anyone ever could be. He'd believed that Darren was his son, and he still loved the boy. Too bad he'd probably never see him again.

If only I hadn't been quite so gullible.

Reaching for his favorite pink satin bra, he slipped his cock and balls through one of the adjustable straps and pulled it tight. His dick was already drooling, but a little more lube improved the glide. None of the women he'd ever dated had even come close to liking the idea of using one of their bras as a cock strap. But what it did to him went far beyond titillating.

His libido shifted into a higher gear as he imagined Tracy's hands on his dick and her mouth on his balls. The first stroke drew a groan from deep in his throat, and his nuts ached for the touch of her tongue, hot on his skin. All the erotic imagery from the night before came rushing back, filling his groin with heat and making his dick bigger and tighter than ever before.

A flick of his nipple rings sent tingles racing over his skin, puckering his nipples as his sex drive kicked in with a vengeance.

The shuddering, quivering sensations began to build as he thought of *her* playing with his cock, taking it in her mouth, and sliding it into her pussy. What the hell would happen when she tied up his dick with *her* bra?

He didn't have to answer that question. His penis did it for him, spewing like a geyser.

Oh, yeah. He wanted her—more than he'd ever wanted anyone. If it wasn't mutual, he could live with that. What he *couldn't* live with was being automatically ruled out because of all the other jackasses she'd dated.

Plan B was looking better all the time.

ಖುಲ

"I've been freaking out all day," Melina announced when Tracy answered her knock on the day of the concert.

As usual, she'd put all of that mental energy to good use. In tight jeans, a ruffled crepe blouse, and a suede jacket—not to mention perfect hair, makeup, and nails—Melina belonged on a magazine cover.

"Like you haven't been a basket case all *week*?" Tracy chuckled. "Just let me grab my coat and we'll go get Joey."

Joey must've been listening for Melina's arrival because he opened his door just as Tracy closed hers. He waved as he stepped out into the hall and slipped a leather jacket over a light blue baseball-style shirt with navy sleeves. "Hey, Tracy. All set?"

"Great outfit," Tracy said. "Your earrings even match your shirt."

"Thanks." She could've sworn he winked. "You're no slouch yourself."

Tracy stifled a snort. Melina and Joey would get all the looks while she disappeared into the crowd. At least, that was the plan. Acknowledging the compliment with a quick smile, she introduced him to Melina.

"So, you're the hero, huh?" Melina said. "Wish I'd been here to see you throw Bryce down the stairs."

"I didn't actually *throw* him," Joey said. "More like aimed him forcefully in that direction." Smiling, he pulled his hair out from beneath his coat—an action that made Tracy's breath catch in her throat.

Tracy couldn't claim to be in love with Joey, but his hair was a different story. She absolutely *loved* it. Maybe that was why she was so attracted to him. If his hair was short, she might not want him at all.

She gave herself a mental slap. She didn't want him *now*. He could shave his head and it wouldn't matter. His hairstyle was his business, not hers—although the skin-head type usually gave her the creeps. She made a mental note to mention that if he ever threatened to cut his long, curly locks.

They went out to Melina's car, and Joey got in the back seat without comment. Throughout the drive to Evansville, she and Melina had plenty to talk about, but Joey was so quiet, there were times when Tracy almost forgot he was there.

Almost.

She couldn't help wondering what he was thinking. The occasional glance over her shoulder proved he hadn't fallen asleep, but not much else. The wink he'd given her was as puzzling as the compliment of her wardrobe—although he'd had to stretch a bit for that one. Evidently, her black sweater wasn't quite as stunning as her Tweety Bird pajamas.

After several cell phone calls to verify their route and destination, they met up with Janet and her son Greg at a steak house near the arena. Tracy vaguely remembered Janet as having filled in at the clinic a time or two. Greg was a tall, handsome blond—too young for Tracy, of course, but then their totally hot waiter came over and introduced himself as Karl. Reminding herself that she wasn't in the market for a man, hot or otherwise, she focused her attention on the menu.

The restaurant was crowded, and they wound up crammed into a booth designed for four people. Tracy sat between Melina and Joey with Janet and Greg facing them across the table. Joey was smashed against the partition, and Tracy's entire left side was pressed against him in an intimate manner.

Not being the designated driver, Tracy took Karl up on his suggestion of a margarita while Joey drank a beer. As the tequila took effect and Joey's body heat seeped into her, her thoughts became increasingly carnal, making her wonder how it would feel to sit naked in his lap with his cock embedded deep inside her, or to suck his cock until he came in her mouth.

Fabulous.

Giving herself a mental shake, she ordered steak and a baked potato with sour cream. Drinking tequila on an empty stomach was her mistake. Once it wore off, she wouldn't have the overwhelming desire to sit on Joey's prick—or suck him off.

Maybe.

Unfortunately, the steak was as warm and juicy as a kiss, and the sour cream served as a reminder of another type of cream she would never taste again if she maintained her vow of abstinence.

Thankfully, her sweater hid the fact that her nipples were hard as rocks. If she'd worn the kind of clingy, low-cut top Janet had on, Joey would've been able to see right down the front of it. As it was, his curls tickled her arm every time she picked up her knife, and despite her best efforts to keep it in her lap, her left hand seemed determined to stray closer to his leg. Whenever he spoke, his deep, raspy voice transmitted vibrations from his body directly to hers. He even smelled good.

He wasn't actually *doing* anything, and she wanted to suck his dick so badly she could almost taste it.

Damn. And he lives right next door…

She wound up behind him as they left the restaurant, and though she tried not to stare, her eyes refused to cooperate, remaining riveted to his cute little ass until he climbed into the back seat of Melina's car. The urge to jump in and cover him with kisses was overwhelming. Swallowing hard, she clenched her teeth resolutely together as she resumed her place in the front seat.

Giving up men was like going on a diet. She never craved triple chocolate fudge ice cream until it was forbidden. Her attraction to Joey was simply a matter of proximity and self-denial.

Those cravings would pass eventually. They always did. This one would, too.

Just as soon as the tequila wore off.

Chapter 12

Tracy and Melina locked their coats and purses in the trunk before heading into the stadium where the opening band was already playing. Tracy's teeth were chattering by the time they entered the building, although whether from the cold or the excitement, she couldn't have said.

"If you want a T-shirt, you'd better get it now," Melina suggested. "They'll be sold out after the concert."

"Good idea," Tracy said. "I'll meet you inside."

"I'll go with you," Joey said.

Unfortunately, after she'd waited in the amorphous line for twenty minutes, Tracy had already decided the music was too loud, and Joey was nowhere in sight.

After briefly considering a blue thong with "BJ Groupie" embroidered on the crotch—which would've been fun even without the innuendo—she chose a brown T-shirt with the band's logo on the front and the tour dates on the back. Nothing sexy about it.

I'm past all that. She ran the T-shirt through her belt so she wouldn't have to worry about losing it, got a drink from the water fountain, and was about to enter the arena when Joey caught up with her.

"What'd you get?"

"A T-shirt," she replied. "You?"

"Guitar picks." His lips curled into a smirk. "How come you didn't get one of the thongs?"

"I should've thought that was obvious."

"Doesn't go with the new you?"

"Not at all." As she passed through the doorway to the arena, her jaw dropped. "Holy shit. There aren't any chairs down there."

"Well, yeah." Joey held up his ticket stub. "This just says floor access. We're in the mosh pit."

Obviously she should've looked at her ticket more closely. "We have to stand for the entire concert? I'll swear, Melina said center stage, seventh row!" She stared at the crowd gathered around the stage in dismay. "Glad I pitched my stilettos."

Joey let out a funny little groan just as Tracy spotted Melina waving at them.

By the time they'd descended the steep stairs to the floor level, Tracy understood the reason for Joey's groan. Melina, along with Greg and Janet, stood to the left of the stage directly beneath what had to be the biggest, loudest speaker in existence.

Conversation was impossible as the first band played for forty incredibly loud, incessant minutes, followed by another twenty minutes of quieter, recorded music. Tracy figured that with two opening acts and a break before the main event at nine o'clock, they would be on their feet for at least four hours.

Oh, joy.

"You don't look like you're having much fun," Melina commented.

"I'm beginning to envy the people in the nosebleed section," Tracy replied. "If the next band is as loud as this one, I'll be deaf before Barton Junction ever makes it onstage."

"That reminds me." She reached into her pocket and pulled out a bag of earplugs. "My husband gave me these."

"Thanks," Tracy said, wishing she'd had them sooner. "Too bad we can't get out from under this speaker."

"Hold your ground," Melina advised. "They'll start pushing when the real show starts."

"I can hardly wait for that." She stuffed the plugs in her ears. "Did we lose Joey?"

"He was here a minute ago," Melina replied. "Maybe he went to the bathroom or something."

Just then, a guy carrying two cups of beer began pushing through the crowd toward the stage.

Melina was visibly annoyed. "I'll bet he was never that close to the front before. He's just trying to look like he's gone out to buy drinks for the others. Grab his ass, Tracy," she hissed. "Anyone who does something that crass is fair game."

Tracy did her best, but he didn't slow down for a second. "He's either immune or too drunk to give a shit."

Joey appeared by her side. "Here." He handed her a cup of beer. "I think you need this. You look more like you're at a funeral than a rock concert."

"I'm saving my energy for Barton Junction," Tracy said. "I've never even heard of these other guys." She didn't particularly care for their music, either.

The next band began playing and the crowd got even wilder. As more guys pushed their way through with drinks held high, she and Melina molested all of them. Tracy's Plain Jane persona must've been adequate cover because no one ever suspected her of being the culprit.

She finished the beer, and, as a result, had to trek up to the restroom during the next break. While she was there, she bought two more beers. After threading her way through the mob, she gave one of them to Joey.

"Did anyone grab your ass?" He was so close his hair brushed her cheek, sending a wave of tingles racing over her skin and making her long to bury her face in his curls.

She shook her head. "Probably afraid I'd douse them with beer."

"Or bite their dick." His breath tickled her ear. "You're a very dangerous woman. Maybe they can sense that."

Dangerous? She'd never been called that before, but the idea appealed to her. If more men were afraid of her, she'd wind up with fewer bruises.

Moments later, the crowd began to move, pushing inexorably toward the stage. She thought she'd lost Joey at first, but then realized he was behind her, pressed even more tightly against her body than he'd been in the restaurant. Rather than spill beer on anyone, she drank it down and dropped the cup.

The lights went down and Barton Junction began playing. She'd never been part of such a writhing mass of humanity before—all moving in time to the same rhythm. The alcohol numbed her inhibitions to the point that she no longer minded being surrounded by complete strangers, and the music seemed to engulf her. With her arms in the air, she screamed along with everyone else, jumping up and down to the beat of the drums.

As she adjusted her rhythm to match the movements of the person behind her, she glanced over her shoulder. Joey was gone. A man she'd never seen before bounced against her butt in an erotic dance while flames shot up from the stage, blasting the crowd with instantaneous heat.

By the end of the next song, Tracy had lost her dance partner and acquired the inevitable drunk, only this time it was a girl. It wasn't until a man came and carried her off that Tracy realized she'd been the only thing keeping the woman on her feet.

Another drunk appeared about the same time the lead singer told everyone to jump up and down and scream during the chorus of the next song. Tracy's new dance partner put his arm around her shoulders and jumped along with her. But when he reached around to hug her at the end of the song, another pair of hands pulled her back. A quick backward glance revealed a familiar face.

Joey, thank God.

As the concert progressed, the pushing stopped and Tracy actually had room to move and breathe. Unfortunately, there were certain frequencies she simply couldn't hear anymore. The words were still discernable, but there was no melody, only the drumbeat remained, and her vision was distorted by the pulsing lights.

The band threw guitar picks and drumsticks into the audience from time to time, drawing screams from the crowd. Unable to imagine anyone actually snatching a guitar pick out of the air in semi-darkness, Tracy never caught anything or even bothered to try.

Joey was still behind her, making her wish she had an excuse to back up against him. He knew exactly how much beer she'd swallowed that night, and it wasn't nearly enough to make her that reckless. Still, one backward step and his dick would be pressed against her ass...

When the pushing began again, Tracy no longer needed excuses; she truly had no choice but to nestle her buns firmly against Joey's groin. Unfortunately, that intimacy didn't mean a damn thing.

Or did it?

ಬಿಲ

By the time the show ended, Joey would've gladly traded rock superstardom for the chance to grab Tracy by the hips and fuck her until she couldn't see straight.

Barton Junction's lead guitarist was as awesome as ever. Joey had studied his style and knew every note. If he'd gone to the concert alone, he could've simply reveled in the music.

But he'd never been in a mosh pit with Tracy Richards before. After purchasing a thong—along with the guitar picks he'd actually admitted to buying—the night had gone steadily downhill.

If that's the right word. He wasn't sure. He'd made himself a promise he wouldn't be too forward with her. Pushy, obnoxious men were the bane of her existence. He'd tried not to get too close, but she was right about being a magnet for drunks. He'd had to intervene several times.

Sitting beside her at dinner had him primed and ready—so much so that the mere mention of stilettos made him groan, and picturing her in nothing but spike heels and that baby blue thong nearly sent him over the edge.

When she'd climbed the steps ahead of him as they left the arena, her ass was practically in his face. Did she have any idea what she did to him? She hadn't been the slightest bit flirtatious and never so much as glanced at the bulge beneath his button fly.

Probably didn't feel it, either.

"My ears are still ringing," Melina said as the three of them crossed the parking lot with Greg and Janet. "Glad we had those earplugs."

Tracy grimaced. "I'm not sure they helped much. After standing under that speaker all night my left ear may never be the same—and that last scream of yours was a killer."

"Sorry," Melina said meekly. "I got kinda carried away."

Joey could certainly relate to that. He'd done his best to protect Tracy from the drunks only to wind up banging his dick against her butt himself. If she'd realized how hard his cock was, she'd have slapped him senseless.

Tracy wrapped an arm around his waist and gave him a squeeze. "What about you, Joey? Were they as awesome as you thought they'd be?"

Her casual touch triggered a gulp that nearly choked him. When his breath and wits finally returned, he replied, "Better. If I could play in a band like that…"

"Don't sell yourself short. You guys are darn good." She gave him another squeeze and let go.

His groin flooded with renewed heat at the same time his heart took a dive. "Yes, but to be really successful you need original material."

"You've *got* original material," she chided. "I know because I've heard you playing it." She arched a brow. "I've heard you singing, too."

This time heat flooded his face rather than his dick. "Sorry," he muttered. "Guess I've gotten louder now that Darren's gone."

"You need to quit playing those songs in an empty apartment and work on them with the band—you know, with drums and harmony and stuff like that."

He shook his head, letting his hair fall forward to cover his face. *If she only knew who half those songs were about…*

Melina laughed. "You sound like a manager, Tracy." She gave Joey a nudge. "Before you know it, she'll have you playing in stadiums all over the world."

"Yeah, right," he mumbled. "Not in a million years."

"You're already a helluva lot better than those other two

bands," Tracy insisted. "They were terrible."

"You seemed to be enjoying yourself anyway," Greg put in. "I still can't believe you grabbed that guy by the seat of his pants."

"Figured I'd better harass the drunks before they started in on me." Tracy's smirk morphed into a frown. "Not sure that approach was entirely successful. I still managed to attract a few weirdoes."

"It's that sweet, understanding face of yours." As Joey shot her a sidelong glance, something else caught his eye. "Hey, what's that?"

"What's what?" Stopping short, she turned to face him.

"This." His hand moved forward seemingly of its own accord to pluck a guitar pick from the v-neck of her sweater.

Probably the closest I'll ever get to her tits.

"Ha! You got one," Melina crowed.

"I'll give you a hundred dollars for that," Greg said, reaching into his shirt pocket.

"No way," Tracy said. "I've got a hundred dollars, but I don't have one of these."

Joey backed away, holding the pick over his head. "Come and get it."

Strangely enough, her eyes didn't seem to be focused on the pick, but on his stomach. She blinked twice, giving her head a quick shake.

"Come on, Joey." She had an odd quaver in her voice as she reached out a hand. "I already gave you a ticket for rescuing me, you—"

"Look at this!" Greg exclaimed. "I got one too. It was in my pocket."

To Joey's dismay, Tracy lowered her hand immediately. "And you were going to give me a hundred dollars for mine."

At that point, Joey would've given him a thousand dollars to keep his mouth shut.

So much for getting into a wrestling match with Tracy.

"What're the odds?" Janet said. "That's pretty cool, finding it in your pocket like that."

"It was more fun finding Tracy's," Joey said with a chuckle. "Here, you can have it back."

She shook her head. "You can put it to better use than I ever could. It might even be good luck."

In Joey's opinion, good luck would've been the chance to put it back where he'd found it. "Really?"

"Sure. You can give me credit on an album cover when you're rich and famous."

He gave her a wink and slid the pick into his pocket. "I'll do that."

They walked out to their cars and, after waving goodbye to Greg and Janet, Joey got in the back seat. Alone.

Melina gasped when she started the engine. "Holy shit. My gas light is on. We'll run out if we have to sit in traffic."

"We're not in any hurry," Tracy soothed. "We can wait here until the parking lot clears out."

If Tracy had been in the back seat with him, Joey wouldn't have minded staying there all night. He was in the midst of a fantasy about her sitting on his prick when Melina startled him back to reality.

"Look at that guy," she said, pointing to a young couple getting into the only other car left in their vicinity. "He is *so* drunk."

By the time Joey glanced up, the man was getting into the passenger side—obviously the girl was the more sober of the two and intended to drive.

"Hmm…cute, too," Tracy commented. "Too bad I'm not interested in that sort of thing anymore."

Melina blew out an exasperated snort. "I remember when you actually *enjoyed* boy watching. I still think you're giving men a bum rap."

"Maybe, maybe not."

The two women began chatting about someone at the clinic while Joey daydreamed about sucking Tracy's fabulous tits and fucking her hot, wet pussy…

"Holy shit!" Melina exclaimed. "She's—"

Joey's eyes flew open. The other car was still there, but the girl was no longer in the driver's seat. She was sitting on her boyfriend, riding him up and down like she was—

"—fucking him."

"I'll be damned," Tracy muttered.

Joey stifled a groan. He couldn't see the man very well, but the girl was quite obviously naked from the waist down.

They're playing out my fantasy while I'm sitting here freezing to death.

A few minutes later, the girl resumed her place in the driver's seat. Her boyfriend's grin stretched from ear to ear.

"He certainly looks happy," Melina commented.

"Yeah." Tracy didn't sound the least bit envious.

Damn.

She glanced in the other direction. "Traffic's thinned out now."

Melina started the car, and they left the peep show behind. After stopping for gas, they began the drive back to Pemberton. Tracy and Melina chatted like the old friends they were while Joey sat quietly, wondering what the hell he should do now.

Plan B.

Melina seemed like a decent sort. She might help him out—might even think it was funny. Tracy might get a kick out of the idea, too.

That is, if she ever spoke to him again.

Chapter 13

"Come on, Tracy," Melina urged as she mixed up a dose of Primaxin. "Louisville is only an hour away, and you'll have a ball. It's a blast trying to figure out what gender everyone is."

For the entire week since the Barton Junction concert, Melina had done her best to convince Tracy to go with her to The Closet Door. Tracy wasn't sure she was ready for the "alternative" nightclub scene—not to mention suspecting Melina of having ulterior motives.

"Would I have to dress up as a guy?" Although she balked at the idea, she suspected the task wouldn't be difficult. She only had to put her hair up in a ponytail and stuff socks in the front of her jeans—and find a way to flatten her boobs.

Well…maybe it wouldn't be so easy after all.

"You'd be an awfully cute one if you did," Melina said. "The gays would eat you up. But then, you're an awfully cute *girl*."

"Thanks." Tracy's reply was automatic. She really didn't give a damn whether anyone thought she was cute or not. "I think I'll stick with being a woman." She paused as another thought occurred to her. "Should I be a girl dyke or a bull dyke?"

"Neither." Melina chuckled. "Unless you've been hiding something from me."

"No. I may *say* I'd rather date girls than boys, but I'm hopelessly heterosexual." A fact she'd discovered when Joey had been bouncing against her butt in the mosh pit. Not that going out with him was a good idea. She couldn't help remembering what he'd said about women not liking him. Was it worth the risk to find out why?

Melina snorted a laugh. "Tell me something I don't know."

"I can't seem to find an opposite-gendered person I get along with, and something tells me I won't find one there."

Melina's eyes widened in innocence. "Did I say anything about finding someone? I just think we'd have fun. My husband might even go with us. He gets a big kick out of the drag queens."

"I'm sure I would too," Tracy admitted. "Unless it's one of those places where you have to stand in line for hours before they let you in."

"I've never had to wait, but I've only been there once."

"Hopefully, it wasn't a slow night." Noting Melina's exasperated expression, she hastened to add, "Don't get me wrong, it sounds like fun. Maybe next Saturday. I'm going to see Joey's band at Cider Hill Tavern this weekend."

"Oh, really?"

"Yes, really. And it's not a date, so you can wipe that smirk off your face."

"But you like him, don't you?"

Tracy's initial response was what she hoped was a nonchalant shrug. "You've met him. He's a nice guy. What's not to like?"

"What's he do for a living besides the occasional gig?"

"He's a cook at Georgio's," Tracy replied, wondering why it mattered.

"He's kinda quiet."

Melina's tone suggested that being quiet was a bad thing. Tracy disagreed. In her opinion, most men would benefit from the judicious use of duct tape. "Maybe that's the way he acts around strangers."

"Not exactly shy, though," Melina drawled. "I mean, he *did* pluck that guitar pick off your chest."

"So what? We've known each other for a while. I even did some babysitting for him before his girlfriend took the baby and left. He was devastated—especially when he found out the baby wasn't even his kid. Between that and what happened with Bryce, I'd have to say we've been together for some fairly significant experiences."

"Significant experiences, huh?" Melina went on, smiling

suggestively. "As in sex with the babysitter?"

Tracy rolled her eyes. "Nothing like that. Trust me on this one."

"It's just as well," she said with a dismissive wave. "He's pretty skuzzy-looking."

Tracy's first reaction to that comment was a flare of indignation that she somehow managed to suppress. "I think he's kinda cute, but what do I know? Bryce was a real hunk, and all he did was rearrange my face."

"Hmm..." She tapped her foot. "So, no danger of falling for Joey?"

"None whatsoever," Tracy replied. She thought she'd handled that rather well, speaking with firm conviction, even while telling one of the bigger lies of her life.

She had Melina convinced.

The trick now would be convincing herself.

ℰℑ

Joey did his best to further his relationship with Tracy, which wasn't easy considering they worked different shifts. Nonetheless, he managed to find several reasons to bump into her or drop by, keeping it friendly while subtly altering their previous pattern.

He didn't purposely play the pity note, but if she thought he was lonely, so much the better. Every now and then she would ask if he'd heard anything from Geena. Unfortunately, he couldn't tell if she was interested for herself or for him.

"I haven't heard a peep, and I don't expect to," he told her after one concerned query when they met—quite by accident—in the laundry room.

"I know it's none of my business, but you seemed so happy together. I don't get it—whether Darren was really your kid or not."

"It's...personal," he said. "I'll tell you someday." She still seemed puzzled, so he added, "It's nothing illegal or horrible. Just something most women don't understand."

"You've told me that much before, but I can't help

wondering—"

"Forgive me. I know it seems weird." He toyed briefly with the idea of just blurting it out.

Not yet. She still needs some...tweaking. "Are you coming to the show tomorrow?"

"Wouldn't miss it." She paused, frowning. "The tavern is non-smoking, isn't it?"

"I wish it was. Whenever I came home after a gig, Geena used to insist that I strip down, take a shower, and throw my clothes in the washer."

She stared at him for a long moment, then pressed her lips together and turned away.

Oh, crap... "I don't smell bad now, do I?"

"No," she replied. "Actually, you smell sort of...Italian."

"Like garlic, you mean?"

She leaned closer and sniffed. "More like pizza—or homemade bread."

"That doesn't sound too bad." Unless it only meant she was hungry. He could certainly smell *her*. She probably thought she'd succeeded in coming across as neutral rather than a gorgeous, sexy woman, but it wasn't working.

Not by a long shot.

She picked up her basket and turned to go. "See you then?"

"You bet."

෨෬

Tracy had never walked into a bar feeling quite so underdressed. Wearing her Barton Junction T-shirt, a pair of nondescript jeans, and no makeup or jewelry whatsoever, she'd merely run a brush through her hair prior to leaving home. Stashing her ID and some cash in her pockets along with her car keys, she went in alone—something else she'd never done. She hoped Joey wouldn't feel slighted, but her plan was to leave after the first set, which should enable her to avoid picking up the usual complement of obnoxious drunks.

She arrived at eight forty-five only to find every table and barstool on the ground level taken. However, the second floor was relatively empty, save for a few people playing darts in the corner, and she was able to get a seat with a bird's eye view of the bandstand.

Despite having been invited, she felt weird about being there at all—out of place and very much alone.

Alone. She'd never been to a bar by herself. She'd always gone with a date or with friends, and she'd always been dressed to kill. Gazing down at the dance floor, she saw herself there in numerous guises—short, tall, blonde, brunette, thin, fat—all different, perhaps, but with one thing in common. They were all on display.

With a shudder, she watched scantily clad women dancing with men whose hands were all over them. She'd been in that same position a hundred times, never realizing how cheap she must've seemed. The need to show so much skin was peculiar. Did men really have to be hit over the head with a woman's sexuality for them to respond?

Men didn't need to wear tuxedos or Speedos to attract women. They only had to be reasonably dressed and relatively clean. Nearly everyone had *some* redeeming characteristic—nice eyes, a great smile, or a good sense of humor. They didn't have to be models or star athletes. Why did women feel the need to dress like exotic dancers?

Then again, this was a place where singles went to mingle with the intent of finding someone. *She* was the odd duck—dressed well enough for the laundromat or the grocery, but certainly not for a night on the town.

Suddenly, she was glad she hadn't seen Joey. She didn't want him to think she hadn't cared enough to put forth the extra effort, even though he might have some idea as to why she hadn't.

A waitress came to take her order, introducing herself as Sherry and eyeing Tracy as though she also thought she looked out of place. "Is your name Tracy?"

Somewhat leery, Tracy nodded in reply.

"There's a seat for you near the bandstand. Joey asked me to look for you. Are you his girlfriend?"

Tracy couldn't help but laugh. "No, I'm just his next-door neighbor." That was about the only connection she could reasonably claim. She couldn't very well mention that he'd been her hero once, and she certainly wasn't a groupie. "If he asks, tell him I'll be okay up here."

Sherry made no comment, leaving Tracy to wonder why Joey would think she needed to sit so close—and also what his description of her had been.

"A woman who looks like she wants to be left alone."

Or, *"A woman deliberately trying to look frumpy."*

She was still mulling over the possibilities when Sherry returned with a bottle of Corona. Tracy reached into her pocket, but the waitress waved a hand. "It's covered."

"No, really," Tracy said, hoping some weird drunk hadn't already spotted her. "I'll pay for it. I'd much rather—"

"No, really. You're Joey's guest."

"Oh."

As Sherry walked away, apparently considering the matter closed, Tracy couldn't help remembering all the guys who'd bought her drinks thinking it gave them the right to follow her home. What was Joey's motivation in claiming she was his guest? Was it simply a friendly gesture, or was there more to it?

The band began playing promptly at nine, and Tracy noted that while Joey was an excellent guitarist, something was missing from his performance. He didn't play to the crowd, didn't grin at the girls or make any provocative moves—not even something as simple as stepping out of his proscribed area during a guitar solo. He might have been hidden somewhere in the shadows or off-stage entirely. She couldn't recall having noticed that when she'd seen them play before—possibly because she'd been with friends and had been out on the dance floor most of the time.

Melina was right. Tracy *did* sound like a manager. She was even beginning to think like one, unconsciously critiquing their performance. The band was technically good, but the connection with the audience simply wasn't there.

They were several songs into the set when Joey stepped up to the microphone, presumably to sing backup. His swift upward glance triggered a double take of recognition, and in an instant, his lips curled into a provocative grin. Suddenly, it was all there—the eye contact, the hip-grinding moves, and the star quality he'd so obviously lacked only moments before.

Tracy smiled back as he came alive right before her eyes—a condition as astounding as it seemed to be catching. His band mates shifted into another gear and the atmosphere of the entire club changed. Whereas before, their performance might simply have been songs played on the juke box, *they* were the show now, rather than the gyrations on the dance floor.

The transformation was nothing short of astonishing, and it had happened the moment Joey's eyes met hers.

Oh, surely not…

ଞଓ

Joey had done his best to engage in the fantasies that enabled him to play so well at their last gig, but it wasn't working. His performance wasn't even up to his usual standards. Brad aimed a few scowls at him, no doubt wondering where the talent had gone. Joey couldn't blame the guy for being annoyed. He was annoyed with himself. Some days were like that.

Days without Tracy.

She was his inspiration and his good luck charm, but the seat he'd reserved for her was empty. He shouldn't have been quite so crushed by her absence. After all, this wasn't the first gig he'd played without a girlfriend in the audience, and it wouldn't be the last.

Tracy obviously didn't see him as a love interest. She was a friend and neighbor and nothing more. All the "tweaking" hadn't done a bit of good. She wasn't knocking on his door. He'd been knocking on hers.

She'd sworn never to get involved with another man. Was there a way to change her mind? He hated the idea of toying with her emotions—something Plan B would do in spades.

Only if I'm desperate.

But *how* desperate? He'd been so close to her the night of the concert. Since then, he'd only received friendly waves and brief chats in the laundry room.

Nothing like what he *really* wanted from her.

He checked the playlist only to discover he had to sing backup on the next song. *Great.* He'd never felt less like singing in his life. Stepping up to the mic, he glanced up.

Holy shit.

Tracy stood there, leaning against the railing like a guardian angel.

His guardian angel.

Relief washed through him, purging his mind of negative energy and setting his spirit free. Singing wasn't a problem now. For him, the crowd ceased to exist. She was the only person who mattered. Any doubts concerning her importance in his life evaporated.

How long had she been there? More importantly, how long would she stay? Would she leave before the break?

He couldn't let that happen—especially now that he'd seen her. He knew the best way to keep her there was to make sure she was entertained. She'd made the comment that the openers for Barton Junction were more to be endured than enjoyed. He would make damn sure she didn't feel the same way about *his* band.

Giving it his all and then some, he called upon tried and true techniques even as he created new ones. His band mates picked up his energy and the music exploded.

No one was leaving yet.

No one.

Chapter 14

Following a quick stop in the upstairs restroom during the break, Tracy figured she'd find Joey, tell him how much she enjoyed the show, and head for home. She didn't want him to feel slighted, she just wanted—

What the hell *did* she want?

"God only knows," she muttered.

As she left the restroom, she spotted Joey sitting at the table where she'd spent the evening. Slouched in his chair, he seemed more defeated than triumphant, toying with an empty beer bottle.

Her empty beer bottle.

He glanced up as she approached, his smile conveying pleasure along with a touch of relief. "I thought you'd gone home."

"Not yet," she said. "But I was thinking about it. I'm kinda tired."

"I had a seat for you downstairs." A brief frown furrowed his brow. "Didn't Sherry tell you?"

"Yes, but I felt better up here—not sure why. Thanks for the drink."

He nodded as though he understood her need for solitude. "I didn't see you for a long time. I thought you weren't coming."

The catch in his voice made her chest tighten. Perhaps she'd been more important to him than she realized. "I said I would."

"Yeah, you did." He sighed. "I guess with you that must mean something."

Another painful twinge touched her heart. Was he thinking about Geena?

Probably.

A change of subject seemed in order. "You guys really sounded great tonight. I guess practice makes perfect." She gave him a wink. "Or is it that Barton Junction guitar pick?"

"Both," he replied. "Along with a little inspiration."

"I can't argue with that." She didn't ask him to elaborate. Her presence had nothing to do with his—or the band's—performance. She wasn't *that* special. They'd simply been playing long enough to warm up. She'd let her imagination run away with her.

Stupid.

"I'm glad you came," he said. "Playing for a crowd is hard for me. It helps to see a familiar face."

At least wasn't tossing out the *I saved your life* card—not that he needed to. That card had already been dealt—but would she feel beholden to him for the rest of the life he'd saved? Or would the score be declared even at some point? "Do you want me to stay?"

"That's up to you." Rising from the chair, he nodded toward the stairs. "Come on. I'll introduce you to the guys. Brad's wife is here and so is Lenny's." A grim smile quirked his lips. "I could never bring Geena."

Tracy didn't have to ask why. She couldn't claim to be anything more than Joey's neighbor, but at least she was old enough to get past the bouncer.

Most people would've condemned Joey for getting mixed up with such a young girl to begin with. Even before she'd learned the truth about their relationship, Tracy thought they were mismatched. Sure, Joey was cute, but Geena was blonde, beautiful, and built like a brick shithouse. Girlfriend or neighbor, Tracy felt like a poor substitute.

She followed him downstairs and across the crowded, smoke-filled room. "I could see you better from where I was."

"Maybe. But you can see Brad and Lenny better from here—*they're* the good-looking frontmen. Billy likes to hide behind his synthesizer. And then there's Dave. He may be stuck behind his drums, but he's a real ladies' man—supposed to be hung like a horse."

"I see..." Truth be told, the only dick she was interested in was

Joey's. Not that she would ever admit that. She couldn't quite figure him out. One minute he seemed to only want to be her friend, and the next, well...she wasn't sure about that, either. He'd seemed a lot different in the mosh pit.

What happens in the mosh pit stays in the mosh pit.

"Is that a warning or a recommendation?" she asked.

He shrugged. "Both, I guess. We've got a table by the bandstand. Want to hang out with us for a while?"

The "us" presumably meaning the band and possibly their wives and girlfriends. "I dunno. My hearing still hasn't recovered from the last time I got too close to an amplifier."

"You don't have to stay long."

"Okay," she relented. "Lead on."

She followed him to a table to the right of the bandstand where he introduced her as "my friend, Tracy Richards" before pointing toward a somewhat anorexic dishwater blonde. "That's Cynthia Caruthers, Lenny's wife, and Angie Winters—" he nodded at a petite brunette with the longest, thickest eyelashes Tracy had ever seen, "—who has the dubious honor of being married to Brad."

Brad, a working-man's version of Brad Pitt, stood behind his wife, grinning as Joey pointed out Lenny, the lanky bassist, and his brother Billy, who looked more like a balding accountant than a keyboard player.

"And I'm Dave Flynn."

Tracy smiled at the shaggy-haired drummer as she took a seat beside Cynthia, doing her best to focus on Dave's mischievous blue eyes rather than his groin. "Nice to meet all of you."

Cynthia leaned closer. "So, are you Joey's new girlfriend?"

Tracy fought the urge to roll her eyes. "Uh, no. I'm his next-door neighbor." She was getting tired of having to say that. Maybe claiming to be his *lesbian* neighbor would be more interesting. It would certainly eliminate any mention of Dave's dick.

"I still can't believe what Geena did to him," Cynthia said, shaking her head. "That was downright cruel."

As noisy as the place was, Tracy doubted Joey could've heard that comment, and a quick glance in his direction proved it. Laughing at some jibe from Dave as they resumed their places on bandstand, he seemed oblivious. "Yeah. He's been pretty torn up about it. She seemed like such a sweet girl."

"I guess she fooled a lot of people."

Was Geena truly the only one to blame? To hear Joey tell it, he'd expected her to dump him—whether Darren was his child or not. She wondered if Cynthia knew why.

The next set began, making conversation impossible—which was just as well.

Tracy wasn't sure how she would've phrased the question anyway.

Joey couldn't tell if Tracy was having a good time or not.

This was a mistake.

No, it wasn't. They were forming a connection.

Maybe. Maybe he was the only one feeling any of it. Damn, she was hot—she couldn't help it. Heat filled the air around her like an aura of—

Of what? That bit about having a sweet, understanding face was only a fraction of her allure. Cynthia and Angie were both pretty women, and they were as dolled up as every other girl in the bar, but Tracy drew his eyes like a magnet.

He was beginning to regret bringing her down from her perch at the edge of the balcony. He could at least see her up there—and she could see him. God, she'd set him on fire with those eyes. Was she watching him now?

A glance over his shoulder caught her gaze. She'd angled her chair away from the table, putting him directly in her line of sight.

That had to count for something. Still, if she could only see him from behind, he'd have to work on giving her a good show...

He sank his teeth into his lower lip as he imagined her hands on his hips, pulling his bare ass back against her, gliding her fingers around to his dick. Taking it in her grasp, she pumped him until he spewed cum clear across the room, then smacked his ass for not waiting for her…

She could take all her annoyance with the male sex out on him if she liked. He'd gladly lie across her knee and let her paddle his butt until he spooged in her lap. And if she tied her bra around his dick, he'd obligingly spew in her face or anywhere else she wanted it.

His balls ached as his fingers played that Ibanez the way he wanted to play her, plucking the melody from every sensitive spot in her body until she sang out in ecstasy. He longed to get his fingers wet in her pussy, probing and teasing until her climax sucked him in. Most of all, he wanted to bury his dick inside her and dance until he couldn't move anymore.

What would it take to break through that wall she'd put up around her emotions? She hadn't given him a single clue she might be interested in him—playing it so cool, while insisting that part of her life was over and done with.

Looking back at her again, he almost wished he hadn't. The biggest drawback to playing in a band was that it left your woman unprotected. Tracy sipped a margarita while a swarthy, foreign-looking dude with bushy eyebrows and a shaved head pulled a chair up beside her, leaning close enough to whisper in her ear.

Damn. I should've left her upstairs.

Joey's fingers fumbled on the strings as he recalled the last time he'd come to her rescue with this same instrument in his hands. Afterward, he'd been pleased to have gotten rid of Bryce without damaging the guitar. Right now, however, breaking the Ibanez over this fucker's bald pate seemed a perfectly reasonable course of action.

He didn't have to face the audience. Hell, with the wireless system, he could walk off the stage and out the door if he liked. What he couldn't figure out was why Cynthia and Angie weren't doing anything to discourage the creep.

Because she's my neighbor, not my lover.

He'd introduced her as "my friend, Tracy Richards."

Last time he'd do *that*.

He was already moving toward her when the dude pulled away from Tracy and staggered to the side exit clutching his belly like he was about to hurl.

Given that Brad had screamed into the microphone at that same moment, he wasn't completely sure what had just happened. Was the man drunk or had he fallen victim to that dangerous woman with the innocent smile?

As her smile became more of a smirk, he suspected the latter.

Tracy rose from her chair, waved to Cynthia and Angie, and headed for the stairs, unsure as to why she opted to return to her perch on the upper level rather than leaving.

Maybe because I don't want to run into that jackass in the parking lot.

Plus the fact that she was too buzzed to drive. She'd accepted the drink, figuring Joey had ordered it. Then that creep sat down beside her, making it patently obvious who the real culprit was.

The nerve of that man! It wasn't as if she'd been wearing a sequined halter top or a see-through blouse. She'd been sitting with two other women, minding her own business when that jerk took her hand and stuck it in his fly.

Opting for revenge rather than outrage, she'd slid her hand further into his pants, given his nuts a squeeze that would've expelled every drop of juice from the average lemon, and yelled "Get lost!" in his ear at the top of her lungs.

I should've bitten his damned dick.

Stopping off at the restroom, she gave her hands a thorough washing and stared at her reflection, slowly shaking her head in amazement. "Why me?"

A glance at her hands provided the reason. No wedding ring.

Her sister had worn her ring for years after being widowed and had found it to be a highly effective form of man repellant. Even Travis had been fooled by it at first.

That's what I need. Nothing flashy or impractical like her friend Beverly's engagement ring had been. Just a plain, gold band. She could probably get a nice, gold-plated style for twenty bucks at Wal-Mart.

And that store never closes. She could pick up a ring on the way home and never be bothered by another man as long as she lived. The idea was so perfect, she couldn't believe she hadn't thought of it before.

She left the restroom, flagged down a passing waitress, and ordered a Coke. When it arrived, she paid for it herself and drank it quickly, hoping to flush the alcohol out of her system. By the time the set was finished, she felt as though she could drive home without incident and was on her way down when she met Joey on the stairs.

"Too loud for you?" he asked.

"Nope, too many drunks."

Joey winced. "I was afraid of that. I saw that guy staggering out the side door. What exactly—"

"The son of a bitch put my hand in his pants!"

"And you—?"

"Squeezed his nuts 'til he screamed."

With his lips pressed tightly together, Joey was obviously trying to stifle his laughter, but his shaking shoulders gave him away.

"But it won't happen again," Tracy declared. "I've got an idea. I'm gonna buy a wedding ring."

His eyes widened. "You're getting married?"

She snorted a laugh. "Don't be silly. I don't need a husband. I just need a ring. Worked for my sister, so it oughta work for me."

"How many margaritas have you had?"

"Just the one." She paused, frowning. "Speaking of which, I'd better get that ring before I go to the drag queen show with Melina—although we aren't going for a couple of weeks. I've got time."

"A drag queen show? Honestly? Where?"

She waved a dismissive hand. "Some club called The Closet Door—as in that closet they've all come out of. I may've mentioned it to you before. Anyway, I'm sure she's right and we'll have a blast, but right now, I've had just about as much fun I can take for one night. I'm getting too old for this shit."

"You're what, thirty?"

She shrugged. "Just imagine what a party animal I'll be at fifty."

"I guess neither of us feels much like it these days." He smiled grimly. "We've both been through a lot. I felt sort of dead myself tonight until I saw you."

So, she *hadn't* imagined it. "I saw that—figured you were just getting warmed up."

He shook his head. "It was *you*."

"Oh." She couldn't think of anything else to say. Despite her best efforts, he was getting to her again. If *he'd* been the one to put her hand in his jeans, the outcome would've been completely different.

"We're playing some new songs tonight," he went on. "You said we needed to work more on the harmony, and there's one in particular I think you'll like."

"A song you wrote?"

"No, but it's real pretty."

Joey singing harmony on a pretty love song would probably be her undoing. "Well, okay, but I'd rather stay up here. Don't want my horny friend finding me again. He might be a little sore."

Crossing his arms, he leaned against the banister, chuckling. "You're really tough on balls, aren't you?"

"Which is probably why I should date women—although I'm still not convinced it's the way to go."

"You never know," he said with a wink. "You might meet someone who'll convert you."

"I doubt it. Besides, I don't think that's how it works." She hesitated, considering the idea for a moment before shaking her head. "That relationship crap is too much trouble anyway. You should know all about that."

"Maybe," he said. "But what happened with me wasn't all Geena's fault."

"You keep saying that, but even Cynthia thought what she did to you was cruel."

Geena had done some of the worst things a woman could do to a man. Not only had she used him up and spat him out, she'd broken his heart and made him look like a fool. Joey hadn't exactly sworn off women as a result, but he probably should have.

"We should make a pact," she said. "Anytime I start to take the plunge, it's your responsibility to talk me out of it—and vice versa. We could call it Dating Anonymous."

"That's a thought." His lips curled into an enigmatic smile. "But what happens if we both fall off the wagon at the same time?"

Chapter 15

Tracy stared at Joey for a long moment. Did he mean that the way it sounded? "Hmm…hadn't thought of that." A wedding ring on her finger certainly wouldn't fool him. *He* could make her fall off the wagon in a heartbeat. "Bad idea. Guess we're both on our own."

"I guess so." His smile faded slightly. "If you don't mind my asking, why does Melina think you'd enjoy a drag queen show?"

"She's been to one before—says it's a real hoot, so…" She shrugged. "Might be because of Bryce and all the other creeps I've been dating. Maybe she thinks I'll prefer cross-dressers or lesbians. I don't know."

"Would you?" he asked. "Prefer cross-dressers, I mean?"

"Who knows? I've never met one—at least, not that I'm aware of. Besides, it depends on the person, doesn't it? I mean, there are bound to be some real shit-head cross-dressers out there, too, wouldn't you think?"

"I guess so." Pushing away from the banister, he held out a hand. "Come on, I'll walk you back to your table."

Given what had happened the last time a man had taken her by the hand, she should've declined the offer. But this was Joey, not that bald-headed freak, and he tucked her hand in the crook of his arm, rather than his pants.

I guess there are a few gentlemen left in this world.

As she resumed her seat, he leaned over the balcony rail, his gaze directed toward the bandstand. "I shouldn't have asked you to come downstairs. This really is a better vantage point, and I liked being able to look up at you."

Since Tracy didn't know how to respond to that, she was somewhat relieved when Brad called out over the microphone, "Hey,

Manzetti! Where are you?"

"Better get going," she advised. "And knock 'em dead, or whatever it is people are supposed to say to rock stars for encouragement."

He grinned. "That'll do."

The dance floor was packed when the band began playing again, and the dancing was more blatantly sexual than ever. Tracy had enjoyed that exhilarating rush many times in the past—the close physical contact mixed with alcohol and the promise of sex—but her feelings were totally different this time. Up in the balcony, isolated from the crowd, she felt like an anthropologist observing the mating rituals of some primitive culture rather than someone who'd once been a part of it herself.

Until she looked at Joey. His moves had been riveting before, but now she longed to strip him naked, exposing his entire body to her gaze and her touch. Her fingers itched to sift through his hair and trace the sensual line of curls running down the center of his chest to his cock. She'd caught a glimpse of that treasure trail in the stadium parking lot when he'd held the guitar pick over his head, teasing her. She couldn't have cared less about the pick. Her eyes had been focused on that enticing patch of skin.

Her mind drifted back to the mosh pit and the thrust of his groin against her bottom, the heat of his body pressed against her own. If only they'd been naked then. Her nipples tingled as she imagined his hands caressing her bare breasts, and the thought of his cock sliding between her legs made her pussy ache with need. She could almost hear their sweat-slick skin slapping together to the beat of the drums.

Lost in her fantasy, she teetered on the brink of orgasm as the song ended. When the applause died down, Joey turned his eyes upward, his gaze locking with hers. "This is for you, Tracy."

The crowd roared their approval as he played the opening riff. Wrapped in each other's arms, the couples on the dance floor moved in a sensuous rhythm while Brad sang the first verse. Spellbound, Tracy let the music flow over her until Joey's raspy baritone joined in perfect harmony with Brad's fervent tenor on the chorus, tightening her scalp and sending thrills racing over her skin.

The second verse evoked the pain of separation and loneliness before segueing into an achingly beautiful guitar solo. As the two men sang the final chorus, tears spilled unheeded down her cheeks.

Stunned, Tracy hardly noticed the thunderous applause, only joining in after several awestruck moments. As the next song began, Joey's gaze met hers again, and in that brief instant, she could almost believe he was playing for her and her alone.

Then the truth struck with a blinding flash of insight. He couldn't have been singing for her because, never having been together, they'd never been parted. Geena and Darren were the ones he'd lost.

Shoving away from the rail, she chastised herself for letting her imagination run riot. This was simply a performance technique—focusing on a memory that enabled him to convey the song's message to the audience. Those words weren't even his, only echoes of another songwriter's emotions.

But why dedicate the song to her? She may have been his inspiration, but that didn't necessarily mean he cared about her in the romantic sense. He was on the stage, playing his heart out. But were those feelings real or were they part of the act?

Dazed and confused, her first impulse was to run, to leave the bar before he noticed she was gone.

Then reason prevailed.

Joey had simply followed her suggestion to play songs that made the most of the incredible harmony between his voice and Brad's. *That* was why he'd dedicated the song to her. It didn't have anything to do with love or lust or desire. It was only his way of thanking her for her advice.

She knew what she had to do now. She would stay until the end of the set, congratulate him on a superb performance, and go home. Alone.

Like a good little friend, neighbor, and manager wannabe.

When the set ended, she hurried down the stairs. Joey met her with an enthusiastic hug—a hug she returned while somehow controlling her own exuberance.

"You guys were so great." She wiped away a tear. "You even made me cry."

"I-I'm glad you enjoyed it." Releasing her, he stepped back, brushing the hair from his face, a question in his eyes.

She gave him what she thought he wanted to hear. "The harmony was fabulous, and, honest to God, you played like you were channeling Eric Clapton, Stevie Ray Vaughn, and Slash all at the same time. Great moves, too—*totally* hot."

His gaze dipped downward—possibly with embarrassment—and yet, he seemed to be waiting for something more.

What the hell does he want from me? Money?

Abandoning the impersonal, objective approach, she gave him a warm smile. "Thanks for dedicating that song to me. I'd forgotten what it was like to feel special."

"It was the least I could do." He drew in a breath as if about to say more, but seemed to think better of it and simply shrugged.

Was the score between them even now? Or was she missing something?

Probably. Being intuitive wasn't her strong suit. If it had been, she'd have steered clear of ninety-nine percent of the men she'd let into her life.

But what about this one? Was he different?

She had to admit that despite her hopes, she had absolutely no idea. Avoiding his gaze lest she throw her arms around him and kiss him senseless, she contented herself with a touch, barely grazing his arm with her fingertips. "Guess I'll say goodnight then."

"Goodnight, Tracy." He nodded, smiling even as that strange, defeated aura seemed to blanket him again. "Thanks."

"Anytime."

Joey watched Tracy walk away, feeling like the biggest idiot to ever pick up a guitar. After all those beautiful, sexy love songs, she'd missed the point entirely—or was purposely ignoring his motives.

I should've kissed her.

He had no idea what she would've done if he had. She'd told him repeatedly she didn't want another man, and the way she'd dealt with that creepy dude was a perfect example of what she was capable of. Joey didn't blame her a bit for squashing the guy's balls, but he'd pass on getting his own face slapped.

Then again, if she wanted to slap his *ass*, he would gladly bend over and bare it.

Wishful thinking.

That song dedication would've scored serious brownie points with most women, and he could think of a few who would've responded by offering to suck his dick. Too bad he wasn't looking for a cocksucking one-night stand.

He wanted Tracy.

But how to get her?

Should he simply bite the bullet and tell her how he felt? He knew he wasn't responsible for the way other men had treated her, but he was still paying for it. He had to overcome that prejudice somehow, and as things now stood, he didn't have a whole lot to lose.

This wasn't the first time he'd faced prejudice, and it certainly wouldn't be the last.

Okay. Plan B it is.

The new approach would require research and planning. Joey had never won any prizes for his intelligence, but he was sure he could handle this project. He already had some of the necessary equipment, and any further information could easily be found on the Internet. All he needed was an accomplice.

And he was pretty sure he knew who to ask.

ഔരു

The winter doldrums had set in with a vengeance, and Melina's excitement over the upcoming visit to The Closet Door was already grating on Tracy's nerves. After her most recent nightclub experience, she didn't feel like going to a show of any kind. All she really wanted to do was to hole up in her apartment like a monk in a garret and sip hot soup until spring. It wasn't until Melina began extolling the virtues of antidepressants that she attempted to put up a better front.

On Friday evening, however, the soup had no effect on the emptiness or the chill, and what she thought was the flu turned out to be strep throat. She kept thinking it would go away, but finally wound up in the ER early Sunday morning after having spent a sleepless night convinced she had somehow contracted the West Nile virus. She had all the symptoms—fever, headache, stupor, and confusion—at least she *thought* she did. Fortunately, strep was treatable with antibiotics. The West Nile virus was not.

She slowly improved, and by the time she saw her own doctor on a follow-up visit, she was feeling okay except for her ears. They were still plugged so tight, she felt like she was walking around with her head wrapped in cotton and was convinced there was something wrong with the speakers in her car.

She wore her Barton Junction T-shirt to the appointment, causing a bit of a stir.

"What does your shirt say?" Dr. Powers asked. "I'm having a little trouble reading the script."

This from a doctor. "Barton Junction," she replied.

"What's Barton Junction?"

"A rock band. Speaking of which, would you check my left ear? I can't hear out of it very well. It bothered me for a while after the concert, but it's even worse now."

Arching a brow, he stuck his otoscope in her right ear. "Ever hear of Lawrence Welk?"

"Yep. My grandmother danced with him once."

"He's not so loud. Maybe you should listen to him."

"Not gonna happen. Never been crazy about his music—and since he's been dead for a number of years, I doubt I could see him in concert."

He took a quick peek at her long-suffering left ear. "Well, your ears look fine. No fluid or infection and the eardrums are intact. You really should stay away from rock concerts, though."

Although he obviously didn't see the point, his nurses were terribly impressed that she'd caught a guitar pick—and completely understood why she would've given it to Joey.

Joey.

Their paths hadn't crossed since that night at Cider Hill, and she had no idea where he was or what he was doing. She'd blamed her morose attitude on illness and the weather—Melina had suggested Seasonal Affective Disorder—but *he* was the real reason.

She missed him. Simple as that. Apparently no longer needing her support or a shoulder to cry on, he was living his life without her.

Melina was obviously worried. Tracy could see the concern in her eyes as she dragged her to exercise class at least three times that week.

"Exercise is all a person needs to improve their mood and their health," Melina insisted.

Tracy disagreed. She'd been working out alone, trying desperately to get herself out of the pits. It wasn't helping. She couldn't sleep, couldn't eat, and spent most of her evenings at home on the verge of tears.

Nor did her luck improve. On the day she decided that cleaning her apartment was the occupational therapy of choice, her trusty Kirby bit the dust.

She dragged it off to the repair shop, arriving at one-fifteen only to find that the proprietor was permanently out to lunch. The clock on the door was rather ambiguous—it could have been pointing to twelve-thirty or one-thirty—so she decided to wait. She'd been sitting there about ten minutes when a car pulled up beside her, a woman with flyaway gray curls behind the wheel.

"He's not back *yet*?" the woman asked.

"Nope. How long's he been gone?"

"I was here at one, and decided I had time to go get lunch," she replied around a bite of her hamburger. "Helluva way to run a business, isn't it?"

Tracy nodded. "I'll give him 'til one-thirty. Then I'm gone."

"No shit. There's another place on the other side of town that has parts."

"I think I need more than parts," Tracy said. "I need service."

After a few minutes of waiting, the woman called her daughter who looked up the address and phone number. Tracy's phone barely had a signal in that location, but she called anyway. A man answered, rattling off several garbled words, one of which at least *sounded* like vacuum.

"Do you service Kirbys?" she asked.

The man said he did and that the shop was located at Nineteenth and Maple. Tracy and her new friend both decided they could find it.

Unfortunately, the numbered streets were interspersed with roads named Hill and Vine, which made finding Nineteenth somewhat unpredictable. Tracy was driving through an area she'd never been before when she spotted what she thought was her new friend's battered Cadillac pulling into a parking lot.

The road sign was obscured by a snow-laden pine until Tracy was right up on it, necessitating a rather hasty right turn once she'd confirmed that it was indeed Nineteenth. After meandering through a parking lot, she crossed a small side street, entered the repair shop's lot, and parked next to a hedge. Pleased that she'd found the place without mishap, she was getting out of her car when she was hailed by a man on the other side of the hedge.

"Hey! You know, there's a reason why cars all have turn signals."

Momentarily taken aback, Tracy found herself explaining why she hadn't signaled instead of telling the bastard to fuck off or go piss up a rope. Then, to top it all off, she had to repeat herself because he couldn't hear her. Suppressing the urge to jump the hedge and slap the shit out of him, she turned on her heel, got her Kirby out of the trunk, and hauled it inside.

"See, we found it!" her fellow vacuum-repair-shop-seeker said with a triumphant grin.

"Yeah. I almost missed the turn, though, and some jerk fussed at me for not using my turn signal. Now that I think about it, he must have actually turned off the main road and followed me through the parking lot to tell me that."

"Did you rip him a new one?" she asked hopefully.

"Nope. He took me by surprise, and I couldn't think of anything mean enough to say. I'll have to work on a snappy comeback for next time. If I'd been expecting it, I might have said something like 'Thank you *so* much. I'm sure no asshole ever had to tell *you* that'—insinuating that he's an asshole without actually saying it, but—"

"I usually just smile and wave, myself," she confided. "It confuses the hell out of them."

While that tactic would've been perfect for this situation, Tracy didn't think it would've been as effective in the others she'd faced recently—neither the Bryce incident nor the one with the freaky bald guy at Cider Hill. "Thanks, I'll try to remember that." She took a deep breath, only then realizing just how shaken she was. "Any idea why men are all such jerks?"

The woman patted her arm. "They can't help it, dearie. It's in their genes."

Tracy snickered. "Is that genes with a 'g' or jeans with a 'j'?"

"Both."

Chapter 16

As Tracy dressed for an evening with Melina and her husband at The Closet Door, her only concern was warmth. With temperatures in the twenties and no need to be sexy or provocative, she donned the same sweater she'd worn to the Barton Junction concert with a lightweight turtleneck underneath it. That it had a picture of Eeyore embroidered on the collar was a statement of sorts, the morose donkey's perpetually glum demeanor being very similar to her own. She had to give Melina credit for sticking by her.

I'd have given up on me a long time ago.

Her new, independent lifestyle wasn't all she'd thought it would be. True, she didn't have to cater to anyone's whims—and no one had bloodied her nose in quite some time—but she couldn't seem to work up a good fantasy without Joey as the star. She even went so far as to knock on his door a few times. He never answered.

Melina and Dan picked her up promptly at six, and when they arrived at the club at a little after seven, Tracy's first impression was that she was sadly underdressed. As always, Melina was gorgeous, but even in an emerald green sheath with a plunging neckline, she couldn't hold a candle to the others. Everywhere Tracy turned, another ravishing beauty caught her eye—and those were just the ones wearing tuxedos.

Tracy stared at a tall woman in spike heels and a red dress that screamed for attention. "That *has* to be a guy."

Melina leaned closer. "It's hard to tell, isn't it? Even the bathrooms are unisex so no one has to give away their secrets."

"No urinals, then?"

"It would be kinda tough to whip your dick out of a pair of pantyhose, don't you think?"

The mental image alone was enough to give Tracy a near-terminal case of the giggles.

Melina grinned. "See? I told you this would be fun. You're laughing your ass off and we're not even inside yet."

Tracy wiped the tears of laughter from her eyes. "Yeah, but these people might not appreciate it if I sat around cackling at them all night."

"Everyone has a great time," she insisted. "And don't assume that just because someone appears to be one gender that they automatically belong to the other. I mean, I look like a woman and I am one, and some of the guys really are guys. The fun is in trying to figure out which ones aren't."

"So, what do you do, turn them upside down and look?" Tracy's grandmother had made a similar comment once, and at the time, the issue hadn't been quite so ambiguous.

"Oh, no," Melina said. "You can't be as blatant as that, nor is it appropriate to ask. You have to look for the clues."

"Which are...?"

"Not gonna tell ya," she taunted. "Besides, they aren't always foolproof."

The show had already begun when they were shown to their table, and the singer onstage was as stunningly beautiful as she was talented.

That must be a clue. Any woman dressed to the nines with perfect hair and makeup *had* to be a guy because women didn't have to work that hard to look like girls. The ladies on stage had to be male by default—what was the point of having a female entertainer in such a place anyway? This theory was proven correct when the current performer pulled off his wig to reveal himself.

Their shirtless waiter had incredible pecs and a face so pretty he should've been a girl. "Hi, I'm Duane, and I'll be taking care of you tonight. Do you know what you'd like, or would you like to hear the specials?"

Already beginning to relax, Tracy grinned. "Could you give me a Screaming Orgasm?"

Duane batted his long dark eyelashes and pursed his lips. "Absolutely."

Melina punched her in the arm. "That's the spirit! Drink up. Dan is designated driver tonight. We're gonna have a blast."

Tracy had to admit she was having fun—and it didn't take a psychologist to figure out why.

No pressure. Without the roiling emotions she'd felt while watching Joey's band, she could simply relax and enjoy the show. Aside from Melina and Dan, she didn't know a soul, and the opinions of strangers were totally irrelevant. On top of that, being surrounded by so many amazing-looking women rendered her effectively invisible.

Or so she thought.

Tracy was sipping her second drink when Melina gave her a nudge. "I think you have an admirer."

Tracy blinked. "What—who?"

"Over there," she replied, indicating a woman sitting a few tables away. "She's been staring at you for a long time. I bet she's working up the nerve to ask you to dance."

"Bullshit," Tracy scoffed. "What makes you think she's looking at me?"

"I've been watching her," she replied. "She never took her eyes off you when you went to the restroom."

Scowling, Tracy took another sip of her drink. "Are you sure she isn't a guy?"

Melina shook her head. "I'm pretty sure she's one of the lesbians."

Great. Was this the nice, butch girlfriend with a tow-truck she'd wished for when her alternator died? Following Melina's gaze, she spotted a striking brunette wearing a denim jacket over a pink, French-cut top and a short leather skirt. The tops of her knee-high boots were just visible beneath the table.

"She looks sort of familiar," Tracy said after a moment's careful scrutiny. "But I can't place her."

"She reminds me of Cher," Melina said.

Tracy stole another glance. Melina was right. She *did* look like Cher. "Hmm…a younger version, maybe. Not as young as during the *Sonny & Cher* years—more like the *Moonstruck* era."

"She's very pretty," Dan commented. "Wouldn't mind dancing with her, myself."

Melina gave her husband's arm a playful slap. "Don't you even *think* about it."

"Hey, that's *my* woman," Tracy quipped. "Lay a hand on her, and I'll beat the living shit out of you."

Dan chuckled. "I'd like to see you try." At around six-two and a good two-twenty, any fight with him would've been over in a heartbeat.

"Watch yourself," Tracy cautioned, doing her best to sound tough. "Us bull dykes can be pretty mean."

Her second glance at the woman was met with a dazzling smile. Throwing caution to the wind, Tracy smiled back, and watched, spellbound, as her admirer slowly stood and began her approach.

"Whoa, shit," Tracy muttered, wishing she'd actually followed through with the wedding ring idea. "I think I just made a mistake."

On her feet and picking her way between the tables, the girl wasn't merely pretty, she was stunning. As her slim hips swayed, her beaded shoulder bag caught the light in sparkling pulses, drawing attention to her tight skirt. Her pink sweater fit snugly over a pair of perfect breasts, and a sapphire pendant drew the eye to cleavage that was only hinted at. Her dark, softly curling hair was pinned up on one side, revealing a large hoop earring with a sapphire stud perched above it. Tracy tore her eyes away long enough to glance at Dan, who was practically drooling.

"Hi, there," she said in a soft, breathy voice.

Melina cleared her throat. "Tracy Richards, I'd like you to meet Luciana Bellomi."

Whipping her head around to glare at Melina, Tracy had to wait a second for her brain to catch up.

I must be drunker than I thought.

"Oh, Melina," Tracy groaned. "You *promised*."

"Call me Anna." The gorgeous brunette pulled up a chair and sat down. "Forgive me for staring, Tracy, but you're just about the cutest girl in the entire club." With a fluid, sensuous move, she crossed her legs in a flash of glossy leather and three-inch heels.

Rendered speechless, Tracy could only gape at her, wondering how anyone could even walk in those boots, let alone do it with such grace.

Melina laughed. "Isn't she though? I keep telling her that, but she doesn't believe me. She always says she's too fat or too plain or something equally ridiculous. You'll set her straight, though, won't you?"

Anna's lips curled into a mischievous grin. "I'd much rather she *not* be straight, if you know what I mean."

Dan shouted with laughter while Melina aimed a grin at Tracy. "You *go*, girl."

Heat flooded Tracy's face as she dissolved into helpless giggles.

God, I must sound like a damned drunk.

"Oh, she's cute all right." Anna's exotic gaze swept Tracy's entire body. "Dimples, big brown eyes, and that *smile*."

No one, male or female, had ever looked at her like that—a circumstance that made Tracy feel strangely uninhibited and more than a little aroused. She sat up straighter. "Would you like a drink?"

Anna laughed lightly. "I should be the one buying *you* a drink. I would have done it before, but I wasn't sure you'd accept it."

With a shock, Tracy realized she *would* have accepted it. This woman was getting to her on so many levels, she couldn't figure it out. "Maybe we should buy each other a drink. What would you like?"

"I'll have what you're having," Anna purred. "It looks…intoxicating."

That explains it. Two Screaming Orgasms were enough to make—

No. No matter how much she'd had to drink, Tracy shouldn't be openly staring at another female with such raw, naked lust. But the fact remained that something about this *particular* woman intrigued her. "That's putting it mildly."

Anna glanced around as though searching for a waiter, then gave Tracy an apologetic smile. "To be honest, I'd much rather dance with you than share drinks."

Sitting at the same table was a far cry from getting up on the dance floor together. The one implied very little, while the other indicated a decided sexual interest. Tracy may have danced with women before, but not in a place like this, and *never* as an excuse to get her hands on them.

And God help me, I want that excuse.

With a nod, Tracy got to her feet and followed Anna to the dance floor. She didn't recognize the song, nor did she care. Her only desire was to get her arms around Anna. She was hot and beautiful and that song was too damned fast to allow for much in the way of close dancing.

Or so she thought.

With the seductive grace of a belly dancer, Anna sashayed her hips, easing backward until her leather-clad bottom brushed Tracy's upper thighs. Although their positions were reversed, Tracy couldn't help recalling a similar dance in the mosh pit with Joey and the feel of his dick bouncing against her ass. She was every bit as turned on now as she'd been then.

What the hell is wrong with me?

Reaching behind her, Anna took Tracy's hands and placed them on her hips. Tracy adopted a wide stance, pulling back hard to grind Anna's firm backside against her—her what? Crotch? Groin? She wasn't a guy. She didn't have a dick, but her pussy ached with lust for this woman.

Tossing a smile over her shoulder, Anna straddled Tracy's right leg and rode back on it, rubbing her hot cunt on Tracy's thigh.

And then the song ended.

Tracy nearly cried out in frustration, but seconds later, as strobe lights pulsed from above, a rap song with a hip-grinding beat began to play. Dancers on and off the stage took up the rhythm, most of them appearing to be doing exactly as the explicit lyrics suggested.

With a squeal of delight, Anna spun around, draping her arms around Tracy's neck. She obviously knew the song well enough to sing it while she danced, never missing a beat or a single lyric.

The raunchy language, coupled with Anna's hot breath on her cheek, filled Tracy's mind with erotic images—chief among them sucking a hard, dripping cock just prior to getting nailed with it. Tracy didn't want to hurt Anna's feelings by making such an admission—the music was too loud for conversation in any case—but she had a sudden overwhelming urge to ask one of the female impersonators to loan her his dick.

Maybe if I got down on my knees and begged...

No. Anna probably wouldn't care for the idea, and, strangely enough, she wanted Anna to be happy.

The song was a long one, and by the time it ended, Tracy could feel her own creamy pussy with every move, and her jeans stuck to her thigh where Anna had been riding her. The brunette's sultry smile promised even greater delights, and again, Tracy caught something familiar in her expression, but she still couldn't place it.

As the dancing continued, Tracy wondered if—or when—Anna would make the next move. Not that Tracy had any clear idea what that next move might be. Melina had played dumb at first, but she obviously knew the girl. Was this a test? Or did Melina seriously believe Tracy would be happy with a female partner?

Pleading exhaustion, Tracy headed back to their table. Dan and Melina had undoubtedly witnessed every erotic move on the dance floor, making the situation somewhat awkward. Anna followed, apparently having no intention of deserting Tracy just yet.

"Well, well, *well*..." Melina drawled. "You two certainly looked like you were having fun."

Still unsure of Melina's motives, Tracy didn't know whether to smack her or give her a hug. "Sure did." After signaling to Duane, she collapsed in her chair.

Anna sat down beside her with undiminished grace. "Tracy's a very talented dancer."

Tracy snorted a laugh. "If I'm any good at all, it's because I was following your lead."

Dan scratched his head. "Which one of you should be leading? Anna or Tracy?"

"Oh, hush," Melina said.

Duane arrived, looking slightly disheveled, as though someone had run impetuous fingers through his perfectly styled locks. "What'll it be?"

"How about another Screaming Orgasm?" Tracy glanced at Anna. "Can I buy you that drink?"

"Oh, no," she said. "Not now. I have to be able to drive home."

Tracy should've been relieved, but for some reason, her heart took it as outright rejection and sank to her toes. "Oh. I see." Sucking in a fortifying breath, she held out a hand. "Well, it was nice meeting you, Anna."

"Silly girl," Anna said with a suggestive wink. "Do you really believe I'd leave here without you?"

Chapter 17

Anna hesitated. "I *can* take you home, can't I?"

Tracy gaped at her. "I, um, dunno. I don't have a car here, if that's what you mean." Her eyes narrowed. "Are you sure you want to do this? I live about an hour away." *And I'm a straight girl at heart who has no idea what she's getting herself into.*

"I can't think of anything I'd rather do right now than take you home," Anna replied. "Is that a yes?"

Tracy glanced at Melina, who immediately threw up her hands in protest. "Don't look at me. If you want to go home with someone you just met, you go right ahead."

Put like that, it sounded risky and foolish, but no more so than that second date with Bryce had been. *All the more reason to say no.* Then again, Melina apparently knew Anna well enough to introduce her to Tracy. "Are you saying it wouldn't be safe?"

Anna's stricken expression should've been reassurance enough, but Melina shook her head. "That isn't what I meant. I'm sure—"

"But I'm not—" Anna blurted out. She stopped there, casting her gaze downward. "You can trust me." Her mesmerizing blue eyes rose to lock with Tracy's. "I won't hurt you."

My God. Was it *that* obvious? Tracy's bruises were gone, and her nose was back to normal. Had Melina told Anna about Bryce? She glanced at her friend, whose shrug and apologetic smile suggested she had done precisely that.

She turned to Anna. "It isn't that I don't trust you. I just can't promise anything—"

Anna pressed a gentle finger to Tracy's lips. "I'll take that chance."

Tracy was still wrestling with the improbability of being

attracted to another woman—an attraction she'd never felt in her entire life. With Anna, however, it was the only thing she could think about.

"You don't have to decide right this minute," Anna went on. "What happens next is up to you."

Tracy wasn't sure how to reply.

Duane, however, was amazingly attentive. "Drinks all around then?"

Tracy hesitated, gnawing her bottom lip. There was a lot to be said for being too drunk to give a damn—or make an enlightened decision. Unfortunately, the effects of alcohol didn't last very long.

Unless I'm drinking champagne. She had no desire to repeat her New Year's Eve blackout. No matter what happened between her and Anna, she wanted to remember it.

Getting to her feet, she picked up her coat and purse. "No drinks for me. We're leaving."

If nothing else, the tears in Anna's eyes should've convinced her she'd made the right decision.

Tracy bent down to give Melina a hug. "Thanks for the introduction. You two be careful driving home. I'll call you tomorrow."

Melina smiled, then shot an unreadable look at Anna. "Don't make me sorry I did this."

"I won't," Anna said.

As they left the club together, a mist of fine flurries made a sparkling coronet of Anna's dark curls. Tracy hesitated at the curb, shivering.

Anna slipped an arm around her. "Are you cold—or nervous?"

"Maybe a little of both."

"Me, too."

"How long have you known you were…different?"

"Seems like forever," Anna replied. "I've tried to hide it, but it always comes back to bite me in the butt. I've never tried this approach before, though. Maybe it'll work, and maybe it won't." She shrugged. "Right now, I feel so lost, I'll take anything you're willing to give."

"Yeah. I know the feeling." Too bad she was getting it from Anna instead of Joey. Obviously that liaison wasn't meant to be. "Don't know how much I have left to give."

Anna nodded. "Come on. I'll take you home." Leading the way to her car, she unlocked the door.

Tracy's eyes filled with tears as she opened the passenger side, and she was crying in earnest by the time Anna slid behind the wheel. How could she possibly tell Anna she didn't want her now? That the only person she really wanted didn't want her? Evidently, sobriety was not the best mental component for one's first homosexual encounter.

Maybe I should've had that drink after all.

Anna seemed to take Tracy's tears in stride, opting for a time-honored means of distracting hysterical women—albeit one normally used by men.

She kissed her.

Unlike the quick peck on the cheek one woman might be expected to give to another, this soft, sensuous kiss shook Tracy to the core.

"I've wanted to do that ever since I first saw you tonight," Anna whispered. "I knew it would be magic."

Perhaps it *was* magic. No longer crying, Tracy's thoughts had taken an abrupt turn for the erotic. "Kiss me again," she sighed. "Your kisses make me forget all the sad things."

"That's the idea." Sliding a fingertip down Tracy's cheek, she touched the corner of her mouth. "I want to see you smile. This night is for you, just you, and no one else. Do you understand me? I'm going to make love to you like no one else ever has, and when I'm finished, I'll go or I'll stay. It's all up to you."

Tracy nodded mutely before their lips met again in a kiss that enveloped her in a sensual haze, reawakening her desire. "Head north on Highway 45. I'll tell you where to turn."

Smiling, Anna kissed her again. "Now, you're talking." Starting the engine, she backed out of the parking space with all the flourish of someone who knew they were about to get lucky. "Are you hungry?"

"Starving. I'd kill for fries and a chocolate shake."

"Me, too." Anna's exotic gaze slid sideways as her lips curled in a seductive smirk. "I need to keep up my strength. I've got a strap-on in my purse, and I'm gonna fuck you like you've never been fucked before. You'll forget all about the guys you've been with. You'll only remember me."

So, one of us has a dick after all. "This could be my lucky day."

"Girl, you have no idea."

༄༅

After stopping for shakes and fries, they drove on, talking and laughing at nothing in particular while listening to Anna's extensive CD collection. She was like a girlfriend and a boyfriend combined, making Tracy feel like a silly teenager with no inhibitions whatsoever.

Who needs alcohol when you're having this much fun?

The sexual tension exploded when Anna reached over to tease Tracy's nipples with her long, frosty pink nails. "You aren't wearing a bra, are you?"

"I figured I could get by without it since I'm wearing two shirts."

"That is *so* hot," Anna purred.

Grinning, Tracy leaned into Anna's caressing hand. "Wasn't thinking about anything but comfort at the time."

Anna moistened her lips with a swipe of her tongue that made Tracy's pussy clench. "How about losing the sweater?"

"I can do better than that." Yanking off the offending garment, she eased her shirt up, exposing her breasts to Anna's gaze.

"My God, you're beautiful," Anna whispered. "Hot…seductive…and sexy as hell."

"Touch me."

Tracy's mouth went dry as Anna slid a hand over her bare skin, flicking a taut bud with her fingernail. "How much farther?"

"Not far." She cleared her throat. "We're all most there."

"Good. 'Cause I'm about to die here. I need to suck your tits and eat your pussy *so* badly…"

Arching her back in a silent plea, Tracy moaned as Anna fondled her breasts at will.

"I want you to come in my face, Trace. I want to feel your juice running down my chin."

"Keep that up and I won't have any juice left," Tracy gasped.

"Oh, I doubt that. There's always more where that came from." Anna withdrew her hand. "But I do need to keep my eyes on the road."

Panting with need, Tracy pulled her shirt down. "Turn left here. My apartment building is on the right."

"Gotcha."

Anna parked the car, then pulled Tracy into a kiss that went so far beyond the first one as to be something else entirely. With tongues entwined and hands that couldn't seem to get enough, Tracy didn't care if Anna was male, female, or an alien from another planet. She wanted her. And she wanted her *now.*

Drawing back, Tracy nodded toward the building. "Second floor. I'll race you." Snatching up her belongings, she wrenched open the door and leaped out, hitting the ground running.

Even with a head start, Anna caught her at the top of the stairs. Unlike the last time Tracy had been pursued, she was excited rather than fearful, leaning back against Anna as she unlocked the door. Anna's hands were everywhere—teasing her nipples and fondling her ass.

"Mmm…" Tracy wiggled her butt against Anna's hand. "I love that." She swallowed around the lump in her throat as one of the kinkier activities she enjoyed came to mind. "D–d'you like being spanked?"

Anna's sharp inhale provided the answer. "Oh, *yeah*… Not hard, though. Just enough to give me a bit of a sting. Makes my d— uh, gets my juices flowing."

"Same here." Tracy pushed the door open. "We're gonna have *so* much fun."

With Anna close behind her, she slipped inside and barely had the door locked before Anna began stripping off Tracy's clothes.

"What a pretty naked lady," Anna purred as her hot blue eyes roamed over Tracy's nude body. "I think she needs her bottom smacked for getting it on with another girl."

Already on the brink of orgasm because Anna was dressed and she wasn't, simply hearing those words sent a gush of moisture down Tracy's legs. Anna pulled her close and kissed her, sliding her tongue in deep as she took Tracy's ass in a tight grip and wedged a leg between her thighs.

"I wanted you like this on the dance floor," Anna murmured. "Hot, wet, and totally..." she sucked Tracy's earlobe into her mouth "... *naked*."

Growling, she moved on to Tracy's neck, sucking the skin hard before taking a step back to inspect her handiwork. "Oh, yeah. I'm gonna put one of those on each side of your ass. Right after I've spanked it."

Shuddering with unprecedented levels of desire, Tracy let out a groan as her knees gave way beneath her. Anna held her up, reaching down to deliver a stinging slap. "Do you like that?"

"Yes!" Tracy gasped. "I want you so bad I can't stand it." Anna's next blow landed right in the middle of Tracy's ass, the shock waves jolting her pelvic organs like a dick slamming into her from behind. "Oh, God," she groaned. "What are you *doing* to me?"

"Do you want me to stop?"

"No," she wailed. "Don't stop. *Please*."

Tracy didn't know if Joey was in his apartment or not. It was late enough for him to be home after work, but too early if he was playing a gig with the band. The very *last* thing she wanted was for him to think she needed rescuing again.

This would be so *hard to explain.*

She'd never met a man yet who enjoyed being spanked—and couldn't imagine that Joey would, either—but keeping her voice down was almost impossible.

Anna sat on the couch, pulling Tracy across her lap. "I want you to do this to me sometime. Not tonight—this night is all for you—but soon."

Tracy lay there, moaning in anticipation. What would be like to have her hands on Anna's firm ass, fondling and spanking it until it was hot and red?

I want more.

Rising up on her hands and knees, Tracy thrust her hips backward, exposing her heated genitals so Anna could strike them more easily. She was nearing orgasm when Anna held back for a moment, breaking her rhythm. The anticipation of the next blow was mind-bending in its intensity, and when it finally landed, Tracy went over the edge, shuddering as her climax racked her body without mercy.

Anna's breath was hot on her cheek. "I know what you want, what you like, and how to do it. I have an advantage over any of your other lovers. I pay attention to what feels good to a woman, and I refine it, practicing until I know better than anyone how to make you feel any way I want you to. You'll get addicted to me. No one else will ever be able to compare after this."

Tracy longed for the strength of will to turn around and do the same things to Anna, but, limp with exhaustion, she could barely move.

"This is only the beginning," Anna whispered. "I've got more treats in my little bag of tricks. You won't know what hit you."

"I'll get you back someday," Tracy promised. "I'll make you scream."

"Yes, you will—but not today. Let's go into the bedroom. I can work better there."

Rolling off the couch, Tracy staggered to her feet and into Anna's surprisingly strong arms. "Go ahead, make my day." Giggling helplessly, she added, "I've always wanted to say that."

"And now you have." Anna shot her a sultry smile. "And I *will* make your day. All you have to do is lie down and wait for me. I'll be there in a minute."

Chapter 18

Tracy stumbled into the bedroom wishing she could've watched Anna putting on her fake penis, but perhaps the shock value of seeing it already in place would be better. Either way, Tracy had a feeling she was in for a letdown because as much as she'd always enjoyed sucking cock, sucking a dildo held no fascination for her whatsoever. Neither did going down on another woman.

Makes me want to bite Bryce all over again for messing with my mind.

Thrusting that thought firmly aside, she keeled over onto the bed.

When Anna returned, just before she turned out the light, Tracy caught a brief glimpse of her lacy pink bra and a harness with a nice, hard cock thrust through it.

"Is your pussy wet, baby?" Anna's voice sounded strangely husky in the darkness. "I hope so, because I want to eat it and make it come and then fuck it until you can't take anymore. Would you like that?"

In that instant, the heat was back, full force. "Yes," Tracy whispered. "Oh, God, yes."

Tracy waited breathlessly as Anna eased onto the bed. Moments later, soft lips closed over her nipple, and her new lover licked her into yet another frenzy of desire.

"I–I'm not sure what you want me to do. I've never—"

A finger touched her lips. "You don't have to do anything, Tracy. I'll still be here in the morning unless you throw me out tonight. After that, I'm yours to do with as you please."

She'd obviously been thinking too much at a time when she should only be focusing on feelings. "Well, the first thing I'm gonna do is paddle your behind," Tracy declared. "Then maybe I'll fix you breakfast."

Anna laughed. "I hope you do, but right now, I've got a deliciously hot pussy to eat. And don't worry, sweetheart. I washed my face. Wouldn't want to get lipstick all over your clit, now, would we?"

"I'm so wet I doubt if it would stick, anyway. But thank you, just the same."

"You're welcome," she said. "I also took my nails off so I wouldn't scratch you. They were just for show. Can't stand having long nails all the time."

"Me, either," Tracy said. "Aside from the fact that nurses are supposed to keep their nails short."

"You're a nurse, then?" She eased down between Tracy's legs. "Well, in that case, I expect you'll like having someone take care of you for a change. Anyone ever do that for you?"

"Rarely," Tracy replied. "And not at all, lately, except—well, maybe once." She pushed the image of Joey wiping the blood from her face resolutely aside. He wasn't here. Anna was. Thinking about him was like cheating on her.

"You just lay back and let me take care of you. I'll take you places you've only dreamed about."

"Hey, I've been with guys who knew what they were doing—well, maybe not *that* much, but—"

"None of that, now," Anna scolded, "or I might have to spank you again."

"Sounds fabulous."

"Oh, I do like you, Tracy," she whispered. "You're the perfect woman."

Tracy had longed to hear that all her life. Unfortunately, she'd always assumed she would hear it from a man. "You might change your mind when you get to know me better."

"I doubt it—although that *is* a woman's prerogative."

Warm breath on her sensitive flesh was the only warning Tracy had as Anna's tongue teased her labia so lightly she might not have touched her at all. A tantalizing breeze followed by a hot tongue came as a shock, and she kept it up, alternately blowing and licking until Tracy was nearly insane with the overwhelming need to climax.

Time stood still as Anna slid two fingers into Tracy's vagina and curled them up to milk her G-spot. When Anna's lips closed over Tracy's clitoris, her orgasm detonated like an atom bomb.

Tracy barely had time to recover before Anna penetrated her with the strap-on, which, after the initial chill of the lubricant, was surprisingly warm. Had she soaked it in hot water? Tracy didn't know and didn't care as Anna fucked her with that cock from every possible angle, finding sensitive spots Tracy didn't even know she possessed.

"You've obviously done this before," Tracy said between moans.

"Yeah. Tell me if I get too pushy. I've had complaints about fucking too hard."

"You won't hear any from me. I like the way you fuck."

"Thank you," Anna said with a chuckle. "But I haven't really let loose yet. You might not like that part."

"Warn me, and I'll try to prepare myself."

"No problem," she said. "See how you like this."

Shortening her stroke, she gave Tracy several shallow thrusts before diving in deeper on the next. Continuing that same rhythm, she soon had Tracy writhing like a fish on dry land.

"Where the hell did you learn to do all of this?"

"Oh, the usual places," Anna replied. "*Penthouse, Cosmo,* other girls—and guys."

Tracy was incredulous. "It's a wonder you don't have girls lined up outside your door."

"Not lately." Anna's breath caught in her throat. "Hold on, Trace. Here comes the big gun."

Anna must have been one to get off on doing another girl, because Tracy could've sworn she climaxed. With a groan, she rammed Tracy with a force that sent her spiraling off into orgasm. After several more hard thrusts, she paused, panting. "Had enough?"

"Yeah," Tracy replied, barely able to breathe herself. "You poor girl. You must be worn out."

"Sort of," she admitted. "I could probably stand a little sleep now."

Although Tracy could have gone on all night, she didn't want to seem too greedy. After all, a strap-on dick might be able to hold up forever, but she couldn't reasonably expect Anna to.

Withdrawing gently, Anna rolled over, dropping a warm kiss on Tracy's cheek. "Good night, Trace. I'll see you in the morning."

Tracy stared up at the ceiling. Miranda would have a cow, and so would the rest of the family. Beverly would never understand—well, maybe she would, considering her attitude toward her ex. Melina... What on earth would she say, having been the instigator?

And for that matter, what would Joey think?

As she drifted off to sleep, a more lowering thought occurred to her.

Would he care?

⊛⊗

Tracy awoke to the sound of deep, even breathing that wasn't her own.

Anna.

She'd stayed all night, just as she'd promised—something Tracy truly wished she hadn't done. As always, the cold, clear light of day highlighted her mistakes. Sex was one thing, but dating or living together? Marriage was out of the question—at least in Indiana.

But did she really *want* to marry a woman?

And never suck a dick again? Ever?

I must've been drunker than I thought.

What in the world would she say to the poor woman? Thanks for a good time, but I'm hopelessly heterosexual?

Although Tracy knew she couldn't have seemed that way the night before, Anna must've known what she was up against. Melina had to have told her that much. Too bad she hadn't gone with Anna to her place or a gotten a room at a hotel. Sneaking out of her own apartment was out of the question.

Might as well wake her up and get it over with.

Rolling onto her side, Tracy propped herself up on her elbow, gazing down at the beautiful woman sleeping beside her.

Only it wasn't a woman.

It was Joey Manzetti.

Chapter 19

Joey didn't look anything like a woman now—except for his hair, which was already starting to rebel, the sweat of the previous night's exertions having brought out the curl. His makeup was gone, and a set of false front teeth lay on the nightstand. The rest of his disguise had all been clothing and attitude. A quick peek beneath the covers proved it.

He'd apparently worn the strap-on harness over his own cock, the initial cold wetness presumably the result of a lubricated condom. He hadn't shaved his legs, which explained the boots and the fact that he hadn't removed his pantyhose until after Tracy had fallen asleep. Most of the hair on his chest and stomach was still there—only shaved down to the neckline of that pretty pink top he'd worn.

The reason for his insistence on pleasuring her without allowing her to return the favor was perfectly obvious now. If she'd put a hand between his legs, she'd have found his balls, and no way could he have convinced her *they* were fake. Tucked up inside his pantyhose, she hadn't felt them.

The most surprising thing was that he hadn't given himself away while they were dancing. "Anna" had been riding her leg, oozing pre-cum through his clothing, so his dick had to be there *somewhere.*

Guess I should've pumped the female impersonators for details.
Or Melina.
Closing her eyes, she stifled a groan.
My best friend... I'm gonna wring her neck...
She'd known exactly who Anna was—had even introduced her.
God, I feel so fucking stupid.

She'd felt so much at ease with Anna—had never truly considered her as a stranger. She'd seemed familiar, not because she looked like Cher, but because she was actually the sweet little rock star who lived next door. And with Melina there to vouch for her...

Oh, yes. The *how* was obvious. What Tracy couldn't figure out was the *why*.

Sure, she'd joked about dating women instead of men, but had Joey actually believed her? Had Melina?

Was this *her* fault? After all, she'd done her damndest to hide her feelings for Joey. Evidently, he'd been interested. She could see that now—buying her drinks, dedicating songs to her, not to mention that wild dance in the mosh pit. *She'd* been the one to turn a blind eye to his romantic overtures. If she'd given him the slightest bit of encouragement, would he have bothered with this charade? Surely he wouldn't have needed to if she had. He could've simply asked her for a date.

She was missing something. Something very *important*...

For answers to her questions, all she had to do was wake him up and demand an explanation. Unfortunately, she was a tad embarrassed—aside from the fact that she'd promised Anna breakfast and a spanking. She tried to recall if she'd said anything about Joey to his face—her face—Anna's face.

God, I'm so confused.

She didn't think she'd mentioned him, but during the course of a very peculiar evening, she could've said just about anything. At least she hadn't mentioned the part about wanting to borrow a drag queen's dick.

She obviously didn't need to do that now—not with Joey lying in her bed. His was the only dick she'd wanted to suck anyway, and she couldn't imagine any man objecting to a woman going down on him. Any *straight* man, that is.

Slipping out of bed, she padded into the bathroom to pee and brush her teeth—two nighttime rituals she'd neglected to perform the previous evening and was now regretting.

A glance in the mirror had her shaking her head in disgust. "Oh, yeah, Tracy. Way to go, girl. You thought you were being so open-minded, allowing yourself to be seduced by a girl, and she turns out to be a guy in a skirt."

Which, she was forced to admit, required a bit of an open mind at that. A moment later, her breath caught in her throat as the answer to her questions struck her like a bolt from the blue.

Joey *liked* dressing in women's clothes.

It made perfect sense. The entire evening had been his way of killing two birds with one stone—getting a self-confessed man-hater into bed while at the same time demonstrating his predilection for wearing pantyhose and mascara. He'd said he'd never tried "this approach" before. Obviously, his intention was to let her know from the start that cross-dressing was important to him. But if that was the case, why had he concealed his identity?

Or had he? Perhaps he hadn't been hiding at all. Perhaps *she'd* been the one too blind to see him for who he actually was.

I'm stalling. She knew that because she was still scrubbing her teeth even though she was fairly certain there was no enamel left on them, let alone plaque. Spitting out the toothpaste, she rinsed her mouth with warm water the way she normally did when she was planning to—

"Goddammit," she growled at the mirror. "I *am* going to suck his blasted cock, and if he doesn't like it, he can take his falsies and go home."

"I have no intention of leaving yet, Tracy," Joey said as his amused reflection came into view. "Just let me run a little water through it, and it's all yours."

૪૦૦૩

Arching a brow, she shot him an evil glare. "And good morning to you, too, *Miss Anna*."

"Good morning, Tracy," Joey said, adopting Anna's voice and coy smile. "I had a great time last night. Would you care for an encore?"

"It wouldn't be the same without the skirt," she said with a sardonic smirk. "Does that spoil it for you?"

He switched to his normal voice. "No. I like being a guy."

"I'm *so* relieved." Her sarcasm never wavered. "I was afraid I was going to have to get my own strap-on and fuck your ass with it."

"Sounds fantastic." Sauntering over to the toilet, he raised the lid and held his cock down to pee.

"Nice dick," she commented when he was finished. "You little skinny guys kinda let it all hang out, don't you?"

"I suppose we do," he replied. "I'm surprised it still works after last night. You have no idea how hard it is to walk—let alone dance—with a hard-on pulled back between your legs." As she turned to face him, he got a better view of her rosy nipples and felt his dick begin to respond. *No hiding it now.* "Don't suppose you've got an extra toothbrush?"

Without a word, she pulled open a drawer and rummaged around until she found one. Slapping it into his outstretched hand like a scrub nurse passing instruments to a surgeon, she shook her head in disbelief. "Is *that* what you did with it? How on earth did you get it to stay there? Duct tape?"

He shook his head. "Panty girdle. I was never so glad to get out of anything in my life."

Her gaze remained directed toward his cock as he began brushing his teeth. "I've never liked them, either—girdles, I mean—and I'm not real crazy about pantyhose."

A downward glance revealed his stiffening cock wiggling back and forth as he brushed. At least she seemed to like the look of it. Considering how well she'd responded to "Anna," he'd begun to have doubts, particularly in light of all the *I'll never date another man again* comments. Still, she *had* to have recognized him.

"Serves you right for trying to fool me."

"Oh, yeah?" he countered. "Like last night was really torture for you." He rinsed out the toothpaste and smiled. "Thanks for playing along."

She returned his smile with a blank stare. "What do you mean, playing along?"

It was his turn to be amazed. "You actually didn't know who I was? And you still let me bring you home and spend the night with you?"

"Yep. I thought you were this gorgeous little lesbian named—what was it? Luciana Borelli? Hell, Melina *introduced* you." She shrugged. "From the moment I said I was giving up men, I knew she was bound to have a lesbian friend or two waiting in the wings."

"You really thought I was a girl." He couldn't believe it. Sure, he'd done his best—for several reasons. "But I've got this huge Adam's apple." He tilted his head back. "How could you possibly miss it?"

She peered at his neck. "I wouldn't say it was *huge*—although it's more prominent than any woman's I've ever seen. Wasn't looking for it, I guess. Plus, your hair was sort of curling around your neck, and maybe you kept your chin down. Oh, hell, I don't know why I didn't notice it—aside from the fact that I'd had two very potent drinks before you ever came over to our table."

"Well, I'll be damned," he said. "Maybe I have a future as a drag queen."

She waved a dismissive hand. "Nah, you're too short to be a drag queen. Drag queens are tall and stately and exotic—*and* they sing like women. I've heard you sing, Joey. Your voice is way too deep."

"B–but what about when we were dancing together? You heard me singing then."

She chuckled. "Yes, but you were singing in my left ear. It hasn't been the same since Melina screamed in it at the Barton Junction concert—and in case you didn't notice, the music in that club was really loud. I could understand the words, but that's about it." Her gaze landed on his dick again. "Is that your ambition? To be a female impersonator?"

"Not really," he admitted. "It *would* be fun, though."

"So that's not the real reason you dressed up as Anna."

Swallowing hard, he shook his head. "It's more of a–a...fetish.

Wearing women's undies turns me on."

"And the mere thought of it has a similar effect?" She was openly staring at his dick now—*and* licking her lips.

Good sign…

"Yeah, right," he said with a snort. "Like you standing there naked doesn't have anything to do with it."

"But why dress up as girl to seduce me? You could've just *said* something." Her eyes narrowed with suspicion. "This is that mysterious flaw women don't like about you, isn't it?"

He nodded. "If you couldn't stand the idea—if you'd told Anna to get lost—you wouldn't have ever known it was me. And I'd still be able to look you in the eye." He drew in a breath. "I really like you, Tracy. But you were so down on men—and I honestly don't blame you for that—but since I *am* a man, I didn't want to fuck it up before we ever got started."

"And the thought that this little charade of yours might piss me off never occurred to you?"

He *had* perpetrated a bit of a fraud, but at least she wasn't wigging out about the women's undies part. "Not really. *Are* you pissed at me?"

"Dammit, I ought to be!" She crossed her arms, scowling—clearly oblivious to how totally hot she was in that pose. *All she needs is a whip and a corset.* "I mean, shit, Joey, you got me to have sex with a girl!"

"No, I didn't. I'm a *guy*."

"But I *thought* you were a girl, which amounts to the same thing."

Considering he had a real cock between his legs—out in plain sight and getting harder by the second—Joey didn't see it that way, but he was beginning to understand her point of view. "Okay. Yeah. I get that, but are you okay with it now? With me being me, I mean."

Her scowl never wavered. "This is why Geena left you, isn't it?"

"You mean aside from the fact that she tried to pass off another man's child as mine?" Teeth clenched, he held up a hand. "Forgive me. I'm still a little touchy about that. But it just goes to show how fuckin' gullible I am. I mean, you think *you* were easily fooled." He barked a mirthless laugh. "You've got nothing on me, Trace. I believed every bit of that crap she laid on me."

"So, tell me," she began. "What happened with Geena?"

Geena might've blabbed it all over town, but Joey had never told this particular tale to another living soul. The fact that he was about to divulge the gory details to Tracy was indicative of how much he trusted her. "I'd been doing the laundry and was folding her underwear. I thought she was asleep—Darren was teething and had run her ragged the day before, so she was pretty tired. Anyway, I tried on one of her bras and got this raging hard-on. So, of course, I had to, um, do something about it, and she caught me."

"Let me get this straight," Tracy said. "She caught you jacking off while you were wearing her bra?"

He nodded. "Pants around my feet and spraying cum all over the clean laundry."

She swallowed hard and glanced at the ceiling before she spoke. "Maybe she was more upset about having the clothes messed up than anything else. Did you at least offer to wash them again?"

He gaped at her in disbelief. "You're kidding me, right?"

"I'm just trying to help," she protested. "To hear you tell it now, it seems kinda funny. But I guess it wasn't at the time."

"Probably the most devastating moment of my life." One he would never forget as long as he lived. His own mind-numbing embarrassment. Geena's outrage. Darren crying after hearing his mother screeching at the top of her lungs...

"Yeah." She paused, her expression thoughtful as she nodded with apparent understanding. "Like that scene in *American Pie* where the kid's father catches him with his dick in the pie."

As she spoke, his mind's eye drew back from that awful memory, enabling him to see it from a different perspective—almost as though it had happened to someone else.

Suddenly, it wasn't just funny. It was *hilarious.*

His laughter exploded. "God, I never thought I'd be able to

laugh about it," he gasped between chuckles. "Thanks, Tracy. You have no idea how much better that makes me feel."

"Glad I could help."

"I certainly couldn't have expected Geena to laugh about it. She's got a gay brother. It tore their family apart when he came out. I'd managed to keep my little quirk hidden from her for a long time, but sooner or later, they always find out." He shrugged. "Afterward, she told me she'd found my stash of goodies. She hadn't said anything because she wasn't sure whether that stuff was from a new girlfriend or an old one. In her mind, catching me wearing her bra was worse than cheating on her."

"Which is why you tried this *different* approach with me?" Lips pressed in a firm line, she seemed to hesitate. "Is there anything else you need to tell me about?"

"I think that pretty much covers it."

"Nothing…kinky?"

"Well, there *is* the spanking thing—and I think you'd make an awesome dominatrix, but—" He paused as he realized what she was getting at. "I won't beat you up, if that's what you're asking. Not my style at all."

"Glad to hear it."

"What about you? Please tell me you don't *enjoy* punching guys in the balls."

"Actually, I prefer licking, sucking, and fondling—which you would already know if you'd taken off your pantyhose last night."

"Guess I should have." A glance at his reflection had him shaking his head. "I still can't believe you thought I was a girl. I thought I looked pretty good, but—"

"Pretty good?" she squeaked. "My God, you were beautiful! Melina and I thought you looked like Cher, and Dan wanted to dance with you. He was practically drooling."

"No shit?"

"No shit. Your makeup was amazing, and my hair could *never* do what yours did." She ran a hand through her straight locks. "Maybe I need a perm."

"You're beautiful just the way you are." Taking a step closer, he sifted his fingers through her hair before tracing the curve of her cheek. "I wasn't kidding when I said you were the cutest girl in the club."

"I-I'm glad you think so." She glanced downward as though struck by sudden shyness, which was odd considering the wild night they'd spent together.

"I *know* so." With a knuckle beneath her chin, he lifted her face to his. "What about it, Trace? Wanna hook up with a cross-dressing lead guitar player?"

Chapter 20

Gazing into his twinkling blue eyes, Tracy wondered how in the world she hadn't recognized them the night before.

Must've been the eyeliner.

"You're on," she said. "Just promise not to pee on the toilet seat."

"Wouldn't dream of it." Grabbing her by the waist, Joey hauled her, giggling, back to the bedroom. "Now, about my dick. You *did* say you wanted to suck it—right?"

"Absolutely." She hopped onto the bed. "Let me have it."

"Like I said, it's all yours." He crawled in beside her, covering her face with soft kisses. "You're sure you won't change your mind if you catch me wearing your undies?"

"Only if you won't let me play with your dick—and I'd just as soon swallow what comes out of it, if you don't mind. It's much neater than spewing all over the place."

Groaning, he moved closer, aiming his drooling penis at her lips. "Where the hell have you been all my life?"

"Right next door for the past year or two." She paused to admire his cock. He certainly had a nice one, even if it was slightly out of proportion with the rest of him. "You were too busy with Geena and Darren to notice."

"Oh, I *noticed*," he admitted. "I'd have to be blind not to—whether I was already involved with someone or not."

She ran her tongue over the head of his thick shaft. "I'm gonna be terribly upset if Geena ever changes her mind." *There. I've said it.*

"I'm pretty sure I've seen the last of her—*and* Darren." With a grim laugh, he rolled onto his back. His dick landed on his stomach like a caveman's club, the head kissing his navel. "But let's not talk about that right now. I, um…could I borrow a pair of your panties?" He shook his head, seeming slightly stunned. "God, I can't believe I actually asked you that."

"Ask me anything you like. As long as you aren't using your fists, I'm game." Tracy went over to the bureau. Opening a drawer, she surveyed her collection of nylon bikinis and plain cotton briefs—none of which screamed cross-dressing lead guitar player. *Guess I should've bought one of those Barton Junction thongs after all.* "Any particular kind?"

"Bikinis or briefs," he replied. "Thongs don't work as well."

That certainly sounded interesting. "How so?"

"They aren't as strong."

Even *more* interesting. She arched a brow. "Will I ever be able to wear them again?"

"Of course you will. I just like to poke my junk through the leg holes, and then give the panties a twist."

"And this does…what?"

"Makes my dick so hard you won't believe it—the ultimate cock ring. And, if you don't mind, I'd rather they smelled like you."

"A used pair, you mean? Really? Seems like my nose'll be a lot closer to them than yours will."

"Yeah, but I'll know you've had them on." With a wink and a shrug, he added, "It's mostly mental anyway."

"Oh, we're *mental*, all right." She started to fish through the laundry basket, then remembered that the pair she'd worn the night before had been soaked a couple of times. *He'd probably like that.* "Certifiable, in fact. No wonder Geena was so upset. I can't imagine what she would have done if she'd seen us last night."

"Trust me, it wouldn't have been pretty," he admitted. "She can screech louder than any woman I've ever known."

"Yeah, well, I'm guessing not too many women have been treated to the sight of you in a bra," she reminded him on her way out to the living room. "You might be surprised."

Retrieving her underwear, she returned just as Joey ran a

fingertip over his cockhead.

"Hands off, big guy," she warned, aiming her panties at him as though shooting a rubber band. "That dick is *mine*."

"Just getting it ready for you." He inhaled deeply as her warning shot landed on his face. "These are from last night, aren't they?"

"Uh huh." She sat down beside him. "Do they smell okay?"

"Perfect." He wasn't kidding about the effect. His cock was already so hard a cat couldn't scratch it.

"Are you sure you need that?" she asked as he threaded his dick through the leg holes.

"It gets better." Twisting the fabric, he tightened the "noose" around his genitals. Veins popped out all along the shaft, and the head looked like a ripe plum.

"Okay. You're right. That's about the hottest cock I've ever seen."

Pre-cum oozed from his slit as she leaned closer to run her tongue over the smooth glans. Slick and salty, he served as a reminder of what she would've missed had Anna actually been female. Tracy had never particularly cared for the taste of a dick after it had been inside *her*. How in the world was she supposed to enjoy the taste of another woman?

She wasn't gay. Bryce had simply made her crazy enough to think it might work.

No. This had nothing to do with Bryce—and everything to do with Joey. On a subliminal level, she must've known who Anna really was—his scent or some mannerism had registered with her subconscious, allowing her to respond to Anna as she would've responded to Joey. She'd never been attracted to another woman in her life—and she wasn't attracted to one now. She had no desire to see Joey repeat that performance. He didn't need to. She was sucking his cock and it tasted like a *him*—not a *her*.

He was even a nice guy. Sure, he'd spanked her the night before, but, unlike having her face used as a punching bag, spanking was something she actually enjoyed. Unfortunately, mentioning that preference had a tendency to backfire, and a couple of guys had gotten carried away. Joey, on the other hand, had done it perfectly—and if what he'd said about liking it himself was true, she was anxious to return the favor.

But right now, she was in heaven. Joey's pre-cum coated her face, and she licked his balls thoroughly. His scrotal skin was soft, pliable, and delightfully furry while his hot, hard cock gleamed like a beacon. Viewed from her current perspective, her decision to give up men was ludicrous. She loved men's bodies. It was their personalities she couldn't stand.

All her life she'd been looking for a soul mate—someone who could share her life as well as her fantasies. And she had some *serious* fantasies—hot, exciting, and dangerously seductive…

Was last night's episode a favorite fantasy of his or had he only done it out of necessity? He'd said he liked being a guy, but—

Yeah, right. A guy who gets off on wearing lingerie. Masquerading as Anna could've been a real turn-on for him, despite that fact that he hadn't enjoyed the panty girdle. She could easily understand him having a fetish—after all, no one could explain why they liked certain things.

What he might not understand was that his unusual preferences weren't the only ones to be considered. She had quite a few of her own—several of which she'd never shared with anyone. Joey had taken a tremendous risk in revealing his sexual quirks. Did she have the courage to do the same?

He certainly seemed happy to accommodate at least *one* of them. Apparently realizing how much she enjoyed his cock syrup, he pumped it out continuously. Her pussy ached as she watched beads of viscous fluid well up from his slit and slide down his cockhead.

She pulled her panties off him. "I don't think you need these anymore. You couldn't possibly get any hotter, unless you want to smell them."

"Give them here," he said. "I'm starting to hurt from being so hard anyway."

While she'd enjoyed his tight balls, they were even better loose.

She licked and sucked them, sliding his wet dick between her cheek and shoulder. Pausing as a question occurred to her, she glanced up at him. "How the hell did you hide these babies from me last night?"

He grimaced. "It's called 'tucking.' Basically, you push them back up the tract they originally descended through and use pressure to hold them there. I wasn't sure I could do it—some guys can't—but I did. Feels really weird."

"No shit. But how did you know to do that? Did you ask a female impersonator for directions or what?"

He shook his head. "I Googled it."

"Should've guessed."

Women's undies might've been a turn-on for him, but a cock in her face did amazing things for Tracy. Aroused to the point she dripped on the sheets, she rested her head on his stomach and reached beneath him. Cupping his butt in her hands, she urged him to fuck her mouth—anxious to taste his cum.

His cock was unbelievably hard as his breath shortened to a pant. Knowing his climax was only seconds away, Tracy altered the angle slightly to keep his semen from shooting straight down her throat. Instantly, his body tensed and he let out a yelp.

Convinced she'd scraped his dick with her teeth, Tracy backed off to apologize just as his cock erupted in her face.

Having always preferred to hold on and swallow, Tracy had never taken a direct hit before—but she *liked* it. Leaning closer, she pressed the head of his spewing cock against her cheek. With the next warm jet of semen, a snarl rose from her throat and her core contracted, sending a flood of moisture down her thighs.

Writhing in ecstasy, she slid his cum-slick cock over her lips and sucked him in. Her orgasm detonated, and she lay helplessly, her face covered with semen and her mouth full of cock, groaning as uncontrollable spasms racked her body—spasms that seemed to go on forever.

Tracy had heard about continuous orgasms, but she'd never achieved anything close—until that moment. She relaxed slightly as her climax began to abate, only to be struck by another wave of tight, muscular contractions. After several cycles, the intensity gradually dropped until finally ceasing altogether.

Releasing him, she rolled onto her back, gasping for breath. "I think I've just discovered a new preference."

He cleared his throat with apparent difficulty. "Did you just do what I think you did?"

"Yes, and if you ever want to come in my face again, you go right ahead. That was incredible."

"Same here," he said. "I don't think I've ever yelled like that before."

With a giggle, she wiped his cum from her cheek. "And here I thought I'd gotten a tooth into you. Guess not, huh?"

"Nope—although, considering your history, I should've expected something like that. Glad I didn't chicken out. You're very talented."

"Yeah, '*Cosmo*, *Penthouse*, other girls—and guys,'" she said, quoting him. "By the way, the information I've gotten from other girls has all been talk as opposed to actual experience. You haven't—?"

"No, I haven't had sex with another man," he grumbled. "Guys talk too, you know."

"Just checking. After last night, can you blame me for wondering?"

"Did you see me dancing with any men?"

"Well, no, but—"

"I'm not gay or bisexual," he insisted. "Given the cross-dressing thing I might *seem* that way, but, believe me, I'm not. I like girls. Period."

"Okay, okay," she said, stroking his balls. "Didn't mean to get your panties in a wad."

He burst out laughing. "I never dreamed I'd ever be able to talk about this stuff with *anyone*—let alone joke about it. This is so great, you have no idea." His voice trailed off, and he winced. "Too bad we didn't get together a long time ago. Might've saved us both some serious trauma."

Tracy knew precisely what he meant, but as she thought back to her younger days, she realized their relationship wouldn't have worked—at least, not with the same potential for success. Naïve and innocent with dreams of a storybook romance, she probably would've reacted to Joey's idiosyncrasies just as Geena had done. Relics of that sweet young thing remained, but her perspective had changed. A lot.

Her younger self wouldn't have wanted Joey. She would've chosen a tall, handsome god of a man with no sexual peculiarities whatsoever. She'd always been attracted to that type, Bryce being the most recent example. Too bad he'd only *looked* the part.

"I doubt it. We wouldn't have appreciated each other nearly as much if we'd gotten together, say, ten years ago. I don't know about you, but I've changed."

Joey's heart took a nose dive. "You wouldn't have wanted me back then—would you?"

She shrugged. "Maybe not. I led a rather sheltered life until I went to college. It's been different since then. I've dated lots of controlling, opinionated assholes—guys who seemed nice enough at first, but the better I knew them, the more I disliked them. I was a lot sweeter in the beginning. Getting knocked around has kinda soured me."

Joey despised those men for hurting her. If she stuck with him, no one would ever hurt her again. Not if he could help it. "You're not sour," he said gently. "You're one of the sweetest people I've ever met."

Tracy snorted a laugh. "Not really. Everyone assumes I am, probably because half the time I'm wearing Winnie the Pooh scrubs. They don't mean anything. They're just a carryover from when I worked in the emergency room. Sick kids respond better to nurses who have cartoon characters printed on their uniforms."

She was joking, of course, but he wasn't smiling. "There's more to it than that. I mean, you *are* good with children—I never worried about Darren when you were looking after him—but you also have a very kind, warm heart."

"Stop it," she whispered. "Just…stop."

"Stop what?"

"Saying nice things about me," she replied. "I'm not…used to it."

"You know, you're a whole lot more sensitive than you let on," he said with a scowl. "I've probably seen more of that side of you than most people—but you've learned not to show it, haven't you?"

"Very perceptive." She glanced away, wiping her eyes. "Must be the musician in you."

"Hey, I may not have many brain cells, but I can see the vulnerability behind the cynicism."

"There's a song in that," she quipped. "Shouldn't take you more than an hour to write it." Tears glistening on her cheeks, she got to her feet.

"Tracy, wait. I'm sorry. What Bryce did to you wasn't funny."

She stared at him. "Who said anything about Bryce?"

"You didn't have to. He's the reason you let Anna bring you home last night. You really thought a woman could do a better job of loving you than a man. Didn't you?"

She sank back down on the edge of the bed. "I never could understand why guys were so mean—like I had *Punch Me* tattooed on my forehead." She plucked at the sheet, not meeting his gaze. "I mean, was it too much to ask for a man to love me and not crack me in the nose for ordering a Big Mac?"

"Jesus. Is that *really* what happened?"

"Oh, yeah. Told me I could have whatever I wanted, then busted my nose because he didn't like the way I ordered it. If you hadn't been there he'd have killed me—and all because of a burger and fries."

"You haven't seen him since, have you?" Joey certainly hadn't stopped watching for him. Red trucks still triggered an immediate response.

"No. I checked the dating service. He'd been labeled as unsafe by several other women. Dunno how I missed that the first time around. Too stupid to live, I guess."

"You're not stupid. You couldn't have known something that trivial would set him off."

Shuddering, she rocked forward, hugging her arms over her breasts. "I should have. Shit like that happens to me all the time. The crazies always seem to find me."

That doesn't sound good. "I hope you're not including *me* in that group."

"You? You're the craziest of all—none of the others have swept me off my feet while wearing a bra—but you're also the best."

At least she hadn't qualified that by adding "so far."

Joey wanted to be the best thing that ever happened to her. If she would only give him a chance, they could be so much more than friends with benefits. They might actually love each other someday. Deep down, he suspected he was already on the brink.

"I'm glad you think so. I'm really sorry about last night—tricking you, I mean. I shouldn't have done it, but I was desperate. I've been going nuts for weeks, trying to get somewhere with you, and after what happened with Geena, well…you can understand why I didn't just blurt it out. I honestly didn't think the ruse would go on as long as it did. I figured you'd see through my disguise and we'd have a good laugh and still be friends—or you'd slap me silly and tell me to get lost. But when you kept playing along, I wasn't sure *what* to do. I had it all planned, but I never dreamed it would work—and then I was scared to death it wouldn't."

Joey held his breath, waiting for her to speak. For a long moment, she simply nodded, still rocking back and forth like a grieving child with no other source of comfort. "I wish I could—"

Her voice broke on a sob and her face contorted, displaying more misery than Joey had ever witnessed. Enfolding her in his arms, he held her while her body shook with violent, gut-wrenching sobs.

I did this to her. This is my fault.

Love was all about trust, and he'd blown it. Sure, he could hold her, offer her comfort—they'd done that much for each other before—but she would never trust him with her heart. Not after what he'd done.

People had been telling him he was stupid for most of his life. Right now, that was exactly how he felt.

Chapter 21

Joey's resignation was evident in his sigh. "Are we about to have the inevitable discussion about what a bad idea this was?"

"Possibly."

"Can't it please wait until tomorrow? I'm not ready for this to end. Not yet." He paused, then added, "Okay, not ever."

Tracy responded with another sob. As Joey stroked her hair, she breathed in his scent—praying it wouldn't be for the last time.

"Are you gonna tell me why you're crying or do I have to just sit here and wonder?"

She shook her head. "You'll think it's silly."

"Try me," he cajoled. "I can't think of anything sillier than what I've told you about myself. It couldn't be *that* bad."

Viewed in that light, he certainly wouldn't get any arguments from her. The trouble was, she wasn't completely sure herself. "I'll let you know when I get it figured out."

"That doesn't sound very promising. This is all my fault for confusing you, isn't it?"

Raising her head, she wiped her eyes. "Not entirely. There are things that bother me sometimes. I can't explain it any better than that. I enjoyed being with you last night, and this morning, too, but—"

His body sagged around hers. "You want me to leave now, don't you?" He blew out a sharp exhale. "Shit."

"I don't know *what* I want you to do. I don't want either of us to get hurt—and I certainly don't want to lose your friendship. It's just that every time I meet a guy, we start off okay, and then after a few dates, everything goes straight to hell. I *never* get it right, and I'm beginning to think I never will. I don't want that to happen with us."

"And the solution is to call it quits after one night?" She'd been avoiding his gaze, but he cupped her face in his hands, forcing her to look at him. "Look, I know it's risky, but please, don't end this before we ever begin. I know it seems like I pulled the wool over your eyes last night, but, believe me, I was more honest with you than I've ever been with anyone."

He swallowed hard, tears shimmering in his eyes. "You wouldn't believe the kind of ridicule my girlfriends have dished out when they discovered my little secret." He paused, shuddering. "But you seemed open enough to handle it, and you make me feel like I'm *worth* something. I know I'm not very smart and I'll probably never amount to much, but do you have *any* idea what it means to a guy like me to hear you call me your hero?"

"But you *are* my hero," she whispered, her voice cracking with emotion. "After so many jerks, I can't believe I finally found you." She fell into his arms, a sobbing mass of pent-up emotions that had been repressed much too deeply for far too long. She doubted she'd cried that much since she was Darren's age.

Darren. Someday Geena would realize she'd walked out on a terrific guy. Tracy didn't know Darren's real father and didn't want to, but she was quite sure she wouldn't have taken him over Joey. Not a man who would dump a pregnant girl, leaving her desperate enough to pass off his child as someone else's.

Geena wasn't some nasty, heartless bitch. She was a nice girl, and Darren was an adorable child—a child Joey had believed to be his own son since birth. Joey had to have feelings for *him*, even if he despised Geena for what she'd done. They'd always seemed so happy together. Would he forgive her and take her back if she asked?

As unlucky in love as Tracy had always been, she could easily see herself falling in love with Joey only to have Geena show up with Darren on her hip. She should've been used to misery by now. Why did it matter so much that the affair would end someday? How was this one different?

With a sudden jolt of enlightenment, she understood.

I love him.

She hadn't loved any of the others. *That* was the difference.

As she saw it, her despair could begin now or later.

She opted for later. *Much* later.

Joey couldn't help smiling as he dried Tracy's tears.

I'm still her hero—even after dressing up like a girl and seducing her. Who'd have thunk it?

He'd never been anyone's hero before. Granted, given Tracy's history, he didn't have much competition, but being a hero wasn't everything. Once the gratitude wore off, he could still write songs for her, sing for her—

And give her breakfast in bed.

"How do you like your eggs?"

She let out a shaky laugh. "Um, cooked?"

"Cooked it is." Hopping out of bed, he pulled the covers up over her and pressed a kiss to her forehead. "Be right back."

He hadn't worked a morning shift in years, but he could still whip up a decent omelet—depending on what he found in her refrigerator. While the coffee brewed, he discerned that she did indeed have eggs, butter, milk, and cheese. After finding a skillet, he got started.

His culinary efforts were duly rewarded.

"Oh, wow," she said after the first bite. "This is fabulous. I never thought of putting smoked provolone in an omelet before."

Joey responded with a self-deprecating shrug. "Necessity being the mother of invention."

"Meaning?"

"That was the only cheese you had."

She chuckled. "Gotcha. Just goes to show how seldom I make omelets. Then again, if I ate like this every day, my undies would be way too big for you."

"There's no such thing as too big," he assured her, "only too small."

She snorted a laugh. "You'll never have that problem with me. I've always been kinda hippy." She ate a few more bites. "Mind telling me just when and how you decided you liked that sort of thing?"

He didn't have to ask what sort of "thing" she was referring to. "My sister had just starting wearing a bra, and she kept going on about how uncomfortable it was. I couldn't imagine what all the fuss was about—once you've worn a jock strap, how uncomfortable could a bra be? Anyway, one day while she was off somewhere with her friends, I tried on one of her training bras. I got so hard I had to jack off—which was also the first time I ever did *that*. It's been a turn-on for me ever since."

"Sounds reasonable," she said. "What I don't understand is why anyone would hold it against you. I mean, there are lots of stranger preferences."

"BDSM stuff, you mean?" He shrugged. "Yeah. Guess I just got hung up on the wrong girls."

"And *I* always fall for guys who like to beat me up."

"Oh, surely not *always*."

"Well, no." She took a sip of her coffee. "Seems that way, though."

"I can think of at least one man who won't ever abuse you."

She gave him a brief smile but didn't say anything. If she only fell for guys who liked to beat her up, did that mean she *hadn't* fallen for him?

I'm reading too much into this.

"No, you aren't the type," she finally said.

She might has well have said he wasn't *her* type. Was she having second thoughts—again? She'd seemed fine with the sex—and breakfast—it was all this *thinking* that made everything so awkward.

Maybe sex was all she wanted. He'd admitted to being desperate for her attention while she'd never claimed to have any romantic interest in him at all. She'd only agreed to a hook up. What if she only wanted a fuck buddy?

"I still don't understand why Geena would leave you because of something so trivial. Sure, she was upset, and yes, Darren wasn't your child, but you couldn't have been her only option. I mean, she had to feel *something* for you or she wouldn't have stuck with you as long as she did."

"I'd like to think so, but in looking back, I can't help wondering if I wasn't simply convenient." *And gullible.* He hated to keep harping on that, but it was true. He'd swallowed Geena's story—hook, line, and sinker.

"Did she ever tell you she loved you?"

Geena said the words all the time, but they'd always been tossed at him—a quick, *Love you!* whenever she waved goodbye or ended a phone call. He couldn't recall that she'd ever looked him in the eyes and said it like she truly meant it. "Yeah. But *I love you* is an easy thing to say. Only words."

She pressed a napkin to her lips. "Do you think she was looking for an excuse to leave?"

"Maybe," he replied. "She didn't even want to talk about it. It was 'I'm outta here' and she was gone." Even now, the memory made him shudder.

A touch of her hand reminded him he wasn't alone. "That still seems so...harsh. I can't believe she wouldn't have regretted it afterward. What if she came back saying she made a huge mistake? What would you do?"

Tracy was obviously looking for some assurance that he would choose her over Geena—not that he blamed her. She'd already endured enough pain. Unfortunately, the choice wasn't that simple. "I honestly don't know. I was pretty torn up at the time—she had me good and fooled. If it weren't for Darren..."

"You miss him, don't you?"

"Oh, yeah. I catch myself wondering how he is, how much he's grown. It's like giving a kid up for adoption—always wondering where they are, what they're doing, if they're happy...stuff like that."

She nodded as though she understood. "I had a miscarriage

once—never even knew whether it was a boy or a girl—and even though I never got to hold my baby or hear its voice, neither did anyone else. Your situation is different. If I were in your place..." She shrugged. "What Geena did may have been unforgivable, but Darren was innocent. Yeah. Tough choice."

"I still can't decide whether I was blind or flattered or just plain stupid. I mean, I liked Geena, but she was so much younger than me. I never *dreamed*... It all happened so fast, and when she told me she was pregnant, I didn't question it—even though I'd always used a condom. Not that they're a hundred percent reliable, but—"

"Do you think it might've been because you *wanted* a baby?"

He hesitated. "I'm not getting any younger—pushing forty and never married... Yeah. Maybe I believed her because I wanted to, not because it made any sense." Taking her empty plate, he got up from the bed, grumbling. "I guess that makes me stupid, gullible, *and* old." Scowling, he added, "None of this is recommending me to you, is it?"

A tiny smile touched her lips. "You might be surprised. Your honesty is...refreshing."

"Then I'm forgiven?"

"Yes, I believe you are." Her smile broadened to become a diabolical grin. "But I *do* owe you a spanking."

"You like me, don't you?" he said with a smirk. "Come on now, admit it. You do."

She threw up her hands in protest. "What's not to like? You're a nice guy, and you've been awfully good to me so far. No one, and I do mean *no* one, has *ever* fixed breakfast for me. And I love your hair."

"Would you still like me if I cut it?"

"Just as long as you didn't shave your head." With a shudder, she added, "Skin-heads give me the creeps."

"I'll try to remember that. Okay, let me see if I've got this straight. All I have to do is be nice—meaning no punching you in the face for ordering a Big Mac—no super-short haircuts, and breakfast in bed once in a while." He nodded. "Got it. What else?"

He looked so cute standing there naked, she was about to suggest that he never get dressed, but immediately dismissed the idea as impractical. "That's probably enough for now."

"You can think about it while I get rid of these dishes."

Stunned by the vision of his cute little ass as he scurried out to the kitchen, Tracy hadn't thought of a thing by the time he returned.

"About the sex," he said as he hopped on the bed. "You like being spanked—I can handle that part, easy. You had a freakin' orgasm when I came in your face—I can do that anytime you like. You liked getting nailed by a girl in a strap-on—didn't mind getting it pretty hard, either. No problems there." He tapped his chin. "Chocolate shakes, French fries, and oral sex. That covers what I know so far. Care to add anything?"

"Sexy rap songs and cock syrup," she said, barely stifling a giggle.

"Consider them added to the list. Is that it?"

"Just one more," she said. "I want you to give me a private concert sometime, but without your clothes."

He waggled his brow. "Got a thing for long-haired, naked musicians?"

"You bet." She slid a hand between his legs. "With big, hard dicks and soft, hairy balls."

"What on earth made you think you'd like being with a woman?"

"Mean guys," she replied. "But you aren't mean, so you've saved me from a lifetime of pretending to be a lesbian when my heart really isn't in it."

"You seemed to like Anna pretty well, though," he countered. "How do you explain that?"

She shrugged. "On some subconscious level, I must've known she was you."

"Ah, then you *do* like me." With a wicked smile, he leaned in for a kiss—her first real kiss since discovering his true identity. Soft and sensuous, his lips turned her insides to mush, flooding her core with heat and making her toes tingle.

"Anna" had been right.

It really *was* magic.

Chapter 22

"I like you much better as a guy," Tracy whispered against his lips.

"Glad to hear it. I never want to have to tuck up my balls again as long as I live."

Easing her down onto her back, Joey covered her body with his own, nudging her legs apart and stroking her with the head of his penis. He wanted to slide his dick over every last bit of her, the high points and the low, delving into every nook and cranny. She was like candy, and his sweet tooth had been denied for far too long. All those weeks of wanting her, unable to touch, to taste, to fuck… Getting his fill of her seemed impossible; he was insane with the need to be inside her.

Her hands were everywhere, stroking his cock, his balls, and his ass. "You feel so good I can hardly stand it." Her soft, wet kisses drove him wilder still, and as they trailed down his neck, he wondered again how she'd missed such a uniquely masculine trait. His skin was already rough, despite having shaved twice with a four-bladed razor, praying his beard wouldn't give him away. All that preparation was forgotten as she sucked his skin where his shoulder met his neck.

He moved forward over her, intending to offer her his cock, but she had other ideas. After giving his dick a kiss and painting her lips with his cock syrup, she twisted sideways beneath him, ending up halfway on top of him, licking his butt before sinking her teeth into the muscle.

"Oh, God," he groaned. "You're killing me, Trace."

Seconds later, she landed a stinging, open-palmed slap on his ass. The impact went through him like a shock wave, forcing juice from his dick and a gasp from his throat.

"Again?"

"Don't stop," he pleaded. "Please, don't stop."

She crawled out from under him, leaving him on his hands and knees with his ass in the air. Alternately slapping and biting, she drove him to the brink of insanity, making him desperate for things he didn't even know he'd craved.

He cried out in frustration when she stopped just short of his climax.

"Don't move," she said. "I'll be right back."

She took a bottle of lubricant from the nightstand and picked up the harness. "Don't suppose you've got the dildo that goes with this?"

His balls clenched, and he held his breath, fighting his ejaculation with every muscle in his body. "In my purse on the dresser," he gasped. "I figured I ought to have it in case you wanted to see it."

Gritting his teeth, he squeezed his eyes shut. If he watched her put it on, he'd come all over the place. *Not yet.*

Unfortunately, he could still hear as she adjusted the Velcro fastenings and tore open a condom packet. The bed dipped as she settled in behind him. "I think you might want to wear this." Hooking his bra around his chest, she pinched his nipples before covering them with the lacy fabric, sending lightning strikes of lust straight to his groin.

"Hurry, Trace. I'm gonna lose it…"

Cold lubricant ran between his buttocks and down over his nuts. "Sure you can take something this big?"

"I don't know. Try it anyway. My *God*, that feels good." The words burst from him as she teased his anus with a fingertip, massaging the tight sphincter until he was frantic with need. "Fuck me, goddammit," he yelled. "I don't care if it hurts."

"Okay, baby, you asked for it." Pressing the blunt head of the dildo against his asshole, she pushed in gently, then backed off and tried again.

Joey gulped in a breath as she delved deeper and deeper inside him, letting out a whimper when her skin finally touched his.

"I'm in." Sliding her hands over his hips, she leaned forward to fondle his cock and balls. "Feel okay?"

His throat too tight to speak, Joey replied with a nod.

"It's best if you take it from here," she said. "If I do it wrong, it'll hurt like hell. Done right, it's so good it'll make you cry."

Already on his hands and knees, he rocked back, driving her in deeper. His mouth fell open and his eyes crossed. Evidently, he was doing it correctly. Each backward thrust and withdrawal ratcheted the intensity to a new level until, with a guttural cry, he took the final plunge.

Cupping his cockhead, Tracy caught his hot cream in her hand. His orgasm triggered hers, and she jack-knifed away from him, pulling the fake penis out of him rather abruptly. Joey's loud hiss could've been due to pleasure or pain. She'd always heard that pulling anal beads out at the moment of climax would quadruple the pleasure, but she didn't know if a penis would have the same effect.

Apparently, it did. Tumbling onto his side, Joey's orgasmic contractions continued unabated, his eyes open wide as semen spewed from his cock.

Slathering him with his own juice, she went down on him, sucking as much of him into her mouth as she could hold while her own climax raged on.

As her ecstasy ebbed, she released him, savoring the slow rise and fall of his chest and the steady beat of his heart.

"Okay," he said, clearing his throat. "I'm adding that one to *my* list. That was…well, I don't know *what* that was, but, *damn*…"

She crawled up beside him. "Not planning to look for a boyfriend, are you?"

He shook his head. "No possible way. That wouldn't have been half as good with anyone else."

"That's a relief," she said. "And it *was* pretty incredible." She sucked in a breath. "Now if I can just get out of this thing…"

He ran a finger along the strap on her hip. "You look totally hot in that harness."

"So did you. I can't wait for you to wear it without the pantyhose."

"No problem," he said. "I had a helluva time with all that. I had to practice for *days*."

"Did you also practice getting a condom off one of these things?" she asked after her first failed attempt. "I think it's stuck."

"Just take the whole thing off and dump it in the sink. We'll clean it up later. Right now, I just want to lay here and hold you."

"Sure thing. Be right back."

Her "penis" bounced like a drumstick all the way to the bathroom. Giggling, she unfastened the harness and stepped out of it. "I'm taking off my dick, now. First time for everything."

After washing her face and hands, she snatched up a towel for Joey. Thankfully, she hadn't noticed any blood on the dildo, and she tried not to think about what might've happened if she'd had to take him to the hospital. Explaining his injuries would've been embarrassing to say the least—and was the main reason she hadn't gone to the ER after the episode with Bryce. Even HIPAA couldn't stop a good story from circulating.

She returned to find Joey lying asleep on his side, the lacy pink bra still strapped around his chest. Never having cared to sleep in one herself, she unhooked it for him. He didn't appear to be bleeding, so she toweled off the lube and snuggled in beside him for a nap. She would keep this unusual sexual experience a secret, knowing they would have tons of fun with it. Someday she would tell him about her biggest turn-on.

But not yet.

༄༅

A deep inhale proved she was still there, spooned up against him. *That went better than I ever thought it would.* Joey still couldn't believe Melina hadn't given him away—although her wide-eyed shock of recognition surprised him a little. Obviously, his disguise was more convincing than he thought—not that he hadn't put a great deal of time and effort into it.

Melina had been game—up to a point. "I'll introduce you to Tracy," she'd said. "But that's *all* I'm doing. She's had her mind messed with enough."

"No worries," he'd assured her. "She'll figure out who I am pretty quick. We'll have a good laugh, and maybe she'll see me as a potential boyfriend."

"Seems like she would've done that already—if she was interested."

"Maybe. But I get the feeling she's ignoring the signals because she doesn't want to get involved with men in general—not me specifically."

Melina snorted derisively. "That's about as clear as mud."

"Yeah, well, this whole thing is kinda murky."

"No shit. Why can't you just ask her out?"

"It's…complicated."

"Uh huh. Yeah. We'll see—but if you hurt her, I'll rip your balls off."

He'd gotten *that* message loud and clear, and he'd intended to reveal himself much sooner if Tracy *didn't* recognize him. Unfortunately, somewhere along the way, he'd wussed out. If Tracy didn't want to admit to being attracted to a man, he figured he could play that game.

Too bad it wasn't really a game.

Tracy hadn't surprised him—well, not *a lot*, anyway. Beneath that sweet, understanding exterior, she had the soul of a…a what? A dominatrix? A sex goddess? A hot, sexy, kinky—

At the moment, his dick didn't care that she was anyone but Tracy Richards, the girl next door.

That didn't take long.

He nuzzled her neck, dropping kisses anywhere he could reach. "You awake?"

"Mmm…yeah." She turned over in his arms. "I was having the nicest dream. There was this girl in my bed who turned out to be a guy with the most luscious cock and an adorably furry stomach."

Chuckling, he pressed a kiss to her shoulder. "You actually *like* my hairy belly? Everybody else tells me I should have it waxed."

"Oh, no. Don't ever do that. I like the way it tickles my cheek when I'm sucking your dick." She ducked her head under the covers. "Speaking of which…"

Seconds later, *he* was the one being tickled. As her lips touched his stomach, he could hardly stand it, erupting in a peal of laughter.

"Ah, so you're ticklish, are you?"

"Apparently," he gasped.

She tried it again with a similar result. "I like hearing you laugh," she said. "It makes me feel good." She paused, her lips parted as though she'd been stunned by a sudden realization. "Holy shit. We're having *fun*. I'm in bed with a guy and we're *actually* having fun.'"

"You mean you've *never* had fun with a man?"

"Not really, and hardly ever in bed. I *like* acting silly or playing around with some of the kinkier stuff. Never felt like I could, though. Men are too serious—always telling me to act my age, making me feel like I'm on trial or something—which isn't fair, really. I'm entitled to as much fun as the next person."

"You've never been allowed to be yourself." Having seldom been granted that luxury himself, Joey knew the feeling.

"Exactly. I always felt like I had to live up to someone else's expectations. Seems like someone is always telling me what to do—like only *they* know what's best for me. But who knows *me* better than I know myself? Maybe it's my face." Her sidelong glance ensnared him. "Do I *look* stupid?"

"No. You don't look stupid—far from it. But I do have a theory about that."

"Really? Let's hear it."

"When people know you're smart, they try to make themselves seem smarter by giving you advice."

Her mouth twisted in contemplation. "Interesting… Do you suppose they do it subconsciously or on purpose?"

"I'm guessing it's usually subconscious. Most people don't think things through that hard. I know I don't."

Tracy chuckled. "Maybe not, but we do have some deep conversations, don't we?"

"And we're *supposed* to be having fun," he said with a rueful laugh. "I think what I'm trying to get at is that you and I aren't judging each other."

She nodded slowly. "Yeah. You wear lingerie, and I had sex with a girl—it's like the pot calling the kettle black."

"But you didn't have sex with a girl. You got nailed by a guy in drag." He gave her a wink. "Big difference."

"Oh, it's *big* all right," she said, taking his cock in her hand. "What do you say we try it without the harnesses and strap-ons and see how it goes?"

"Sounds fabulous." Joey could scarcely believe his luck. He was in bed with Tracy. No costumes, no paraphernalia. All they needed was a condom, and he had several of them in his purse.

On that thought, he started laughing and didn't stop until tears ran down his cheeks.

She arched a brow. "What's so funny?"

"I was thinking that all we need is a condom, and I have plenty of them in my p–purse."

"Nice purse, too. Might borrow it sometime."

"Sweetheart, you can *have* it. I don't need it anymore." Rolling onto his stomach, he took her in his arms and kissed her long and slow and deep. His dick rested against her hip, drooling with anticipation.

Nothing kinky this time. Just a good, straight, vanilla-sex fuck.

Unless, of course, she wants to be on top.

"Speaking of condoms, do I need one?"

She nodded. "Yeah. I've never been able to tolerate birth control pills. Sorry. They make my lips break out whenever I eat anything acidic."

"Now, *there's* an interesting side effect."

"Yep. Just as weird as the rest of me."

"You aren't weird. You're sexy and sweet and I'm gonna fuck you silly." Lowering his head to her breasts, he licked one nipple while teasing the other with a fingertip. "Nice tits," he murmured. "I took my nipple rings out to play Anna. Didn't want them getting caught in my falsies."

"Ooh, sounds hot."

"Figured you'd like them." A tremor ran through her body as he flicked her nipple with his tongue. "They're in my purse, too. Be right back."

Within seconds, he returned to her, wearing nothing but a condom and two silver hoops.

She licked her lips. "Oh, wow...they're big enough to get a finger through them—even the tip of my tongue."

He winked. "That's the idea." Parting her thighs, he slid inside without preamble. "My God, you feel good."

Knowing she would feel even better without the rubber, he longed for a time when he could glide his naked cock into Tracy's hot, wet pussy—which, of course, he couldn't do unless they were married or at least intending to have a baby.

What a concept.

That decision had been taken out of his hands the last time—whether he'd been the *real* father or not. The mere thought of making a conscious choice to have a baby made his balls ache to comply. Instead, he took it slow and deep, undulating his spine, fucking her with full, even strokes.

Her eyelids drifted downward and a smile curled her lips. "Oh, yeah..."

Pushing himself up with his hands, he hovered over her, the silver rings dangling mere inches from her lips. He closed his eyes as her breath rippled his skin just before she took the ring in her mouth. "Mmm... Love that..."

Tracy responded by tonguing his nipples until he was sure he'd go mad. "I thought about getting mine done. Does it hurt much?"

"At first," he admitted. "After that, it's a real rush when someone tugs on them." He held his breath, trying desperately to erase the sizzling image of Tracy with nipple rings from his mind. "God, I almost came just thinking about it."

"Well, then," she whispered. "Guess I'd better do it, huh?"

Instantly, his head snapped up and his dick erupted with enough force to turn his toes inside out. "Whoa, momma..."

"Hang on, Joey." She chuckled. "You ain't seen *nuthin'* yet."

Chapter 23

Tracy's alarm clock elicited a much louder groan than usual. Having sent a rather cryptic text to Melina's phone—*Fantastic weekend with you know who. Details on Monday*—she was reluctant to go anywhere near the clinic. Melina would undoubtedly want to hear all about it, and though that weekend had easily been one of the high points of her life, there were a great many *details* Tracy had no intention of sharing—particularly the part about the strap-on.

Damn, the man was hot. If she'd known Joey was packing that much heat, she'd have pounced on him in the laundry room a long time ago. Despite having to work Sunday evening, he'd still managed to rock her world before bedtime. His flavor lingered on her tongue and the memory of his body was so real she could almost feel him—hot, hard, and indescribably delicious. In hindsight, she should've paid more attention to her gut reaction instead of trying to convince herself he wasn't really interested.

Still, interested or not, it couldn't last. No one could keep up the kind of pace they'd set.

Maybe it's a good thing we work opposite shifts.

Or not. She was finally getting a taste of the kind of life—the kind of *man*—she'd always wanted. Who'd have thought Prince Charming would show up in a skirt?

Rolling over, she hit the snooze button. *Another ten minutes...*

Her nose disagreed. Coffee...*definitely* coffee. And eggs.

Oh, my God. He's still here, and he's fixing breakfast. Again.

After a quick stop in the bathroom, she threw on a robe and stumbled out to the kitchen. "Smells great. Looks great too—and I'm not talking about the food."

Clad only in a pair of low-slung jeans and his nipple rings, Joey shot her a smirk as he gave the eggs a quick flip. The effect couldn't have been any more titillating if he'd been naked.

I need coffee. Bad.

"Wish you didn't have to go to work," he said.

"Me, too." She heaved a sigh. "Don't guess we'll have many more days like yesterday."

"Meaning?"

"Oh, you know…that first flush of sexual excitement thing." She waved a dismissive hand. "Impossible to maintain."

He arched a brow. "I don't know about that. My dick is working better than ever."

"Really?"

He nodded. "Except for when I was a teenager. Couldn't keep it down then."

She poured herself a cup of coffee while attempting to imagine him as a teen. "I bet you were really cute."

"Nope. I was little and skinny with a bad case of acne. My hair was so curly I could barely get a comb through it."

"Sounds like me, except for the curls and the skinny part." She stuck two slices of bread in the toaster and pushed the lever down. "I've never been skinny in my life."

"Tracy," he began. "Could we…I don't know, just *enjoy* this, and not think it to death?"

"What d'you mean?"

"This." He waved a spatula back and forth between them. "Us. We've had one helluva good time so far. Let's not fuck it up by overanalyzing everything—or worrying about it being temporary."

"Go with the flow?"

"Yeah. And we don't have to expect fireworks every time we get together. We can do crazy things, but we can do normal things, too. Like going to movies and shopping and stuff like that."

And get married and have babies. She had to bite her tongue to keep from saying it aloud. "Normal. Yeah. Normal sounds good." Taking a sip of her coffee, she let the hot brew slide down her throat, easing the painful lump forming there. "Should we pitch the strap-on?"

"That isn't what I mean." He blew out a breath. "What I'm trying to say is that I want us to be more than fuck buddies or friends with benefits—or at least not rule out the possibility."

"A long-term relationship?" She was scared to death to call it love.

"If you want to look at it that way, yeah. Long-term."

Did she dare to hope he meant forever? Was it even remotely possible? If her history was anything to go by, it probably wasn't. But he wasn't like the others—not even close. She took another sip, wishing for something stronger than Colombian coffee. "So, we jump in with both feet and let the chips fall where they may—is that a mixed metaphor? Never mind, you know what I mean."

"It doesn't have to be a leap of faith. We aren't in any hurry. Let's take the time to enjoy it."

Tick, tick, tick went her biological clock. She's always intended to have children before she was thirty—one of those promises she'd made to herself after her pediatrics rotation in nursing school. Plenty of normal, healthy kids were born to older mothers, but maternal age was still a factor in a good many birth defects. And she was thirty-one…

This is not the time to be thinking about that.

Considering what he'd gone through with Darren, Joey might want another baby right away, or he might shy away from the idea entirely. Losing a baby hadn't made Tracy want a child any less. If anything, it made her that much more anxious to try again.

"Okay," she finally said. "Let's just let it happen."

Joey hadn't been kidding about the state of his dick—proving that he didn't need to *wear* Tracy's undies to itch to get into them. Strange, how the first woman to ever be okay with the idea seemed to eliminate the need—or at least diminish it.

He plated up the eggs while she buttered the toast.

Like an old married couple.

This time, he wasn't going to rule out that option. He thanked his lucky stars he hadn't married Geena. But Tracy? He wanted her sitting across from him at the breakfast table every morning of his life.

It was much too soon to ask her, but how long should a guy wait when he'd already made up his mind? Six months? A year? The fact that he'd never truly contemplated marriage made it difficult, and he'd come dangerously close to blurting it out when she walked into the kitchen. The realization that it wasn't the right moment was the only thing that stopped him. He only hoped he would recognize the *correct* moment when it arrived.

As a songwriter, he should be able to do that. Unfortunately, most love songs were about bad luck and heartbreak rather than happy endings. Off the top of his head, the only happy-ever-after songs he could think of were "This Magic Moment" and "Signed, Sealed, Delivered." Surely, there were more than two. Then he remembered "Faithfully."

Okay, that's three...

After polishing off his eggs, he leaned back in his chair. "Go ahead and get ready for work. I'll clean up."

She swallowed the last of her coffee. "You're spoiling me. You know that, don't you?"

"I'm gonna give it my best shot."

"Promises, promises," she drawled, giving him a kiss that promised something else entirely. "Thanks for the chow."

While Tracy went off to take a shower, Joey caught himself humming "Signed, Sealed, Delivered" as he washed the dishes. He'd played that old Stevie Wonder song a thousand times, but those lyrics had never meant quite as much as they did now. He truly was hers, and his future really was in her hands.

Wow. He should've been scared, but he wasn't. The tough part was over—he'd played his weakest hand and was still in the game. If he'd been any more elated, he'd have been floating.

Paulina had gotten quite a kick out of him at Georgio's the night before. He'd been floating then, too.

"Make sure you don't mix up the salt and the sugar while

you're up there on cloud nine," she'd cautioned him. "I've already lost a waitress. Don't want to have to fire a cook."

"You won't have to fire me," he grumbled. "Speaking of waitresses, had any nibbles?"

"Not really." Paulina doused the pizza dough with sauce, then fired handfuls of onions and mushrooms at it. She said it helped the veggies meld with the sauce, but it was kinda scary to watch. Her specialty was chicken cutlets. Wielding a mallet that looked more like a carpenter's tool than a cooking utensil, she seemed to enjoy pounding them into submission. "I might have to get you to wait tables."

"Better not fire me, then, huh?"

She shot him a grin. "Wouldn't dream of firing *you*, Joey. Best cook I ever had."

Paulina probably wouldn't like it if the band made it big and he had to quit his job. But she'd get over it—might even post his photo on the wall to add a touch of atmosphere to the dining room.

Like the Hard Rock Café.

Joey barely stifled a laugh. A guitar and an autographed picture on the wall in a Hard Rock Café probably made a lot of musicians feel they'd made the big time—perhaps even more so than a gold album. Never having gotten either one, he wouldn't know.

There were a million rock star wannabes—and that was just in the States. Bands from Britain and Europe—hell, even Iceland—were topping the charts. What chance did a bunch of guys from Pemberton have? Especially since there weren't that many venues for live music in town.

We have paying gigs.

He had to remind himself of that—frequently. In Nashville or LA, talent scouts might be more apt to see them, but they'd probably be playing for tips.

Brad had resisted the idea of doing a demo, even though Joey was sure he'd written several songs that had hit potential. Brad was happy with things as they were and believed they were better off playing songs everyone knew—which was true for the kind of places they played.

Joey was a tad more ambitious, and now that he didn't have a baby and a—God, he'd almost thought *wife*—he wasn't tied to Pemberton anymore. Uprooting a family was one thing, but Tracy… Hell, nurses could get jobs anywhere. She could come with him.

Strange, he'd never thought of relocating before. Something had always held him back. What was different now? Even before he'd had Geena and Darren to consider, he'd never given the idea any serious thought.

I didn't have Tracy then.

He wasn't sure he had her now. She'd referred to him as her hero, but did he still need to make her proud? Did her input as a "manager" make a difference? Or was it simply her acceptance of his fetish and the way he played when fantasizing about her…

Perhaps that was why he'd never strived for stardom. He'd never truly been inspired before and certainly didn't think he was good enough to play beyond the local level. Tracy inspired him in ways he'd never imagined.

Especially when she walked out of the bathroom with her hair twisted up in a towel. Naked.

He glanced at the clock and blew out a sigh. "Don't suppose you could be a little late, could you?"

She shook her head. "Melina will give me enough hell as it is." With a swift, downward glance, she crossed her arms over her breasts. "Sorry. I wasn't sure you'd still be here."

Swallowing hard, he reached for a dishtowel to dry his hands. Truth be told, he *never* wanted to leave. "What makes you think that about Melina? I'd expect you to rip *her* a new one, not the other way around."

"Trust me, I thought about it—at first. How did you ever talk her into introducing us?"

"She wasn't crazy about the idea—in fact, that was all she said she'd do—except for threatening to rip my balls off if I hurt you."

"Now, *that* I can believe." Tracy giggled. "Of course, you could always tuck them up so she couldn't find them."

"I'd rather not have to."

"No shit." She hesitated, lowering her eyelids as though stricken with sudden shyness. "I don't think she'll have any reason to be after your balls anytime soon." Pausing again, she exhaled with a sigh. "I've never been happier in my life—and I ought to be thanking her."

"So should I."

Tracy smiled. "I could kick myself for being so blind. All this time, my hero—and the sexiest man alive—was living right next door."

The sexiest man alive? In a bra and pantyhose? There's hope for me yet. "Well, I *did* have a girlfriend and a baby."

"Yeah. Maybe that's it."

As her shrug emphasized her cleavage, Joey's mouth went dry. If she didn't put her clothes on soon, she was gonna get nailed right there in the middle of the kitchen floor.

"I never thought of you as being available, and then there was that giving up men business." She snorted a laugh. "Who knows? That last date with Bryce may turn out to be the best thing that ever happened to me."

Tracy was quite possibly the best thing that had ever happened to *Joey*. He'd had more fun in one weekend with her than he'd ever had with Geena or anyone else. For the first time in his life, he felt free to express himself. It was…liberating. "Funny how things turn out."

"Every cloud has a silver lining? Yeah. Something like that." With a sigh, she headed back toward the bedroom. "Guess I'd better get dressed and go to work."

As she walked away, Joey discovered a new motivation for seeking fame and fortune. If he earned enough money, Tracy wouldn't have to work. She could do as she pleased—and he didn't wish that just so he could fuck her anytime he liked. He'd never once considered being the sole breadwinner when Geena moved in with him—they'd barely scraped by as it was. Nor had he ever aspired to owning a house big enough for a family. Tracy made him think about backyards, swing sets, and bikes in the garage.

Tracy not only inspired his talent, she fueled his ambition.

Whoa…

Chapter 24

In Tracy's opinion, leaving Joey was perhaps the most asinine thing Geena had ever done—except perhaps letting what's-his-name get her pregnant to begin with—but then, the motivations of a nineteen-year-old were anyone's guess. Thus far, Joey was the best man Tracy had ever had the pleasure of spending time with, and unless Geena had been madly in love with that other dude, Joey's fetish was no reason to call it quits. The best she could tell, he'd been a good father to Darren, and she knew for a fact he was a fantastic lover.

There were other considerations, of course. Restaurant cooks weren't exactly overpaid and neither were small town rock bands. Joey never said what Darren's father did for a living—although if he was Geena's age, Tracy doubted he earned megabucks. Geena *had* to have been in love with the guy—which meant the likelihood of a change of heart with respect to Joey was unlikely.

Maybe I really don't *have to worry about that.*

Melina was less optimistic. "He does have a history with her. I mean, *I* wouldn't welcome her back, but I'm sure he loved that baby."

"Yeah, he did," Tracy admitted.

"She may also know something about Joey that you don't. And he *did* try to trick you. I'm not sure I'd trust him after that."

"But you went along with it," Tracy insisted. "You even pointed him out to me."

"You probably won't believe this, but even though I knew he would be there, I didn't recognize him at first."

"Well, then, I'd better not hear any ragging on *me* for not realizing who he was."

Melina's eyes nearly popped out of her head. "You mean you really thought he was a girl?"

"You *told* me he was one of the lesbians—and I was working on my second Screaming Orgasm at the time."

Melina was in the process of putting a needle on a syringe and nearly dropped them both. "I figured he must've come out to you while you were on the dance floor."

"Hell, no," Tracy exclaimed. "*Anna* got me so damned hot, I was ready to fuck her."

"Jesus, what did you think when you—"

"Went to bed with a woman and woke up with a man?" Tracy's laughter bubbled up inside her. "I was tickled shitless."

"Wait a minute. Are you saying you slept with him thinking he was a *woman*?"

"Yeah. Put *that* in your pipe and smoke it."

Swallowing hard, Melina thankfully put down the needle before she stuck herself. "How on earth—?"

Tracy threw up her hands. "He said he had a strap-on in his purse—wore the harness and everything. He thought I knew who he was and was playing along."

"But why dress up as a woman to begin with?"

"That's my fault for saying I wanted to date women. I figured you'd found some nice lesbian for me."

"Okay. Let me get this straight. He thought you didn't like men, so he posed as a woman. And when you told me you weren't interested in him, I take it you were lying?"

Tracy grimaced. "Yeah—straight through my teeth. I tried to talk myself out of it, but you can't help who you fall in love with. I was so sure Geena would realize what an idiot she'd been and come back, but I couldn't help myself."

"Are you saying you're in love with him?"

Trust Melina to catch me on a slip of the tongue.

"Maybe." Tracy'd had a hard time admitting it to herself, let alone anyone else.

"But you let *Anna* take you home," Melina reminded her.

"What were you thinking about then?"

"Figured you'd bring that up. I told him I thought maybe it was because on a subconscious level I realized it was him."

Tracy had been on the receiving end of some pretty skeptical looks before, but this one was in a class by itself. "Yeah, *right*—and you honestly didn't know you were with a guy until the next morning? Weren't you paying attention in anatomy class?"

"Hey, when Anna said she had a strap-on, I believed her. Why wouldn't I?"

Melina's skepticism was replaced with knowing wag of her head. "He must have gotten you so damned drunk."

"On a milkshake and fries? Not likely. I wasn't drunk. I was just looking for someone I could be happy and comfortable with and who wouldn't beat the living shit out of me at the drop of a hat. I had a blast with him as Anna. She was loads of fun and sexy as hell. Joey'd been trying to get my attention as himself, but I wasn't listening because I couldn't stand the thought of being with him and then having Geena come back. I *still* can't."

"Do you really believe she'll come back?"

Tracy blew out a breath. "Honest to God, I don't understand why she left him to begin with. I mean, I know *why*, I just don't get why she would leave him for something so trivial. He's awesome. She had to know that."

"Maybe it wasn't trivial to her." Melina shrugged. "Would it really be the end of the world if she *did* come back? He isn't the only fish in the sea."

Tracy took a long moment to form her reply. "I know that. But you've got a husband and two kids and a house and a dog and a cat. I'm over thirty and I've never had anyone—at least, not for long. I don't even have a frickin' goldfish. And Joey is an absolute sweetheart. Do you have any idea how few of those I've run across in my life? I know it sounds stupid, but it's the truth.

"I want to be loved, Melina. Not tolerated—or abused. I'm *sick* of it. I want to have kids and go to school plays and baseball practice and all that stuff. I want to watch my kids grow up and then grow old with someone who loves me. I don't want to be alone forever. I've been trying to convince myself that I can do it—and I will if I have to—but all that crap about your career being enough to satisfy you is just that. Crap. I need to love someone, and I need it so bad I was willing to try it with a woman. Imagine how I felt when that *woman* wound up being the one man I've been trying so hard to resist."

"Well…I'm glad it turned out that way," Melina relented. "But I don't want to see you get hurt. I still can't believe you were willing to go home with a woman. Even with an introduction from me, it was risky."

"Which proves how desperate I was. Actually, I took more of a risk with Bryce. Joey didn't beat me up, he just—" Tracy broke off there as a smile crept across her lips.

"Just *what*?" Melina prompted.

"Blew me away," she replied. "And it's too late to stop it now. I'm *crazy* about him. He's sweet and sexy and adorable. He's been through a lot too, and the last thing I'd ever want to do is hurt him."

"Mind telling me why his girlfriend left him?"

"It's…personal."

Melina's interrogatory glare would have done a district attorney proud. "Personal, huh? As in…?"

Tracy refused to be intimidated. "Personal," she said firmly. "You're acting as though Joey was the one who beat me up. Trust me, he's nothing like Bryce."

"But I *worry* about you, Trace." Melina actually had tears in her eyes. "I never want to see you covered with bruises again."

"I know, and thanks for caring, but if I get any pain out of this relationship, it won't be physical."

No, it wouldn't be physical.

But it would certainly leave scars.

ಸಿಂ

By Thursday morning, Joey was beginning to believe he'd died and gone to heaven. Tracy was not only going with the flow, she was fast becoming an integral part of his life. Granted, they only had late nights and early mornings together, but the thought of coming home to climb into her bed made everything worthwhile. He might've enjoyed making pizzas and playing in a band, but he enjoyed being with Tracy a helluva lot more.

He'd made love to her every night and fixed breakfast for her every morning, but it wasn't enough. He wanted to do something really special for her. But what?

He sent her off to work with a searing goodbye kiss when he finally remembered her list of preferences the morning after "Anna" had fucked her senseless. With a devious grin, he picked up a pen and began scribbling down lyrics. Sexy, sensuous, *pornographic* lyrics…

His dick was drooling by the time he'd finished writing the song. Hoping it would have a similarly titillating effect on Tracy, he snatched up the Ibanez and worked on the riffs until it was time to head over to Georgio's—allowing time to shop for an appropriate wardrobe. Oh, yeah…Friday night was gonna be *fun*…

ೞ೧೪

At five o'clock on Friday, Tracy was locking her door when Joey stuck his head out of his apartment. "Before we head out to dinner, would you mind listening to a new song real quick?"

"Sure." Not having completely recovered from the wild day they'd had at the clinic, she was happy for the opportunity to sit down. She'd put in fifteen catheters and four PICC lines, not to mention eight or nine dressing changes. She didn't bother to count the IV's she'd restarted.

Following him into his apartment, she took a seat on the couch. With a wink, Joey switched on the amp and plugged in his guitar and then, to her orgasmic delight, stripped down to nothing but a black lace thong. When he turned away to slip the guitar strap over his head, the sight of the leather strap across his back and the strip of lace between his buns nearly triggered a seizure.

"Holy shit," she whispered. "I can't decide whether you look better from the front or the back."

He wiggled his ass before turning to face her again. "Am I making your pussy wet?"

"Oh, yeah." She stared at his thong with open fascination. "You are so totally *hot*..."

"I know." With a seductive smirk, he ran his fingers down the neck of the guitar, picking out a long, sensuous riff. "Wanna fuck me?"

"Always," she replied. "But play the song first."

"I will, but don't forget, you're my groupie tonight. During the breaks, I'm gonna kick back while you suck me off." The thong barely contained his dick as it was, but his quick pelvic thrust threatened to rip the lace.

She let out a whimper. "Will you spank me afterward?"

He flicked a brow. "Absolutely."

Tracy's pussy was already on fire as he began playing the song—one she'd never heard before. With a strong rap beat, it had more melody than the typical rap song and an intricately beautiful guitar accompaniment.

I like the way you always reach for me
There's lots of heat in everything I see
I want to feel you going down on me
I want to feel your love surrounding me
You're all I want, I want it all for me
You're so hot, baby, suck me...so hard

Tracy was creaming her jeans by the first chorus, and if the lyrics alone hadn't done it, his moves certainly would have. He made Elvis, Rod Stewart and anyone else she could think of look like a bunch of minister's wives at a church social, grinding his hips as though trying to fuck her from across the room.

I want your body, pretty baby
I want to eat you, sweet lady
I want to fuck you, sexy lady
Don't ever let me go, baby

You're so hot, baby, suck me...so hard

From her position on the sofa, his dick was right at eye level—he'd even shortened the strap so the guitar didn't hide it—and when he unsnapped one side of the thong, the tiny scrap of lace slid to the floor. Free of restraint, his cock bounced with the beat as he began the second verse.

I want to show you what you do to me
I want to feel you getting hot for me
Don't ever tell me you don't want me
Just open wide and bring your love to me
I'll take you for a fuckin' ride on me
You're so hot, baby. Fuck me...so hard

By the time the song ended, his cock was dripping and Tracy was stripping, throwing her panties at him like any self-respecting groupie.

"Where on earth did you find that song?"

He flipped the strap off with a flourish and set the guitar back in the stand. "You said you liked sexy rap songs, so I wrote that one for you."

"You wrote a rap song for me?" she squealed. "No shit?"

"No shit," he replied. "Ready to give me some head?"

"Oh, God, yes. Anything you want."

"Damn, you're easy," he said with a grin.

She threw her shirt at him as he advanced toward her, his sword at the ready. "Aw, why don't you just shut up and fuck me?"

"Oh, no," he said, sliding the head of his cock across her lips. "You're my groupie, and I'm the hot-ass rock star. Suck my dick, baby."

She gave him a big, long swipe with her tongue, getting a mouthful of syrup as she shuddered with desire. "Not getting LSD, are you?"

"You mean Lead Singer Disease?" He rubbed his cock along the curve of her cheek. "Not very likely seeing as how I'm not the lead singer. How about LGD?"

"Lead Guitarist Disease?" She shook her head. "Doesn't have

the same ring to it."

"Maybe not, but would you suck my dick anyway?"

She shot him a coy grin. "Say please."

"Tracy, sweetheart, would you please suck my dick?"

"Sure thing." She trailed her fingers over his pulsating penis. "But I want the thong on you with your dick sticking out of it."

Snatching up the thong, he snapped it into place with his cock off to one side. "Like that?"

"Oh, *yeah*," she whispered. "*All* guys should wear black lace undies."

He sighed, sliding his slick cockhead past her parted lips. "Mmm... I think I love you, Trace."

The next two verses had a slightly different rhythm, and he sang them without the guitar, rocking his hips to the beat while he fucked her face.

You like my hard cock when it's covered in lace
I'll stick it in your mouth, and I'll rub it on your face
Lick my dick, baby, suck it to the base
You make me want to come all over the place
Eat my cum, baby and don't leave a trace
You're too hot, baby, suck me...so hard

Lick my dick, baby, suck my balls 'til I yell "ouch"
You make me wanna shoot my wad right into your mouth
I'll fuck you in the kitchen, and I'll fuck you on the couch
I'll fuck you in your pussy, and I'll fuck you down south
Don't stop baby, fuck me...so hard.

On the final note, Joey fired off a round that hit Tracy in the face and splattered all over her chest.

I'm losing it...

Yanking off the thong, she pulled him down on the couch and rolled him onto his back. With an ecstatic moan, she buried her face in his groin, then rose up to glide her cum-slick tits over his cock and balls. As she gazed up at him through lashes mascaraed with his semen, Tracy knew that if Geena ever *did* come back, she would fight tooth and nail for him. Geena had relinquished her claim, and Tracy wasn't about to let him go. Ever.

He's mine now.

Chapter 25

Joey had a feeling they weren't going to make it to dinner that night—especially when Tracy took his hand and pulled him upright.

Stretching out across his lap, she tossed her hair over her shoulder and wiggled her butt. "Spank me."

At least my dick isn't stuffed in a panty girdle. The last time he'd spanked her, he was afraid his dick would never straighten out again. Now he wasn't sure it would ever get soft. "I'm not sure I want to." He fondled the smooth skin of her bottom. "I think I'd rather kiss it."

"Smack it a few times, and you can do anything you want with it."

Joey closed his eyes, biting his lip. If he hadn't just come all over her tits, he probably would've shot another wad. "You're killing me, Trace."

"Hey, you're the one wearing thongs and singing sexy rap songs. I'm just the groupie responding to your hotness."

He had his own ideas about who was the hotter of the two, and it certainly wasn't *him*. Sinking his fingers into her soft flesh, he didn't know which he wanted to do first—spank her, bite her, kiss her, or lick her. "Maybe, but you've still got the most succulent behind I've ever seen." Giving her a slap that stung his palm, he crawled out from under her to lie between her outstretched legs. "I need to bite it."

Tracy let out a groan as he sank his teeth into her ass. "Whatever you say, Mr. Hotshot Rockstar. I'm all yours."

Growling, he pressed a kiss to the back of her leg. "Roll over. I want to give you my own version of a screaming orgasm."

She flipped onto her back and spread her legs wide. "Eat me."

Joey dove in face first, sliding his tongue between her labia. "My God, you taste good." Not quite as sweet as honey, but the consistency was similar. "I'll have to write another song about that."

"Too bad you can't sing and lick me at the same time."

"I could try—or I could record the song and play it back while I suck your clit. Mmm...soft, wet, sweet...the possibilities are endless. It'll be the biggest hit ever." Closing his eyes, he lapped at the tight nub, loving the way it twitched against his tongue.

"I already like it, and I haven't even heard it yet." She gasped as he thrust his tongue inside her, stretching it to the limit. "I like that, too."

"Just returning the favor." He paused, flicking her clit with the tip of his tongue before sucking it hard. "I wouldn't want to lose my groupie to the lead singer."

"Never," she whispered breathlessly. "They're just a bunch of cocky bastards who don't know when to shut up."

"Don't like guys who run off at the mouth, do you?"

"Nope. Especially not when they're doing what you're doing. Although it does feel nice when you talk with your mouth full."

"Hmm...maybe I should try singing after all."

"Humming is nice. Better than a vibrator."

"I'm glad you think so. I'd hate to be replaced by my own strap-on."

"Trust me, you're better. I like the way you tease." She let out a sigh as she settled deeper into the seat cushion. "I don't think I'll scream, Joey. It feels fabulous, but I'm too comfortable. I have to work pretty hard for that kind of orgasm."

"No problem. I'm having a good time here."

"You say the nicest things," she murmured. "Go ahead. Knock yourself out."

He gave it his all and was ultimately rewarded when she had a whopper of an orgasm. Rising up off the couch, she grabbed him by the hair and pressed his mouth against her pussy. She even screamed.

Nope, not letting this one get away. Even if he had to tie her to the bed with her own bra.

On the thought, his balls tightened, threatening to unload another shot. "Be right back." Retrieving a condom from the back pocket of his jeans, he rolled it onto his cock with trembling hands. This woman did things to him no one had ever done. Turned him into a rutting stag. Made him want to fuck her until he couldn't fuck anymore.

Resuming his place between her thighs, he pulled her feet up onto his shoulders and took the plunge. Good, but not as good as it would be without the latex between them.

I want to make a baby.

He would marry her before he did that. Right now, he just needed to fuck her. Give her pleasure and make her moan.

Glancing down, he watched his dick gliding in and out of her hot body. She was like candy—or an addictive drug—and he knew he could never get enough of her. Now that he was inside her, the sense of urgency eased enough for him to play around with different angles and rhythms. He wanted to spend the rest of his life finding new ways to drive her wild. Pushing in as hard as he could, he wiggled his hips back and forth.

Her swift inhale made him smile. She was so responsive, never holding anything back. If something felt good to her, she let him know. He loved the feedback—instantaneous and uncensored.

"Hey," she whispered. "How about playing with those nipple rings?"

"You mean you want *me* to do it?"

"Oh, yeah… So fucking hot…"

Releasing his hold on her legs, he flipped both nipples just hard enough to hurt a teensy bit, sending a lightning bolt to his dick. "I won't last as long," he warned.

"Doesn't matter. I want to watch you make yourself come."

He could've argued that he could make himself come simply by sticking his dick in her pussy, but didn't bother. "Play with your tits, baby. Show me what you like."

"That thing you just did. Doesn't it hurt?"

"Yeah, but it has another effect. Try it."

Pressing her middle fingers against her thumbs, she gave each nipple a hard flip.

And had an orgasm.

At least, that was what it looked and felt like. Her upper body snapped up off the couch, and her pussy squeezed his cock like a vise.

"Holy cow," she exclaimed. "*That* was different!"

"If you do it too often, you'll get sore, but yeah, every once in a while is good."

"*Shockingly* good." Her eyes widened as she gave her head a quick shake. "Wow."

"You have to be careful with the nipple rings, too—can't tug on them too much."

"I'll be careful," she promised, then frowned. "I'm still thinking about getting mine pierced. Do you know if it affects your ability to breast feed?"

He laughed. "Doesn't affect *my* ability at all."

Scowling, she gave his hair a yank. "You know what I mean."

"Yeah. I've known some women who didn't have any trouble at all and others that did."

"Hmm… Maybe I should wait, then."

If it hadn't been for the condom, Joey would've made her pregnant right then. She could make him come harder and faster than anyone else ever had—and sometimes without any warning whatsoever.

"Will you make up your mind?" she demanded, giggling. "First you come when I say I *will* get them pierced, and now you come when I say I ought to wait."

Joey had to take several deep breaths before he could speak, and he *still* gasped out his reply. "Maybe it's because we're talking about your tits." At least, that was the easiest explanation. The other one involved babies and breastfeeding.

And we've only been together for a week.

Was this what happened when you found the right woman? He

certainly hadn't felt that way when he and Geena first got together. He'd freaked out when she told him she was pregnant. On the other hand, if Tracy were to make a similar announcement, he would've been ecstatic.

Huge difference.

"Guess I'd better wear an all-concealing sweatshirt to dinner. Wouldn't want you to jizz in your jeans during dessert."

Dinner? "Yeah, right. Dinner. Where are we going?"

"I'm not sure we ever decided, but I'm going to assume it wasn't pizza."

"You got *that* right. How about a steak?"

"Perfect."

ഇൻ

Considering the fact that her most recent dinner date involved the drive-thru at McDonald's, Tracy would've settled for anyplace she could sit down and order a meal from an honest-to-God waitress. She liked Mickey D's food well enough, but she had a feeling she might wind up with a drive-thru phobia.

Not with Joey.

Hell, Joey could've taken her to the grocery and she'd have been happy.

There it was again—that sense of normalcy. The everyday stuff like buying toilet paper and milk—the most mundane errand would turn into a fun date if she was with Joey. Watching guitar practice had been an unexpected bonus.

She pulled on her jeans, a little sad that he was putting his pants on too. "How often do you and the band get together to practice?"

"Whenever we can. Working different schedules makes it tough."

"Would you mind—that is, could I come with you sometime?"

"Sure." He shrugged into his shirt. "Cynthia and Angie show up once in a while. Dave's brought women before—and I mean that in the plural sense."

"Does more than one at a time, huh?"

Joey chuckled. "I wouldn't know about that, but I've heard rumors."

She studied him for a moment. "Do the guys in the band know about your eclectic taste in underwear?"

"Wouldn't surprise me if they did, but nobody's ever said anything. I mean, *I* never told them, but—"

"Some of *your* women might have?"

"It's possible, but I doubt it. Not sure the guys would care. It's not like it affects my guitar playing—at least, not adversely. They'd probably complain more if I stopped." He glanced downward, seeming to give an inordinate amount of attention to tying his shoelaces. "And then there's you."

"Me?"

He nodded, still not meeting her eyes. "Remember that night at Cider Hill?"

"Yeah. You said you played differently because I was there."

"That's right, I did." His gaze finally met hers. "I gave some of my best performances while fantasizing about you. Brad wanted to know what I was on during that New Year's Eve gig. All I'd had to drink was water. I was high on *you.*" His voice dropped to a whisper. "And you weren't even there. I tried to duplicate it at Cider Hill and couldn't do it—maybe it was because I'd asked you to come, and I didn't think you had. I'm still not sure, but as soon as I saw you…"

"Are you saying I need to be there for you to play well?"

"I don't know. Maybe." Tugging at his lip with his teeth, he drew in a ragged breath. "I'm not sure I want to find out. I think I'll be okay now that we're…together." He smiled, his eyes bright with unshed tears. "We *are* together, aren't we?"

She nodded slowly. "I believe we are—that is, if we aren't too scared to admit it."

"It *is* kinda scary. We've been having a lot of fun, but we both know how much it can hurt when the fun's over. I *really* don't want this to end."

"What would make it end—for you, I mean?"

His sigh reflected all the tentative hope she felt herself. "I can't think of a single thing."

A quiet voice in the back of her mind told her to let go. To embrace the fear and uncertainty, to stop thinking and just feel. "That's all I needed to hear. If you want me, I am *so* yours."

Chapter 26

I ought to pinch myself.

Joey slid in behind the wheel of his car, stunned by the realization that after everything he and Tracy had done together, this was their first real date. They'd had so much fun when he was Anna. Could they duplicate that chemistry and excitement?

At least Tracy wasn't crying this time. He hoped she could put her past behind her enough to enjoy herself. Battered women carried scars that often went unnoticed, and the last time she'd been on a date with a man—at least, a man she *knew* was a man—she'd gotten the shit beat out of her.

He stole a glance at her as she buckled her safety belt.

Oh, yeah. The nerves were *definitely* there—the rough clearing of her throat, the quick swipe of a fidgety hand over her nose followed by a brief touch to the side of her head. *He* knew she wasn't in any danger, but she was plainly remembering another date that had gone sour in a heartbeat.

"There's a new restaurant over by the cinemas that's supposed to be really good," he said. "Would that be okay with you? It's bound to be really crowded, but—"

"Hey, as long as you don't freak out when we have to wait for an hour."

He laughed. "I'm not wound quite that tight."

"Glad to hear it." Although she was smiling, constraint colored her voice.

Unsure as to his best course of action—should he open the topic for discussion or ignore it?—he fished in the console and handed her the box of CD's. "Lady's choice."

He wanted to kiss her again, just to prove he wasn't going to backhand her in the nose, but when she popped in *Stevie Wonder's Greatest Hits* and skipped to "Signed Sealed Delivered," he knew he had her.

"We must be on the same wavelength," he said. "I've been humming that song for days."

Her grin was genuine this time. "I know. Now I want to hear you *sing* it."

She turned up the volume and started singing, and just like that, they were back to the same vibe they'd had the night he'd been wearing mascara and a skirt. Granted, he was wearing the lace thong, but *still...*

They'd reached the first stoplight when the song ended. Tears sliding down her cheeks, Tracy reached for him, giving him the kiss he'd longed for. "Thank you so much for being sweet and normal and reasonable—and fun."

Although he might argue with the normal part, the reasonable description fit him to a T. "Don't need a big, hairy Neanderthal to protect you?"

"Nope. A man with a guitar is all the protection I need."

Aw, hell... "I love you, Trace. I truly do."

She started to lean toward him again, but checked herself. "That isn't a guy on the rebound talking, is it?"

"Rebound? No way. That's a totally smitten, love-drunk, songwriting romantic who's finally found the perfect woman talking."

"Oh, my…"

When the ensuing kiss was interrupted by the horn-honking motorist behind them, Joey released her with a wink. "Hold that thought."

She hadn't said *I love you*, but Joey didn't have to hear the words. He could *feel* them.

And they felt incredibly good.

༄༅

Tracy walked into the restaurant still reeling from something as simple as a drive across town.

No. It was more than that. It was…she didn't know *what* it was.

Elation? Joy?

Love?

After being warned about a forty-five minute wait, Joey took the pager from the hostess without batting an eyelash. "Why don't we wait in the bar? She said we could eat there if we find a place to sit."

Tracy nodded and followed him as he threaded his way through the throng. "A lot like the mosh pit in here, isn't it?"

He tossed a grin over his shoulder. "Music isn't quite as loud. Want a drink?"

She didn't like champagne enough to ask for it, but it seemed appropriate somehow. Still, tequila was her friend. "How about a margarita on the rocks?"

"You got it."

Tracy leaned against a room divider topped with trailing plants and studied the décor—anything to keep her eyes and hands off Joey's hot ass and gorgeous hair. The rustic brickwork seemed vaguely Italian, and tropical fish swam in a tank behind the bar with TV screens high on the wall above it. Joey ordered their drinks and paid for them, handing her a margarita before taking a swig out of a bottle of Blue Moon.

In that instant, the money issue hit her. Margaritas were expensive. "Thanks. How about I pay for dinner since you got the drinks?"

A flicker of emotion crossed his features too quickly for her to register whether it was hurt, annoyance, or simply acknowledgement. "You can pay next time."

I should've kept my mouth shut.

Money wasn't an issue if she didn't choose to make it into one. Still, without Geena's income, Joey was bound to be a little strapped paying rent on a two-bedroom apartment. Tracy's one-bedroom cost her plenty.

"I'm just thinking about the drinks you bought for me at Cider Hill."

He actually laughed. "That's one of the perks of being in the band. We don't pay for drinks. Neither do our dates."

"I hadn't thought of that." When the waitress told her the drinks were covered, Tracy assumed she meant that Joey was paying for them. Perhaps she'd misunderstood... "Must be nice. Nurses don't get perks of any kind."

"Not even a free Band-Aid?"

"Nope. Well...maybe a free flu shot and a TB test every year, but that's about it."

"Ever thought about a different career?"

She shrugged. "Not really. I like the clinic and the people I work with. Just wish our hospital hadn't been sold to one of the big healthcare conglomerates. After telling us everything would be business as usual, they've instituted one change after another—and none for the better. Staffing sucks, and half the time we don't have the supplies we need. Pretty soon they'll have us wearing matching uniforms and acting like a bunch of Stepford nurses." Shaking her head, she pasted on a smile. "Enough about that. We're here to have fun, not drown our sorrows. Right?"

"Right. But if you could quit and be a stay-at-home mom, would you do it?"

She only had to think a second before snorting a laugh. "When half the nurses I know are working two jobs to pay for daycare and their deadbeat husbands? Not likely."

"Let's say you didn't have a deadbeat husband. Would you miss going to work every day?"

Tracy shrugged and took a sip of her drink. "I'd miss the people. I'm probably closer to them than I am to my sister. Melina and I are pretty tight."

It was his turn to snicker. "I've noticed."

"Yeah. The ball-ripping threat didn't surprise me a bit." She hesitated before furthering her reply. Did he really need to know all of it? Maybe he did. "There was a time when I thought of nothing beyond being a wife and a mother. But with Miranda as an example of what can happen even with a happy marriage, Mom insisted I go to nursing school so I wouldn't have to depend on a man to support me—and I never have. Not sure I could do it now. It would be...strange."

He took a sip of his beer. "I can understand that. Be nice to have the choice, though—wouldn't it?"

"Yeah. But I don't." She shrugged. "Moot point."

Joey nodded and didn't say anything for a moment or two. "We're practicing at Brad's place tomorrow afternoon. Want to come along?"

"On one condition."

He eyed her expectantly.

"I want you to play some of your own songs."

He shook his head, grimacing. "Brad never wants to do that—and he's the bandleader."

"Doesn't he want to make the big time?"

"Not really. He's afraid he'd have to spend too much time away from his family. He and Angie have a three-year-old and a baby. I can't blame him for that."

"But to not even *try*? That seems sort of—"

"Inconsiderate? Maybe."

"Have you ever thought of going solo or starting your own band?"

Joey gaped at her like she was nuts. "I'm not good enough to go solo, and we've been together a long time."

She arched a brow. "I've heard you sing, and I've heard you play—your own songs, too. I'm no music critic, but I think you're selling yourself short."

"I *am* short."

"No jokes now," she warned. "You're talented and you know it. And besides, what good is all my inspiration if you're going to keep on doing the same routines?"

"I'm not arguing with you. And yes, I could start my own band, but it's tough finding the right people. I might have better luck auditioning for an established group that needs a new guitarist. That sort of thing happens all the time—even Barton Junction's current drummer isn't the original."

"Yeah. Might be worth keeping a lookout for them." She glanced up just as an older couple got up from the bar. The woman gestured at her chair. "Look, they're giving us their spot."

"Great," Joey said. "I'll take the pager back to the hostess."

Tracy had an idea he'd been pleased by the interruption, but she wasn't going to let the subject drop. If Joey's ambitions were being stifled by Brad, well...Joey could easily be a lead singer himself, despite his protests to the contrary. He had a unique quality to his voice—not to mention a totally sexy style. Brad might've been the handsome frontman, but Joey was the one who'd drawn her eye.

Because you already thought he was hot.

No. That wasn't all of it. When Joey shifted into high gear, the whole band had gone with him. She hadn't imagined that. He had star potential, and getting the big break had as much to do with luck as it did talent. Unfortunately, Pemberton, Indiana wasn't the place for big breaks.

But if he were to leave town...

Tracy wasn't sure she wanted to encourage him to do that. He'd said he couldn't think of anything that would end their budding relationship. Leaving Pemberton just might do it.

You're thinking too much. Tracy knew she tended to overthink things, and it always amazed her when others claimed not to share the same affliction. Even reading Eckhart Tolle's *The Power of Now* hadn't cured her.

Maybe I need to read it again...

A glance at the doorway caught his return, making her suck in a breath. He was so *totally* hot—and her head wasn't the only one that turned. It might've only been the hair, but right now she didn't care. Shocking as it seemed, he was hers—something else she couldn't quite wrap her head around.

Climbing onto the barstool beside her, he draped an arm around her shoulders and kissed her. "Did you miss me?"

"Absolutely."

When he was there beside her, she had fewer doubts—although nothing could completely shut down her annoying brain.

Tequila is my friend, and Joey loves me. She took another sip. Funny how being happy was almost as much of a drain on her as being miserable and lonely. Reminding herself to live in the now, she leaned closer to Joey and inhaled his scent, smiling as his hair tickled her cheek.

"I could get used to this," she said.

"What? Hanging out in bars with not-so-famous rock stars?"

"No." She closed her eyes and focused on the moment—one she wanted to remember and cherish for a long, long time. "Hanging out with *you*."

Chapter 27

After a night of love and blissful slumber followed by a breakfast to die for, Tracy went with Joey to Brad's house for practice.

"You really *are* a garage band, aren't you?" Tracy chuckled as she took a seat in the corner of the cleanest garage she'd ever seen.

"If you can call this a garage," Brad said. "It's never had a car in it."

"Do the neighbors ever complain about the noise?"

Brad shook his head. "It's sealed up pretty tight. I insulated the walls and added a double layer of drywall and acoustic foam panels to cut the flutter echo."

She glanced around the room, noting the thick, padded carpet and heavy curtains. "The band must be doing pretty well for you to afford to do all this."

Brad shrugged. "Depending on the size of the venue, we can get up to five hundred bucks for a forty-minute gig. Seemed worth it."

As much as he'd put into the retrofit, Tracy had an idea it could easily be used as a recording studio. They already had what appeared to be a decent mixer and plenty of microphones. All they needed was a little software and a recording system.

Too bad Brad was so resistant to the idea of producing a demo. According to Joey, he considered the band to be more of a hobby than a lifestyle. She couldn't blame him for that. Lots of musicians opted to stay put rather than go out on the road.

During a break, the guys discussed the arrangement of a new song they were learning while Tracy did a search on her phone. For about four hundred dollars, they could get a digital multi-track system with built-in CD burner. One gig would pay for it.

She considered gifting them with one herself, even though it was a tricky offer to make, especially since she didn't know the guys very well. Perhaps an alternate approach would be best...

"Ever thought about renting this place out as a recording studio?" she asked Brad.

"Not really," Brad replied. "Anyone who used it would have to have their own equipment."

One glance at Joey was enough to assure her that he knew exactly why she'd asked that question. "But if they did, would you consider it?"

"Maybe. Might actually pay for itself eventually."

Figuring she'd put enough of a bug in everyone's ear, she simply nodded and let the matter drop.

As they continued with the practice session, Tracy became even more convinced that they were missing an incredible opportunity. She'd seen the size of the crowds they could draw. Granted that was only in Pemberton, but she was sure that with adequate promotion they could fill a larger venue. If they were to play in Louisville or Indianapolis, they might actually get noticed.

She had to ask herself what her motivation was and decided it wasn't so much what she would get out of it as Joey's girlfriend as it was for Joey himself. She hated to see his talent hidden under a rock and doubted he considered making pizzas a viable alternative to stardom. When they played The Wallflowers' "Sixth Avenue Heartache," she was sure of it. Having a gravelly voice similar to Jakob Dylan's, Joey sang the lead with Brad providing the harmony. And the guitar solo...*wow*.

You idiot. It wasn't very high quality, but her *phone* could record a song, and with acoustics like this...

"That was awesome! I *love* that song. Would you mind playing it again?"

Brad shrugged. "Sure."

༄༅

"You are one tricky little woman." Joey stowed his guitar in the trunk of his car, unable to suppress a grin.

Tracy arched a brow. "Why, whatever do you mean?"

Her innocent tone and sly grin didn't fool him for a second. "Let's just plug your phone into the audio jack on the way home and play back everything you recorded."

"Was it that obvious?"

"Probably only to me since I'm the one who can't keep his eyes off you. Did you buy that digital recorder you were looking at?"

Her eyes narrowed. "And you think *I'm* a tricky little woman. I've got *nothing* on you."

"Did you buy it?"

"No—although I *was* tempted. You might as well admit it, you've thought about getting one yourself."

"Yeah. Just never had the money to spare."

Her incredulous gaze was augmented by a slow wag of her head. "You guys have no idea how good you are, do you?"

He shrugged. "Maybe not. But lots of bands make their own CDs on those recorders and pass them out to their families at Christmas. Most of them are crap. We've never done that."

"Yeah, well, if you did, they wouldn't be crap—far from it." She stared at him for a long moment. "What do you really want, Joey? You could have it all if you put yourself out there."

"The new manager speaks?"

"Maybe. Tell me you don't want it, Joey. Tell me and I'll let it drop."

He wanted it, all right. In the past, he'd simply been too chicken to take the plunge. *But now?*

Her encouragement made a huge difference and her confidence in him made him capable of so much more. Everything about her made him better—in so many ways. "Okay. You're right. I want it. And I want it with my own songs."

"Just what I needed to hear." She waved her phone. "I'm going to send this to some friends who own a club in Louisville—a big one. I'd rather be sending a demo of original material, but this will do. Do you trust me?"

He sputtered out a laugh. "Do I *trust* you? Good God, Trace. I'd trust you with my life."

Her smile warmed the cockles of his heart. "I can't promise a recording contract, but I'm pretty sure this will get you a show. Are you willing to travel that far?"

"*I* am. Don't know about the others—especially Brad. We've never had an offer like that."

"I find that hard to believe—and I'm not just saying it because I love you."

Joey gulped in a breath, momentarily unable to focus on anything besides those last three words. "I–I didn't have you to love and inspire me before. I wasn't that good—hell, *we* weren't that good." He pulled her into his arms. "Do you really love me, Trace?"

"Oh, *yeah*."

He couldn't believe his luck. Somewhere, somehow, he must've done something to deserve her. Was it simply because he'd rescued her from Bryce? Or did good deeds really result in better karma?

He didn't have any answers, and at the moment, he didn't particularly care. His lips met hers, and he slid his hands down her back to cup her jean-clad bottom, pulling her against his stiffening cock. Lost in the scent and feel of her nestled in his embrace, he kissed his way to her ear. "We'd better get in the car before someone calls the cops or yells at us to get a room."

"I'm all for that." She sighed. "I love being your groupie."

"I think we might have to promote you to manager—especially if you get us a gig in Louisville."

"Do I get a percentage?"

"Of what?"

"Of you."

"No worries there, babe. You can have a hundred percent of me every damn day."

༄༅

Tracy hadn't seen Linda Taylor since she'd moved to Louisville six years ago, but Linda hadn't forgotten her. There were advantages to keeping your Christmas card list up-to-date.

"I listened to the songs you sent," Linda said. "Those guys are damn good. I'm sure Jackson will offer them a gig—although probably for less than we usually pay because they're unknown here."

"I don't think they'd mind that. What bothers me is that the bandleader is something of a homebody."

"Doesn't like to travel, huh? Are you, um involved with him?"

"Not exactly," Tracy replied. "I'm more into the lead guitarist."

"Gotcha. Hey, do you want the credit if we ask them to play here?"

"No. In fact, I'd rather you didn't mention my name at all because if this backfires, I don't want anyone pointing fingers at me."

"What about your boyfriend? Does he know?"

"Yeah. But he can keep a secret." *Trust me on that one.* "They play at a place called the Cider Hill Tavern fairly often. Anyone could've seen them there." Tracy gave her Brad's contact information before doing a little catching up. "Still working at the hospital?"

"Nope. Had to give it up. Should've said something in my Christmas card, but I'm finally pregnant!"

"Congratulations! You've been trying forever."

"No kidding. After so many miscarriages, I've been afraid to tell anyone," Linda confided. "This time my doc put me on bed rest right away. I'm bored out of my mind, but I've only got three weeks to go."

"Boy or girl?"

"It's a boy. Jackson is freaking out."

Tracy chuckled. "I'll bet he is." Jackson Taylor had never struck Tracy as the fatherly type—or one to freak out about anything. A giant of a man with bushy red hair and the longest, thickest beard Tracy had ever seen, he looked more like a biker than a successful businessman—although he *had* started out as a bartender.

"Melina's got two kids now, doesn't she?"

"A boy and a girl." *A husband and two kids and a house and a dog and a cat.* All those things Tracy had never been able to acquire.

"What about you and the guitar player? Any plans?"

"Not yet. We've known each other for a while, but we only got together a week ago."

"Recently divorced?"

"No, recently dumped. He's my hero, actually."

"Care to share the details?" Linda drawled.

"It's, uh, complicated."

"I imagine so. If you come along with the band, you'll have to fill me in. Unless someone cancels, we're booked for the next two months. It'll be interesting to see what happens between now and then."

Understatement of the whole fucking year. "No shit. In the meantime, keep in touch. I want to hear all about that baby—pictures, too."

"Trust me, if all goes well, there *will* be pictures and lots of them." She paused. "I hope everything works out between you and the guitar player."

At one time, Linda had been as close a friend as Melina. She knew Tracy's history all too well.

"Me, too, Linda," Tracy said. "Me, too."

Chapter 28

Joey may have promised Tracy could have a hundred percent of him every day, but by the following Friday, only getting late nights and early mornings with him had her desperate for the weekend.

Then she got an idea. A perfectly *wicked* idea…

She went to Georgio's for dinner. Alone. After ordering the lasagna and a glass of Chianti from a blonde waitress named Sandy, she sat back in her booth and waited.

When Sandy brought her entrée, one bite of the lasagna nearly triggered a foodgasm.

"Everything okay?" the waitress asked when she stopped by a few minutes later.

"Amazing," Tracy replied. "I think I need to compliment the cook—personally."

Sandy shot her a wink. "I'll send him right out."

Tracy's only fear was that Joey wasn't the only cook. However, she needn't have worried because it wasn't long before Joey came sauntering out of the kitchen. Meeting his look of surprise with a purposely bland expression, she hoped he would get the message.

Apparently, he did. "Sandy said you wanted to speak with me. Is everything okay?"

With a deep sigh, Tracy raked his body with a sizzling gaze that rested on his groin for a moment before returning to meet his eyes. "So *you're* the one," she purred. "*Terrific* sauce. I've never had better lasagna anywhere, and I've been to Italy—twice."

Her blatant lie reinforced the masquerade. "Why, thank you, ma'am," he said, his perfectly correct and polite reply in sharp contrast to the carnal glint in his eyes. "I was afraid you were going to say you'd found a long, curly hair on your plate."

"I should have," she drawled. "It would've given me an excuse for a more *private* word with you. Heaven forbid you should lose your job, but I'd hate for such gross negligence to go unnoticed—or unpunished."

His eyes flashed at the mention of punishment, encouraging her to take it a step further. "If, for example, I were to find a long, curly hair in my *dessert*, I think I'd have to do something about it. Later, perhaps—after you get off work."

"I'll see what I can do." His lips curled into a provocative grin. "I'll bring your dessert myself."

"You do that."

Otherwise, the poor waitress will have a cow.

When Tracy ordered her dessert, she made a point of asking Sandy to have Joey bring it out.

"No problem," Sandy said with a knowing smile.

Moments later, Joey came out of the kitchen with a piece of cheesecake smothered in raspberry sauce and placed it before Tracy with a flourish. "Your dessert, madam," he said, sounding a bit like an English butler. "I trust you will enjoy it."

Glancing down at her plate, Tracy nearly choked when she spotted a rather *short*, curly strand trailing from the edge of the dish, held in place by a droplet of clear, viscous fluid. For a moment, she teetered on the brink of a screaming orgasm right there in the middle of the restaurant.

How he'd managed to do it without anyone else noticing, she couldn't begin to guess, but if his saintly expression was anything to go by, that hair hadn't come from his head. Tracy was pretty sure it wasn't attached to the plate with a droplet of corn syrup or honey—or anything else that might have come out of a bottle.

Discreetly removing the hair with a fingertip, she transferred it to the front of her shirt to trail from the vicinity of her right nipple. She tasted the fluid, which was slightly salty.

Definitely not corn syrup.

"You are *so* bad," she said, her tone laced with reproach. "However, your presentation deserves high marks." With another sultry glance, she waved dismissively. "Go on back to work, baby. I'll deal with *you* later."

The corner of his mouth twitched, and he gave her a brief nod before returning to the kitchen, his swagger more pronounced than ever.

The cheesecake was fabulous, and Tracy lingered in the cool, dark booth, savoring every luscious, creamy bite. When she finished, she paid the check and left, intending to return after shopping for a few items she'd sworn she would never buy again—namely, a pair of high heels and a short skirt, plus a little something extra special for Joey.

Having made her purchases and changed her clothes, she returned to the restaurant and waited outside in her car with the doors locked. The parking lot was deserted by that hour, and she sat impatiently, her anticipation level nearly reaching the boiling point.

Finally, he left the building.

Unlocking the doors, she rolled down the window, calling out to him as he headed for his own vehicle. "Hey there, bad boy. You wouldn't be trying to leave here without me, would you?"

"Oh, no, ma'am," he replied. "I would *never* do that."

"Then get your cute little ass over here. I've got something for you." She dangled a scrap of red satin out the window. "I've been wearing this all evening, dreaming about what you'd look like in it. I'll let you have it if you'll get in the car with me."

He eyed her warily. "I thought I was going to be punished, not rewarded."

"Oh, you will be," she assured him. "Unless you're a *very* good boy."

With a cocky smirk, he went around and slid into the passenger seat. "I can be as good or as bad as you want me to be. You just tell me what you want."

"The customer's always right?"

"Something like that." He plucked the G-string from her fingers and held it up to his nose, inhaling deeply. With a satisfied smile, he lounged back in his seat. "What are you planning to do to me for rubbing my dick all over your plate?"

"First, I'm going to take you for a little ride, and then we'll see." She started the engine and drove to a dark corner of a nearby lot. Parking the car, she slid her seat back as far as it would go. "Take off your pants and put that on."

He arched a brow. "Is that the reward or the punishment?"

"The reward."

"No way." He dropped the satin garment in her lap. "I'd look like a fag in that."

"That's not a very nice thing to say. Besides, I disagree. I think you'd look totally hot wearing nothing but that."

"I'm not doing it." He set his jaw in defiance. "You can't make me."

"Perhaps not, but I can make you wish you'd said yes."

"How?"

Pivoting slowly in her seat, she leaned back against the door, spreading her legs wide as she rested a seductively clad foot on his shoulder. "I'll make you watch but not touch."

She stopped his lunge toward her with a spike heel applied to the side of his neck, forcing his head back. His hair swung back from his face, cascading down his back. He looked wild, and Tracy fought a brief skirmish with the desire to let him do anything he liked. Taking a deep breath, she gradually regained control.

"Not so fast." She pushed him away. Slowly. "You can have anything you want—eventually. You just have to play along."

His eyes were mere slits. "I'm not wearing that thing."

"Shh…" she whispered. "Just watch."

Reaching down, she teased her labia apart, coating her finger with her own hot juice before circling her clitoris with a fingertip. Joey let out a loud groan and reached for her.

She dug her heel in deeper, stretching his neck even further. "Unzip your pants. When you get them off, you can have some of this."

"Can I lick it?" His voice was a hoarse whisper, his eyes alight with lust.

"At least once," she replied. "Let me see your cock."

Growling in frustration, he reached down and exposed himself. "Is it big enough for you?"

She surveyed him with a critical eye. "Yes, but it's much too plain. Here." With a stroke of luck she couldn't have duplicated if she'd practiced for hours, the G-string landed on his slick cockhead and stuck there. "Dress it up a little."

"No. I won't do it," he said, his adamant tone displaying a determination to delay his gratification that was nothing short of heroic.

"Pants off all the way, or no pussy." She gave him another nudge with her heel and teased her clitoris again. "Hot, slick pussy... You want it, don't you?"

"Yes," he hissed.

"Take off your pants and put that on, and I'll give you the ride of your life."

"And if I don't?"

She smiled devilishly. "Then I'll spank your cute little butt until you'll do anything I tell you to. You'll be begging to wear whatever I say."

He sucked in a breath, and his cock pulsed, sending a rivulet of shining fluid pouring from his slit.

"You like that idea, don't you?" Slipping off her other shoe, she raised her leg up to stroke his cock with her foot. "Your dick likes it too."

Knowing Joey as well as she did, Tracy knew he couldn't decide whether to submit to the spanking or put on the thong. Either one was enough to send him into ecstatic oblivion, but she was offering him both—and the anticipation was undoubtedly driving him nuts.

"Which do you want?" she prompted. "A spanking or the thong?"

"Both," he growled. "I want it *all*."

In an instant, she released him, spinning around in her seat to tuck her legs beneath the dashboard. Seizing his hand, she yanked him across her lap and shoved his pants down, rubbing his bare ass while he groaned with pleasure. His breath hitched as she drew back her hand, and he let out a satisfied grunt as she gave him several loud, stinging slaps.

"Okay," he yelled. "I'll wear it."

"That's more like it," Tracy said. "I want you naked except for that."

Joey stripped off his shirt and skimmed his jeans down the rest of the way, kicking off his shoes along with them. Then he slid the red satin band on over his legs.

"Put the waistband under your cock and the crotch between your balls. Then pull it up tight in the back."

His cock had been incredibly hard the time he'd used her panties as a cock ring, but it was about to split apart now. Tearing open a condom packet, she attempted to roll it down over his engorged penis and failed. "It doesn't fit."

"Fuck me anyway," he pleaded. "I'll pull you off before I come."

At that point, Tracy didn't care what he did as long as she could get him inside her. Climbing onto his lap, she sat down, delighting in the feel of his unsheathed cock plunging into her pussy. This was it—her biggest, hottest turn-on—and not simply because there wasn't a barrier between them. She wanted this one to *count*.

He was going to have to pull her off because she didn't intend to move from that spot until long after he'd shot her full of semen. Grinding her hips into him, she bit her lip in an effort to regain control, but the thought of his cum-slick cock inside her rendered her efforts futile.

Joey leaned back against his seat, thrusting upward with a force that made her bounce. Moaning her appreciation, Tracy wished he could continue those long, penetrating strokes all night. Unfortunately, his excitement level was too high, and all too soon, he tightened his grip on her hips, his fingers digging into her flesh as he prepared to pull her off.

"No!" she screamed. "Don't—"

Too late. He was gone from inside her, his breath coming in loud gulps as his ejaculation shot across her bottom, covering her with cream. Tracy might have been screaming with frustration, but her body climaxed anyway as his hot, slick cock slid between her butt cheeks. Doubling over, she gripped his shoulders, burying her face in the curls nestled on his neck.

He'd undoubtedly assumed she was warning him not to come inside her, but that wasn't it at all. She longed for him to fill her with his seed, to plant it where she wanted it to grow. Tracy had conceived before, but she'd never delivered a living, breathing child—something she wanted to do more than anything in the world.

Not this time.

Swallowing her disappointment, she slid off of his lap and back into the driver's seat, opting to continue the act she'd begun. "Go on home now, baby. I believe I've punished you enough. Let that be a lesson to you not to do such a thing ever again."

He grinned sheepishly, no doubt blissfully unaware of the turn her thoughts had taken. "Yes, ma'am. I've learned my lesson. Next time I won't mess up your plate." With a wink, he added, "I'll just stick my dick in your mouth."

Chapter 29

Joey couldn't quite put his finger on the problem, but he had the strangest feeling he'd made a mistake of some kind.

"I'm not sure you got the lesson I was trying to teach," Tracy said with a sardonic smile. She nodded at his groin. "You might want to wear your own undies home. That's bound to be uncomfortable."

He placed a possessive hand on his satin-clad balls. "No way. It's mine now. I'll wear it if I want to."

"It sure did fabulous things to your cock. That's the first time I ever had trouble getting a condom on anyone. Might need to stock up on a larger size."

"They've always fit before." He tried another wink. "You may be onto something."

She returned his wink with a skeptical glance. "I'll bet you say that to all the girls."

"Not a single one." He couldn't tell if she was still role playing or not. "You're special, Trace. Haven't I made that clear?"

"I don't feel very special as a rule," she grumbled. "More like last week's newspaper with the good coupons clipped out."

Joey swallowed hard in an effort to tamp down his rising panic. Didn't his opinion carry any weight at all? Everything had been going so well. Had he missed something?

Maybe it's PMS. He hadn't been close enough to Tracy to know how hormone fluctuations affected her. Then again, maybe she'd had a really rotten day at the clinic.

"You're *very* special to me. Shit, nobody's *ever* given me a red G-string before."

That at least drew a smile. "The cashier probably thought I was buying it for myself."

"You mean you actually went into a shop and *bought* it for me?"

She snorted a laugh. "I didn't have much choice. I got rid of all my sexy stuff weeks ago—remember?"

"Yeah, I remember." Never having the guts to walk into a store, he'd ordered all of his stuff online. "That place you went to...could we go there together sometime?"

Her peal of laughter was devoid of cynicism—finally. "Are you kidding me? Your dick would get so hard you wouldn't be able to walk."

"I'd still like to go," he insisted. "Modeling thongs for you would be a blast." The mere thought made him quiver with anticipation.

"Your dick would drool all over everything you put on. I mean, *I'd* love to find a spot of your joy juice on my underwear, but I doubt anyone else would." She paused as though considering the possibilities. "Wish I'd known you liked lacy undies before I gave everything to the Goodwill."

"Yeah, right," he grumbled. "I'm sure I would have spoken right up at the time. Wish I had, though. I'll bet you had some really hot stuff."

"Being quite the exhibitionistic slut, I had lots of pretty things," she said with a chuckle. "It never occurred to me that I could find the perfect man without having to dress like a hooker. Speaking of which, how *did* I get your attention?"

The perfect man? Me? Wow... "It certainly wasn't because you were an exhibitionistic slut—which I doubt you ever were. I liked you from the first moment I met you."

"That's only because I held the door for you the day you and Geena moved in. As I recall, you were carrying a couch."

"Sure was. Then when Darren was born, you were so good with him..." He paused, closing his eyes for a moment to squelch the memory. *Best not to take that any further.* "And the way you handled Bryce showed a lot of spunk."

"Spunk, hell. I thought I was dead."

"Far from it," he said with a chuckle. "I once saw a cartoon of a mouse giving the finger to a hawk as it was about to strike. The caption said something about a last act of defiance. You reminded me of that."

At least she's smiling.

Sighing, he raked a hand through his hair. "I was still so fucked up. But that day we exchanged phone numbers and you gave me the concert ticket—"

"Aha! I knew that ticket had something to do with it."

"—and you *kissed* me and called me your hero. My dick hadn't been hard in weeks, but I got a *serious* tingle." He shrugged. "After that, my imagination ran wild, especially at the concert. I wanted to fuck you so bad I could hardly stand it."

She sucked in a breath. "And I *wanted* you to."

"You sure had *me* fooled. I wasn't getting any encouragement at *all*. That stint as Anna was pure desperation. My imagination did a pretty good job of it, but honest to God, Trace, you blow me away every single day."

"You mean I *blow* you every day."

"That, too." He shot her a smirk. "Race you home."

"The loser gets an ass whippin'?"

Joey groaned like a man who hadn't been laid in months as opposed to mere minutes. "Mmm, yeah. I'd like to get yours stinging hot and fuck the hell out of it."

"Considering the size your cock got the last time, I'm not sure I want it in my ass."

"Can't blame you for that, but at least with ass fucking, a condom is optional."

She squirmed in her seat as though imagining his dick in her butt. "Okay. But try not to get arrested or have an accident on the way home. That would be bad."

"Don't worry. I'll be careful."

Her lips curled in a seductive grin. "And I'll be driving *slow*."

༄༅

By the time Joey reached their building, Tracy's car was nowhere in sight. Dashing up the stairs, he hurried into his apartment. He already had the music in mind—an instrumental album with a driving beat—setting the perfect mood and rhythm for sex. After turning on the stereo, he found a bottle of lube and a few other items and set them on the end table. Then, with the door open wide, he leaned against the jamb and waited. Moments later, she came through the outer door at the foot of the stairs.

"You're late," he said, tapping his watch. "Where the hell have you been?"

"Out," she replied as she reached the landing. Breezing past him, she pitched her purse onto the couch.

Joey closed the door, raising his chin in what he hoped was a pugnacious manner. "And just who were you out *with*?"

She shrugged. "Some guy who cooks at Georgio's. He makes the best lasagna in the world and he's *totally* hot. I've probably still got his cum on my ass."

Joey gulped, unable to decide whether to act outraged or not. Either way, his balls were about to explode.

"Want to see it?" Turning her back to him, she bent over. Her skirt was so short he could see everything, including the wet spot on the hem.

"Why you little *slut*." In a few quick strides, he was on her. Grabbing her around the waist, he yanked up her skirt and pushed her over the back of the couch. His first open-handed slap made her butt jiggle.

"I knew that would make you mad." Tossing a provocative smile over her shoulder, she gave her bottom a shake. "Come on, Joey, spank me. I am *such* a bad girl."

"No, you aren't," he said, but gave her another smack anyway. "You're the perfect woman, remember? And I'm gonna fuck the hell out of your red-hot ass."

She gasped as he hit her buns with the side of his arm. "Do it then. Get your dick wet and nail me in the ass. *Now*."

He certainly didn't need to get her pussy wet. Her juice was already halfway down her legs. Stripping to his skin, he slid his cock between her thighs, coating it with her moisture before gliding up to tease her anus. "You've got the most beautiful butt I've ever seen in my life. It makes me want to fuck like nothing else in the world—even red satin G-strings, and you *know* what they do to me."

She giggled. "They make your dick humongous."

"Oh, yeah," he groaned. "I'm gonna fuck you 'til I'm ready to come, and then I'm gonna pull out and jizz all over your ass again. Would you like that, baby?"

Her reply was more of a long, tortured moan than actual words.

"I'll take that as a yes." Snatching up the lube, he dribbled it between her butt cheeks and doused his dick with it. Pressing his cockhead against her anus, he began a slow, steady in-and-out thrust, delving deeper with each stroke. "So good, baby. So *fucking* good..."

Dancing to the beat of the drums, he fucked her in every possible direction, the way he'd wanted to fuck her in the mosh pit. Only this was better—much, *much* better...

He leaned in to growl in her ear. "Have you figured out yet why rock guitarists are so hot?"

Moaning, she shook her head.

"We've got the moves, Trace. I can fuck on the beat or fire off a riff and drive you completely insane—and I can keep it up for a long, long time, especially since I've already come once tonight."

By that point, the only sounds she seemed capable of making were high-pitched whimpers. Using her anal sphincter as a pivot point for his cock, he stirred his dick inside her like an oar swirling through lake water.

"I can play you like a guitar, too." He reached around to tease her clitoris with a calloused fingertip. "Just let me get my fingers on you, baby, and I'll have you screaming in no time."

"Cocky bastard," she gasped.

"Of course, that's *nothing* compared to what I can do to you with a guitar pick."

Retrieving a pick from the end table, he pulled her up off the couch and reached under her shirt. Using his fingers on her left nipple, he stroked the right with the pick.

Tracy arched against him in total surrender. "Do my clit!" The words seemed to burst from her lips.

He went after her clit with the pick, playing a long riff while still fucking her ass.

"Oh, my *God.* No one has *ever*…" An orgasm shook her, leaving her open-mouthed and helpless in his arms.

She was finished, but Joey wasn't. The next song had a strong, erotic beat, and he laid her over the back of the couch again, working her with short, firm thrusts. He hadn't been lying when he'd said he could keep it up for a long time, but he was almost disappointed when his body finally signaled his climax. Pulling out, he shot blasts of hot cum all over her gorgeous backside.

"I've always liked playing that song—and I knew it would be good for this." Placing his palms on her butt, he massaged his semen into her glowing skin. "Everyone on the dance floor looks like they're about to rip into each other, and now you know why." Landing another loud smack on her bottom, he hauled her into his arms and spun her around to face him. "Kiss me, Trace," he whispered. "Promise you'll never leave me."

She drew in a ragged breath and fell against him, pressing her lips into his. "Never. You'll have to throw me out."

"No danger of that," Sliding his hands down her back, he grabbed both cheeks and pulled her hard against his groin. "I'm never letting you go. I'll chain you to the wall if I have to. You're *mine*, baby."

"And you're mine. Any little groupie chick who gets within ten feet of you is toast."

"I like the sound of that." He devoured her lips, groaning with ecstasy as their tongues met. "From now on, every time I pick up a guitar, I'll be playing *you*—I'll feel you in my hands and play you for all I'm worth. The girls in the audience will think I'm hard because of them, but you're the one I'll be fantasizing about. Just *you*."

Chapter 30

Tracy had to hand it to Linda, she and Jackson had worded the offer well, plus they'd waited a few weeks before contacting Brad—possibly to defer suspicion from Tracy.

"It's a bar called the Comstock Lode—one of the biggest venues of its kind in Louisville," Brad said at the start of a Sunday afternoon practice session. "They've heard about us and know we're good, but they'd like for us to play some original material—the whole 'world premiere' thing. Since nobody's ever heard of us there, I guess they figure they need something extra to draw a crowd. The date isn't until the eighteenth of May, so we've got six weeks to prepare." He glanced at Joey. "I know you've got plenty of songs, and I know I've been resistant, but—"

"You want them now," Joey finished for him—although how he managed to say it without a trace of smugness or even a smirk, Tracy couldn't imagine.

She sat in her usual corner of Brad's garage keeping her mouth firmly shut, determined not to say anything that might give away their mini-conspiracy.

"We don't need songs from an *amateur* songwriter," Dave protested. "I've got a friend in Nashville who's actually *sold* a song."

Tracy literally had to bite her tongue after that comment. In her opinion, Dave was well on his way to getting Lead Singer Disease, and he was the damn drummer.

Fortunately, their group wasn't called the Brad Winters Band for nothing. "We've heard all about your buddy," Brad said. "He writes country, not rock."

Scowling, Dave muttered something unintelligible and

wandered off while the other guys gathered around. All of them seemed excited—even a little relieved—when Joey started pulling pages out of a thick binder.

According to Joey, Dave had always been a bit on the cocky side and having chicks crawling all over him had done nothing to improve his humility. Tracy had to admit—if only to herself—he *was* a handsome devil, and his girlfriend was no slouch. Unfortunately, he'd recently ditched her for Kiki, a blonde bimbo with big tits and a proclivity for tube tops and cutoffs that covered less of her than the average bikini. Considering it was mid-March with the most recent snow still on the ground, Tracy shuddered to think what the girl would wear in July.

Their first experience with Dave's latest squeeze had come the week before at a small bar south of town called The Castaway. Tall, slender, and tan, Kiki had the look of someone who'd been around enough to have plenty of room for Dave's reportedly over-sized cock.

Somebody better smack me before I say that aloud.

Not being judgmental as a rule, Tracy might've felt differently if Kiki hadn't had the audacity to tell her Joey was ugly. Undoubtedly, she'd never seen him in drag.

"I'd punch her lights out if she said that about Lenny," Cynthia had said as Kiki sashayed away to make goo-goo eyes at Dave during the first set.

"I prefer verbal sparring," Tracy said. "Unfortunately, engaging in a battle of wits with an unarmed person has its limits."

Cynthia nearly spewed her mojito and thereafter chuckled anytime she glanced in Kiki's direction, whispering "Bimbo Alert" whenever she approached.

Angie didn't seem to care for her, either. "Should we ask her what she thinks about calling tuna Chicken of the Sea?"

"I'm almost afraid to," Tracy had replied.

But now, Kiki was at home nursing a bad cold, and Joey was handing Brad a stack of sheet music. Tracy couldn't help seeing it as a turning point—for all of them.

"I'll run in the house and copy these real quick," Brad said. "Then we can get started."

She and Joey exchanged a wink. For a guy who didn't want to venture far from home for a gig, even Brad seemed pumped.

The first song they chose was "Drifting Sand" a rock ballad with a uniquely beautiful melody, a guitar solo worthy of Eric Clapton, and harmony that sent chills racing up and down Tracy's spine. The verses could have applied to anyone, but the chorus made it perfectly clear who Joey's inspiration had been.

A hero isn't what I thought I'd ever be.
But I see it in your eyes each time you smile at me.
My life before was built on drifting sand
And I can't let the world see who I truly am.
But you, my love, only you understand.

Knowing the song better than anyone else, Joey sang the lead vocal. Tracy's connection to the song and the departure from the playful raunchiness of Joey's usual style might have explained its impact, but she wasn't the only one with tears in her eyes when the final chord sounded.

"Holy shit, dude," Brad exclaimed, rubbing his face on his sleeve. "That's–that's fuckin' *beautiful*."

Joey shrugged. "We can tweak it a little more—Billy can probably improve on the keyboard accompaniment—and it'll sound better with you singing the lead, but it's—"

"No," Brad insisted. "*You* need to sing the lead. Jesus Christ, how long were you planning to hide shit like that under a rock?"

"I didn't write it all that long ago," Joey mumbled, rubbing the back of his neck. "It's probably my best song."

"If the others are even *half* as good…" Brad shook his head, still seeming stunned. "Damn."

When Dave rolled his eyes and started to speak, Tracy caught him with look that pinned him to his stool. If he kept on with that crap, she had an idea that, like Barton Junction, these guys wouldn't make the big time with their original drummer. She, for one, wouldn't miss him.

Or Kiki.

～･～

The next six weeks went by like a blur. About the only thing Tracy noticed during that time was that spring had finally arrived. One day she'd been wearing her winter coat, and the next, she was thinking about turning on the air conditioning. "I'm just glad it warmed up. It's such a pain in the ass to keep track of a coat or a jacket in a bar."

"Don't worry," Melina said. "It'll be warmer in Louisville anyway." She closed the drawer of the Pyxis machine after selecting her patient's meds. "You never did tell me the name of his band. Would I have heard of them?"

Tracy snickered. "Not unless you've started hanging out in *straight* bars."

"Ah, so Joey isn't doing the cross-dressing thing on stage? Too bad. He'd make one helluva female impersonator."

"You actually have to be able to *sing* like a woman to be a female impersonator," Tracy reminded her. "Joey's voice is way too deep and raspy for that. But to answer your other question, they call themselves The Brad Winters Band."

"*That's* original," Melina said with a smirk.

"Wasn't my idea, and I'm not sure using Joey's name would make it any better. Still, it *is* Brad's band. His name, his garage..." She hesitated. "While we're on the subject, if you don't mind, I'd rather you didn't mention that other *performance* to anyone—Miranda in particular. I'm not sure she'd understand."

"She's not *that* much of a prude, is she?"

"I wouldn't say she was a prude at all," Tracy admitted. "To hear her tell it, she and Travis have a lot of fun together. But I'd still rather that charade not become common knowledge." Not so much for Joey's sake as for hers for not recognizing him. She'd never live *that* down.

Tracy had invited most of her friends and family to the show in Louisville. Miranda wasn't sure she could get the night off, but

Travis's cousin Alan and his wife Emily planned to come, as did Miranda's son, Levi, who was bringing along his girlfriend, Tabitha.

Melina wagged her head. "I dunno…That's got to be one of the best *how we got together* stories ever."

"Yeah, well… Someday I'll tell it to my grandchildren, but not my sister. Not yet, anyway. I'm the black sheep of the family as it is."

"What about the rest of the band? Have they heard about it?"

"No, and they'd better *not* hear it from you."

Tracy narrowed her gaze as Melina's expression shifted to wide-eyed innocence. "Would *I* do that?"

"You introduced me to a lesbian who turned out to be a guy. Seems to me you'd be capable of just about anything."

Melina snickered. "Only good things, Trace."

Tracy chuckled along with her. "I certainly can't argue with that. Being introduced to Anna was one of the high points of my life."

"I just hope it stays that way." She paused. "You *are* happy with him, aren't you?"

"Deliriously happy—except for that part about waiting for the other shoe to drop."

"You always were one to overthink things."

"I know," Tracy groaned. "*Believe* me, I know."

ஜஓ

Joey's knees felt like rubber as he climbed the steps onto the stage of the Comstock Lode. He'd played in a lot of clubs, but never one so big he couldn't see the bar from the bandstand. The dance floor alone was as big as Cider Hill.

He knew Tracy was out there somewhere. She'd texted him when she arrived with her friends and family, he just couldn't see her. They were the second band on the card for the night and the place was packed. He and the guys had gotten there early enough to hear them, and they were good. Joey didn't see anything wrong with their performance, unless it was that they seemed to ignore the audience.

Tracy had made a point of telling them they needed to connect with the crowd. "Banter with the audience is important," she'd said. "Otherwise they might as well be dancing to canned music." Joey certainly couldn't argue with that.

"You okay, dude?" Brad asked.

"You mean aside from the guy with a jackhammer in my gut?"

"Yeah. That."

"I'm okay." He wiped a hand over his brow, not surprised to find he was already sweating. "Never thought it would happen like this, though. I'd always imagined I'd be playing my songs for a hometown crowd. You know...people who will say something nice even if they think it's crap?"

"They won't think that—whether they know you or not. Don't you think I know a great song when I hear it? And even if "Drifting Sand" isn't the next megahit single, they're not going to hate it— unless you forget the words."

"No chance of that." He knew he could play it, too. With Tracy there and that red G-string hugging his balls, he could pretty much guarantee an outstanding performance.

If my nerves don't kill me first.

He plugged in his amplifier and adjusted the gain. "I just wish we could've tried out these songs somewhere else first."

Brad chuckled. "What? My garage doesn't count?"

"You *know* what I mean."

"Yeah. I do." He nodded at the crowd. "Your woman's waving at you."

Joey put up a hand to shade his eyes from the glare. "Where?"

"Right there," Brad said, pointing a finger. "Better go get a hug for luck or whatever it is you do whenever she's around."

Joey stared blankly at his friend. "What are you talking about?"

Brad snorted a laugh. "Do you really think I haven't noticed the difference in you? She's been good for you, man. Don't let her get away."

"I won't." Joey finally spotted Tracy—although how he'd missed her in a shirt as red and shiny as his thong he couldn't begin to imagine.

Jogging across the stage, he ran down the steps and onto the dance floor. When he reached their table, he barely registered any of the others sitting there. Tracy was the only one he saw. Flinging his arms around her, he did his best to kiss her lips off.

"You're gonna be great," she said, returning his kiss. "But first, you need to meet Levi."

A blond young man with a shy smile got to his feet and held out his hand. "You're Joey? Tracy's new boyfriend?"

Joey nodded, smiling as he shook Levi's hand. "Nice to meet you, Levi."

Levi scowled at him. "Are you being nice to Tracy?"

"Um, yeah," Joey replied, somewhat taken aback.

"You'd better be," Levi said. A moment later, he cocked his head, a puzzled frown furrowing his brow. "Has anyone ever thought you were a girl?"

Tracy's gaze met Joey's as she let out a whoop of laughter and pulled her nephew into a hug. "He's not a girl. He's a sweet, long-haired, guitar-playing rock star."

"Oh, okay, okay," Levi said, waving a hand. "I get it now."

So did Joey. With that one remark, his nerves vanished. Tracy introduced him to Levi's girlfriend, Tabitha, and Alan and Emily as "cousins-in-law or something" who were starry-eyed newlyweds. Melina and her husband waved from the next table, but his mind was only on Tracy. He was her hero, and she was his inspiration.

He would make her proud.

Chapter 31

Tracy watched in awe as a star was born.

Eddy Van Halen had nothing on her Joey—and neither did The Edge, Slash, or any other guitarist in the history of rock 'n' roll.

I'm prejudiced.

She told herself that numerous times, but apparently her opinion of Joey was shared by most of those present—and there were *a lot* of people there. The band's covers of rock standards were well received, but when Brad announced, "Here's a little something new from our own Joey Manzetti," the crowd went wild.

Joey sang "Drifting Sand" with an intensity that gave her chills, and he played the guitar solo with unsurpassed skill and style. It wasn't simply a good song; it had all the makings of a classic.

Thunderous applause erupted before the last reverb faded, and Tracy's brief one-hit-wonder fear was immediately dispelled when the next song—one of Joey's hard rock compositions—had people tearing up the dance floor.

Alan leaned over, speaking directly in her ear in order to make himself heard. "He's damn good."

Tracy sucked in quavering breath. "Oh, *yeah.*"

With a wink and a wicked grin, he added, "If he fucks half as well as he plays that guitar…"

Tossing her head back, Tracy laughed for sheer joy. "Better."

Especially when he's wearing my undies.

Tracy had heard reports of Alan's incredible stamina, but she preferred quality to quantity. Emily seemed very pleased with him, however.

Everyone has their own perfect mate.

Alan and Emily had found theirs, and so had Miranda and

Travis—perhaps even Levi and Tabitha. Now it was Joey and Tracy's turn. He might've been rocking the house down, but whether he was mobbed by autograph hounds and well-wishers when the set ended or not, Joey was going home with *her*.

Alan nodded at Emily. "Want us to take Levi and Tabitha home so you can have Joey all to yourself?"

"That'd be great." She hadn't planned it that way, but the prospect of another road trip similar to the one she'd taken with Anna would be the perfect ending to an evening of triumph.

At least Joey's *home* was next door to hers. She was already wishing they'd moved in together, although Joey tended to practice at his place and spend the rest of the time in hers. Tracy didn't know whether to hope he would earn enough as a musician to quit his job at Georgio's or not. Either way, she still wouldn't see enough of him.

Unless he earns enough for both of us.

Which was a concept she hadn't considered. However, thinking back, she realized Joey had. His question about whether or not she would miss her job had related to that very issue. Had he expected this to happen? Or had he simply been engaged in wishful thinking?

She glanced at her nephew. "What about it, Levi? Are they good or what?"

With his trademark theatrical smirk, he gave her an enthusiastic thumbs-up. "Oh, yeah. Awesome."

Tracy held out a hand, unable to sit still another moment. "Dance with me?"

She'd expected him to reply with a dismissive wave and was therefore astonished when he jumped to his feet. "Sure!"

The dance floor was so crowded they could barely move, but Tracy didn't care. She was dancing again, and Levi, who to her knowledge hadn't done any dancing since a rather memorable third grade music program version of "Y.M.C.A.," was right there with her. She glanced up at Joey, playing his heart out and grinning at her like the happiest man on earth.

Moments like this were so rare. Closing her eyes, Tracy let her heart fill with love for him—and for life itself—until it burst, radiating joy from deep within her soul.

❧☙

In an instant of total clarity, the crowd, the sights, the sounds all converged to become the twinkle in Tracy's eyes.

Overjoyed.

At last, Joey understood the meaning of the word, and she was the source—the beginning, the ending, and everything in between.

If he'd been sitting down with his guitar in hand, that flash of insight would've become a song. It still would. The drive home would give him the opportunity to find the right words, but time spent alone would recreate the feelings.

The set ended and his world dissolved into a surreal maze of feminine squeals, hugs that squeezed the breath out of him, pens thrust into his hand, and pictures taken with his arm around total strangers. Somehow, somewhere, he found Tracy, pulled her into his arms, and kissed her like the precious jewel she was.

The trappings of superstardom were commonplace for many performers, but he had an idea all of those people whose names were on every tongue could remember a moment like this—an event untarnished by everything that came after and unsurpassed in its significance. Tracy was part of that. He wanted to make sure she always would be.

He pressed his lips to her ear. "Will you marry me, Trace? Whether I play concerts in the Superdome or make pizzas for the rest of my life, I don't want to do any of it without you." With a sigh, he added, "I don't even want to try."

Her fingers tangled in his hair as her breath cooled his overheated skin, but it was her reply that sent a torrent of tingles down his back. "Oh, yeah. I'll be there. Beside you all the way."

A surge of emotions welled up inside him, making him hold her even more tightly than before. Despite the noise and the crowd, they shared a level of intimacy he'd never felt with anyone. She was uniquely his, just as he was hers.

"Let's dance, babe," he said. "Just you and me out there on the dance floor."

She nibbled his earlobe. "If you dance half as well as a girl named Anna, I'll have to take you home and fuck you."

"Promises, promises…"

The twinkle in her eyes was augmented with tears. "I love you, Joey—and in case you weren't paying attention, yes, I *will* marry you."

"I've waited a long time to hear that from the woman I love. I was beginning to believe it would never happen." Holding her face in his hands, he kissed her until he had to stop to breathe. "You've made a believer out of me, Trace."

For once, a slow song played at the perfect moment. He caught a glimpse of Levi and Tabitha out on the floor. Levi must not have done much in the way of slow dancing because she obviously had to coach him. But he seemed to be catching on rather well.

Joey would be a part of a family again—a *real* family. He would have sisters and brothers-in-law and Levi would be his nephew. Maybe someday he and Tracy would have a baby. A baby that was truly his—not one passed off as his out of a mother's desperation. He couldn't have loved Darren any more, but this time, he and Tracy were going to do it right. They would make the *choice* to bring a child into the world.

He could hardly wait to get started.

୧୬୦୧

Don't spoil it.

Joey was holding her, he'd asked her to marry him, and she'd accepted. Tracy tried to revel in the joy, but her efforts to quash the questions were for naught. The little voice inside her head hounded her just as it always did, shifting her focus from joy to doubt as reality began to creep in.

Could she be the wife of a rock star? He'd be on the road half the time. Then again, no one had made any offers—yet. Was she putting the cart before the horse? Maybe he could simply be a songwriter—get his songs published and sit back and rake in the royalties.

No. She'd seen him up there on the stage and watched him shine. There'd be no holding him back now—whether it was with Brad's band or not. If necessary, he could join another band or start one of his own. Brad was a good singer, but Joey had been the star of the show tonight. A blind man could've seen that.

What did the others think? Were they jealous, or would they embrace the opportunity and run with it?

Turning her head, she buried her face in Joey's hair and inhaled his masculine scent—the tang of his sweat, the subtle aroma of his aftershave, the sheer *maleness* of him. He was so *alive*—his warm hands splayed on her back, the easy movement of his body against hers, the steady rhythm of his breathing. She would be dancing with this man for the rest of her life. Somehow, that realization soothed her, allowing her to escape from her own mind for a time.

She finally understood why she'd expunged every trace of all those other men from her life—not to make room for herself, but to make room for *him*. Still, he had two bedrooms and not much furniture. It made more sense for her to move in with him. Of course, if they moved to a new place, Bryce couldn't find *her* and Geena couldn't find Joey.

Two less things to worry about. Although, truth be told, she hadn't thought about Bryce for a while now.

No worries. People said that all the time, but what would it be like to actually have nothing to worry about? Tracy would probably never know—at least, not until her brain no longer functioned. She bit back a laugh. By the time she didn't have any worries, she wouldn't even be aware of it.

Shut up, brain. Let me enjoy this.

Opening her eyes, she gazed into Brad's excited countenance as he tapped Joey's shoulder. "Dude, you're not gonna believe this."

"Not now, Brad." Joey didn't even turn around, simply tossing his words over his shoulder.

Joey couldn't see Brad, but Tracy could. He looked like he was about to come completely unglued. "This is *important*, man. There's a freakin' talent scout here, and he's waving around a recording contract."

"Later," Joey reiterated. "This song only has another minute to go. Give me that much."

"Whatever," Brad grumbled. "Thought you'd be excited."

"I am," Joey said. "But right now, I'm dancing with my fiancée, and I don't want to talk to anyone."

"Fiancée?" Brad echoed. "When did *that* happen?"

"About two minutes ago."

"Oh." Brad shrugged. "Gotcha—and congratulations."

"Thanks," Tracy said. "I promise to deliver him to you promptly." She'd been engaged to him for two minutes, and already she had to share him.

And so it begins…

Chapter 32

Tracy had already planned on driving Joey home, and in light of their engagement and the resounding success of the show—plus the fact that Levi and Tabitha weren't in the back seat—it should've been memorable. What she *hadn't* expected was that triumph would set so poorly with him.

"Contracts make me nervous," he said. "I never dreamed...well, maybe I did, but the reality is... I dunno. Just wish I knew what we're getting into."

"Have a lawyer look at it," Tracy suggested.

"I doubt if we can afford one."

"They aren't *that* expensive, and it would be worth it to get some legal advice up front instead of finding out you got screwed two years from now."

"A lawyer might try to screw us too."

"Maybe," she admitted. "Think of it as a pre-nuptial agreement. If you were marrying an heiress, you'd want to know what you'd get to keep in the event of a divorce, wouldn't you?"

His blank stare remained fixed on the dark highway ahead. "That sounds like you aren't expecting it to last."

She hoped he wasn't referring to their engagement. She didn't think so, but the doubt persisted. Smiling, she did her best to gloss over her own uncertainty. "Hey, not all bands stay together forever. Hell, the Beatles broke up when they were sitting on top of the world. Nobody's immune."

He shuddered. "I can see it now—all five of us, each with his own lawyer, battling it out. I want to focus on the music. I don't want to be a part of all that crap. It would ruin everything."

"Maybe, but it's a fact of life, and if you're ever going to make it big, you'll have to deal with it. You should know that by now. You can distance yourself up to a point, but sooner or later, it all comes down to one thing."

"Yeah. Money." He sounded so bitter Tracy could scarcely believe he was the same man who'd proposed to her on the dance floor. Then again, the contract offer hadn't been an issue at the time—only his superb performance and their love for each other.

That one shining, perfect moment...

Tamping down her concerns, she kept her tone as matter-of-fact as possible. "Of course it is. If you can get someone to promote you, you're in. If you don't, you're not." She was hesitant to say more because she had a stake in his success that she didn't have before his proposal. She hated to seem greedy, but she and Joey weren't the only ones involved. "Look, it doesn't matter how good the music is if no one hears it. I'm sure there are lots of fabulous acts that are stuck in small clubs because they weren't willing to play the game. Success comes at a price. You have to decide whether or not you're willing to pay it. *All* of you have to decide."

"I know. *Believe* me, I know." With a sigh, he finally managed a bleak smile. "I honestly never thought we'd be faced with this decision. The truth is I *like* playing small clubs and weddings. Those huge stadiums lack intimacy. I've heard lots of big names say they miss the interaction with the audience, and I'm pretty sure I'd miss it too."

"Then that's something you and the guys need to discuss. It's easy enough to avoid becoming rich and famous. On the other hand, having thousands of people screaming every time you wiggle your hips has got to be a rush. You *know* the Rolling Stones have more than enough money to live on. They keep performing because they love it. There's no other explanation."

"Like we'll ever be that big," Joey muttered.

"Maybe not. But if you don't take the first step, you'll never find out."

"I still can't believe Brad is so gung ho. He never even wanted to *listen* to my songs before." He shook his head. "I don't get it."

"You never know how people will react when faced with that situation. Then again, he may be having second thoughts too."

"Yeah. I mean, look at me. I never thought *I'd* be having second thoughts." He heaved a sigh. "Would you look at the contract?"

"Sure. But I'm no lawyer, so don't stop with my assessment. If there's anything about it you don't like, don't sign it. Chances are it won't be the only offer you'll get."

"Maybe not." He was silent for a long moment, shifting uncomfortably in his seat. "You won't…I mean, will you still marry me even if I *don't* sign the contract?"

Thankfully, the highway was four lanes wide and reasonably straight—as well as deserted—because otherwise they might not have lived long enough for either of them to sign anything. Regaining control of the car following a long, open-mouthed stare, she took a deep breath. "Joey. I said yes before Brad told you about the contract."

"Yeah, but you knew it was coming, didn't you?"

"No, I didn't."

"But those friends of yours who own the place—"

"Didn't say *anything* about a talent scout being there."

After all we've been through, he's doubting me?

Joey drew in a breath as though about to speak, but she cut him off again. "You're gonna have to trust me on that one. Who knows? Maybe those guys show up anytime a new band plays there—but even if they do, and even if I'd known about it, that *still* wouldn't guarantee an offer."

He nodded. "I'm sorry. I didn't mean it that way. Oh, hell… I'm not sure *how* I meant it. I thought I was ready for this. I wanted to make you proud and make a better life for both of us. But practically the second I proposed, Brad was trying to drag me off to talk to that talent scout. It all happened so fast—*too* fast. I barely had a minute to enjoy the fact that you'd agreed to marry me."

"Yeah." Her smile was bittersweet. "I didn't see you again until it was time to leave."

"See what I mean? I love you, Trace, but I'm so afraid I'll fuck it up. In case you haven't figured it out yet, I'm not the smartest guy on the planet. If I was, I'd be doing something besides making pizzas for a living. Sure, I can play guitar and make up songs, but—"

Tracy could scarcely contain her laughter. "Joey, *sweetheart*, do you have any idea how many rocket scientists would give their left nut to be a rock star?"

"Maybe..." A smile twitched the corner of his mouth.

"Honest to God, you're a bigger worry wart than I am! We should be celebrating, not...whatever it is we're doing." With a fake scowl, she shook a finger at him, hoping he'd take the hint and lighten up. "And if you say one more word about being stupid, I'm gonna take you home and paddle your cute little butt."

Joey never missed a beat. "I'm so stupid a dog could beat me at checkers."

"That does it. The second we get home, you're getting your ass whipped."

He chuckled. "What would it take to get you to tie me up first?"

"Tie you up? To *what*? My bed is a sleigh and yours doesn't even have a headboard." Tracy might've been laughing right along with him, but her pussy contracted at the mere thought. "Isn't it enough for you to put on a bra?"

"Maybe," he drawled. "Depends on how you make me wear it."

"*Make* you wear it? You mean you want *me* to wrap it around your dick?"

A quick glance revealed his teeth sinking into his lip as he wagged his head. "Uh, no. Not this time."

"I don't get—"

"You'll need two of them."

The mental image hit her like a brick through the windshield. "Whoa, shit."

We're gonna have fun tonight.

Tracy truly was one in a million.

And she's all mine.

"See? You're a *lot* smarter than I am," Joey said with a smirk.

"You got that without me having to explain it—which is good because I'm gonna jizz in my jeans if I say much more." His dick was already making a valiant effort to pop open his fly as it was.

"Yeah, well, you're the one who thought it up. I only have to do it to you." She frowned. "Wait a second. Does what you just said about me being smarter count as you saying you're stupid?"

"If you're looking for a reason to tie me up, then yes, it does."

"Hmm...tied up and spanked... What about fucking you with the strap-on?"

With that kind of enticement, Joey had to come up with something fast. "I'm so stupid that the cat the dog beat at checkers could whip me at tic-tac-toe."

"Yep. That's pretty stupid. I'll have to nail your ass for that."

Okay, the pants have got to go.

Reclining his seat slightly, he flipped open the top button of his fly. "Wanna see my dick?"

"Absolutely. If I'm going to be your wife, I need to familiarize myself with it."

"Good plan." Undoing the rest of the buttons, he pulled his cock out from beneath the red satin thong. "This is why I want to marry you. Even when I feel like shit—whether I *should* feel that way or not—you can still make my dick hard."

She snorted a laugh. "The number one prerequisite for a wife, I'm sure."

"You bet. A woman who can make your dick hard when she's mad at you...it's tough to beat that."

"I'm not mad at you," she protested.

"You should be. I was a total jackass for ever doubting you."

"If you think *that's* being a jackass, you've obviously never met any of my old boyfriends—or my ex-husband. Believe me, they have jackassdom down to a fine art." She glanced at his dick, which was sticking straight up and gushing like a fire hydrant. "On the other hand, showing me your awesome cock while I'm driving borders on cruel and unusual punishment."

"Want me to make it spurt for you?"

She sucked in a breath so hard she choked on it. "Dammit, Joey!" she said when she recovered. "You aren't helping!"

"Since I'm such a bad boy, I'll jack off for you and then you can spank me when we get home." He glanced at the clock. "It'll take us at least another half hour to get there. Trust me, I'll be ready to go again."

"If I don't drive into a tree."

He winked. "You keep your eyes on the road. I'll tell you when to look."

Her subsequent whimper almost made him tell her to pull over, but he suspected she was as anxious to keep going as he was.

"How about taking your pants off all the way?" she asked.

"Anything for my woman." Shoving his jeans down to his ankles, he started to take off the thong.

"Leave that on," she said. "Just put it underneath your balls so the waistband holds them up."

Joey had to hitch the thong higher in the back, but he certainly couldn't complain about the results. His scrotum was pulled so tight, his nuts gleamed in the soft glow from the dash.

"That's perfect," she said with a hoarse whisper. "I hope you know you're making my pussy wet."

"That's the idea."

"It isn't just wet, either. It's aching for the feel of your cock." Her sidelong glance caught his gaze. "Your *naked* cock."

"Birth control isn't an issue anymore, is it?"

"No. I want to have your baby, and I don't see any point in putting it off."

Running a hand over his cockhead, he let out a groan. "I want to plant babies in you, Trace. I *liked* being a father. I'm ready anytime you say."

"I'm about due for a period, so it probably won't happen tonight, but yeah. I'm not getting any younger."

"Maybe not, but you get more beautiful every day."

"Sweet talker." She was practically purring. "See if you can hit the windshield with your cum."

"Sure you don't want me to hit *you* with it?"

With a moan, she lurched forward, nearly smacking her head on the steering wheel. "Oh, yeah…spray it all over me."

"Whatever you say, baby. This dick is all yours." As hard as he was, it wouldn't take long. The faster he came, the more recovery time he'd have.

Not that he'd need it. Being tied up and spanked was one thing. Having *Tracy* do it—*and* fuck him with the strap-on—was almost more than his mind could handle.

"You want to suck it, don't you?" Gripping his shaft, he slid his fist from the tight, purplish head all the way to the base. As much as he enjoyed jerking off, doing it while gazing at Tracy was even better. She was as gorgeous in profile as she was when she glanced toward him, her lips curved into a seductive smile.

"You know I do. When I've got you where I want you, you'll be helpless to resist. I'll tie you up and lick…your…dick." She emphasized each pause with a swipe of her tongue over her lips.

Joey's hand stilled on his cock. His next breath hissed in through clenched teeth, and he held it, squeezing his eyes shut—desperate to stave off his climax for a few more minutes. Of course, if she kept saying shit like that, his damned dick would probably go off all by itself.

"I won't tell you what else I'm going to do to you, but two can play *this* game. Come for me, Joey. I want to watch your balls tighten and your dick spurt." Without even touching him, she was still in control. "Play with your balls, baby. It won't feel near as good as it will when I suck them, but I want you to get as much pleasure out of this as you possibly can."

He was so close, he could feel his ejaculation building, the tension skyrocketing with each passing second. "Remember the night when I was Anna, and you showed me your tits?"

"Of course I do. I wasn't *that* drunk." She shot him a wink. "I'm not drunk at all now, and I'm not going to be. I want to remember every tiny little thing that happens tonight, from spanking your butt to tickling your balls and fucking your ass."

"Show me your tits again." One glimpse and he'd spew all over them. Every muscle in his body was coiled like a spring.

She shook her head. "Nope. I'm driving. Gotta keep my mind on what I'm doing or we'll end up in the hospital—or worse. You're gonna have to come all by yourself."

One sharp inhale and it was all over. Joey's nuts slid up in his sac and his cock erupted, splattering Tracy with a line of cum that stretched from her cheek to her elbow.

Like Mount fuckin' Vesuvius.

Her tongue darted out, seeking the droplet of semen at the corner of her mouth. "Mmm…delicious. There'd better be more where that came from or you are in *so* much trouble."

Chapter 33

By the time they reached the outskirts of Pemberton, Tracy had chewed her lip enough to draw blood while mulling over every possible way a woman could restrain a man using two bras, but only one that was perfect for fucking him in the ass.

"I want to spend tonight at your place," she said as she parked the car. "You've got more *stuff* than I do."

"Meaning the strap-on?"

"Um, yeah—among other things."

She knew he had more goodies. Butt plugs, anal beads, and several types of restraints, to mention a few. "How come you've got all those toys? Somehow, I can't see Geena—"

He cut her off with a snort. "I never used *any* of it with her. She was strictly the vanilla-sex type."

His reply certainly matched Tracy's opinion of Geena, but it didn't answer her question. "So…?"

"I had a girlfriend who loved being tied up." He paused, shaking his head. "She just couldn't stand the thought of me putting on her panties."

"Her loss." In Tracy's opinion, loaning him her underwear was a small price to pay for the sexual freedom she'd had with Joey. He was one in a million—always ready to try something new or play along with any erotic scenario she could imagine.

And best of all, she trusted him.

Where there is no trust, there can be no love. She'd heard that somewhere, never realizing how true it was. She certainly knew it now.

She was going to marry him. The date and any other specifics were immaterial. This time, it would be a *'til death do us part* kind of marriage. She could feel it deep down in her soul—a feeling she'd never had with anyone—and the awesome sex only illustrated the level of trust.

He would be famous someday—perhaps sooner than he knew—and he would still be hers, no matter how many groupies threw themselves at his feet.

Popping the trunk release, she got out of the car, shivering in the cool night air. "Need some help with your gear?"

"Sure." He handed her a guitar. "Think you could carry this?"

One glance at him proved the weather wasn't responsible for her shiver. *He* was. "If it gets us inside quicker, I'll carry *everything*."

"No need for that." The light from the street lamp glinted off his curls, making him more appealing that ever—if that was possible. "So...any thoughts as to when we should get married?"

She didn't hesitate. "I'd do it right now if we could."

"Think you could take Monday off?"

They could get a license and be married the same day in this state. But this was still the real world and he wasn't rich and famous. Risking the day job wasn't an option—yet. She blew out a sigh. "Not unless I call in sick. Might be better to request a day off next week before the new schedule comes out."

"Sounds good." He shot her a grin that promised more fun to come. "But right now, we've got an engagement to consummate."

"How's your dick?"

"Rarin' to go. How's your spanking hand?"

Her pussy clenched at the mere thought of smacking his adorable ass. Swallowing with difficulty, she aimed a smirk at him. "Never better."

"I hope you've got some really strong bras." Hauling his amplifier out of the trunk, he shouldered another gig bag.

"Yeah, right," she grumbled. "Like I've got any other kind now."

"Do you hear me complaining?"

She closed the trunk, and they headed toward the building.

"Well…no."

"Guess we know what to get each other for—what's next? Memorial Day?"

"Yeah. We sorta missed Easter, and St Patrick's Day before that. I didn't even get any green beer."

"I should've gotten you a green bra with shamrocks on it." He hitched the bag higher on his shoulder. "Or maybe some pasties. Can't think why I didn't. You'd look awesome with shamrocks stuck to your tits."

Tracy burst out laughing. "Oh, I do love you, Joey. Honest to God, you make me laugh, make me hot as hell, play guitar like a freakin' rock god…" Stepping sideways, she craned her neck to plant a kiss on his cheek. "You're just plain awesome, you know that?"

He sniffed, protruding his lower lip in a mock pout. "Does that mean you won't spank me?"

"And you're every bit as weird as I am," she added without missing a beat. "I'm gonna tie you up, paddle your butt, and eat you alive. Then I'm gonna lay back while you fuck the snot out of me—without a condom."

"That'll do for a start."

"For a *start*?" she echoed. "Not sure I'll have any energy left after all that."

He shot her a wink. "There's always tomorrow."

"Um…it's *already* tomorrow."

Tracy's description of her plans for the night nearly had Joey dropping everything and dragging her into his apartment.

Everything, that is, except the Ibanez.

Nope, not gonna risk that sucker again.

That guitar was his life—and so was Tracy. The thought of fucking her without a condom, spilling his seed inside her body had him shivering with anticipation that went far beyond being tied up and spanked. She was affecting him on a level he'd never imagined.

"In that case, we'd better hurry before my dick goes off again."

Her laughter echoed across the parking lot. "All the more reason to smack your ass."

After they reached the building and climbed the stairs, Tracy unlocked the door to his apartment. Once inside, Joey plunked down his gear and started peeling off his clothes until he was down to the satin thong, which did nothing to contain the goods. His painfully hard cock stuck out above the waistband and his balls hung out on either side, the cool air raising goose bumps on his scrotum.

"Good boy," she purred, patting his bare butt. "Wait here. I'll be right back."

He nodded, biting his lip and silently praying she wouldn't dawdle. As the door closed behind her, he stole a peek at his cock. Purple-headed and drooling, it was so tight and shiny it might have been made of glass.

By the time she returned, pre-cum was running down his leg. She hadn't changed her clothes, but the collection of scarves and lingerie draped over her arm made his nuts ache.

Her gaze raked his nude body. "I see you've managed to stay in the mood while I was gone."

"Oh, yeah. No problems there."

She tied one end of a scarf loosely around his neck, leaving the long end dangling like a leash. "Let's go."

With a quick yank on the makeshift leash, she led him into the bedroom. Pulling back the covers, she pushed him onto the bed. "Now that I've got you where I want you, I'm gonna do things you never even *thought* of."

Joey could barely contain his lust. "The suspense is killing me, Trace. Do me. Now."

After making a careful selection from the items she'd brought, she tossed the rest onto the bed. Two bras dangled from her fingers, one pink satin and the other a lacy teal. "On your hands and knees, big guy."

He did as she asked, facing away from her, quivering with anticipation.

Peeling the thong to his thighs, she ran a hand over his butt, then cupped his balls. "I just love these—firm, furry, and delicious."

His cock pulsed, spurting a jet of pre-cum onto the sheets.

She responded with a stinging slap on his ass that made his balls jiggle. "Bad Joey, getting the bed all wet."

"I'm gonna do worse than that in a minute." His throat was so tight he had trouble getting the words out—and the scarf around his neck had nothing to do with it.

"Go ahead and come without me if you like. But remember, you *will* be punished." With a steady downward tug on the scarf, she pulled his head and shoulders down onto the bed, leaving his ass up in the air, naked and vulnerable. He tightened the muscles, squeezing his butt cheeks together.

Not yet.

"Trace, I'm not kidding. If you want me to fuck you..."

"Doesn't matter." She edged closer, whispering in his ear. "You go right ahead and come if you have to. I'll lay back, spread my legs wide, and play with my clit until your dick gets hard enough to fuck me and fill me with cum."

"That oughta do it," he gasped.

"I can't wait to feel your hot, naked cock inside me. That night in the car was fabulous... I wanted you to do it then—wanted to feel you pumping me full of your sweet cream."

"You weren't worried about getting pregnant?"

"No. Not then, and certainly not now. I love you, Joey. I can't wait to have lots of babies with you and watch them grow."

"Wow." His voice was low-pitched and breathy with awe. She was saying sweet, wonderful things—the kind he'd never expected to hear from anyone—and was driving him absolutely wild at the same time. "I love you too, Trace." He wiggled his hips. "Now spank me until I jizz all over the bed."

Giggling, she gave him another slap. "Bet you can't."

"Bet I can. You just watch me."

Kneeling beside him, she gave him the spanking of his life. His cock swung up and down with every lick, the heat flooding his groin until his balls felt like lead weights. Fisting his hands in the sheets, he thrust his ass backward, welcoming each stinging blow.

His climax was almost in sight when she paused. "Had enough yet?"

"No!" he shouted with a violent shake of his head. "Don't stop until I come."

She hit him again, low on his ass, dangerously close to his nuts. "One more…"

The next strike was more of a punch, landing squarely in the middle. In an instant, his eyes snapped shut as his cock erupted, spewing semen onto the bed in long, ball-wrenching spurts.

He'd barely finished when he felt her hands on his arm, pulling it back until his elbow rested on his knee. Even with his head turned to the side, he couldn't see a thing, but he knew what she was doing. Wrapping a bra around his arm and leg, she fastened the hooks, effectively tying his elbow to his knee. Then she did the other side.

Tracy let out a groan. "Oh, God. That is so fuckin' hot." She slapped his ass again. "Don't move."

The bed dipped and she left him there. He knew she was only donning the strap-on, but the time still passed with excruciating slowness.

Finally, after what seemed like an eternity, she returned. "Did you miss me, baby?"

"You know I did," he replied. "Fuck me, Trace. Fuck me *hard*."

"Don't worry." The lube was cold as she dribbled it over his asshole and then slid a finger inside. After adding more lube, she snapped the lid shut. "I'm gonna *nail* your ass."

With a slow advance and retreat, she worked the dildo inside him. Once fully hilted, she popped him with a series of quick, hard thrusts, sending shock waves rippling throughout his body. Her subsequent progression to long, slow strokes made him wish he could see her—to watch her undulating hips ramming against his ass, her creamy breasts rocking on her chest, her luscious lips curling into an intoxicating smile…

Holding his hips tightly in her grasp, she plunged into him, setting a rhythm that lulled him into blissful tranquility even as it drove him to the far reaches of ecstasy. The pleasure continued its relentless climb until the platform of his existence seemed to drop out from under him, leaving him suspended in time and space for the split second before he fell, plummeting into orgasm.

With a cry, he tumbled onto his side, straining against the bonds that held him. Tracy seemed to understand his need to be released, for she unhooked each bra, allowing his back to arch and his cock to thrust forward. He wouldn't have thought he'd have anything left in him to ejaculate, but apparently, he did.

What he *didn't* have was air in his lungs—having gone out with a whoosh, threatening never to return. His cock tingling and his nuts aching, he finally relaxed enough to take a breath. Opening his eyes, he beheld the most beautiful thing he'd ever seen in his life—Tracy, the woman who would soon be his wife.

Life... Wife...

At last, his poetic soul understood why those two words rhymed.

Chapter 34

If anyone would've told Tracy Richards six months ago that she'd get her jollies fucking Joey Manzetti with a strap-on, she'd have had them committed.

And I've done it twice.

Stripping off the harness, she made a quick run to the bathroom to clean up. She climbed back into bed and pulled Joey close, sitting cross-legged behind him, his head and shoulders resting on her lap.

"Poor baby." She traced the line of his brow. "You've got to be all fucked out."

"Not yet," he murmured. "Give me a minute."

With a gentle laugh she lifted his head and kissed him on the nose. "I'll give you the next fifty years *if*—" Scooping up his hair, she divided it into two sections and spread it out over her thighs. "—you promise never to cut your hair."

"So, I get to be a ninety-year-old man with hair down to my butt?"

"Yep. Promise me."

"I promise." Sighing, he reached up to stroke her cheek. "What we have is so much more than I ever dreamed of. I'll do my best not to screw it up."

With everything Tracy had been through, she was finally on the brink of the happily ever after, and Joey obviously felt the same way. Unfortunately, fear and doubt could destroy it in the blink of an eye. All she had to do was believe—to have faith in another person who deserved that faith.

The ramifications were shocking. She could actually go on through life, making plans, having children, and loving Joey the way she'd always wanted to love a man. In turn, he could become a star or he could make pizzas forever. Either way, he would still be hers—faithfully.

"C'mere." Shifting sideways, he untied the scarf from his neck. "I want to hold you."

As she slid down beside him, he flipped the scarf over her head, using it to pull her into his arms. His lips melted into hers, renewing her passion. She'd never enjoyed kissing a man as much as she loved kissing Joey. That fact alone should've proven he was the one.

"Cold?" he asked when she shivered.

"A little, but that's not where the shiver came from. *You're* the reason for that."

"Mmm…" He kissed her again, then sat up to pull the covers over them both. "Can't have you being even a *little* cold. It's my job to keep you warm and happy."

"Funny how so many men can't even do that much."

Snuggling in beside her, he nuzzled her neck. "You *are* happy, aren't you?"

"*Deliriously* happy—one of those this-can't-be-real-somebody-better-pinch-me kinds of happy." She refused to acknowledge the part about waiting for the other shoe to drop.

I'm not going there—ever again.

"Good. That's just the way I want you." Kisses followed, accompanied by caressing hands and warm touches. His lips drifted down to her breasts, taking his time, leaving no place unloved.

Sighing, she lay back, giving him full access to her body. It belonged to him now—was his to entice and enjoy as he wished.

His body called to her on the same level. She'd already spanked him and fucked him. Now she was going to love him, submerged in a deep sea of love and desire. The feel of his hair, his skin, his body delighted her, making her wonder why she hadn't craved him even before Geena left him.

I was stupid and blind.

And she respected Geena and Joey's relationship. That was the difference. A difference that no longer mattered—especially not when she was in bed with the man she loved—a man who loved her enough to ask her to marry him and mean it.

Joey played her body like a well-tuned instrument, stimulating all the right places in all the right ways, easily bringing her to climax before parting her thighs and sliding his stiff cock into her waiting body. Moving slowly and deliberately, he pushed her pleasure to a peak, let it glide back to the beginning, then took her there again. Never rushed, never hurried or frantic, but easy, lovingly, with a desire to please and entice, rather than dominate.

When at last he reached his own climax, filling her with all he had left to give, she was content to drift dreamily off to sleep, to awaken with the dawn, still cradled in his arms.

ഗ‍ര

Joey had gone to sleep expecting to wake up to Tracy's loving kiss and sweet smile. Unfortunately, what he got was Brad's ringtone playing "We Will Rock You."

"I'm gonna kill him," Joey grumbled. Snatching the phone from the nightstand, he noted the time before switched it on. "Seven o'clock? This better be good, dude."

"What?" Brad shot back. "You think a recording contract isn't a good enough reason to call?"

"Of course it is. But you can't tell me they want us in the studio at *this* hour."

"No, but don't you think we should talk about what we want to do?"

"I didn't get the impression there was a time limit on the offer," Joey pointed out. "And we're already getting together to practice this afternoon."

"I know, but we need to talk *before* then."

"Why? You're the one who's been so hesitant to take the next step. It's your band, which gives you more say than any of us. If you want to sign the contract, then sign it. Granted, they're my songs, but if the band wants to record them, I certainly won't object to raking in the royalties. Not sure what more there is to discuss."

"Maybe not, but Dave—well, you know how he is. He's gonna be trouble. I can feel it."

"Are you saying you want to ditch him *before* we sign the contract?"

"Maybe. I'm just wondering if he could sue us for doing it."

"You're asking *me*? Shit, I'm no lawyer."

"Yes, but you've got Tracy, and…"

"She isn't a lawyer, either."

"Yeah, but she's a pretty sharp cookie, and she's had some great ideas. We might want to hire her as our manager."

"Maybe. I'm not going to speak for her—"

"Just talk to her about it. See what she thinks. She's coming with you this afternoon, isn't she?"

"Dammit, Brad! We only got engaged last night, and she just woke up. We talked some on the way home, but—"

Brad snickered like a high school freshman caught hanging out in the girl's locker room. "You've been fucking all night, haven't you?"

"Something like that." Tracy stirred beside him, her sleepy-eyed smile having a predictable effect on Joey's morning wood. "We'll talk it over and call you back, okay?"

"Okay." Brad blew out a breath. "Look, I know this is all coming at us pretty fast, and we don't need to make a decision right away, but the sooner the better."

"I dunno. Tracy seemed to think that wouldn't be our only offer. We might want to wait a bit."

"I hope she's right. I know I was excited last night, but I've read through this contract several times now, and to tell you the truth, it doesn't look all that great."

Joey rolled his eyes. "Have you done any research on what *is* a good contract?"

"Well, no," Brad admitted. "It just doesn't seem like much money—and there's this part about having to recoup manufacturing and marketing costs before we get *anything*."

"Everyone thinks recording artists make a bundle, but most of them probably don't make enough for beer money. We may be better off not signing with anyone until we've generated more interest. I'm just glad I listened to Tracy and got those songs copyrighted before we performed them."

Tracy gave him a nudge.

"Listen, I've got to go," Joey said. "We'll talk later."

"Okay. Let's be smart about this."

"We'll do our best. See ya."

Joey switched off his phone and fell back against the pillow. "Brad wants us to be *smart* about this. Why do I get the feeling we're already in over our heads?"

"You can't be if you haven't signed anything," Tracy said. "I still say you need to talk to a lawyer—one who specializes in entertainment legalese. There's bound to be one or two in Indy or Louisville—Linda or Jackson might even know of one—and Nashville's probably thick with them."

"Yeah. I don't mind admitting I'm scared. I mean, I want it—but I don't." He raked a hand through his hair. "It's hard to explain."

"It's a big decision, but I'm sure you'll make the right one." She leaned over and gave him the kiss he'd wished for when the phone rang. "What do you say I fix breakfast this time?"

"I'll help." He waggled his eyebrows. "Naked breakfast sounds fabulous."

Flipping back the covers, she hopped to her feet, giggling. "Only if you fry the bacon."

"I can do that." One glimpse of her beautiful behind was enough to make Joey forget all about food. Unfortunately, his stomach chose that moment to let out a growl. "Then again, you'd look great in nothing but an apron. More of a tease that way."

She aimed a pointed stare at his groin. "Doesn't look like you need teasing."

"Yes, but your nipples are doing the same thing," he retorted.

"Cold air will do that," she said, crossing her arms over her breasts. "Can't help it."

His heart took flight as realization struck. "Wow. I just realized we'll have mornings like this for the rest of our lives. Awesome feeling."

This time, he got the sweet smile *and* the kiss. "It certainly is."

❧☙

After less than ten minutes of practice, Tracy was convinced that the entire band—with the exception of Joey—had somehow contracted Lead Singer Disease overnight. Dave's arrogance was a given, but even Lenny was acting like a prima donna, and Billy—the keyboard player who hardly ever opened his mouth—was well…mouthy. Brad stopped singing after every third line, questioning every note.

Having repeated her suggestion that they find an entertainment lawyer before signing anything and pointing out the potential disaster of hiring a rookie manager—meaning herself—she sat, arms folded and foot tapping in irritation. Joey's thought about auditioning for a different band was sounding better all the time. He could publish his songs and leave these guys in the dust.

The songs were his, after all. But the lawsuit potential was still there, particularly if the contract offer was revoked if he left the band.

Be careful what you wish for…

She did some research while they played. The record company appeared to be legit—they even had some big names in their stable, Barton Junction among them. She was a little surprised that they would even be checking out local bands. Still, there were bands that were signed before the guys finished high school. This was an older group. Like new recruits to the armed forces, record companies probably preferred to pick kids up young before they knew any better. Young talent always seemed to find a market quicker.

Still, good music was good music—no matter the age of the songwriter or the performers. She could only do so much on her phone. Her time would've been much more productive had she spent it at home with her laptop. At least that way she wouldn't have had to sit through a practice that made her want to tear her hair out.

Finally, she couldn't take it anymore.

Taking advantage of a lull, albeit a rather strained one, she glanced around the room. "You guys played like pros last night, and you got a contract offer. Why would you want to change stuff around now?"

"Thought you didn't *want* to be our manager," Dave groused.

Tracy was a little surprised he didn't tell her to shut her mouth. "I never said that. I said you need a manager who knows something about the music business. I don't. But what I *do* know is that you shouldn't mess with success. If someone liked your music enough to offer you a contract, then that's the kind of music you should play. Now is *not* the time to be making major changes. Now's the time to prove last night wasn't a fluke."

Joey shot her a look of thanks, but it was Brad who spoke. "Yeah. You're right." He sucked in a breath. "Let's forget about the contract. We've got a gig in Bloomington in two weeks, and we should play like we always do."

Tracy sighed with relief. No telling what would happen next, but at least they wouldn't be shooting themselves in the foot.

Chapter 35

"So, he asked you to marry him, huh?" Melina shot Tracy a sidelong glance from her seat at the desk. "Seems a bit sudden."

Monday morning had come much too quickly for Tracy. Joey hadn't been scheduled to work at Georgio's Sunday night, which gave them the entire evening together, but the clinic was still the very last place she wanted to be.

Melina's gaze narrowed with apparent suspicion. "You aren't pregnant, are you?"

"No, but it wouldn't matter if I was." In fact, Tracy would've been overjoyed. As much unprotected sex as she and Joey had been having, she was on the alert for pregnancy symptoms like a hypochondriac looking for a brain tumor.

"Hmm… Still seems damn sudden."

Trust Melina to elicit the same hair-tearing impulses she'd had at band practice. "I didn't say we were getting married tomorrow. We're *engaged*—not fixing to run off to Vegas. And why do you always have to be the voice of reason? Shouldn't you leave that to my family?"

"You think Miranda will be happy for you?"

"Well, yeah. She and Travis are happy as clams—they'll be tickled shitless, and my parents will be thrilled."

"Then that leaves me as the voice of reason, doesn't it?" Melina's smug smile morphed into a frown. "Wait a minute. You haven't *told* them yet?"

"Aside from the band, you're the first," Tracy admitted. "I wanted to get…settled into the idea first."

"Chicken shit."

"Yeah, well, after having to face them at Christmas with black eyes and a busted-up nose, can you blame me? I told them about Joey rescuing me from Bryce, but—" She paused, mirroring Melina's frown. "No, wait. Mom and Dad weren't home for Christmas. But they know I'm dating someone. Anyway, if Miranda had been there on Saturday, I probably would've told her about our engagement. As it was, that recording contract kinda overshadowed everything else."

"Is he having second thoughts?"

"About me or the contract?"

"Both, I guess." Melina closed her laptop and leaned forward, her expression earnest. "Look. We've been pals for a long time, Trace. I don't want to see you make a mistake—one you might regret for the rest of your life."

"Why would I regret marrying Joey?" At the moment, Tracy couldn't see it as anything but a win-win situation. "We're perfect for each other—not to mention head over heels in love."

"Maybe. But he's at a point where his career is probably going to take precedence over everything. Are you ready for that?"

Tracy shook her head. "It's not gonna happen that fast. Contrary to popular belief, there's no such thing as an overnight success."

"Listen, I was there Saturday night. I saw Joey play and I heard his songs. Trust me, something's going to happen. Something *big*."

It took Tracy several seconds to realize her mouth was hanging open. She closed it with an audible smack. "You really think so?"

"I *know* so. You weren't the only one he impressed. The whole place was going wild. That had to be the most electrifying performance I've ever seen—and I've been in the mosh pit of a Barton Junction concert."

"Not to mention The Closet Door," Tracy drawled. "Don't forget, I was there, too." Unable to decide whether to take Melina's predictions seriously or not, Tracy felt the need to break the tension somehow. Even so, her snicker was a little forced.

"No jokes now," Melina said. "This is serious. I'm asking you—do you think you can compete with that kind of success?"

"Compete? Why does it have to be a competition?"

"It might not be. But you might want to see what happens first. Give it a few months—"

"I already said yes." *And I told Joey I'd marry him on the spot.* Somehow, letting Melina in on that little secret seemed like a bad idea.

"Just don't rush into it. That's all I'm saying."

Tracy had an idea it wouldn't end with that. "Okay. I promise. No hasty marriages at the county courthouse." She'd already put in a request to take the following Friday off and deemed it best not to mention what that day was for. Still, a marriage license was only good for sixty days, which probably wouldn't be long enough to satisfy Melina.

Then again, it wasn't Melina's marriage license.

ഩര

As she'd expected, Tracy's family was thrilled—especially Levi. After a quick visit to her parents on the way home from work, Tracy made a run out to Miranda's farm, her unplanned arrival coinciding with Levi's.

"I like him!" Levi said. "He plays guitar really good—even if he does have hair like a girl."

"Don't you be telling him to cut it," Tracy warned. "I love his hair."

"I hope you love more than *that*," Miranda said with a wry smile.

"I do. He's sweet, talented, and simply the best."

Miranda hugged her, wiping tears from her eyes when she drew back. "You're sure you want to marry him? I mean, you've only been dating for a couple of months, right?"

Tracy didn't know exactly how long it had been, but it went beyond that first date with "Anna"—perhaps even before the Barton Junction concert.

Probably the day Bryce beat me up.

Yeah. That was it. Unfortunately, neither of them had recognized that fact at the time. "If I hadn't been so stubborn, it would be closer to five months, but that's water under the bridge now."

"When's the wedding?"

"Umm...not sure." She didn't have to tell Melina—or Miranda. Or anyone. She and Joey could get married as soon as they got the license. "Does it matter?"

"Only if you want any of us to be there."

Tracy felt her face growing hot beneath Miranda's close scrutiny. "I'm not sure that matters, either." In many ways, it was already done. Only the legal formalities remained. Her mind drifted back, stripping away the filters of convention, and she caught herself speaking without thinking. "I think the *real* wedding was that show in Louisville."

"Sorry I wasn't there."

Miranda had been matron of honor when Tracy married Bob—playing a classic role in the traditional ceremony with white satin and flowers. That celebration seemed so long ago now, it might've happened to someone else. *All* of it seemed that way.

Tracy was a different person with Joey. She'd found her true self—a woman who didn't necessarily adhere to conventions, didn't think the same way, or look for pleasure in ways that didn't satisfy.

Funny how she'd never thought of life as a continual quest for pleasure, but perhaps it was. Pleasure was a very powerful motivator, and the need to feel something—*anything*—was every bit as strong. Perhaps that was why she hadn't followed through with her plan to abandon the opposite sex. Somewhere, somehow, she needed them. Needed to hear their voices, needed to touch them, and make them feel something in return. But not *them* in the plural. *Him* in the singular...

Miranda startled her out of her reverie with a loud clearing of her throat. "I'm not sure *you're* here now. You look like you're about a thousand miles away."

"Not quite that far," Tracy said with a hasty smile. "I just realized something, that's all."

"Hold that thought. It looked like a good one."

"It was."

Her introspection continued during the drive home. That need to feel was why lukewarm coffee didn't satisfy. Why soda lost its appeal without the bite of the bubbles or the chill of the ice. Why tequila was her friend when she wasn't getting any...

Interestingly, none of those things had seemed as important since she'd found Joey. Giving and receiving. Him with his music, her with...*what?* Her love for him, her passion? Senses needed to be stimulated. If not in one way, then certainly another.

Arriving home, she climbed the stairs to her apartment, the outer door reopening just as she inserted her key in the lock.

A frisson of fear swept over her until she stole a glance over her shoulder and saw not Bryce entering the building but Geena.

She wasn't nearly as lovely as Tracy remembered, nor was Darren on her hip. Her hair was lifeless, her expression distraught.

"Hi Tracy," she began. "D–do you know if Joey's home?"

Tracy stared at her, speechless.

"I called his cell number a while ago, but it went to voicemail. I would've gone to see—"

"He's working at Georgio's tonight," Tracy blurted out, finding her tongue at last.

Geena nodded. "I was afraid of that. I didn't want to go there. Too many people we both know..." She drew in a shuddering breath. "I'm sorry. I just want—*need*—to talk to him." Her shoulders sagged, taking her entire body along with them. "I made a terrible mistake."

Tracy couldn't think of a single thing to say—and even if she had, her mouth didn't seem capable of doing anything but gaping like a goldfish.

"I should never have left him. I was so stupid." Shaking her head, she glanced up at Tracy. "I–is he...okay?"

"Yeah." With that one word, Tracy's brain slid back into gear. "He's fine—the band even got a contract offer. They played a terrific show in Louisville. You should've seen it."

A weak smile played across her lips. "I was there—borrowed my cousin's ID to get in. They were incredible."

She hesitated. "Geena...what happened? Why are you here?"

The girl's smile disappeared, replaced by a grim set to her jaw. "Trey's as much of a bastard as he ever was. I was a fool for leaving Joey. I...I need to tell him that."

Tracy's heart slid to her toes. "You want him back?"

A mirthless laugh escaped her, and she shook her head in a manner devoid of hope. "I think I burned that bridge pretty effectively. I only want to apologize."

Once more at a loss for words, Tracy noticed her heart was beating again—pumping blood the way it always did, although her ears felt prickly and hot.

"I treated him so badly—didn't realize I had it so good." She paused, frowning. "Well, maybe I did." Her gaze sank to the floor before flicking back up to meet Tracy's eyes. "You two are together now. Aren't you?"

Tracy nodded her reply.

"I saw you on the dance floor. You looked so happy."

Geena must've been watching them when Joey proposed. Tracy didn't know whether to add insult to injury by telling her that. "*Very* happy."

"Did he tell you why I left him?"

"Yeah."

With a shrug, Geena leaned back against the door. "Probably doesn't bother you a bit, does it?"

A smile tugged at Tracy's lips—the first since Geena's arrival. "Not at all. I've got a few quirks myself."

"You're better for him," Geena said. "Closer in age, more...tolerant."

Tracy was a little surprised Geena was able to grasp that idea—although she seemed to have matured slightly over the past six months. That time couldn't have been easy for her, but it had to have been worse for Joey. Tracy doubted that Geena's anguish had been anywhere near as severe as his. No one had taken Geena's baby from her. Joey had lost everything.

"Why did you do it—to begin with, I mean?" Tracy asked. "I know why you left him, but why lie to him?"

"I was stupid and scared," she said bitterly. "At first, I thought being with Joey would make Trey jealous. When it didn't, I sorta…panicked."

Tracy'd been that age once—had been equally naïve, if not more so. "Do you still want to talk to him or would you rather I did it for you?"

"Might be best if you told him," she said. "I'm not sure I could find the courage to come here again."

"I can understand that." No doubt it would be best if Geena and Joey *didn't* meet again—especially if Geena was thoughtless enough to bring Darren with her, which she hadn't done this time. "Where's Darren?"

"My mom's watching him. She's encouraged me to go back to school so I can get a better job. Obviously I'm going to have to be the one to provide for my son. Trey is totally worthless."

On that last word, Geena burst into tears. Tracy never thought she'd be the one to comfort Joey's ex, but here she was, rushing down the stairs to hug the poor kid.

Then again, Geena's actions had resulted in Tracy's own happiness. Perhaps she *did* owe the girl a hug. But no way was she giving Joey back to her.

That ship had sailed.

Chapter 36

If it hadn't been for Darren's involvement, Joey would've counted Geena's departure as one of the best things that could've happened to him. "She was such a child. I mean, I knew it, but at the time…oh, hell, I suppose I'm as gullible as any guy when it comes to a pretty face."

Tracy sat up in bed and whipped around to face him. "Excuse me?"

"You know what I mean. I'm not saying I'd do it all over again if I had the chance. It was more a matter of timing."

"Timing?"

Tracy's responses were getting progressively shorter, leading Joey to suspect he'd blundered somehow. "Yeah. Not like with *you*. We had the chance to get to know each other as friends before we became romantically involved. Geena had only worked at Georgio's for a couple of months when, all of the sudden, we were moving in together."

She seemed slightly mollified. "Yeah. Hopefully, we'll last longer."

"We're gonna last a *lot* longer." Joey dropped an arm around her shoulders and pulled her close. Her peculiar mood was understandable, but it hadn't improved even after she'd told him about Geena's visit. He had an inkling there was something else…some undercurrent of emotion he hadn't expected and couldn't identify. "You feeling okay?"

"Yeah."

Once again, her reply was too immediate, too brief. "Did something bad happen at the clinic?"

This time, she hesitated. "No. Not really. Just Melina ragging on me for getting engaged so quickly."

In Joey's opinion, their marriage wasn't happening rapidly enough. "What about you? Do *you* think we're moving too fast?"

"No," she replied. "But I wonder… You and Geena—I know the circumstances are completely different, but what you just said about pretty faces is part of it. Rock stars have women chasing after them all the time. I know that's not how you met Geena—or me—and I'm not saying you'd ever be unfaithful—" She stopped there, shrugging. "Oh, hell, I don't know what's bugging me. It's probably nothing—nerves maybe."

Joey suspected she'd already put her finger on the problem. She simply didn't want to admit it. "Are you saying you'd rather we *didn't* sign that recording contract?"

"I didn't say that. Besides, it would be very selfish of me—especially since I've already criticized Brad for holding you back."

"Yes, but now that we're engaged, what happens to my music career affects us both. That was Brad's reason for not wanting to take the band to the next level. He knows how much strain fame and fortune can put on a marriage."

Taking his hand, she laced her fingers between his as though trying to strengthen the bond between them. "Yeah. And when you asked me to marry you, there was no contract offer."

Joey could understand her concerns—although it was the exact opposite of the doubts he'd had. He'd expected her to be disappointed if the band *didn't* make it big. Unfortunately, the flipside of that coin was almost as bad. "Does one automatically rule out the other?"

"Not necessarily. But the fact that they happened at almost the same time puts a different spin on things. Remember how we talked about doing normal stuff together? Doesn't seem like we ever get the chance to do that."

"We will. We're only getting started."

"But what if—" She paused again. "What if it never gets any better? Even if you don't reach the rich and famous level, what if we're always working opposite shifts and spending weekends in

Brad's garage or at a gig somewhere?"

"We wouldn't be the first couple to live that way. Geena and I—" It was his turn to hesitate. "I, um, see your point."

If Joey had his way, Tracy would never have to work again. That was his goal. Lots of women wanted exciting careers and complete independence. Tracy would never be a clinging vine—she simply wasn't the type—but he sensed that she and her nursing career weren't joined at the hip. "At least you don't work nights. I don't think I could stand not sleeping with you."

"Same here. Maybe we can work something out—different jobs or schedules." She snuggled closer, resting her head on his chest. "I just wish we had more time together. I feel like I never see you except in bed."

"Is that a complaint—or is that what's really been bothering you?"

"Maybe—but I'm leaning more toward it being a fear of the unknown. The not knowing what to expect or how to plan for it. Not knowing which decision will be the best for everyone concerned."

"Does anyone *ever* know that?"

"No. But up to now, my future has mainly been determined by my own choices. Now it's up to someone else. It feels weird."

Joey had faced similar issues when he and Geena moved in together. "I know the feeling. I'd been going it alone for so long, and then suddenly I had Geena and Darren's needs to consider. Yeah. Completely different perspective."

"Guess I should stop worrying and take it one day at a time, huh?"

"That's all we *can* do—for now." He gave her another squeeze. "Feeling better?"

"Much." Her sigh stretched into a yawn. "Too bad that overnight success thing couldn't happen tonight. Be nice not to have to get up at the crack of dawn."

"No shit. Think you can sleep now?"

"Maybe—although it might help if you'd, um, knock me out."

"My pleasure." With a wink, he reached over and turned off the light.

Funny how he didn't seem to need bras and other sexual accoutrements for these late-night encounters. Tracy was in his bed, primed and willing. That he was already rock-hard was a given.

Rolling over, he kissed her long and deep, then slid inside, loving the way her wet heat wrapped around his cock. He rocked into her, her sighs touching him like nothing else ever had—like nothing else ever could.

This wasn't just sex. This was making love with Tracy, the most beautiful, wonderful woman in the world. This was Barry White singing "You're the First, the Last, My Everything."

Baby-makin' music.

Oh, yeah...

೫ಌ

"Ready?"

"You bet." Joey held the door of the courthouse as Tracy stepped inside.

Friday morning had arrived so quickly, Tracy still felt like she should've been at work. The band's practice the previous Sunday afternoon had gone incredibly well. Even Dave behaved himself, although with Kiki along for the ride, he didn't need to play the jackass role. She did it for him.

"He has *got* to get rid of her before we make the cover of *Rolling Stone*," Joey said afterward.

"Yeah. I can see the tabloid headlines now, 'Drummer's flame ignites inferno.' Literally."

"I can't *believe* she'd light up a cigarette in Brad's garage. I thought he was gonna have a stroke."

"No shit—but I have a feeling she won't make the same mistake twice." Tracy wouldn't have minded if she never had the opportunity to make that mistake again. Unfortunately, Kiki seemed quite taken with the idea of being a rock star's main squeeze and, as a result, had latched onto Dave like a leech.

But now, Kiki and Dave were forgotten as she and Joey handed over their driver's licenses and Tracy's divorce papers.

Joey eyed her speculatively. "Made a decision yet?"

"Still thinking."

"Never had dreams of being a June bride?"

Actually, Tracy had plenty of dreams, and she'd already decided that June tenth would be an excellent anniversary date. Never having celebrated an anniversary before—she and Bob had split up before even reaching the six-month mark—she couldn't recall the date of her first wedding, although she was pretty sure it was in September.

The nineteenth. *What a time to remember.*

Despite telling herself the flutter in her stomach was only nerves, she had her suspicions. She just wasn't ready to tell Joey yet.

Don't want him to think I'm marrying him because I'm pregnant. Any similarities between her and Geena were to be avoided at all cost.

The clerk was smiling when she handed over the final documents. "When's the happy occasion?"

"What?" Tracy blurted out. "Which one?"

Chuckling, the heavyset blonde arched a brow. "The wedding?"

"Oh. Yeah. Right. The wedding." She felt her neck getting hot and fixed her gaze on the clock, noting that it had one of those jumping red second hands and a crack in the glass cover. *Nine-thirty. June tenth.*

"Is there something I should know?" Joey asked.

"Nope. Must've been thinking about the gig in Bloomington. Dunno why."

"Uh huh."

Joey didn't sound convinced—aside from the fact that he had to know she'd missed a period.

She still wasn't prepared to admit it. Not yet. After one miscarriage, she knew better than to count her chickens before they hatched.

Interesting choice of metaphors…

"Reason I asked is 'cause we've got a judge available for the next hour or so," the clerk explained. "Just sayin'…"

Oh, what the hell… Tracy glanced at Joey. "Got your garter belt?"

He threw up his hands. "You were supposed to bring it—not me."

She knew full well he was wearing the red thong she'd given him. "For good luck," he'd said. Apparently, it worked.

The clerk seemed confused—her heavily shadowed eyes darting from Tracy to Joey and back again. "*His* garter belt? Are you sure…?"

"Never mind," Tracy said. "Tell the judge we're ready whenever he is—or is it a she?"

"She's a she." The clerk winced. "At least, she *says* she is. To be honest, I'm not really sure."

"You mean she's a little…butch?" Joey suggested.

"Kinda," the clerk admitted. "But that's okay." She waved a dismissive hand. "Different strokes and all that."

Tracy's eyes met Joey's. "Sounds perfect."

༄༅༆

Tracy swallowed against the rising nausea as she hung the catheter bag on the side rail. She'd probably put in five hundred thousand catheters in her career—*okay, so that's an exaggeration*—but nothing like that had *ever* made her sick.

Generally speaking, the only thing that grossed her out was having to suction the snot out of someone, which was one reason she'd left the ER and avoided the ICU. Working in the clinic was no guarantee against the possibility, but still…

This is different.

Gathering up the remains of the insertion kit, she stuffed it in the trash bin, hoping she didn't end up puking on it. While a trash bag made a convenient emesis basin, it would still be embarrassing, particularly since her patient was fully alert. Stripping off her gloves, she tossed them in after the kit and squirted sanitizer on her palms. With a terse, "Be right back," she pressed her fingers to her lips and hurried from the room.

She barely made it to the nurse's restroom.

Married four days and already puking my guts out.

There'd be no hiding it from Joey now. She couldn't stand the thought of getting his hopes up for what might be a false alarm. Her first pregnancy had ended at eight weeks for no particular reason. She hadn't fallen down the stairs or taken any weird drugs—just lost her baby and Bob in one fell swoop.

That won't happen this time. Different situation altogether.

Different reasons for marrying, different father—hell, Tracy was different herself, not to mention older. That was the scary part. She hadn't been able to carry a baby to term at the age of twenty-three. What hope did she have at thirty-one?

Melina stuck her head in the door. "Are you okay?"

Tracy wiped her lips with the back of her hand. "Yeah."

"Preggers?"

No point in denying it. "Preggers."

"Done a test yet?"

"Not sure I need to. Sore boobs and nausea. Not much else it could be."

"True. Feel up to changing a dressing?"

"Maybe. How bad is it?" Tracy had changed a few that, to quote George Carlin, could've knocked a buzzard off a shit wagon. This was not the time to make a similar attempt.

"Not sure," Melina replied. "Looks kinda dirty on the outside."

With a violent heave, Tracy leaned over the toilet.

"Guess not. So, tell me…what does Joey have to say about all this baby stuff?"

"Haven't told him yet," Tracy gasped, barely able to speak for the spasms gripping her abdomen.

"Don't think you'll have to."

The paroxysm eased, enabling her to stand up straight. "Hey, at least we're married."

Melina's eyes ignited in green flame. "Why, you little—" Clearly unable to think of anything bad enough to call her best buddy, her tirade ended with taut cheeks and lips pressed into a thin line.

"Scamp? Bimbo? Golddigger?" Tracy suggested.

"None of the above. When were you gonna tell me?"

"After that 'don't rush things' speech of yours, I was thinking about next Christmas." She'd be six months pregnant by then, which would be far more difficult to conceal than morning sickness— especially if she showed up at the Christmas party wearing a Baby's First Christmas T-shirt.

"You don't even have a wedding ring," Melina said with a sniff.

"An unfortunate side effect of an impromptu wedding. Although, if I'd ever gotten around to buying that pretend wedding ring from Wal-Mart, I wouldn't have that problem."

"A *pretend* ring?"

Tracy pulled a paper towel from the dispenser and doused it under the tap. "Didn't I ever tell you about that?"

"No, you didn't." Sometimes Melina had no sense of humor whatsoever.

And I'm the one who's puking...

"You know how Miranda used to wear her wedding ring to keep men away?" As Tracy pressed the cold, wet towel to her face, her nausea subsided—a little. "I was going to do that."

"Why didn't you?"

Good question. She'd come up with the idea after her ball-crunching encounter with that weird skinhead guy at Cider Hill. Why hadn't she followed through?

Because it wouldn't have fooled Joey.

"Don't remember," she lied. "Besides, we're going shopping for rings on Sunday. The guys are getting a pretty decent paycheck for the show in Bloomington. Figured we ought to buy them while we were flush."

"Let's see now..." Scowling, Melina crossed her arms and

began tapping her foot. "You got pregnant. Then you got married, and next you're buying rings. Doesn't that seem a little backward to you?"

Despite her nausea, Tracy giggled. "Geez, Melina. You left out the part about Anna having sex with me before Joey did."

"Silly me," Melina drawled. "How could I ever forget that?"

"Oh, and get this—the judge who married us was a lesbian."

"Figures." Melina's scowl persisted.

While her blessing wasn't strictly essential, Melina *was* Tracy's best friend. "Aren't you at least a *little* happy for me?"

"Ecstatic." This time, she smiled. "You go, girl."

Chapter 37

At least I can see the bar.

Joey's eyes swept the interior as he stepped up onto the bandstand. Bloomingbirds's might've been smaller than the Comstock Lode, but it was easily twice the size of Cider Hill.

Moving up in the world.

He wondered what it would be like to play something the size of the arena in Evansville. Probably no different—maybe not even as good—and they'd be too removed from the audience. Except for the noise and the lights, they could've been playing in Brad's garage.

No. For one thing, in Brad's garage, he never had any trouble spotting Tracy. He liked having her where he could see her. She was his inspiration as well as the anchor that kept him grounded. His heart began to race until he finally spotted her sitting at a table with the other wives, the lights reflecting off her hair.

Oh, wow…

My wife.

None of his band mates were surprised when he told them about his marriage to Tracy. But when Lenny expressed a desire to have been invited to the wedding, everyone stared at him like he'd lost his mind.

"I *love* weddings," Lenny exclaimed. "It's not like we haven't played at a few. Great food, open bar—and cake! Oh, yeah. Weddings *rock*."

"Our ceremony wasn't anything like that," Joey said. "The judge at the courthouse married us. Granted, *we* thought it was a romantic, spur-of-the-moment idea, but I doubt it would've been much fun for anyone else."

Joey wouldn't have cared where they were or who they were

with. All that mattered was the love he felt when Tracy said *I do*, the fervency of his own promise to love and to cherish, the sweetness of their first kiss as husband and wife…

Swallowing around the lump in his throat, he blinked away the stinging tears and shrugged. "Even if we'd had a big church wedding, we probably wouldn't have had an open bar. Too expensive—especially if you guys were there."

Lenny gaped at him. "You'd have at least had a keg, wouldn't you?"

"Well…maybe a case or two." The problem would've been hiring a band for the event. Joey didn't much care for the idea of playing at his own wedding.

Even after they'd finished setting up for the gig, Lenny wouldn't let the subject drop. "You and Tracy need to have a party. You know…sort of a belated reception? Bad enough I missed the wedding. I want some cake, dude."

"If all you want is cake, how about throwing us a baby shower?"

Lenny nearly dropped his bass. "Tracy's pregnant? *That's* why you got married so fast?"

On occasion, Lenny had been known to display a reasonable amount of intelligence. This was not one of those times. "We got married because we love each other. The baby is…a miracle."

"Yeah, right," Lenny snorted.

"I'm not kidding," Joey said. "Babies are *always* miracles." Despite everything that had happened since Geena dropped her little bombshell, Joey hadn't forgotten the sense of wonder and amazement when he gazed into the eyes of a newborn baby, and he could hardly wait to do it again—with a child he and Tracy had created together.

Seeming to appear out of nowhere, Brad leaped onto the bandstand. "Babies are always miracles? There's bound to be a song in that."

Joey nodded as a melody trilled through his head. "Trust me, I've got several in the works."

"Good thing," Brad said. "You know that talent scout guy? He's here, and he brought along a couple of friends."

"Friends?" Joey echoed.

"Yeah. Barton Junction's tour manager and their frontman, Chuck Thomas."

"You're shittin' me," Lenny exclaimed. "Aren't they in the middle of a tour? They should be on the road with the band, not hanging out in bars."

From the look of him, if Brad got any more excited, he'd probably explode. "They're checking out opening acts."

Joey's jaw dropped. "Holy shit."

With a whoop, Dave flipped his drumsticks in the air, catching them with all the ease of a juggler. "This is my lucky day! Kiki dumped me for a cab driver just in time for us to hit the road. She'll be so pissed."

"A cab driver?" Lenny gasped. "I don't believe it."

Smiling wickedly, Dave seemed to derive perverse pleasure from Kiki's departure. "She said my dick was too damn big and that his was more…*comfortable*."

"You're better off without her, dude," Brad said over Lenny's shout of laughter. "Angie and Cynthia couldn't stand her." He glanced at Joey. "And I don't think Tracy liked her, either."

Joey doubted Dave cared what anyone thought of his choice of girlfriends, but he knew Tracy would be pleased. "Guess that means you and Billy can handle the groupies."

"It's a tough job," Dave said. "But I won't need any help."

Following Dave's rimshot on the drums, Billy shrugged. "I'll take the girls that don't fit you."

For a long moment, no one spoke. Joey eyed Billy with newfound respect. "You go for days without saying a word, and then you come up with something like *that*. Amazing."

Brad cleared his throat. "Yeah, well, we won't *have* any groupies if we don't play well enough to deserve them—or go on tour."

Joey recalled a time when Brad considered going on the road to be his worst nightmare. "What about Angie and the kids? Do you really want to be away from them for that long?"

"Yeah. We all have jobs, too," Lenny said. "I'd probably have to quit mine, and I doubt it'll be waiting for me when I get back."

"We'll cross that bridge when we get to it," Brad said. "Nobody's asked us to do anything yet, and they may not."

"Wish we didn't know they were here," Lenny grumbled. "Playing a gig is tough enough as it is."

In that moment, Joey understood how Tracy felt about her future depending on someone else's choices. "Guess this is our chance to see how well we perform under pressure." He didn't have any fears for himself. With Tracy in the audience, he would play as well as he ever had.

Unless we go on tour and she isn't there.
Shit.

There was *always* a catch. It wasn't that he didn't want her to come along; he just couldn't imagine how a pregnant woman would feel about traveling across the country on a tour bus. She'd have to miss prenatal visits and such—all the little things involved in preparing for a new addition to the family.

Joey did some rapid calculations. Unless he missed his guess, their baby wouldn't be due until March. "Um, what tour are they talking about? Fall, spring, or what?"

"They're in the middle of their spring/summer tour now," Brad replied. "I got the impression this was to finish out the season. Their world tour starts in August."

Lenny let out a low whistle. "Damn. Those guys must be on the road all the time."

"Yeah," Brad said. "That's another thing we need to think about. Leaving our jobs is bad enough, but leaving our families is even worse—and no, I'm not talking about you, Dave. Or Billy for that matter." He glanced at Joey. "Considering what you were saying about babies being miracles and the way you were counting on your fingers a second ago, I'm guessing Tracy is pregnant?"

"She hasn't said anything yet, but I'd bet money on it."

"Something else to think about. Still, our part of the tour would only be about six weeks. In the meantime, we've got a show to do."

"Yeah." Joey nodded. "Let's rock."

❧

Tracy watched Joey perform with the same degree of awe as she had on every other occasion. Would it always be this magical?

Somehow, she thought it would. Just as they'd done at every other show she'd seen, the band electrified the audience, and Joey was the star.

Well...maybe she was a tad prejudiced in that respect.

And he's my husband.

After her discussion with Melina, the next step had been to tell her family she and Joey were married. Her parents weren't the least bit happy about being denied a wedding, but Miranda didn't seem to mind—nor was she surprised when Tracy called.

"I know the feeling," Miranda said. "It's not something you want to have to wait for, especially when you're starting a bit late."

She and Travis had put together a nice wedding in a short period of time. But, of course, Miranda hadn't been pregnant.

"I'm a bit late in other respects," Tracy said, hoping her sister would take the hint.

She did. "Imagine that." A few seconds passed. "March?"

"Um, yeah. Probably so."

"Congratulations! What did Mom say?"

"Shall I quote her?" Tracy drawled.

"Oh, please *do*..."

"'It's about time!'"

"Yeah. That's what I figured. Wow. I'm finally going to have a niece or nephew who doesn't live in Texas or Arizona."

"Hadn't thought of that," Tracy admitted with a chuckle. "Glad I could help."

"I'm so happy for you, Tracy. You have no idea how much."

"I might. I was probably just as happy when you married

Travis."

"I guess we're even, then."

Their conversation ended shortly thereafter with only one topic left untouched—the fact that Tracy hadn't told Joey of her suspicions. Now, here she was, watching him play, trying to figure out how to tell him.

Why was it so hard?

Maybe it was that jinx thing. After she and Bob were married, she told everyone and their mother's brother about her baby.

Then she lost it.

Of course, *not* telling Joey didn't guarantee a damn thing—except that he'd be pissed when he wound up being the last to know.

Still, she hadn't had anything stronger than coffee to drink since that first bout of nausea.

He might notice that.

The longer Tracy sat there, reveling in the band's stellar performance, the more determined she became. She would tell him after the show. Period. No ifs, ands, or buts. Definitely.

How hard could it be? Melina's favorite phrase kept running through her head. *You go, girl.*

Okay, I will.

෪෬

After running the gauntlet of well-wishers and megastars of the music business, Joey finally made it back to the table where Tracy sat nursing what appeared to be a Coke. Never having seen her drink anything alcoholic using Coke as a mixer, her choice only confirmed his suspicions. "Hey, Trace! How'd you like the show?"

Leaping to her feet, she threw her arms around his neck. "You were amazing—as always!"

"Thanks! Guess what? We got another contract offer—a better one. And get this: they want us to replace one of the bands on Barton Junction's summer tour. Evidently, you aren't the only one who thinks their opening acts are terrible."

Tracy's arms went slack and she stepped back, sweeping a lock of hair from her eyes. "H–how long would you be gone?"

"Six weeks—until the end of July."

"But I—we–we just got married. Don't you think—"

"You could come with me if you want. Not sure how much you'd like hanging out on a tour bus—especially since Dave would be there—but they said you could. Oh, and just so you know, Kiki is history." He opted to keep the best part of *that* story until later.

"A tour bus? For six weeks? I dunno… I'm not sure I could get that much time off from the clinic."

"We haven't signed yet, but we need to decide soon. I know a bus sounds really crappy when you're feeling queasy, but they do most of their traveling during the night."

He watched her expression change as she registered the full impact of what he'd said. "Queasy? What makes you think—"

"Tracy, sweetheart, did you think I wouldn't notice? I may not have many brain cells, but I'm not brain *dead*. I've been waiting for you to tell me for a couple of weeks."

"I've been too scared to say it. I'm afraid of jinxing myself…us…the baby."

"Don't be. Trust me, if saying 'I'm pregnant' worked like that, no one would ever have a baby."

She burst out laughing. "I should've known you could put everything in its proper perspective. Sure you aren't mad because I didn't tell you first?"

"Nope. Long as you don't plan on telling me a year from now that it's someone else's kid."

"No possible way."

"Then it's all good."

ಬಇ

Tracy climbed the stairs to her apartment after her last day at the clinic, her mind in a whirl.

Unbelievably, the personnel department was letting her take the next six weeks off. She would have to use every vacation and sick day she had stored up, but it was going to happen. The tour bus would be picking them up at five-thirty the next morning.

For once in her life, she wasn't going to think everything to death. Her gynecologist—who would now be her obstetrician—had given her the go-ahead, as long as she got plenty of rest, took her vitamins, and avoided alcohol.

No worries there.

She'd opened the door and was about to call out to Joey when a man came out of nowhere, seizing her around the waist and wrapping an arm around her neck. His foul breath and body odor turned her already queasy stomach even as frissons of terror knifed through her. She didn't even have to see his face to know it was Bryce.

"Thought you'd sic the cops on me, did you, bitch?"

In that instant, her fear was replaced with anger.

Not this time, asshole.

"No, but I should have. Not that I didn't *enjoy* the idea of you rotting in jail. Actually, I was *hoping* some chick would rip your fuckin' nuts off."

Stomping down on his instep with her heel, she ducked under his arm and twisted away, spinning around to face him.

Her defensive move had allowed her to escape, but so far, he wasn't even reacting to the pain. "Yeah, well, it's just you and me this time, sweetheart. The little fuckwad next door isn't home, or I'd kill him too."

Thanking God for Joey's safety, she put more disdain into her words and posture than she would've thought possible. "Too? Meaning you plan on killing *me*?"

"Oh, yeah. And I'm gonna enjoy every second of hearing you scream and watching you bleed."

Tracy had never seen such insane hatred in anyone's eyes before, but oddly enough, she still wasn't afraid. Even if she died, which she had absolutely no intention of doing, she would die knowing Joey loved her—a love that bolstered her courage and gave her strength.

Without hesitation, she strode forward like a placekicker on a sixty-yard field goal attempt, delivering a punt to the groin Bryce's descendants would feel for generations to come.

If he ever gets the chance to reproduce.

Hopefully, he wouldn't—if he hadn't already. Finally screaming in pain, Bryce staggered backward just as Joey darted out of the bedroom.

This time, he'd had sense enough to pick up the right guitar. Swinging the old acoustic for all he was worth, Joey caught Bryce on the side of the head with a blow that dropped him like a rock and reduced the guitar to a tangle of wires and splinters.

Panting, he glanced at the man's unconscious body before focusing his gaze on Tracy. "You okay, Trace?"

She nodded. "I am now."

He pulled her into his arms and kissed her, only then realizing that he was shaking even harder than she was. "Do you want to call the police, or shall I?"

"Go for it." She collapsed onto the couch as soon as he released her. "This is the only time I've ever wished I had a gun."

"Thank God, *he* didn't," Joey said, whipping out his phone.

"Probably couldn't get one—at least not legally." She wrinkled her nose. "Jesus, he stinks like a derelict on a bender. He said something about the cops being after him. Must've been on the run for a while."

"Too bad he didn't have sense enough to keep running." Joey punched in 911, then gave the dispatcher the pertinent details. "Better send an ambulance, too."

Switching off his phone, he plopped down beside Tracy. "Think we should tie him up?"

She responded with a burst of laughter. "Wanna use your bondage goodies or a couple of my bras?"

"Or guitar strings. He'd *never* break those." He gave her a squeeze. "Although I *do* have a set of handcuffs."

"Really?"

"Yeah. I was saving them for our one-month anniversary. Sorry to spoil the surprise."

She stuck out her foot and prodded Bryce with her toe. "Yet another demerit to add to his list." Cocking her head, she added, "I'm not sure we need to do anything. I hear a siren."

Moments later, the bell rang. Tracy opened the door, letting it swing wide.

"Officer Williams," she said with a heavy measure of sarcasm. "It just had to be you, didn't it?"

A policeman with brown hair and dimples stepped inside, his tall, lanky partner following close behind him. "Hey, Pemberton isn't exactly a megalopolis. We don't have that many guys on the force." He glanced at Bryce's inert form. "Let me guess, the dude who messed up your face decided to pay you another visit."

"Yeah," Tracy said. "But that might be your fault. He seems to think I reported him."

"Glad you finally wised up—or did *you* make the call?" The officer aimed his gaze at Joey.

"Sure did. Right after I bashed him in the head with my guitar."

The taller of the two officers snickered. "You know what they say about smashing perfectly good guitars."

"That one wasn't exactly perfect," Joey said. "I can still play the Ibanez I hit him with the last time."

Footsteps sounded on the stairs just before two EMTs stuck their heads in the open door. "Did somebody call 911?"

"Yeah. Better bring a stretcher." Officer Williams glanced at Tracy. "Don't suppose you remember his name, do you?"

She nodded. "Bryce Hancock. One of my more disastrous mistakes."

"Really?" Kneeling beside Bryce, he slapped on a handcuff. "There's a warrant out for his arrest. You saved us a lot of trouble."

Tracy stared at the officer, plainly puzzled. "But how…? I never reported—"

"You didn't have to," the officer replied. "Seems the girl he beat up last fall finally came out of her coma and filed a complaint."

"Holy shit," Tracy said in a hoarse whisper. "He hasn't beaten up anyone since, has he?"

Joey had no trouble understanding why she would ask that question and wished he'd overruled her decision to keep quiet months ago.

"Just you," Officer Williams replied. "At least, as far as we know."

Bryce was already beginning to stir when the ambulance crew returned. After checking him for injuries and applying a cervical collar, they rolled him onto a stretcher. The police handcuffed him to it—which was fortunate because a moment later, he started pulling against the cuffs and cussing at the top of his lungs—most of it referring to Tracy, and none of it very nice.

"Shut up," Joey snapped. "That's my wife you're talking about."

"You little shit," Bryce growled. "I should've killed you when I had the chance."

"You never *had* a chance," Joey said. "That's twice I've beaten the shit out of you."

"Yeah," Tracy said. "Joey's my hero. You're nothing but a pathetic, woman-beating loser."

The cop glanced at Tracy with surprise. "Wait a minute. You got *married*? Really? Thought you'd decided to date women."

Tracy stared at him for a full second before dissolving in hysterical laughter.

"I don't get it," Officer Williams said. "What's so funny?"

"She tried dating a woman," Joey said, shooting a wink at his wife. "But she decided she liked me better as a man."

Tracy smiled. "Oh, *yeah… Much* better." Wrapping her arms around his waist, she pulled Joey close, giving him a kiss that stiffened his cock and turned his knees to jelly.

Her gaze left his for an instant as she tossed a question at the police. "Are we finished now?"

Officer Williams cleared his throat. "Just need to get a

statement from each of you."

"Well, then, hurry it up," she urged. "Joey and I are hitting the road in the morning."

"Honeymoon?"

"Kinda," she replied. "Although it's actually a concert tour. I married a freakin' rock star, you know."

Joey didn't bother to deny her claim. Superstardom was still a long way off, but with Tracy at his side, anything was possible.

And all of it good.

ABOUT THE AUTHOR

A native of Louisville, Kentucky, Cheryl Brooks is a former critical care nurse who resides in rural Indiana with her husband, two sons, two horses, four cats, and one dog. Her **Cat Star Chronicles** series was first published by Sourcebooks Casablanca in 2008, and includes *Slave, Warrior, Rogue, Outcast, Fugitive, Hero, Virgin, Stud,* and *Wildcat.* Look for Book 10 in 2014. She has one self-published e-book, *Sex, Love, and a Purple Bikini,* and one erotic short story, *Midnight in Reno.* She has also published *If You Could Read My Mind* writing as Samantha R. Michaels. As a member of *The Sextet*, she has written several erotic novellas published by Siren/Bookstrand. Her **Unlikely Lovers** series includes *Unbridled, Uninhibited, Undeniable,* and *Unrivaled.* Her other interests include cooking, gardening, singing, and guitar playing. Cheryl is a member of RWA and IRWA. You can visit her online at www.cherylbrooksonline.com or email her at cheryl.brooks52@yahoo.com.

CPSIA information can be obtained at www.ICGtesting.com
Printed in the USA
BVOW11s2000210515

401395BV00016B/513/P

9 780983 808183